TEMPERED STEELE

M.E. LOGAN

Bella
BOOKS
2015

Bella Books, Inc.
P.O. Box 10543
Tallahassee, FL 32302

Printed in the United States of America on acid-free paper.

First Bella Books Edition 2015

Editor: Cath Walker
Cover Designer: Linda Callaghan

ISBN: 978-1-59493-423-0

Other Books by M. E. Logan:

Lexington Connection
Revenge

Acknowledgments

This was a long-time ongoing book so I will probably skip someone I should acknowledge and thank. I can start with the Alpha: Gail, who read draft after draft and said yes, no, you're kidding, this is better, good, for more years than you could ever guess and end with the Omega: Cath Walker, my editor, who said yes, no, what?, improved, good, okay; as well as all the in-betweens: Vicki, Joan, Sherri, Lisa, Terri, Linda, Lynn, and countless others whose brains I have picked and bounced ideas off.

Thank you all for your encouragement and patience, your endurance. I thank you. Deborah thanks you.

About the Author

A displaced Hoosier, M. E. Logan lives in North Florida with two dogs, umpteen cats, imaginary characters and one real one. She dabbles in antiques, reading and book collecting as well as bringing her imaginary characters onto pages to share with others.

Dedication

To Diane, who never got to read the
final copy before she left.

PROLOGUE

EARTHQUAKE!

December 21, 2012: Breaking News: The U.S. Geological Survey reported a massive earthquake this morning at 8:36 am EST in the Memphis area. Early reports indicate massive damage. Please stay tuned for further details.

Noon Update: A strong earthquake shook the middle of the country early this morning, collapsing buildings and causing widespread damage across several states. The quake hit at 8:36 EST in the Memphis area, with the center at New Madrid, Missouri.

The State Emergency Management has unconfirmed reports of injuries, but because of communication failures there is scant information. Tennessee Governor Nelson issued a disaster declaration, saying there has been widespread damage to buildings and roads. There are unconfirmed reports of fatalities.

Breaking News: The U.S. Geological Survey has reported a massive aftershock at the New Madrid site, strong enough to be felt in St. Louis, Missouri, Cincinnati, Ohio, Nashville, Tennessee.

Breaking News: Another aftershock has been reported.

Follow up three days later: Critical infrastructure (essential facilities, transportation and utility lifelines) has been substantially damaged in the 140 counties surrounding the earthquake zone, including 3,500 damaged bridges and nearly 425,000 breaks and leaks to both local and interstate pipelines. There are approximately 2.7 million households without power. Over 130 hospitals are damaged and most of them in the Tennessee–Missouri area. Injury and death numbers are estimated in excess of 80,000 with continued search and rescue being hampered by difficulty getting access as well as the heavy snowfall and severe winds. Evacuation camps are being set up in neighboring states with estimates as high as seven million people displaced and two million people needing temporary shelter.

Further strong damaging aftershocks are predicted.

* * *

The Great Earthquake has had a direct economic impact on eight states: Alabama, Arkansas, Illinois, Indiana, Kentucky, Mississippi, Missouri and Tennessee. The damages bill for these states may total nearly as much as $300 billion, while indirect economic losses are estimated to be at least twice this amount. Collateral damages to neighboring states are still being tallied. It is the highest economic loss due to a natural disaster in the history of the USA.

To compound the already devastating effects of the massive quake, the National Weather Service has issued a winter storm warning for north-east, north-central and south-central parts of Kansas with predictions of six to ten inches of heavy blowing snow. Residents are warned to be prepared for hazardous conditions and low visibility when driving. Power outages may occur.

The storm will continue eastward and may impact the states hit by the earthquake.

During the President's Address to the Nation on Christmas Eve, just three days after the Great Earthquake, there was another massive aftershock that rocked the chandeliers at the White House. This was captured live.

The United States has had the largest national disaster in its history.

Natural gas and oil transmission line damages affected service as far away as the East Coast and New England.

There are fifteen nuclear plants in these eight states that are being checked for safety concerns.

* * *

West Memphis was eighty-three percent destroyed then buried in a snowstorm. They were still finding bodies in the spring. Ruptured gas lines exploded, burning down several towns. Fire services were helpless when water lines broke as there was no water pressure. Many dams broke and flooded areas below them, but the Kentucky Dam, a TVA project that had produced the largest artificial lake in the eastern U.S., held. Six states filed bankruptcy and the Fed cut services because of lack of cash and resources, inflation rose because the Reserve was printing money without backing. Power grids collapsed. Those left standing continued to be damaged throughout the winter because of lax maintenance, and were not replaced in many areas. The main bridges across the Mississippi collapsed, preventing truck east-west transportation. The west was already suffering a drought. The East Coast rapidly ran out of food causing riots in the cities. Martial law was declared but not before parts of the cities were destroyed.

The Internet was still functioning, but dependent on the towers, many of which have not been replaced.

The insurance and finance industries were hit hard. Medical services were not restored to anywhere near full capacity. Much employment had been in the service industry rather than manufacturing. Both were hit hard when money wasn't circulating. All this happened as the United States was coming out of the worst recession in modern times.

CHAPTER ONE

Five years after the Great Earthquake

"Too rich for my blood," came the comment from across the room. The scrape of a chair and the jingle of coins as someone's winnings were removed from the table followed.

Deborah Steele only half-listened to the poker game in the far corner as she watched the wind whip snow into a growing drift blocking the door of the roadside diner. She took another swallow of now lukewarm coffee as she measured the frost crawling up the window. That ancient heater labored more every time it kicked on and she wondered whether it would last the night. She hoped so. They were lucky enough that the train had reached Lincoln. These days engines rather than the passengers were babied but having a halfway decent train schedule between Richmond and Logansport made it worth the occasional inconvenience. It sure beat the twenty-mile hike she had been making after her truck had died. She just couldn't cost-justify a truck replacement when there was so much she considered more essential. So she had welcomed the news that they were rebuilding the track and now looked forward to the day when it was repaired and ran again all the way to Kokomo. It worked well for her as it was because the train transported the repair crews between Logansport, Richmond and Kokomo. In the morning there was a run to pick up crew and take them up the line, in the evening in reverse. Then they ran a scheduled route midday. If she planned carefully, she had a run whenever she wanted.

As for now, if they were going to be snowbound, she much preferred being at the diner rather than caught in an unheated train. Here were shelter, heat and even hot meals. She had been through enough snowstorms in the past five years that it took little to convince her to spend the night here.

Well, she had wanted some downtime, she thought, as she laced her fingers behind her head and stretched out. She needed to get away from the house occasionally, have some distance so she could see where she was, what she had to do. She just was not cut out for group living and living with eleven women in the house taxed her endurance. Going into town helped, but what she had really wanted was time to just do nothing. She could not remember the last time she had been alone with no agenda, no one needing her for anything. A luxury, and she would take it even if it had been delivered by a snowstorm.

She got up and stretched, wondering if the storm would blow itself out soon or whether it'd snow all night and they'd be stuck here yet another day. She hoped not. While she did appreciate the downtime, there were things she had to do at home. She wandered over to the counter, lifted her cup in question to Luella, the owner who was sitting in a booth gossiping with another of the train passengers.

"Go ahead," Luella waved her behind the counter.

She's probably enjoying the added business, Deborah thought as she glanced around the filled tables.

She returned to stand before the plate glass window, sipping coffee, watching it snow. She had loved snow as a kid, but now she could never see it without remembering the blizzard that hit Memphis after the Great Earthquake. Destroyed buildings covered with heavy wet snow that hampered the search and rescue teams. She had tried to pick out familiar landmarks as she watched on the television but it was impossible. Such devastation. She never could look at snow the same way again.

The death toll had been tremendous, over seventy-five thousand directly from the earthquake. Then the bad winter with massive homelessness, cities running out of food, out of fuel, out of just about everything increased those numbers. Financial failures, the insurance companies almost totally wiped out, the investment companies tanked. Banks toppled. Investors fled. Civil unrest abounded, people went where they could to survive, confronting those already there who barricaded themselves in. Riots broke out and martial law was declared across vast areas. Government was reduced to the most basic level, delighting some, terrifying others. The nation had a big black hole in the middle of the country sucking up all their resources and nothing but need oozing out.

The Great Earthquake had changed her life like it had so many others. She had come home to Indiana to take care of year-end family farm business. If not for that, she would have been there in Memphis when the New Madrid Fault moved with such shocking consequences. She might not have survived. As it was, she lost everything. Well, relatively speaking. She lost her job, her home, her community, a whole lot of friends. But she had a house and land here in Indiana. She had her life. And like most survivors, she wondered why she had been spared.

Slowly, by happenstance, she found family, women who had no one, no resources, women who couldn't survive alone. Some had simply passed through, some stayed.

"Hey, Deborah, want to join in?"

Deborah broke her reflective mood. The poker game. She hadn't played for years, but she'd always had good luck. And from the looks of the snowfall, they weren't going anywhere soon. It would pass the time. Besides, there was always gossip around the poker table. She might learn something.

"Why not?" she said to no one in particular so she picked up her jacket and headed down to the other end of the diner. On her way she passed Todd stretched out on three straight chairs, his hat pulled down over his eyes, apparently asleep.

"Don't get snookered," he commented in a low voice as she went by.

"I'll try not to."

Just as she reached the midpoint a blast of cold air hit them all and the room turned to see the engineer from the railroad crew. A wave of anticipation went through the dozen or so passengers as the moving snowman stomped his boots free of snow and brushed the sleeves of his heavy coat. The scarf fell from his face, dropping clumps of snow at the door on the old linoleum.

"Any luck?" Deborah asked.

He pulled his hat off and slapped it free of snow, looking around to meet everyone's expectant gaze with resignation. He shook his head. "Can't see the tracks. As soon as we get them clean, they're buried again. This whole stretch is questionable. Can't see them—don't run. Sorry. Looks like we're here for a while." Everyone settled back down into their seats, turned back to whatever they were doing to kill time. "Coffee hot, Luella? Sure could stand a mug."

That settled that, Deborah thought as she continued on to the open dining area where the card players had taken over the round table. She could smell the heat from the vent right above them as she tossed her long jacket over a neighboring table. She pulled the chair out and looked around as she sat down, nodding to the players already in the game. She knew two of them. They had farms down by Seven Mile. She had gone to school with them, old county families, same as hers. Another two she only knew by sight, having seen them at the grain elevator or other places she did business. Then there were the two strangers.

She had noticed them when they had boarded the train in Richmond because they had also come from the hotel just like she had. But what had caught her eye was the woman accompanying them. She hadn't gotten a good look at her. The two men had kept her isolated, quick to steer her where they wanted her to go. City people, Deborah surmised. But there was still the question about the woman, who had kept her head down and turned away. She looked for her now.

"What's the game?" she asked no one in particular as she looked around the open room. There was a couple with a kid at one table, a woman knitting at another nearby table, maybe the wife of one of the players, a bored-looking woman bundled up against the cold, her legs stretched out. And then back in the corner booth, about as far from everyone as she could get, she saw the mystery woman.

"Stud. Jacks or better to open. Nothing wild." Brad, one of the farmers she had gone to school with, answered.

Deborah nodded as she hauled change from her pants pocket. These were all small-time farmers. There wouldn't be a lot of money floating around.

Deborah kept glancing back at the woman, at her threadbare jacket thrown across the table, that once upon a time had been denim with a flannel lining, the flannel shirt that at least added another layer. She couldn't see her face but she looked pinched and cold. She sat with her legs drawn up, her arms wrapped about her legs, her face turned toward the windows. Deborah could see the metal bands on each of her wrists, signifying she was contract labor registered with the state. That alone got Deborah's sympathy. Contracts such as these, who had been in one type of conflict or another, and had fallen under state regulation, were never treated well, and she particularly hated seeing female state contracts in the company of men. What was originally protection for them now only marked them as fair game. There was just too much opportunity to abuse them in ways she hated to contemplate.

As if she sensed Deborah's scrutiny, the woman raised her head. Without looking around, she pulled down her sleeves to cover the bracelets, wrapped the shirt tightly around and turned so her back was to the room. Perhaps, Deborah thought, she was merely curling up to conserve body heat but more likely trying to get some privacy from prying eyes.

Deborah accepted her dismissal and turned her attention to the card dealer. Sympathy wasn't always welcome and besides, there was nothing she could do. Chance and luck decided things in life as well as in cards, sometimes bad and sometimes just not so bad.

"Now what I really need is a beer," one of the poker players was saying. "A tall one, ice-cold. Too bad we get stuck in Lincoln."

"Could have been worse. Could have gotten stuck at Anoka." There was general laughter and Deborah smiled. Anoka consisted of a wide spot in the road several miles further down the track, where a general store used to stand. Now it was just another empty building. At least Lincoln had the train station, the diner, a gathering of houses and a church. There had been a convenience store once too but it was long empty. She almost wished they were stuck at Anoka. She'd be close enough to walk home, even in this weather.

"Gotta watch him," Carl, one of the men she knew by name, said, indicating with a crooked thumb the stranger as he leaned to one side in a falsely conspiratorial whisper. "Thinks we're all rubes and he's gonna clean us out."

Deborah nodded. Carl's tone was kidding, friendly, but all the same he was a good judge of character. His cheerful face and hail-fellow-well-met made people underestimate him.

"Name's Gentry, ma'am," the stranger introduced himself. "Came up here from Memphis." Big man, barrel-chested, broad face, sandy hair. Well fleshed, meant he ate well. Wore wool instead of denim, not a laborer.

Deborah caught her breath and focused on her cards. Strange how such casual words could be like a punch to the gut. Memphis. It showed up in the most unexpected places, invariably catching her off guard. She focused on her cards, shut away those memories. "Earthquake zone," she commented in a steady voice.

She wondered if anyone at the table even remembered she had lived in Memphis. Probably not, just that she was from an old county family, had gone away somewhere "out there" and had come back to stay. Memphis was just someplace where some disaster happened. That had been there. They were here, safe and sound. Sorry for them, relieved for me. That was all that mattered.

"Yes, ma-am, that New Madrid Fault hit us hard. Took out over half the city."

Half the city and then almost half the country, followed by a winter with weather that broke the records. Bitter cold and record snows, the Great Lakes froze over. Snowed clear into May. By that time, the refugees had scattered across the country, and somewhere in the mix of people and emergency conditions, came new infectious agents. People said it was like the earthquake had released virulence into the air to kill what it couldn't do directly.

She didn't like remembering that winter. She hadn't handled it well. She had been obsessed with what she had lost, being back where she started when she had worked so hard to leave it behind her. Every time she turned around, she had to deal with another loss. She hadn't found her footing until spring when she finally told herself she could either founder and die or get up and deal with it. She had it better than most.

She had hunkered down then, decided to survive, do what she had to do. She had land, good farmland. She had shelter—a strong, stable house that had withstood years of storms. She was isolated, which meant she was out of harm's way. Her only shortfall had been labor and she would find a solution. She would survive.

The cards went around. Deborah played cautiously, getting the feel of the cards, the players. She always thought you could tell a lot about a person by the way they played cards, and she wondered about the two strangers. And she wondered about the woman in the corner, a state-registered contract. Puzzling.

Not that she had anything against contracts. Contracts were just a means of survival. Based on the old indentured servant labor system, one person promised to provide shelter, food, clothing and care in exchange for so many years of labor by the other. The idea seemed simple in the beginning for business owners who needed the labor but didn't have the cash. Like anything else, it got complicated. Contracts got sold. Some people thought it smacked of slavery and were opposed on principle. Arguments that it wasn't the person who was sold, just the piece of paper that held their promise of labor, didn't sway them. Some people did think of it as just a piece of paper and walked away. So contracts were registered, and although they were a civil matter, the contract terms were enforced by the courts. Walking away or even enticing someone to leave the promised employment was seen as a theft of services, and treated as such. Then it became a crime, and the state got involved. But the state usually didn't have the time or money to enforce the law. If the runaway was found, they were usually remanded back to the contract holder but even the state could run out of patience. Three strikes and they would sentence the runaway to prison for the duration of the contract term.

"You playing or dreaming," Sid asked with a nudge.

"Hmm." Deborah came back with a start. She had been wandering, wondering what that woman had done to be on a state-registered contract. She checked her cards, grimaced and folded.

A contract could be abused, she admitted. That was why they weren't popular. Some holders worked the laborers as hard as they could to get as much out of them before the end date. Some laborers were tricked into signing contracts, thinking they were signing for one kind of work and then being sold for another. Once that contract was signed, the laborer had little or no say about what happened. There were no unions, although labor boards were beginning to become established. Women, if they got pregnant, had that time added to their contract, even though they might work right up until delivery. Then there was always the sexual abuse and exploitation that happened.

Other times, contract laborers were treated as valued employees, taken in as family when they were working in a small business. While they might not be paid cash wages, they benefited in other ways. That's how she treated hers, as family. She couldn't manage without them and tried to let them know it. Karen managed the land, Sara managed the house, Linda took care of the animals. Sue managed the kitchen. Now Beth was the prize, a nurse practitioner. Rae had started doing pottery this winter and that was turning out well. Peg, ah, Peg was in a class by herself. Sometimes she wished Peg had declined her offer of a contract, but then she would have probably left the area. Having her on contract was not the same as having her as a lover, but at least now, she still had her counsel. She sighed. Sometimes she had hard choices. The others were easy. Brea was a solid stabilizing force, and then Kelly was just a flat-out hard worker. She frowned. Now, Bobbi. Bobbi was a problem. Hadn't found out what to do with her yet.

"You in this round?"

She nodded. Back to the card game. The afternoon passed, the snow piled up and she focused on the cards. She threw in a few good hands, bluffed a few, won some, lost some. She thought Gentry and his companion had something going, but she couldn't quite figure out what. They had suggested another version of poker, just to make things interesting. The group went along—stakes were higher. If there was cheating, Deborah wasn't sure how it was being done. Finally Gentry was out of cash but he seemed to think he had a good hand. He started to drag the pot, pulling the amount of his bet out to one side. If he lost, that was the amount he would owe. If he won, it wouldn't matter.

"Can't do that," Sid pointed out. "If you lived here, that's one thing, but you're just traveling through."

Gentry checked his cards again, seemed like it was a hand he had a lot of confidence in, hated to fold. "Got chits from Bank of Memphis."

Brad, the old school-mate, laughed. "Hell, we don't take chits three counties away, never mind someplace like Memphis."

Everyone waited. Gentry checked his cards again. Deborah sat back in her chair, convinced this was what Gentry had been building up to all afternoon. She had a good hand, but she wasn't sure she was going to stay. It all depended on what Gentry was up to.

"Tell you what I'm gonna do," he said like he just seized on a bright idea. "I've got this contract here. I'll put her up as collateral."

Oh, really bad form, Deborah thought as she felt the chill around the table. He's really read this group wrong. Contracts in this area were still respected as people, not pieces of property. It was one thing to set up a contract between two people as a promise of support in exchange for labor, quite another to use a contract as collateral for a loan much less a poker game.

He looked over his shoulder. "Hey, you. Come here."

Deborah watched the woman slowly unfold from her corner. She bent over to push her jeans down her legs and got to her feet. She stood there a minute as if bracing herself then picked up her jacket and started through the tables and chairs with a long lanky stride.

Deborah looked down at her cards, not seeing them, reluctant to watch the woman approach but then she looked up again, compelled. There was no way anyone else could move the same way, that long leggy step, the twist of the body as she weaved through the chairs. The woman stationed herself across the table from Deborah, near enough to be compliant and distant enough to be out of Gentry's reach. Now that she was closer and her head was up, her fading black eye was visible as well as the jagged cut on her cheekbone and the bruise along her jawline. She didn't look at anyone as Gentry went on with her list of accomplishments.

"Experienced, cooperative, has the most amazing skills," and he had that slight leer to his voice until his eyes fell on Deborah. "Good, hard worker, great help around the house, even does work outside, switch hitter so to speak."

The woman glanced at him, betraying surprise which suggested to Deborah that housework accomplishments weren't usually cited, then gave a quick glance around the table. She started at the sight of Deborah. Deborah stared back with as much disinterest as she could muster and the woman quickly looked away.

"Now what do I want with a contract?" Sid complained. He had the best hand showing on the table, a possible straight. "And we can sure see she's a good willing worker."

"I'll cover it," Deborah said blandly, picking her change up and dropping the coins one by one onto a stack. Her words created a bigger chill. She had never before publicly arranged any contracts. Oh, people knew or rather suspected but the contracts had all been privately negotiated and could therefore be tactfully ignored by everyone. She was reasonably sure stories of this poker game would be all over the county by sundown tomorrow night if not sooner, snow storm or not. She wasn't fond of being the subject of gossip or any public scrutiny. She had survived by no one knowing her business, but this was different. "Whoever wins, I'll pay the drag and the contract balance."

No one made any comment in the heavy silence. Deborah just sat there and waited for someone to say something. No one spoke up in protest. The pot had grown large enough that no one wanted to lose. Gentry seemed pretty confident of his hand, but there were some good hands showing. Everyone wanted to win the money except Deborah. She had what she wanted as soon as Gentry tossed the papers into the pot in the middle of the table.

Conversation in the diner died and Deborah felt rather than saw others wander over to watch. From the corner of her eye, she saw Todd take up a position behind her.

The last card went around. Brad drew nothing so he folded. Sid had a possible straight, maybe even a possible flush but Deborah didn't think so. He checked. Carl and Leon, Gentry's companion, both folded. Deborah checked. The last guy folded. Gentry had a possible full house, which Deborah speculated, might have made him overly confident.

"Full house." Gentry turned his cards over. Aces and kings. Sid turned his hand over with a grimace. He had his flush, but not a straight. Too bad. Gentry was already reaching for the pot.

"Not so fast." Deborah flipped her hole cards of jack and ace to match her ten, queen, king, showing all red, all hearts. "Read 'em and weep." A collective breath was expelled from around the table.

"Damn Deborah," Brad burst out with. "I swear to God, things haven't changed a bit. You can still pull those straights like nobody's business."

Deborah permitted herself a small smile. "Inside track with Lady Luck, don't you know?" She dragged the pot in front of her as Gentry stared at her cards in apparent disbelief. Sid shook his head as he picked up his remaining monies. The game was over as far as everyone was concerned but it was already a topic of discussion.

Deborah picked up the folded contract, read the cover sheet. She glanced at the woman who wouldn't look at her, then went back to skim through the rest of the pages. She looked up at Gentry. "Ready to sign the transfer?"

Gentry rubbed his chin. "Well, guess you won it fair and square." Everyone stopped talking and turned to look at him. He looked up at the sudden scrutiny. "Not that I'm implying that there was any cheating going on," he said quickly.

"Better not be," Brad warned. "We've known each other since grade school. You're the odd man out."

Gentry made a show of reaching for his pen from his jacket pocket. "Just wondered if the lady knows what she's getting into. Contracts can be a dirty business."

"Oh, I think I can handle it," Deborah said blandly, halfway expecting someone to say something. There was a silence around the table, a waiting.

"State contracts can be a pain in the a—" He caught himself in time. "There're a lot of extra rules and regs."

"I'll deal with it." Deborah waited and finally unable to delay anymore, Gentry signed. He handed her the papers.

"And the balance I owe you?"

He named a figure and there was a low whistle from someone, a throat clearing from someone else.

Deborah reached behind her and Todd handed over her jacket. She gave a nod of thanks and pulled out her wallet from the inside pocket. Normally she wouldn't be carrying that much cash but thanks to the bank unexpectedly closing she hadn't been able to deposit it. She counted the cash out on the table, then glancing at the small amount in front of him, she deducted the amount he owed the pot. Satisfied, she picked up the cash and held it out to him, her other hand outstretched for the signed contract.

Once Gentry had folded up the money and Deborah had stuffed the contract into her pocket, the tension was broken. "Hey, Luella," Brad hollered. "You got any ham and eggs in the kitchen?"

"Coming up right away." She went through the swinging door to the kitchen. "Anyone else?"

Gentry slowly rose from the table and made a move toward the woman. She stood there, uncertain, looking from him to Deborah, cautiously stepping away as if he would stop her.

Deborah wondered about the byplay as she caught the woman's eye. "You need to come with me," she said in a firm voice. "We need to get acquainted."

With an air of relief, the woman moved further out of Gentry's reach but she didn't come any closer to Deborah than necessary. Deborah stuffed her wallet back into her jacket wondering how she was going to handle this.

"Thought you had a full house," Todd interrupted her thoughts in a low voice behind her.

She glanced at him in puzzlement and then realized he wasn't talking about the cards. "Always room for one more." She saw the woman stiffen and wondered if she heard or how she took it.

He raised his eyebrows in question as he glanced at the woman and then back at Gentry. "Hope you know what you're getting into."

"So do I." She turned back to the woman and pointed to the other end of the diner. "This way."

Halfway down, Deborah ducked behind the counter and stuck her head into the kitchen. "Luella, can I use your office?"

"Sure, go ahead."

Deborah pointed to the door marked Private at the end of the counter. "Down there."

CHAPTER TWO

She considered what she had done purely on impulse. She didn't need another contract. She was close to the limit now both in terms of legalities and house capacity. Maybe it was the woman's bruises. Maybe it was just because Deborah didn't like Gentry's attitude, that she could have some perverse enjoyment in taking something away from him. Maybe it was her rescue fantasies kicking in again. Maybe it was just because.

The solid wood door opened to more of a storage room than an office although to the left of the door there was a desk with a lamp. The walls were lined with shelves, some half empty and others loaded with supplies. Luella had her sources and was known for packing ten pounds in a five-pound bag.

"Go on in." Deborah gave a slight push to the woman's back noting that she jerked away. "Take a seat." She indicated one of several metal chairs in the middle of the room.

"I'll stand," the woman said in a raspy voice.

Deborah gave her a sharp look as she shut the door and flipped the deadbolt, the sound of it sliding home loud in the small room. This was one interview she didn't want interrupted.

The woman stepped back, half turning, providing minimum exposure, a defensive move Deborah recognized. Her hands were clenched, whether from tension or from the thought she might need to defend herself, Deborah had no idea.

"I don't bite." Deborah tossed her coat over the file cabinet at the corner of the desk and held her hand out for the woman's jacket. Reluctantly, she handed it over. Now that they were alone, away from curious eyes, Deborah could openly appraise the whip-thin woman.

Joanna… God, after all these years. If it hadn't been for her walk, I wouldn't have known her. All those bruises. She didn't want to think about how she had gotten them. *So thin, and I thought she was thin years ago. God, didn't she ever eat? Need to put some weight on her. Those clothes. Jeans so thin they could almost be seen through. Running shoes? In this weather? She'd better have something else out there 'cause that tank top and flannel shirt under that jacket aren't enough.* She looked the woman over again. Her hands, the fingers, thin and red, the knuckles skinned. Her dark hair was almost shoulder length but it was a bad cut and hung around her face. Then Deborah met her gaze.

The woman glared back at her, defiant, as if she considered Deborah's appraisal offensive. Her head went up slightly, and she drew herself in. *At least she can still get angry, although that's probably how she got beaten. So she's got some fight left in her. So many have been broken.* Yes, Deborah considered, it probably was offensive but there were lots of things offensive these days and if this was the worst of it, then they were both lucky.

"You know, Joanna," she opened the conversation, "you're about the last person I ever expected to find on contract."

"And you're about the last person I ever expected to find as a contract holder," Joanna responded in that raspy, hoarse voice.

Deborah actually flinched at the sound. Not the words. She was accustomed to the contempt and could deal with that, but the hoarseness was like a physical blow. She had fallen in love with Joanna's voice, listening to it through the speakers in the radio studio library, feeling it envelop her as if it had a texture. Sometimes she thought she had fallen in love with Joanna before she had ever physically met her simply because of her voice.

Hearing it like this was like seeing a fine painting slashed. She gave a small shrug. "I guess we've all landed in different places."

"I've never dealt with a woman contract holder," Joanna went on caustically. "I forget some women take advantage of others just as much as some men do."

"Equal opportunity," Deborah said evenly. *Nothing like bringing out the attitude first thing. In that way, she hasn't changed.* Any idea of Joanna being glad or even relieved to see her could be discarded. "For that matter, there aren't many women contract holders but we do exist. You have a problem with that?" *Might as well get it all out in the open.*

"I don't like contract holders, period."

Well, that's blunt enough. Straightforward as ever. Glad to see that hasn't changed. But Deborah also knew such an attitude could cause trouble. "So why are you on contract then?"

"I never signed a contract."

Deborah raised her eyebrows. "Oh, really?" She reached over and pulled the contract out of the jacket pocket and flipped through the pages. *Damn, there are a lot of transfers.* She finally made it to the signature page. "Looks like a signature here, Joanna. Not your right name, but it's your writing. It hasn't changed much. I still recognize it. And there's the thumbprint." Thumbprints were added, she knew, because lots of people signed a false name and then tried to weasel out of it later. And some were just ashamed. Contracts were usually the last resort for survival and no one wanted to admit their situation was that bad.

Joanna took an angry step forward. "I don't want to be on contract."

That's not answering the question. "So? I haven't found many people who do."

"No!" Joanna took another step forward, her face flushed under the bruises. "I never *consented* to the original contract."

"Ah-ha. Consent." *A key word.* Deborah sat there a minute, staring at Joanna, trying to think of how a person could be on contract without consenting to it. Crime time—some jails and prisons leased out prisoners onto contract—it reduced their overheads. Debt seizure—those usually lasted until the debt was paid. However, she couldn't see Joanna falling into either of those categories. "So tell me, how did this little thing come about?"

"I was shanghaied!"

Shanghaied. That would explain it. Deborah looked down at her leather boots, examined the toes as she considered the ramifications of Joanna's statement. Such things did happen, she knew. Peg and Brea had mentioned it once or twice, about towns to be avoided because of such things. An unfair practice but the bottom line was still that Joanna was on contract.

"You do know what shanghaied means, don't you?" Joanna questioned caustically when Deborah made no immediate response.

"Oh, yes," Deborah said resignedly as she gave Joanna a warning glance. She could not imagine Joanna speaking to Gentry like that, but then again, that might have been why Joanna was bruised. "I'm just more familiar with it being used in terms of nineteenth-century sailors rather than present day contracts."

"Well, the practice is alive and well," Joanna said bitterly.

Deborah shook her head both in dismay that such things happened and sympathy for anyone caught in that situation. "Go on, tell me what happened."

"Small town," Joanna said shortly. "They decided they didn't need any drain on their civic treasury. So they gave us free meal. For the homeless. The food was drugged. When we woke up, we were all on contract, sold to the highest bidder. Kill two birds with one stone. Get rid of anyone who didn't belong. Money in the treasury."

Deborah considered the story as she eyed Joanna. It sounded true enough, but it didn't explain why Joanna had been caught in it. What was she doing in that position? And why was she homeless? Why didn't she have someone to vouch for her so she could get out of it. Deborah had some sympathy for small towns with stretched resources and drifters coming through. There were no easy answers. "Tough luck," she commented in a neutral tone. Maybe she could find out later the parts Joanna was leaving out.

"Luck!" Joanna advanced a step, her fists clenched. "Common decency—"

"Is in short supply these days," Deborah cut in coldly. "Especially for outsiders." Conditions were hard and she couldn't do anything about most of them. She had little sympathy for those still living under old expectations, and frankly, she thought Joanna would have known better. People who couldn't adjust didn't survive.

"It's not right," Joanna said in a voice cold with fury. She said nothing more but from her glare, Deborah got the idea it wasn't from lack of words.

"No, it's not," Deborah admitted. "We've become very self-protective and woe to be for strangers. It's not right but that's the way it is."

She paused for Joanna to add something but she remained silent. Deborah went back to reading the contract more carefully. "I see you appealed it," she said.

"For all the good it did me." There was no mistaking the resentment.

"Then you made it worse by running away. Twice. That brought you under state registration. Do it again and you'll be sitting in a cell." *A waste of resources,* Deborah thought but that was the way things were now. Prisons for profit needed prisoners.

"I've already done it," Joanna said with some defiance. "Twice more."

Deborah started flipping back through the pages. She only saw two.

"No, you won't find it recorded there."

"Why not?" Deborah could think of several reasons, none of them good but it would explain some of the bruises. *Desperation or stupidity?* She never thought Joanna stupid and she hated to think she might have been that desperate.

"If he had reported it," Joanna said evenly, "he would have forfeited my contract. He didn't want that so he took care of it himself." She faced Deborah defiantly as if daring Deborah to doubt her.

God, this just gets worse. Deborah could readily envisage Joanna being insubordinate and taking chances, physical or otherwise. Joanna had always been the more physically active one and determined to the point of foolhardy. "But he wasn't adverse to risk losing you by tossing your contract into a poker pot. There seems to be a degree of inconsistency."

Joanna gave her a knowing pitiful smirk as if Deborah were some rube who didn't know a con game when she saw one. "Oh, he hasn't lost me. He'll be around, late tonight, maybe tomorrow, with some story. Can't stand to lose me, I'm too important to him. Maybe since you're a woman, maybe he'll use the story that contracts are difficult for a woman to deal with, you know, women can't manage anything, much less a contract. He'll offer to buy my contract back, take me off your hands. At a lesser price, of course."

Deborah mulled over that idea. The scam probably worked most of the time. Contracts weren't popular in the rural areas but the lure of having someone at your beck and call to get work done was tempting. Sometimes having an extra pair of hands was just too good to resist. Then, once that contract was in play, the responsibility kicked in. Another mouth to feed, supervision of maybe someone who wouldn't work. And if a contract was difficult? She looked Joanna over speculatively. No one wanted to buy trouble. Deborah could imagine a quick sell back. "Sounds like he's done this a lot."

"Enough."

"And what's your role?"

There was a lightning flash of anger across Joanna's face that she didn't bother to hide. "Role? What makes you think I have any role to play? I'm a fucking commodity!"

Deborah couldn't decide if Joanna had used the word as a profanity or a description. It didn't matter—either way was appropriate. Her attitude alone would have marked her as a difficult contract, and anyone not prepared to deal with that would be shed of her quickly. Deborah shook her head. Joanna's attitude probably played right into Gentry's hands. She would have thought Joanna would have been smarter than that. Her distaste must have shown.

"What? You didn't think contracts could be used like that? Get your head out of the sand, Deborah. Contracts are abuse."

"So's starving," Deborah retorted sharply. Joanna bit back any response and Deborah caught her temper. Joanna wasn't the one she should be angry with. She started again. "Prostitution was around a long time before there were contracts," she managed to say in a milder tone. "Long before contracts, and probably will be long after contracts fade away."

Joanna jerked back as if Deborah had slapped her.

"And I guess I used the wrong word," Deborah went on smoothly. "Although you did give me information I needed to know. I asked what your role was. I should have asked what your choice in the matter was."

"Choice! What makes you think I had any choice in the matter?" Until that point, Deborah had always considered the description "spitting mad" a euphemism but Joanna was spitting mad. "I didn't have a choice being on contract! I didn't have a choice as to who got my contract! I sure as hell don't have a choice as to what he does with me! You have no idea what it's like," Joanna continued shakily when Deborah made no comment. "He 'sells' my contract. And I have to put up with—with whatever they want to use me for." She closed her eyes and turned her head away. "Then he comes back and offers to buy it back. Even if someone decent does 'win' my contract, even if they are reluctant, he leans on them and strong-arms them into finally agreeing to the buyback. My opinion isn't a consideration."

Deborah sized Joanna up dispassionately. She knew all the arguments. She didn't need a difficult contract, and Joanna would definitely be one. She didn't need to bring someone into the house who might stir up trouble. Might? It was almost a given Joanna would. Deborah didn't need an unwilling contract to make everyone else question if they could have made it without her. She certainly didn't need a state-restricted contract with all the possible exposure it would entail.

At the same time, Joanna certainly showed evidence of being abused. She never had been a fighter, more of a persuader. She might have learned some self-defense along the way but she had never been aggressive. Clearly in these times, that was a disadvantage.

"Come here," Deborah ordered suddenly as she moved back on the desk for a firmer seat. "Let me see you."

Joanna abruptly pulled back. "You can see me just fine from where you're at."

Deborah lowered her head and looked up at Joanna. "Don't be dense, Joanna. This isn't the time to show how difficult you can be."

Joanna hesitated but then she came forward reluctantly to stand before Deborah. Deborah caught Joanna's wrist to pull her closer between her spread legs. Joanna let herself be drawn to Deborah. She didn't fight until Deborah let go of her wrists and took hold of the edge of her shirt. Then different emotions rippled across her face as Deborah unbuttoned the threadbare flannel. Apprehension, distaste, indecision, fear, anger—all were held in check until Deborah spread open the shirt and started to push it off Joanna's shoulders. Joanna jerked back, would have stepped back except for Deborah's leg coming up to catch her.

"Don't. Touch. Me." It wasn't a request.

Deborah paused. Defiance. Insubordination if she wanted to play the hard line. Yes, she knew she was pushing the limits, goading Joanna. Still, she needed to see how she would react and yes, she needed to see how badly damaged Joanna was. No matter what their history, they were in a different time now. She needed to deal with a new contract she was taking into her house. Yes, she was being invasive, but this was a responsibility. Joanna was on her very thin grounds for refusing her. At the same time, there was no sense pushing her into a corner and leaving her with no place to go. She dropped her hands.

"Take your shirt off, Joanna," she ordered instead in a quiet firm impersonal voice.

"For what?"

"So I can see how bruised you are." Deborah met her gaze, the angry defiance. "I'm not going to hurt you and I won't touch you." She offered that much as an assurance, not sure whether Joanna would take it or not. "But I do need to see."

"And if I don't?"

Deborah gave a careless shrug. Persuasion was the better choice, and she really did need to see. If she didn't now, she would later because she already knew she had no intention of letting

Joanna go back. "Your choice. Just remember all choices have consequences."

Joanna stood there a moment, uncertainty in her eyes. Deborah watched her clench and unclench her fists and wondered how Joanna was working this out. Surely she had been examined before. "It's invasive," Joanna said finally but they both knew it was no more than a token protest.

Deborah nodded, accepting Joanna's backing down. "Yes, but I have the right to examine a contract as to health and injuries if I doubt the claims of good health and being injury free."

"I have the right to protest." Joanna's voice and manner was stiff, resistant. She might tolerate but that didn't mean there was any trust.

"Noted." Deborah waited. What seemed like an impossibly long time went by before Joanna spread her shirt and slid it off her shoulders to expose the tank top. Deborah noted the bruises on her upper arms where someone had grabbed her hard, another one shoulder disappearing under the shirt. Joanna dropped her gaze as she took the shirt off. "Turn around."

Joanna turned around and Deborah did a sharp intake of breath as she saw the welts and bruises across Joanna's back. She reached out but caught herself before she touched. She had promised and she knew if she wanted to gain any trust, she had to keep her word. "Pull up your tank top. Let me see." Even to her own ears, Deborah's voice was harder, colder, and she saw Joanna shudder before she complied.

Joanna took hold of the lower part of her tank top and pulled it up, exposing her back. She folded her arms tightly across her breasts protectively, leaving the tank top bunched over her shoulders. Deborah examined the bruised flesh, the swelling, welts across Joanna's back from the shoulder blades down. She reached out, not to touch, but to run her hand over Joanna's back just above the heated flesh. The bruises even extended under the waistband of Joanna's pants.

"Explain," Deborah ordered tersely as she dropped her hand.

"I ran away. He found me. I told you, he did his own punishments."

"These look fresh."

"He was just taking me back."

Deborah couldn't stand looking at the damaged flesh anymore. There was no excuse for this kind of abuse. "Pull your shirt down. Turn around."

Joanna pulled her shirt down and turned around. Her exposure had taken some of the starch out of her, some but not all. She didn't meet Deborah's eyes but gazed off somewhere in the distance braced to endure whatever Deborah might do next.

"I'm going to touch you," Deborah said as evenly as she could. She didn't want Joanna to think that she was angry with her. "I don't want to cause pain, so if something hurts, I want you to tell me." She saw no indication that Joanna had even heard her.

She started with Joanna's face, cupping the swollen cheeks, brushing her thumbs lightly against the jagged cut on the cheekbone, like someone's ring had caught her. It didn't feel like there was anything broken. She moved her finger lightly down Joanna's nose. Not even there. Her lips were dry, cracked.

She ran her fingers through Joanna's hair, limp, probably from poor diet. There was an egg-sized swelling on the back of her head. "What's this?"

"I fell," Joanna answered without expression.

Deborah looked her in the eyes, speculating if Joanna was lying.

Joanna looked startled by Deborah's doubt. "Really, I did. Trust me, I wouldn't say a word to protect him." She looked away again. "I slipped on some ice."

Deborah nodded. It was possible. She moved down to Joanna's jaw line, lymph nodes, lightly across the shoulders as Joanna stiffened. Deborah went down Joanna's arms, bruises on the outside indicated she had tried to defend her face. She was so thin, Deborah thought as she examined Joanna's hands. Long slender fingers, broken nails. She turned Joanna's hands over, as she remembered how Joanna had always taken such good care of them. Neglected now but no calluses.

"Are you still ticklish?" Joanna nodded, and Deborah firmly felt Joanna's ribs through the tank top. She could feel a welt there too. She shook her head. Small breasts, narrow hips. "Step back."

Joanna stepped back and Deborah got off the desk. She felt down Joanna's legs, picked up one leg, then the other, felt the ankles.

Deborah straightened up. As she had thought—too thin, soft, damaged. A good diet, some toning up, some healing time. She watched the pulse point at Joanna's collarbone, watched it increase under her gaze. Watched Joanna breathe shallowly. She looked into Joanna's face and saw the pure anger an instant before it was veiled. She didn't blame her.

"You have good endurance," she said quietly. "Now we need to talk." Deborah moved around her and pulled one of the metal chairs over. "Sit down."

Joanna stood there momentarily, then slowly collapsed into the chair. "What's there to talk about?"

"Tell me what he'll do next."

Joanna didn't answer but sat there, staring at the floor. Deborah stood over her, frowning, wondering if Joanna was going to just shut down entirely.

"Joanna," she prompted.

Joanna took a deep breath. "He probably won't come tonight," she said finally with a sigh. "Probably in the morning, if it looks like we're going to get out of here. I mean, as long as we're here, you have to pay for my food and everything."

Deborah nodded. He was a cheapskate besides. She pulled up a chair and sat down beside Joanna. "So he'll come by in the morning and give me this song and dance that I'm too delicate to take on a contract."

Joanna turned to give Deborah a head-to-toe look. "He's not that stupid." She looked away. "But he's used to getting his way. He'll probably try to convince you you're out of your depth, that holding a contract isn't easy. There're rules and regulations, all sorts of things."

Deborah raised her eyebrows. "So? Is that supposed to scare me?" Joanna turned back to look at her, her expression at first puzzled and then questioning. "You're not my first contract, Joanna," Deborah answered the unspoken question. "And you're not my only contract now."

Joanna blanched. "No," she protested faintly, looking ill. "You wouldn't." She shook her head. "I can't. I won't." She made a movement to get up and Deborah caught her arm and pushed her back into the chair.

"Can't what? Won't what? What are you talking about?"

"The only women contract holders I've heard of ran brothels." She shuddered and shook her head. "No, I won't do that. You can't make me."

"You assume too much. I run a farm not a brothel." *Although, God knows, on given days a brothel might be easier.* She tried to imagine the women at the farm in that setting and except for one maybe, it was unimaginable. "Yes, a farm, with vegetable gardens and fields of grain and livestock, cows, pigs, chickens," she clarified. "And yes, I've contracted with women only, but there's nothing going on there that you wouldn't expect on a farm."

Joanna's expression didn't change.

"It's hard work," Deborah went on. "But there's none of this." She ran her fingers lightly over the cut on Joanna's face, the bruises.

"I've seen farm operations with contract labor," Joanna said woodenly. "Might as well be slavery."

Deborah took Joanna lightly by the chin and made Joanna look at her. The woman looked fearful and defiant by turns, only now there was also pain and confusion in her eyes. "I don't do that. I'm not going to tell you it's an easy life. But we've managed to survive. Intact. There's food on the table and a roof over our heads."

"Just one big happy family."

Deborah chuckled as she thought of a few of the residents. She stood up. "Well, I wouldn't say we're all happy about it but I never put a rose garden into the contract. I promised hard work, shelter, food and safety. Happiness and attitude is something you bring into it." She stood looking down at Joanna, trying to imagine how she might fit in. All of her rebellion seemed to have evaporated and Deborah wasn't sure why. The physical exposure? Resignation? The knowledge that she couldn't do anything to stop her? Shame at how she had been treated? "Joanna, I run a good operation," she said, quietly trying to reassure her.

Joanna wasn't having any of that. "Yeah."

"I try to treat everyone as if they were part of my family."

Joanna wasn't mollified. "Yeah. Slaveholders said the same thing about their slaves."

Deborah shook her head. "You're just not going to cut me any slack, are you? Nice to see you can still get right to the point. You could be a regular little spokeswoman for ACTS."

Joanna caught her breath, her whole body stiffened. "You know of ACTS?"

"Against Contracted Temporary Services? Of course, every contract holder does," Deborah replied dismissively. "I understand they're making a real pest of themselves in the southern part of the state, but I haven't seen anyone locally. But that's another matter. I have a farm, seventy-five acres. It's been in my family for generations. So I have contracts to run it." She saw Joanna shudder and she could guess the images that were running through her mind.

"It's not like that," Deborah said quickly. "All my contracts are cooperative. They came to me, we hammered something out we could both live with. They're not open-ended, none of them are binding. They could give me notice any time and leave. I wouldn't stop them.

"You'll come into my house, you'll be treated like everyone else, no better, no worse. You won't be working any harder than anyone else there. And it would be honest labor." She could feel the tension ease. "And when you go to bed at night," she said in deliberate tones, "it'd be your bed and yours alone. No one will force you or coerce you."

Joanna shook her bowed head, made a faint sound of disbelief.

"But there is one thing," Deborah went on. "I expect some degree of cooperation from everyone I deal with. So I'm giving you a choice: you're going to have to tell me what to do when he comes tomorrow or whenever and wants to buy back your contract. If you really can't deal with me holding your contract, if you truly believe your lot won't be improved, that the devil you know is better than the devil you don't, then I'll sell your contract back."

Joanna continued to shake her head. "No, I can't choose. I won't cooperate. Cooperation is capitulation. Do whatever you want but don't expect me to help you."

"I don't consider this as 'help', Joanna. And I don't see it as capitulation. I see it as you having some say in what happens to you. Cooperation is not capitulation. Cooperation is survival."

"No, I can't. I won't."

"Yes, you can. All you have to do is tell me what you want me to do."

Joanna wrapped her arms around herself, bent over as if in pain, all the time shaking her head.

Deborah watched her, sympathetic but keeping her emotional distance. "Joanna, do you really want to go back to him? Do you really want to have your contract sold or won over and over again as part of his scam? Do you want to get dragged into situations that tear down your self-respect? How much longer do you think you can endure this?" Joanna took each question as a body blow. "Do you really think he shows any respect for you or cares about you except as a commodity, and not even a valued one at that?" She leaned forward to Joanna but didn't touch her. "Do you really think that I would treat you like that, that I wouldn't treat you decently?"

Joanna came up so quickly she almost hit Deborah, who reared back. "I don't know! Damn it, that's just the point. I don't know how you'd treat me. I never thought to see you or anyone else I ever knew holding contracts!" There were tears in her eyes as well as all the anger and fire that Deborah could remember seeing. "I don't want to be on contract at all."

Deborah squatted down beside the chair, looking at Joanna eye to eye. She resisted the desire to touch, to try to offer some reassurance, some protection. "No, I suppose not, but it's gone past the point where you or I have that choice."

Joanna glared at her and Deborah knew there was no point in further discussion. Joanna had to give her some leeway. "Joanna, I need you to answer me."

Joanna closed her eyes, shaking her head no. Then as if against her conscious will, the words were torn from her. "I—don't—want—to—go—back—to—him."

Deborah closed her eyes and breathed a sigh of relief. She didn't know if she could have sold this contract back. She opened her eyes to see Joanna stuff her fist in her mouth, shaking with tension. Deborah took hold of Joanna's hand, pulled it down and didn't let go. "See? That wasn't so difficult. And now we have something you and I agree on: I don't want you to go back to him either."

Joanna stared at her with mixed disbelief and hope. *How many times has she heard that?* Deborah wondered.

"You wouldn't—you wouldn't jerk me around on this, would you, Deborah?" Joanna asked in a shaking voice. Tears threatened to spill over. Tears had always been Joanna's undoing. She had always cried easily, and for so many reasons. Tension, frustration, anger, happiness, sometimes just being tired would do it. And she was always furious when others took it as a sign of weakness.

Deborah pulled out her bandanna from her back pocket and offered it. "No, I wouldn't jerk you around." Joanna took the bandanna, buried her face in its folds. "If you're going to cry, do it now, here. I don't want you going out there looking like I ran over you."

Joanna shook her head and Deborah watched her fight for self-control. She had never taken Joanna's tears for weakness, just great emotion. Sometimes she had envied her that. Now she just waited for the storm to pass. There were no tears, not this time.

Joanna finally raised her head, not dry-eyed but in control. She wiped her face, blew her nose. Then she carefully folded the bandanna and handed it back. "I'm all right," she said without shaking, but she avoided looking at Deborah.

Deborah shifted her position to stuff the bandanna back into her pocket but she didn't stand up. The tenuous pact she had established with Joanna could easily be destroyed by standing over her. "I know it'd be a lot easier all around if we could just leave right away but that isn't going to be the case. The snow."

Joanna nodded in faint agreement.

"With luck, in the morning we can get out of here but tonight, well, it might be uncomfortable for you." She paused but Joanna remained silent. "Folks around here don't like strangers and they're still uncomfortable with contracts."

Joanna still wouldn't look at her so Deborah went on.

"It might be awkward because everyone saw how I got your contract. They might be uncomfortable with that, but I don't think anyone here is going to be unpleasant to you because they have been forced to look at something they've tacitly ignored for a while. Me, maybe, but not you."

That was something she would have to deal with. Everyone knowing she held contracts was one thing. Rubbing their nose in it as to how she got this one might be something else. But that was her issue and her problem, not Joanna's.

"You okay?"

Joanna nodded but she was hunched over as if all this was more than she could deal with. And, Deborah considered, it probably was.

Deborah stood up and looked down at Joanna's bowed head. Her defiance had disappeared. She had the demeanor of someone anticipating an unavoidable beating.

"Now." She reached down and took Joanna's hand, ignoring her flinch and instead, feeling how cold her hands were. "We're going to go out there, and I'm going to find a nice warm corner for the newest member of my household. Then I'm going around and make nicey-nice with everyone because you are not the only one who does not think well of contract holders. I need to remind them I've been here. I'm the same person. Nothing's changed except now they know I have them too."

Joanna did look up at this.

"Yes." Deborah was able to smile. "Just a different type of closet." She had hoped for some response from Joanna but she merely dropped her gaze.

"And you." She squeezed Joanna's hands lightly. "You'll have time to process all this without me or anyone else hanging over you. You can take a nap if you need to. The power's still on, and hopefully it'll hold, so we should get a hot meal tonight. I can get you something right now if you need it." She turned Joanna's face to look at her.

Joanna still avoided looking at her but when Deborah didn't let go, she uneasily turned her eyes to her.

"You don't owe him a thing now, and he's not going to hurt you, not anymore. You don't have to be afraid."

Joanna jerked away. "I'm not a child that I have to be protected!"

Touchy. Deborah ignored her tone. "No, you're not a child, but you are a woman on contract. You've run away twice officially. You're vulnerable. I just want you to know that you're under my roof now, so you have my protection."

CHAPTER THREE

Joanna followed Deborah back into the diner. She held her head high and her back straight, loath to admit to anyone, much less herself, just how unnerved she really was. She slid into the corner seat Deborah pointed to. Normally she would have resented being treated like chattel but this time, all she wanted was to be left alone.

Much of her being able to survive was because no one knew her, her face, her voice. Amazing on one hand when in the past, she had strived so hard to be visible but then as anyone in public communication would say, the public is fickle. Yesterday's news lined today's birdcage. If there were still newspapers. If anyone kept birds anymore. And besides, she asked herself bitterly, who would ever expect the founder of the strongest anticontract organization in the country to be on contract herself.

So her invisibility kept her safe for the past year. Safe? She reconsidered that word. Maybe alive would be the better term. She had endured treatment that was the antithesis of safety but she had carried on relatively intact. Although lately, she had felt like she was losing something.

Nothing had shaken her so much as when she had stood there at the table and looked up to see Deborah Steele looking back at her. She'd always been cool under pressure but she had never been so tested as when she saw her ex-lover sitting there, holding cards and calmly stating she could cover the bet for Joanna's contract.

She buried her face in her hands, her long fingers running through her auburn hair. She hadn't been that shaken when the Alcohol Tobacco Firearms and Explosives (ATF) inspectors had come with their news. That was when ATF was still operational and able to investigate acts of arson and bombings.

"A bomb?" she remembered repeating when they told her and her advisory board. "In these offices?"

"Yes, ma'am. That was the plan. And he was pretty close to carrying it out. I understand you were having some repair work done?"

"Yes," her office manager had said. "We've had some vandalism recently."

The inspector had nodded. "Yes, that was how he gained access. He had planned on planting a bomb, we're not sure how he was going to trigger it but he certainly had enough explosives to do the job."

Joanna dealt with it with only minor disruption. She had been receiving death threats for over a year because of her anticontract work so she was in a sense prepared, appalled that someone would actually try to carry them out but still able to deal with them. The second attempt had shaken her. She had been the driver when that big dump truck had bumped them. They were in the fringes of the reconstruction zone so there was lots of heavy equipment on the road. She had thought at first it was just a run-of-the-mill accident and had slowed down preparatory to stopping.

"Jesus!" Rory her assistant had seen something. "Don't stop! Floor it! Get us out of here!"

She had done so, just escaping when the truck bumped her again. God, she didn't think those things could move that fast as she accelerated and the monster truck stayed on her bumper, knocking her once, twice, attempting to make her lose control.

She outran him, thanking God that she had taken that defensive driving course, not the one offered to the general public, but the one offered to security drivers. By the time they could pull into a safe populated location and watch the truck roar by, she had been shaking too much to get out. Rory had stumbled out of the car, to throw up in the nearest trash can.

"What was that about?" her logistics coordinator asked as she came up from the other car that had gone ahead. Then she had seen Rory, still white-faced and sick, and Joanna sitting there in the car with the door open. "Are you all right?"

Her board insisted on a security detail then, and while Joanna loathed the idea of a bodyguard, she knew it was as much for their safety as hers. It helped but it made her more isolated, which she didn't like. And in its own way, it exposed her more. She couldn't slip into anonymity so easily and gather the information she considered so critical. When they found the reward posters for her elimination on the net, they held an emergency meeting.

"Maybe you just need to drop out of sight for a while," William suggested. "You're our most visible spokesperson. We don't want to lose you."

Joanna turned to the young-looking well-built African-American who was also one of the ACTS founders. "I'm not running away," she said firmly. "This just means that someone out there is feeling the pressure."

"That might well be, but my experience also says it also will bring out every crazy who thinks they can make big-time with these extremists. And it's not like you can't run this organization without being here."

So in the end, she was persuaded. She would take the underground up to Canada. She could still be in contact, as long as the web held out. No one would realize for a while that she was gone. She would get firsthand knowledge on how they were spiriting some contracts out of the country. There were counterparts in Canada who would welcome her. So with some misgivings, she agreed.

The worst part of the journey was where the interstate was broken. They were traveling on secondary roads, winding through the countryside. Joanna had actually felt safer until they had paused to eat at a diner in some small town. She had noticed the silence when they entered, the military bearing of many of the diners.

"Local militia," her guide had said in a low voice. "Just be cool."

And she was, even when the hunk dressed in army fatigues slid in beside them and started a conversation. She remained friendly, chatty, gave the cover story she was traveling up to her sister's place in Wisconsin, cities were getting too dangerous. He readily agreed with that, quizzed them as to how long they were staying, were people expecting them, where they planned to stop for the night.

He left, but Joanna noted the glances of authorization that circled the room. But his parting words had been chilling. "You look like that dyke bitch who used to be on the tube. Anyone ever tell you that?"

"Yeah," she said with a laugh. "Won a look-alike contest a couple of years ago."

He wasn't impressed. "Wouldn't mind getting my hands on her, showing her some reality."

"Yeah," she said. "Well, everyone's reality is different."

Jesus, she thought as they left. Some young play soldier was walking around her car, looking at the license plates, at the luggage in the backseat. The man who interviewed her stood at the window watching and at some hidden signal, the man outside drew back.

"Have a safe trip, ma'am," he said politely but it was clear, she was to keep moving.

"Good God, what was that about?"

"Strangers aren't welcome," her escort explained in a small voice. "How's our gas? I don't want to stick around here any longer than what we have to."

"We can make it to the next town, assuming they have gas."

"Let's assume. This place gives me the willies."

Things deteriorated after that. They were going through country where there were fewer cars, more hitchhikers. They got lost for almost half a day. Their map wasn't accurate. Her escort got really sick, but she said it would pass, just a temporary thing.

They stopped at a hotel, phone lines down so no ATM, no credit card, not even the new one with her cover identity. Had to pay cash. Came out the next morning to find the car gone.

She had maps, she had her backpack. Her escort couldn't walk. Joanna assured her she could make it to the next safe point alone. She was athletic, capable. The escort didn't have much choice. She gave her directions. Joanna joined a group walking up the road, hitched a ride with them in the back of a pickup. The lift gave her all the warnings about a lone woman traveling but they were good people. They took sympathy on her and went out of their way to get her close to her destination. She gave a false location of the safe house. She waited and watched them leave before she started to backtrack, to pick up the side road. From the detail on the map, the house couldn't be more than a mile or so off the highway.

However, the friendly house had been destroyed, a burnt shell. It could have been razed because of sickness, to eliminate contamination. It could have been a reprisal. She just knew she had to make it to the next stop totally on her own. That was why she had been alone when she was shanghaied.

Already at a disadvantage of being homeless, no support, no money, this group of laborers had been shamelessly taken advantage of. Sweatshops, hard labor, poor food even for these times, and poorer living conditions. She had spoken up, and had been beaten for it. She managed to file a lawsuit but it had been rejected as frivolous. Then she had escaped but she didn't have the necessary road smarts to survive. She got caught in a round-up. By then she was labeled a troublemaker and she learned that the more savvy contract laborers were just as dangerous as the contract holders.

Gentry had picked up her contract cheaply because she was labeled as difficult, and he turned out to be just a small-time operator on the fringes with big ideas of trying to break into the big time. He used her to open doors, sometimes to the very factions who had been trying to kill her. She wasn't recognized, but she had nightmares about it. She was managing by hiding in plain sight, learning more about contracts from the inside than she had ever imagined. Just one anonymous woman on contract.

Until now. Until Deborah Steele. Contract holder. Farmer? Ex-lover.

She looked down the diner to see Deborah leaning over the counter, talking to the heavyset woman who owned the place. How does a mild-mannered librarian who liked to work behind the scenes at a radio station in Pennsylvania morph into an Indiana farmer who ran her farm with contract labor?

Joanna drew a deep breath. She couldn't afford to go to pieces now, no matter how much Deborah unnerved her. Joanna examined the tall woman dressed in whipcord pants and matching jacket, a turtleneck sweater, calf-high leather boots. She glanced at the long down jacket that Deborah had carelessly tossed onto the seat beside her. Joanna had seen fights over clothing like that, protection against the penetrating cold. In this group of denim and flannel, Deborah stood out as successful, prosperous and a person of influence. No wonder Gentry had put Joanna's contract into the pot. Deborah was everything he usually courted. Except she was a woman.

A woman contract holder. Hard to believe. Joanna didn't want to believe. She'd heard stories, "Hard-hearted bitches, not a bit of mercy in them," she had been warned. "Avoid women contactors like the plague. Most of them run whorehouses, but no matter what they do, they're hard taskmasters. Harder on the women than the men under them, like they don't want to identify with any woman on contract."

"There's got to be good ones," she had argued. She was naïve. "There's good and bad in both genders."

"If there's a good woman contractor, I haven't found her yet."

And since then, all the stories had been similar. Joanna had lost most of her naiveté, learning how cruel holders could be, how they took advantage of every weakness, how they were users, and now she was theirs to be used.

Joanna watched Deborah mixing with the other diners. A farmer. Well, Joanna thought grudgingly, farmers had the best chance of eating. And Deborah did look well fed, but that was the situation for most contract holders. Joanna had heard of situations where the holder sold all the produce, didn't bother feeding the workers, and if they hadn't stolen, they would have starved. So she would have to reserve judgment on that count. Deborah did look healthy, leaner than she used to when she had made excuses not to go to the gym. She appeared well-tanned in spite of the season but then Deborah always did, even though she never went outdoors. She said something one time about Indian blood. There were lines at her eyes, indicating she worked outside now. Her hands were thinner, dryer, calloused. Joanna remembered their touch during their interview. Invasive, yes—harsh, no.

Joanna gazed over the room again, avoiding Gentry's eye. She didn't want to deal with him now, didn't want to have to think about tomorrow. Her mind was still filled with Deborah and how she was going to deal with her.

"You must have me confused with someone else," Deborah had told her the last time they had met. That had been where? God, she couldn't remember. Joanna had been on a speaking tour, traveling around the country, gathering information. The economy was tanking and safety nets for the poor, the elderly, the children, they were all failing. And more insidious was the war on women, as she saw it. One of the speaking engagements had been at the library somewhere in the Midwest where Deborah was working. She had seen the name on the program and wanted to meet this Deborah Steele who had been in charge of some of the arrangements. She wasn't even sure that it was the same Deborah, as their breakup had been years before. Perhaps enough time had passed so they might be friends.

Even now, Joanna could shiver. She had forgotten how Deborah could carry her anger the way a miser saved her money. The icy stranger who ignored her offered hand looked her straight in the eye and denied her. Joanna left that day, realizing the cold stranger was right: she didn't know her at all. Maybe she never had. And she hadn't seen her since.

Perhaps that was the route she should have taken with Deborah now. *You must have me confused with someone else.* Would Deborah have bought it? Probably not. Joanna never had the ability to sandbag the way Deborah did. She could do it past all reason, all logic, no matter what it cost her.

Yet, she had said, "You have my protection." Maybe her statement was worth something. Maybe Deborah would, in spite of everything, protect her. Maybe the disasters had changed her, taught her that she had to hold on to things. Maybe she would protect her because of what they once had. Maybe.

Joanna wondered what Deborah was saying as she mingled. She despised being on contract but she didn't want to be an object of pity either. She could feel their glances, and when she finally got up the nerve to look up and met their gaze she was surprised to see thoughtful looks, curious maybe. One man even raised his finger to his nonexistent hat, and the girl behind the cash register gave a tentative smile.

Confused, Joanna turned to look out the windows. The snow was still coming down but she wasn't so concerned about the weather now. Could Deborah have been telling the truth? Was she just running the family farm and using contract labor? Surely though, she would have heard what Joanna had been doing? No, Joanna decided on second thought, When Deborah turned a blind eye, she really didn't see it. Her comment about ACTS was just casual enough to make Joanna believe she didn't know. ACTS was just an annoyance, nothing personal, just one of those organizations trying to mess with her business.

But even if she didn't know, she was still a holder. And she knew who Joanna really was. All it would take would be one careless comment to the wrong person, drop her name at some holder gathering or just mention it in passing.

"You have my protection." That's what Deborah had told her. But she may not realize just how much protection she required. The question was, Joanna thought with icy chills, *Even if you can protect me from him, who's going to protect me from you?*

She saw Gentry watching her. Would he be safer? Although he was a really nasty guy, he didn't know who she was. She heard Deborah's laughter and turned to see her stop at the booth and talk to the men from the poker game. If it had been Gentry talking to them, she would know what was being said and would already be guessing which one would be first to come around for her later. But Deborah? No, even at her worst, she could not imagine Deborah pimping.

She looked back at Gentry watching her and knew he wanted a word with her, wanted to know how his scam was going to go. She knew if she ended back in his clutches, she'd end up paying for not cooperating with him now. He was killing her by degrees because she continued to defy him. How much longer could she endure that? And Deborah has promised shelter, food, hard work, her own bed. Honest work.

Not much of a choice. As long as Deborah could stand up to Gentry. Had Deborah changed so much that she could be strong-armed into doing something she didn't want to do? Still work with him in case she landed back in his hands or take her chances with Deborah in spite of the dangers?

As it turned out, there was no choice. Every time she moved, Deborah eyed her. When she got up to get a drink of water, to move cramped muscles, whatever, Deborah was right there. Finally Joanna put her head back down on her drawn up knees so she didn't have to see anybody.

"When did you last eat?"

Joanna started and blinked. She must have dozed off a bit. She looked across the table at Deborah and tried to make sense of her question, unaccustomed to any contract holder looking out for her. Deborah even sounded concerned, as if Joanna's answer might actually matter. Joanna shook her head.

"I asked a question. I expect an answer."

Joanna closed her eyes and thought about it. "Last night," she said finally, not adding that the dinner hadn't stayed. She had thrown it up after another beating. Rich food, hotel food, she couldn't stomach anymore. When she looked back, Deborah was gone, down at the other end of the counter by the cash register. She was talking to the older woman again.

Joanna laid her head back down on her knees.

"Eat." The thump of the plate set on the table in front of her made her jump and she jerked upright. Shepherd's pie and homemade biscuits on the side. She looked up in disbelief as Deborah sat a similar plate across the table from her.

"You're eating with me?" was all she could say.

"Of course." Deborah went back to the counter to pick up two cups, one coffee, one hot tea, and returned to the table as Joanna sat up. She set the tea down beside Joanna's plate and pulled out the chair. "Your voice sounded strained. I've brought you some tea with honey and lemon. Thought it might help," she said as she sat down. "Does it still work, the tea?" She picked up her silverware, looked up at Joanna when she didn't respond. "Something wrong?"

Contract holders don't eat with the help. But Joanna couldn't say it. She indicated the tea with a nod. "You remembered."

"I remembered," Deborah said shortly. "Now eat before it gets cold."

Joanna picked up her fork, resisting feeling touched at the unexpected kindness. How could something like a plate of shepherd's pie hit her so hard? Except it was her favorite comfort food, always something that warmed her on cold winter nights, and here Deborah was serving it to her when she was cold and alone and afraid. She wondered if it was deliberate. Diners like this usually had shepherd's pie as a staple, a way to use up leftover meat and vegetables. No matter whether it had been deliberate or happenstance, she had to take it as a gift of Fate. And then the tea. How many times had Deborah brewed tea for her to ease her strained throat? Instead of being reassuring, Deborah's actions were vaguely unsettling, a reminder of just how well she knew Joanna.

They ate without speaking as darkness fell and the plate glass windows turned into mirrors. She squinted to see if it had stopped snowing, if Deborah's prediction of their getting on their way in the morning would also be true. *And to where?* she wondered. She had no idea where they were except in the most general terms. That was what made escape impossible. If she could only get her hands on a map. Years of using a GPS didn't help much now. What she wouldn't do for a paper map, even an out-of-date, wrinkled up, torn apart paper map.

She looked up to see Deborah watching her, her gray eyes heavily hooded. Joanna hauled in her thoughts and deliberately laid her silverware across her plate, signifying she was done.

Deborah picked the plate up without comment, stacked hers on top with her coffee cup but left Joanna's half-filled tea. She carried them away and didn't return, leaving Joanna to reflect and think and worry.

Joanna sipped the tea, soothing on her raw throat. She began to feel better. The meal had helped. Deborah hadn't asked about the name change on her contract. Joanna wondered why. Maybe she hadn't noticed. Maybe she just accepted it as one of life's events. Women marry, divorce. Names change for all sorts of reasons. Maybe she just didn't care. Or didn't want to know. Or it didn't matter.

Joanna finished her tea, looked around. Deborah wasn't in sight and others in the diner seemed to be settling down for the night, picking out their spots. The men were at the other end, and Joanna got that fluttery feeling. It was the time of night when someone usually came to collect her. She swallowed as she assessed her isolated corner. Deborah wouldn't have just abandoned her after all that fine talk, would she? She moved back into the corner, trying to make herself smaller, invisible.

Even if she didn't think Deborah would sell her, she grew uneasy. Her earlier comment that prostitution had been around a long time, would be around after contracts, came back to her. Vaguely she remembered some past conversation years before when they had discussed women's rights. *If she's willing and enjoys it, and he's willing to pay for it, I don't see a problem,* Deborah had said then. Joanna hadn't agreed, arguing about degradation, abuse, levels of power. Deborah wasn't swayed then, so may not be now.

She had to move, she couldn't stand the waiting. Her stomach began to churn. She had been too open, telling Deborah how she had been used, tacitly giving her permission to continue. She had been a fool. She had wanted to believe so badly in spite of all her logic. Hope dies so hard.

She moved cautiously, wondering if she could make it to the restroom unnoticed. As soon as Joanna stood, Deborah came out of the kitchen door, her sleeves rolled up, a dishtowel thrown over her shoulder. "Going somewhere?"

So she was being watched, Joanna realized with a sinking heart. "I need to go to the restroom." Having to ask like a little kid was just one more unchanged humiliation.

Deborah threw the dishtowel down on the counter, and Joanna now understood Deborah had been working in the kitchen. "This way." Rather than go around the counter where she would have had to pass Gentry Deborah led her through the kitchen past the other women who didn't look up. "You all right?" Deborah asked over her shoulder.

Joanna looked at her in surprise at Deborah's concern. "Yes," she answered, taken aback again.

"I mean, I thought the pie would be bland enough for you. If you're sure you're all right, I'll wait out there." She examined Joanna's face. "If you need me, call me."

Maybe she read Deborah wrongly. That feeling lasted until she went out the door.

Deborah had her back to the restroom door, talking to the tall lanky guy who had been asleep on the chairs earlier in the day. Joanna's immediate thought was whether he was her first customer. "So what's he willing to pay?" Deborah was asking.

"Don't know," Todd answered evasively as he eyed Joanna. "Looks like you had quite a win today, Deborah." Deborah jerked around, the look of irritation immediately erased when she saw Joanna.

Joanna stepped back, her mouth suddenly dry as she realized she had interrupted something. Maybe it wasn't negotiations for her services, maybe there was something else going on. She had seen that look of irritation on Deborah before and anger was usually close behind it.

"Yes, Lady Luck has been very kind," Deborah said in an even tone as she reached out for Joanna and drew her closer. "Joanna, I want you to meet Todd Lancaster. He's a friend of ours. Todd, this is Joanna Davis."

Joanna glanced from one to the other. She had seen and participated in too many conversations with hidden signals for her to wonder about this one. Or heard. Still she was surprised when he held out his hand and she took it warily, finding his grip firm, friendly.

"So you'll be joining Deborah's House of Steele," he said with a welcoming grin. "Well, you could do a lot worse. I'm sure she'll take good care of you."

"I'm sure," Joanna muttered, uncertain what to say. She wasn't going to be hypocritical and say she was glad to be there. She glanced up at Deborah for guidance but could see the amusement in her gaze.

"Joanna may need some adjustment time," Deborah said dryly. "She's had a pretty traumatic day. We may have to call it an early night." She looked Joanna up and down speculatively, but Joanna thought she also saw concern. Deborah turned back to Todd but took hold of Joanna's hand, lacing her fingers through Joanna's. Claiming, Joanna thought. "Think the storm'll break tonight?"

He nodded as he glanced at the windows. The lower light back there had less of a mirror effect on the glass so they could see the blowing snow. The snow was finer now compared to the wet drippy flakes earlier, swirling instead of driven. "Be clear by morning, may be cold as a witch's tit but clear."

Deborah gave a slight laugh. "Now how would you know how cold that is, Todd? Have you been slumming again?" She took Joanna by the elbow and was turning her back to the kitchen. "We need to go stake out sleeping space."

Todd laughed. "Listen," he said, becoming serious and causing Deborah to pause and turn back. "You have any problems tonight, you give me a holler." He glanced significantly at the other part of the diner, and Deborah nodded.

"Okay, I will. But I don't expect any." She turned back and they went through the kitchen. "Luella, you leaving the water running? Don't want any pipes freezing."

"They should be good but I'm leaving the oven on anyway."

"You sure that's a good idea? Gas stove, isn't it?"

"Okay, maybe not. I'll turn them off when I come out there. You going to settle in?"

"Yeah, we're taking the floor in the corner, let you more mature ladies have the cushions."

"Sure, they'll be real comfy," one of the "mature ladies" returned and there were chuckles around.

Joanna went where she was told, reflecting on the conversation she had interrupted when she came out of the restroom. She recognized the undercurrents that suddenly not all was as it seemed to be. Was Deborah more than just a simple farmer? As she watched her tip over a table to create some privacy, she realized the woman she remembered really didn't exist anymore. She needed to gather information just as if she had never known Deborah before. She shivered at that thought. She was at the disadvantage. Deborah knew her well enough and Deborah was the contract holder.

"That fellow Todd," she said as Deborah moved chairs around, "said something about a house of steel. What'd he mean? You live in a warehouse or something?"

"No, we have a nice old-fashioned brick country house. House of Steele is a reference to the family name. My house, so it's the House of Steele."

"You never mentioned having a farm back when." She trailed off.

"Didn't have it then. Didn't think I'd get it. Still had relatives alive up here. I inherited the farm afterward."

"And it holds ten people?" She had images of living in a bunkhouse, or cabins maybe.

Deborah turned away to the survey the space. "Steeles always had big families. Great-great-grandpa had oh—twelve kids, I think. Two families. Maybe there were more, just didn't all live in the house at the same time." She made some adjustments to the table and chairs. "Then these last couple of generations thinned out the family. Not so many kids. But it was a great house to grow up in." She surveyed the area. "I think this will do," she announced. "What do you think?"

Joanna nodded without even looking at the space. She had seen lots of signs with the name Steele on them. She thought it was coincidence. She hadn't connected Deborah with these parts. How many other things had she not known? She watched as Deborah took the blanket folded on the chair. "You never talked about growing up on a farm."

"No. When I got to college, all the people I wanted to impress seemed to think if you were from the country you were a hick. I wasn't ashamed of my roots, but I just stopped talking about them, got tired of explaining." She turned around and looked up at Joanna. "I never asked, you have anything else with you?" Joanna didn't understand the question. "Backpack, extra clothes?" Joanna shook her head. "Nothing?"

Joanna held out her arms. "What you see is what I got." She immediately bit her tongue and cringed at the way those words could be taken. She gave Deborah a cautious look.

Deborah was shaking her head as she unfolded the blanket and laid it out on the floor. "Criminal," she muttered. "In this weather." She glanced at Joanna as if to explain. "I think, maybe we need to put this on the bottom. Floor's pretty hard but it's more as a cold barrier. You probably aren't sleeping on your back, are you?" Joanna shook her head. "Didn't think so." Deborah knelt down and felt along the blanket, smoothing out lumps, then turned around and sat on the floor, her back against the booth wall, legs stretched out. She patted the floor beside her for Joanna. "Come lie down, get comfortable."

Joanna knelt on the blanket, still looking at Deborah, sure there would be other demands forthcoming.

Deborah looked at her as if she could read her mind, knowing and mocking and sympathetic all at the same time. "No one's going to molest you, Joanna," she said in an even, emotionless voice. "Lie down, try to get some sleep. You'll need it for tomorrow."

Joanna looked at Deborah's worker's hand. She lay down, warily turning her back to Deborah with one arm doubled up under her head, the other one wrapped around her ribs, trying to conserve heat. She stiffened when she felt Deborah move as she positioned her jacket over her like a blanket and then she felt Deborah against her, hip against her shoulder, thigh against her back. Heat radiated from her, making Joanna more chilled before she felt slightly warmer. She pulled her own thin jacket tighter and closed her eyes.

Sleep wouldn't come. Deborah was too close for comfort. Her thoughts raced. Her ex-lover was a contract holder. And now she held Joanna's contract. Joanna had gambled that sometimes the safest place was in the middle of your enemies but that depended on them not recognizing you. She had managed this for over a difficult, unpleasant year. If Deborah put it all together, what would she do? Would it be safer to trust Deborah, confide in her, or just to chance her silence?

She felt Deborah lean over her. "Still cold?"

She nodded, not trusting herself to speak. Once upon a time, she had been able to handle anything, but this, now? She didn't know if she had the strength or the nerve left.

"It's going to be all right, Joanna," Deborah assured her in a soft voice, almost whispering in her ear. "Everything's going to get better. No one's going to get to you tonight, or tomorrow or any other time." Joanna felt Deborah's arm snake around her, tucking the jacket around her. "Is that better?"

Joanna held her breath until Deborah withdrew her arm, uncertain whether Deborah's question meant the jacket or the promise no one would get to her. Either way was good. She nodded uncertainly.

Deborah stroked back Joanna's hair and pulled the jacket up close. "Go to sleep. It's going to be okay. I promise."

Joanna shivered but the warmth was enveloping her. She ducked her head, could feel Deborah against her backside but no longer touching her. Deborah's presence seemed to surround her and she began to believe that perhaps she had escaped Gentry's clutches.

CHAPTER FOUR

Deborah sat there on the cold, hard floor listening to the wind, someone coughing, someone moaning, someone snoring. She couldn't sleep. The woman at her side occupied her thoughts.

Joanna. Just seeing her again would have been unsettling but to see her like this was a great shock. She had thought with all that she had lost, all she found herself having to do, she would be immune. The new reality was that bad things happened, and if she wanted to survive, she couldn't always do anything about them. So she built a wall around herself to defend what was her and hers. Then someone like Joanna comes back into her world and that protective wall crumbles. She closed her eyes as the memories washed over her.

How she had loved Joanna. She thought she was the smartest, most beautiful, most charismatic person she had ever met. Even as she told herself everyone felt that way about their lover, she just knew her Joanna was destined for bigger and better things than the local radio station in Philly. And yet she could see Joanna's limitations. She was highly strung, she could work herself into a frenzy, she could burn herself out. She would be so involved, so focused on her current project, she'd forget to eat, forget day-to-day activities. So Deborah took care of those: groceries, laundry, made sure she ate, calm her down, hold her when the invariable setbacks crushed her.

Then Joanna had come home with news of a great opportunity. Another station, another city, away from everything Deborah knew. Deborah could have coped better had it been another woman. All she could see at the time was Joanna taking the risk, failing to achieve, being hurt. And besides now, years later, Deborah could admit her own fears. What if she did go with her, and then Joanna found someone else? She would be left with nothing. So Deborah refused, made it into an ultimatum, her or the job, the career, the opportunity.

Foolish. Stupid. Idiotic. She lost.

If living well was the best revenge, then Joanna had had her revenge. The newest star with an immediate following—the right place at the right time. Damn, she was everything Deborah had known she would be. Deborah would watch her on the television and be so proud of her she wanted to cry and at the same time feel lost, abandoned, bereft.

She finally had to leave the radio station where they met, the house they lived in, even the town. She even gave up watching the news as Joanna's career escalated to state, then national. She felt Joanna was haunting her.

Deborah laid her head back on the bench seat and stared up at the darkness. How long had it taken to put all the memories into cold storage? And how long did it take today for that to spill open and all those memories fall out?

She felt Joanna shiver spastically and move against her, seeking heat. "Still cold?" she asked quietly. Joanna gave a ragged nod and Deborah covered her more. She tucked the jacket around her when what she wanted to do was wrap her arms around her, pull her into a cocoon of warm safety. But she didn't dare do that. She dwelt on what might have been. And what it was now: a long cold night.

* * *

Deborah leaned back in the three-sided booth the next morning after breakfast, her feet up on the opposite seat to block Joanna in the diagonal corner. Joanna was edgy, alternating between almost clinging to Deborah and then distancing herself. Made her unpredictable. Perhaps, Deborah thought, Joanna didn't believe she could withstand Gentry. Maybe a night's sleep had made Joanna look at things differently. Deborah knew for sure that she hadn't slept worth a damn.

"Do you think we'll get out of here today?"

Deborah eyed the sun reflecting on the fresh clean snow. "Probably," she acknowledged and watched the railroad crews across the road clear the track. The day was bright and clear after the storm, the cold sharp and brittle, the same as Deborah's mood.

People change, Deborah realized. Look at herself. Work out in all sorts of weather and your skin gets weathered, you muscle up. She remembered when she used to dress for work—heels, make-up. She'd go to the spa once a month. Get a weekly massage. Have a closet full of dresses, and pantsuits and pumps. Nothing flashy, tailored, dressed like old money even when she was starting out to work. A lipstick lesbian, even before they had come up with the term. Now she put on the first thing she could lay her hands on in the morning, usually patched jeans and ratty shirts, unless she was coming to town. Then she dressed a little better, as if she was successful, even when she wasn't sure if they would survive the season.

She looked sideways at Joanna. There but for the grace of God, she thought. Didn't matter how much you planned, how prepared you were. A mess of bad luck and you were on the bottom. Wrong place, wrong time, alone, and look where you landed. She was working herself into a real brooding mood. She could get bitter and ugly then, although sometimes that worked to her advantage. She might scare the piss out of Joanna, and she didn't deserve that. Besides, it wasn't Joanna she wanted to scare.

From her peripheral vision, she saw Gentry coming down the center aisle toward her. There was something about him she didn't like, and hadn't liked when she first sat at the poker table. He was the person she wanted to scare. Gentry paused at the table. He must have heard about her. The man at the poker table would have slid into the booth across from her without so much as by your leave, but he deferred to her saying, "Ms. Steele, might we talk?"

Deborah dragged her gaze from the locomotive starting up. They should be leaving soon, not soon enough to suit her but soon. She watched Gentry with a look that had given many second thoughts about continuing a conversation with her.

"Mr. Gentry. And what might we have to talk about?" She moved her legs and watched him slide into the booth across from her. She saw Joanna move unobtrusively to the corner nearer Deborah.

"I understand you have some experience with laborer contracts."

She watched him for a moment before responding. She wondered idly what the people here had told him. "Someone's been talking."

He rested his arms on the wooden table, a man ready to give some friendly advice to an unsuspecting woman. "You understand though, state contracts, by their very nature, are more difficult to manage than the standard civil contracts."

"So?" She watched the railroad crew scramble over the train cars, opening them up, firing up.

"I understand that you're fairly liberal with your dealings. You might find this type of contract a bit beyond your capacity."

Deborah shifted her gaze from the train to look at Gentry, not even bothering to be offended. "I don't think you know anything about my capability."

"No, I don't," he admitted with a duck of his head Deborah was sure he thought was charming. "But I do have knowledge of her. She's smart. She's a tough cookie. She'll look you right in the face and lie through her teeth. Don't like to talk about such sordid details with ladies but she's a whore, do anything to get some advantage. I'm afraid she just might be more trouble than she's worth to you. I don't even think that Davis is really her name."

Oh really? Deborah could feel the anger, the outrage Joanna was throwing off. There was something else there too. Maybe fear? She had to bite her tongue before she spoke angrily. "You might be exactly right about that," Deborah could finally say in a cool tone.

"Well." Gentry appeared surprised. He glanced at Joanna and then back to Deborah. "I'd make a fair offer."

"Really? Why?" For the first time, she met his gaze directly, challenging him.

Gentry narrowed his eyes, surprised. He glanced at Joanna, no doubt wondering what she had told Deborah.

"You tell me what a terrible person she is," Deborah went on, "but at the same time, you want her back. Why is that?"

Gentry drew back, aware she was very close to calling him on his scam and evidently unsure how to respond. If he called her out on it, he would lose credibility. He'd have a hard enough time with the gossip up and down the line about this deal, never mind being without Joanna.

Deborah heard the train powering up so she wanted to wrap this up. "Now, Mr. Gentry," she went on in friendly advice tones in spite of how she felt, "I don't know how you do it in your neck of the woods, but here, we still treat people on contract with some respect. We don't treat them like assets or chits to be used in a poker game instead of cash. And when I make a contract with someone, it stays made. I don't sell my contracts. I don't see anything in this situation to warrant making an exception." She heard the silence in the diner and realized everyone had been listening. Well, too bad. Everyone in the county knew she held contracts. It was now an open secret.

Gentry drew back, and his eyebrows went up as he eyed Deborah. Another tack. "She might cost you a pretty penny more than what you paid for her."

Deborah gave a small smile that didn't hide her contempt. "That's my affair."

Gentry swallowed. She knew as well as he did that the price she had paid for Joanna's contract wasn't low. A high price usually made an easy buyback, the mark might lose some but at least it wasn't the whole thing. He tried again. "I'm warning you: she's a troublemaker, dangerous. She's a runner."

Deborah sighed in exasperation. Wouldn't this jerk give up? She wasn't selling back the contract. "So? I'll deal with it. I haven't lost one yet."

"Oh, come now," he blurted out in disbelief. "Anyone who's held contracts had at least one who got away."

Deborah appeared to think about it. "Well, I take that back. I've lost one."

Gentry looked around in smug satisfaction. See, she's not any better than anyone else.

"She's in the cemetery."

Gentry jerked back, his expression plain to read that he thought Deborah had hunted her down and she had been killed.

Deborah had had enough. She moved out of the seat, reached back for her jacket and for Joanna. "Come on, they're loading the train."

Joanna looked a little startled at Deborah's revelation. She scooted across the seat, glancing at Gentry to see his surprise as she got to her feet. Deborah put her hand on Joanna's back lightly, moving her along. She turned back to make one parting shot at Gentry. "MY cemetery."

Once on the train, Deborah pointed a white-faced Joanna to the seat next to the window. Deborah knew she would have some explaining to do but that would come later. Right now, the day was clear and bright, the snow fresh and clean, deep enough to appear level across the fields. Deborah took the outside seat and stretched out, her feet up on the seat across from her, again pinning Joanna in. She knew the car would not be crowded and she wanted to discourage anyone from sitting there. She didn't want to talk to anyone, not even Joanna. Maybe especially Joanna. She folded her arms across her chest and closed her eyes. Time for a catnap. She figured she'd have about twenty minutes.

Deborah woke immediately when the whistle sounded. "Ready for a walk?" she asked rhetorically as she got to her feet and picked up her jacket. Joanna looked out the windows for a station. She stepped into the aisle in front of Deborah. "Train doesn't come to a complete halt," Deborah said quickly as they moved toward the door at the end. "So be prepared to step down lively and move away quickly." Joanna pulled on her jacket, breathing hard. She cringed visibly as she went by Gentry.

"Fucking dyke," Deborah heard him mutter as she went by. She waited until she got down to the door and then she turned back.

"Damn right," she announced loudly, startling him as well as the other passengers. "Proud, in-your-face dyke. And you'd better not forget it." She followed Joanna out the door and shut it behind her.

The wind was sharp in their faces, and Deborah took a good cleansing breath. Joanna was holding tight to the railing, looking back down the empty tracks, looking apprehensive when there was no station in sight. The train slowed, the landscape ceased to be a blur and then became bushes and mounds of snow as they listened to the air brakes. Deborah put her arm around Joanna's waist and pulled her back, tightly against her. "Train does a rolling stop," Deborah explained into Joanna's ear. "Just go down the steps and swing off. If you fall, roll away from the tracks. Takes a knack, but the snowbank should be a good cushion." She put her hand on Joanna's shoulder to steady her as she released her. Joanna looked over her shoulder at Deborah in disbelief. "You can do it," Deborah assured her.

Joanna went off first, hesitant but Deborah's hand was firm on her back. Deborah made sure Joanna was clear as she jumped, fell and rolled. Deborah shook her head, it was a little scary the first couple of times. She still got nervous. She stepped off into air, let go into that instance of suspension and then the thud as she landed, on her feet this time. That was good, made a good impression on Joanna, showed her it could be done. Her bad mood lifted but didn't completely disappear as she walked back to Joanna.

Joanna was shaking the snow off and rubbing her shoulder when Deborah reached her. "Some day," Deborah said casually, "we may get to have this as an official stop."

Joanna turned around looking at the open desolate fields. "Why?"

Deborah merely chuckled in reply and turned her around. The train had picked up speed and moved on down the tracks, revealing the huge abandoned store, cement porch across the front, broken windows, a half-collapsed garage beside it.

"This way." Deborah led Joanna across the tracks and the windswept road. She detoured around the edge of the buildings where the snow had drifted high and then over the cleared ground to the back door. She slowed as she approached the door, looking for disturbed snow. She pushed the door open with her shoulder and stepped in. She examined the floor for tracks, for any evidence of someone else being there before she motioned Joanna in. Light from the windows showed what might have been the main storage room. "Take a seat," she ordered. Deborah pointed to the bench off to one side.

Joanna sat, shivering. She hunched over, stuffing her hands in her pockets.

"You were right—he did want you back. He just didn't try very hard." She went around the room, checking the built-in cabinets, shelving, the jumbled wood, broken equipment. Every time she came here, she could see the building's possibilities. Right now, she and Joanna were alone, in some semblance of a shelter. While it wasn't the best location for a private chat, it was what was available. Once they reached the house, opportunities would be gone. As much as she knew those women and loved her house, sometimes she would swear the walls were glass and every room was bugged. There was no way to keep a secret there. She went back and stood before Joanna. "Did he?"

"You didn't give him much of an opening."

"Told you I wouldn't consider it."

"Holders lie."

"And contractees don't?" Deborah put her foot up on the bench almost against Joanna's hip and leaned forward, her elbow resting on her leg. Joanna looked ill, not just physically. Deborah had seen women scared sick, and those shocked and dazed from tragedy. She had seen them running scared, and that's what Joanna looked like now. "Look at me."

For a moment, she didn't think that Joanna would obey but finally she did look up into Deborah's face. Her expression was a mixture of defiance and apprehension. "Joanna, what's the deal? What's going on?"

Joanna stared back at her, saying nothing.

Deborah had thought all night long about what Joanna had told her and there were things that just didn't add up. "You contracted under a false name. You were isolated enough to be shanghaied. What *aren't* you saying?"

Joanna set her jaw, clenching her hands inside her pockets.

"Are you hiding from someone, running away?"

Joanna grimaced. "Just leave it, Deborah," she said in a tight voice. "You won a contract in a poker game. It doesn't matter how I got on contract or why or anything else. What's one more body in your holding? I'm just another pair of hands, aren't I? Another laborer? Nothing else matters."

It matters, Deborah knew. "I didn't ask you about it last night," she said in an even voice. "I didn't figure you'd say anything with everyone else around, but now, here, it's just you and me, no one else. I want to know."

"Yes, I can imagine," Joanna came back cuttingly. "You always did like knowing so you could manipulate things behind the scenes. You always did want to be a person of influence. Well, you've certainly come into your own now, I guess. Land, contracts, people to do your bidding, your own little fiefdom. You always had one way to do things—your way. Now I guess you've really been able to have that. A big fish in a small pond."

"Better than no pond," Deborah said evenly. If she knew Joanna well enough to know she was hiding something, Joanna still knew her. "And it was certainly large enough to land you, wasn't it?"

"Don't expect me to be grateful!"

"Evidently not." But she did expect gratitude. Deborah knew that about herself. She expected a give-and-take relationship from all the women she had contracted with. Joanna had nothing to give, not her willingness, not her cooperation so there was nothing left for her to give but gratitude. *No good deed goes unpunished* came to mind, Todd's favorite line when they discussed strategies. She gazed down at Joanna, knowing she had done the right thing by her and knowing at the same time, it was going to change her world.

"All right, Joanna, if that's how you want it. I'll tell you what I'm going to do," Deborah said in a chilly tone. "And you can handle it however you want. I'm going to forget that I ever knew you before." Joanna closed her eyes. "I'm going to forget that we ever lived together, that we ever slept together, that we ever had any sort of a relationship. That we ever loved each other. If we ever did."

Joanna gave a quick start, her hand reaching out before she caught herself. She dropped her hand back into her lap and looked down at the ground, "Did what we had really mean so little to you?"

Deborah pushed off from the bench, refraining from the sudden urge to kick it over. She stepped back from Joanna, needing to have her out of reach. "Ask yourself that question, Joanna. You were the one who left."

Joanna's silence answered her.

Deborah moved away, turned her back on Joanna and counted to ten. She had thought if she confronted Joanna when they were away from everyone, Joanna would talk to her. She had not expected a flat denial. If Joanna couldn't trust her, she needed to find that emotional distance to be able to treat Joanna as a stranger. She could do it. She had done it before, she could do it again.

Finally she came back to stand before Joanna. "Here's what is going to happen, Joanna *Davis*," she said with biting emphasis on Joanna's assumed name. "I'm going to take you home and introduce you to my house simply as a new contract. You'll have a roof over your head, you'll eat every day and you'll work at anything that's assigned to you. Your papers say that you're a state-registered contract so I'll have to treat you like that. Your papers say that you're a troublemaker but I'll give you the benefit of the doubt, a clean slate. If you want to cause trouble, I'll deal with it. You want to keep your nose clean, that would be great. If not." She shrugged. "That's up to you."

"And what am I supposed to say when anyone asks?" Joanna asked woodenly.

"No one's going to ask anything. Certainly not about us. If they ask anything about you, you can say what you please. I don't care." Joanna drew a deep breath but kept her gaze on the floor.

"I've never taken on an unwilling contract," Deborah continued, "so I'm going to be feeling my way. I don't have any preconceived notions so what you do and how you act will set the tone of your conditions."

"And how am I supposed to act?"

"Cooperation would be nice but that's your choice."

Joanna turned her head away.

"You have any questions?"

Joanna looked from one wall to the other, avoiding Deborah. She tried to say something so Deborah waited. Joanna licked her lips, tried again. "Did you kill her?"

Deborah frowned in true puzzlement. "Kill who?"

Joanna swallowed. "The one who got away."

Deborah started to laugh and then stopped. The question probably was pertinent and scary for someone who had run from past contracts. "Hetty died of pneumonia in her own bed."

Joanna looked up at her and Deborah could see the terror.

"She was eighty-three and had been with me for two years. She died with her loved ones around her and she has been greatly missed by all of us."

Joanna's color returned a little. "You made it sound like…" She trailed off.

"Well, I wasn't trying to sound like Lady Bountiful," Deborah pointed out caustically.

"No, I guess not," Joanna agreed faintly.

"Any other questions?"

"What will I be doing?" Joanna drew a shuddering breath. She appeared resigned, maybe more at ease, as if she were more able to deal with the contract holder/contractee relationship.

"Anything and everything, manual labor. We all live together, share and share alike. We all do whatever needs to be done to keep going. It's hard labor for all of us and there are days when we're too exhausted to think. You're coming in at a slack season but within a few weeks, there will be field work that will almost kill us. Let me be clear on that part, Joanna, we all work."

"Including the contract holder? I have a hard time believing that."

"Including me." She saw the disbelief in Joanna's look. "Now every one of those women came to me and they knew that I didn't hire, I contracted. Every one of them sat down with me and we hammered out a contract. No one was coerced or forced or trapped. Not everyone is happy with being a contract but it was a choice they made so if you want to be unhappy about being on contract, you'll find souls to agree with you. The only difference is that they chose to do it and you didn't."

"A slight difference that puts me in a completely different class."

"Maybe, but you'll be treated like everyone else. The only way you'll be treated differently is when your actions call for it or what these new rules require."

"I'm sorry. I can't be grateful," Joanna warned. "I'm not going to be one of those contracts who kowtow to the holder. When you say jump, I'm not going to ask how high on the way up."

Deborah gave a mocking laugh. "Well, then you should fit right in, Joanna Davis." She now shivered. The room was getting colder if that was possible. She saw her breath in imitation smoke, and she turned back to look at Joanna. She was still shivering but her face was flushed. Now it was time to put her memories of Joanna back into their little box and lock the door again. This was just another contract with all the duties and responsibilities that came along with it.

Deborah brought her hands to her own face and then reached out to lay her hand against Joanna's cheek. Joanna evaded her. "Stay still," Deborah ordered. Joanna swallowed as Deborah bent over and took Joanna's face in her hands. Joanna felt terribly warm. "Look at me." Her eyes were bright, too bright. Deborah shook her head. Damn, she should have guessed that Joanna was run down, her system shocked. She looked over Joanna's inadequate clothes again. Well, there were some things she could do. "Come here."

She took Joanna's hand and led her to the southeast corner of the building, still open but it had a few hours of sunlight and wasn't quite as chilled as other areas. "Take off your shirt."

"Take off—are you crazy?" Joanna burst out.

"Of course." Deborah was already peeling off her jacket, her inner jacket and dropping them on the floor. She glanced up at Joanna. "Move. In case you haven't noticed, it's cold in here."

Angry but conditioned to obey, Joanna took off the jacket and the flannel shirt. She glanced around to see if they were alone as she shivered. "What's this? Can't take a cold shower? I didn't think I'd have this effect on you."

"Yeah. Neither did I." Deborah pulled off her sweater then her silken undershirt. She paused as Joanna pulled her tank top up and over her head. The cold air caused gooseflesh and erect nipples on both women. Joanna shivered convulsively.

Deborah pulled off her undershirt and immediately pulled it down over Joanna before the shirt could lose her body heat. "Get that tank top back on."

Joanna pulled the tank top back over her head as Deborah picked up her sweater and held it out for Joanna, ignoring her own cold for the moment at least.

"You'll be cold," Joanna protested.

"Not like you are. Come on, hurry up." Joanna slipped her arms into the openings and pulled the sweater on as Deborah picked up her own jacket and quickly put it on.

"You still put out heat like a blast furnace," Joanna observed as she pulled on her shirt.

"Yeah. Great for this weather. Kills me in the summer." They quickly dressed, Joanna's fingers fumbling either from cold or fever. Deborah took over and finished buttoning up the shirt. "Feel better?" Joanna nodded unsteadily. "It should hold the body heat in better, keep you a bit warmer. You really don't have enough layers. I don't suppose you have a hat?"

"A hat?"

"Stay there."

If Joanna was ill, they were still too far away from the house, too far for Deborah to carry her. She went down the hallway, moving carefully but quickly. She checked the tab she had left on the door before she opened it and picked up her backpack and more importantly, the sawed-off shotgun.

Joanna stood there, a solitary figure in the open area, bathed in sunlight. She had pulled the jacket closed and stuffed her hands into her armpits. She looked up at Deborah's return and her expression was that of a soul abandoned, alone and vulnerable. Her expression was almost more than Deborah could bear.

Stop it, she told herself. *You take in lost puppies too.* She pulled the stocking cap out of the backpack and stuffed it inside her own shirt to warm it. "Here." She pulled gloves and scarf out of her pockets and handed the gloves to Joanna. "Put these on. You're not dressed for the cold." She took the scarf and wrapped it around Joanna's neck, pulling open her jacket to tuck it in. Joanna pulled on the gloves as she avoided looking at Deborah.

"We've still got a walk ahead of us. About three miles." Deborah pulled the cap out of her shirt and put it over Joanna's auburn hair, down far enough to cover her ears. "Think you can make it?"

"Do I have a choice?"

"We'll make it," Deborah answered. She looked Joanna over again. "I'm going to have to clothe you from head to foot," she muttered, thinking of what extra clothing she had.

"I can't do it," Joanna said through chattering teeth. She wrapped her arms around herself.

"Yes, you can," Deborah answered firmly. "You will." She took hold of Joanna's shoulders, made Joanna look at her. "And when we get there, there's a hot meal, a warm bed, clean sheets." Joanna shook her head. "Yes," Deborah repeated. Then unconsciously, she pulled Joanna to her. She hadn't yet zipped up her jacket and now wrapped her outer jacket around Joanna.

"Oh, God, you're so warm." Joanna burrowed against Deborah, shivering.

Deborah closed her eyes and wrapped her arms around Joanna, holding her tight. Skin and bone, but she could feel how Joanna still fit against her, and for the moment, the years fell away. She wanted to hold her and protect her and keep her safe from harm. She wanted to kill whoever had hurt her, to promise her safety and security. She rested her head against Joanna's, felt Joanna's breath on her neck.

"You're so warm," Joanna repeated as she moved into Deborah's arms. They stood there for an instant and then Joanna pushed away. "You always treat new contracts like this?" she asked harshly.

Deborah tried to tell herself it was just the sudden cold air rushing in where Joanna had stood that took her breath away. "No," she replied. "But I don't want you sick and risk losing my investment." She turned away and picked up her backpack. This putting Joanna back into a box wasn't going to be so easy this time.

* * *

Joanna didn't remember much of the walk to the house. She recalled the cold and the vast expanse. When she went back later, rewalked it, she was surprised at how easy a walk it was, almost a stroll in the park. That first time, though, was a killer. Snow was calf-deep in spots, the sunlight reflected on the bright snow was blinding, the cold was bitter. The silence smothered her, nothing but the crunch of the snow, Deborah's heavy breathing and her own labored gasps. Her shoes were inadequate her feet were soon soaked and then numb. The smooth snow hid the uneven terrain below. She fell twice, the second time twisting her ankle. The first time she had pushed herself to her feet, ignoring Deborah's outstretched hand. The second time, she was grateful for the assistance. She had stood there, testing her ankle, wincing and trying to hide it.

"Twist it?"

Joanna nodded.

"See that grove of trees?" Deborah pointed with the shotgun to a dark spot against the bright snow. "That's where we're going."

Joanna groaned. It looked like an impossible distance. Then she felt Deborah's hands on her and she jerked away. She stumbled and started to fall again and Deborah caught her, pulled her back to her feet, turned her around so the sun was on her back.

"You really don't like being touched, do you?" Deborah commented as she took hold of Joanna's jacket and unsnapped it. She pulled out the scarf and rearranged it across Joanna's face, wrapped it around her head. "Warms the air you breathe, won't hurt so much. Lungs hurt?" Joanna nodded, losing her pride enough to answer. "May cut some of the glare also." She bundled the jacket closed and snapped it back up while Joanna stood there like a little kid. "Let's get moving."

After that it was just a concentrated effort to put one foot in front of the other, to follow the dark shape of Deborah in front of her. The distance seemed endless, the air she breathed a knife. She didn't remember Deborah coming back to wrap an arm around her. She never remembered going over the hill, just stumbling and rolling down some distance. Then Deborah was pulling her up, and she couldn't even help.

"No, please," she pleaded, her arms up in protest. "I can do. I'll do it. Don't hurt. Please, I just slipped."

"It's all right, Joanna." Deborah pulled Joanna to her feet, held her, supporting her a moment before they started again. "We're almost there. Just a bit further. Let me help you. I'll get you inside. There's a warm bed waiting, something hot to drink, dry clothes."

Joanna almost choked. Whenever had she had that? It would be enough if she had some space that was warm and dry. She leaned on Deborah because she needed the support, because her legs felt like rubber, because she didn't know where she was going. The next thing she remembered was going into darkness, and some god-awful pounding noise.

"Yo! I need some help out here!" Then warmth hit her like a wall and there were many hands on her. She sank into oblivion.

She came up twice, the first time when they were undressing her. She struggled, panicky, crying out, feeling terribly sluggish, incoherent, striking out and hitting something solid. Her wrists were caught, held firmly, and she was pinned against the bed.

"It's all right, Joanna," a familiar voice assured her. "No need to be afraid. You're safe."

She struggled to control her panic. "No, don't. Please."

"We're not going to hurt you, just need to get you out of these wet clothes, into something dry. Hush. It's going to be all right."

Nothing's ever going to be all right. But she recognized she was trapped and fighting wouldn't help. She could only endure. She didn't fight as she was sat up and she bowed her head against a warm shoulder, gasping for breath.

"It's all right," the soothing voice repeated over and over again, holding her and supporting her as the wet layers were pulled off. "Don't be afraid, I've got you right here."

There was a gasp when her shirt came off. "What the fuck?" came the rough voice behind her.

"Shut up," the familiar voice said without losing the soothing tone. "She's been hurt, and we need to show her something different. Here Jo, drink this."

There was a cup held to her mouth and she eagerly drank and then gagged at the taste. She was pushed back as the vile-tasting liquid came right back up.

"Ugh, whew!"

"If you can't stand the sick room, then get out," another voice said. "Deborah, you okay?"

"Yeah. Always told you that stuff tasted like you're killing us. Help me get this off her."

Joanna was limp as clothing was removed again, another gown pulled over her head and the cup again held to her lips. "Take it straight down, Jo. Don't taste it—just chug it. That's good. Now just hold it in. Atta girl. There, isn't it good to feel warm and dry. Promised you that."

She was lain back in the bed and she curled up onto her side to a fetal position. "Cold."

Her feet were rubbed with warm hands, a warm something placed at her belly and she curled around it. Covers were tucked over her and she buried herself in the pillow. The last thing she heard was, "God, Deborah. She caught you good. You're gonna have a shiner for sure."

The next time, she woke up much more coherent. She came awake suddenly, not moving, her heart pounding, alert mentally. She looked around with as little movement as possible and didn't recognize anything in the white room. She lay in a single bed with a firm mattress, warm blankets and a pillow beneath her head. She moved slightly and realized that she had nothing on but an unfamiliar gown. Someone magically appeared at the bedside. The oval face of a stranger with light brown hair and sympathetic pale blue eyes examined her. There was a hand against her cheek, a light touch. The head turned away and said something. Joanna caught the name Deborah. At least that was familiar, not welcome but familiar.

"Bathroom," she announced, firmly, strongly she thought but it came out so soft she could barely hear it. She struggled to get up, afraid the woman—did she know it was a woman and not a man? Then there was an arm around her waist and she was sitting behind a screen on a chair with a chamber pot. She closed her eyes, needing privacy, wishing, unable to speak.

"I'll be right back." The woman left.

Alone. Relief. Oh, what a relief. She rested her elbows on the chair arms and buried her face in her hands as she tried to remember. Deborah. Snow. Cold. Walking. Deborah taking her home. She had Joanna's contract. Oh, God, it would be better to sink into that darkness. She lost her balance and started to pitch forward only to be leaning against a soft body.

"Back to bed with you."

The bed was still warm, and the room was so bright, sterile. There was a window. Bright blue sky and white walls. Clean. Restful. She was exhausted. She closed her eyes and sank into that darkness again.

The next time she awoke the room was dark except for a small light in the corner. She looked around, still trying to make sense of everything when she saw the sleeping figure in the recliner. She moved, and in trying to turn over, moaned. The figure immediately came over to her.

"Thirsty." She managed to rise up a bit on her elbow as the woman poured something from the carafe into the cup and sat down beside Joanna. Joanna pushed the cup away. "Not—not that stuff." *Terrible noxious stuff they poured down me. Fixed them, threw it up. They only poured more down.*

"It's just water," Deborah said. She helped Joanna sit up. "None of Beth's curatives." She held the cup and this time Joanna took it. "I know, the tea earlier was pretty bad but it does its stuff."

Cool, wet water. Joanna could only take a swallow before she pushed the cup away. "Terrible." She leaned against Deborah. "That other stuff—poison."

"No," Deborah assured her. "Actually it keeps us pretty healthy."

"Where? Am I?"

"My place. In the infirmary. Do you remember coming down the hill?"

"Fell." *Head over heels, snow down her shirt. Cold, oh, God, so cold.*

"Yes. We were close enough that I could carry you."

"Protect your investment."

"That's right." Deborah sounded amused.

Joanna rested her head against Deborah's shoulder, Deborah's arm around her. She wanted to pull away but she didn't have the strength. No, that wasn't even it. Being enclosed in Deborah's arms was like a safe port in a storm. "I didn't want to leave you." She had to take a breath between each word.

"Could have fooled me." Deborah very gently laid Joanna back down on the pillow, helped her turn over, pulled the covers up to tuck her in. She leaned over Joanna, supporting herself on her arm. "Go to sleep," Deborah soothed. She brushed back Joanna's hair, stroked her face.

"Didn't think you'd remember me." Joanna settled into the bedding. She felt Deborah's light touch. She didn't have the energy to protest about being touched. Wasn't sure she wanted to. The touch was strangely comforting.

"How could I forget?" Deborah leaned over her.

"No one ever loved me the way you did."

"Glad I gave you something. Didn't do me any good. Now go to sleep. You're safe. That's all that matters right now."

Joanna took a deep breath and was asleep even before she exhaled.

CHAPTER FIVE

"Nice shiner." Beth Mitchell wrapped the oversized flannel shirt tighter around her as she took a seat in the morning meeting in Deborah's office. The front of the house was always colder and she had just come from the sick room.

"Hmmm," was Deborah's only response about her swollen half-closed eye. "And our patient?"

"Pneumonia, just a light touch. She's terribly run-down, so exhaustion and the cold all contributed. Looks like she got a terrible beating. That didn't help." The broad-faced brown-haired woman gave Deborah the questioning eye across the big wooden desk. "You do pick them up in strange places, don't you? This one was at Luella's?"

"Traveling through," Deborah commented without further explanation.

Sara Pierce wandered out of the adjoining office. "Did you read this?" she asked, as she flipped through the pages of the contract. "In its entirety?"

"No. I was a little more occupied with other issues. Why?"

"Just wondering. Real different from the standard one." She wandered back into her area and started pulling file drawers open. "Whole different set of rules. Hope you knew what you were letting yourself in for."

"What did you have in mind for her?" Karen LaMont asked as she stretched her long legs out in front of her and her arms across the back of Beth's Windsor chair. She was the only one with nothing to report but since she was the work manager, Deborah thought it was good that she sit in.

"Hard worker, knowledgeable. Good organization skills. Team player. Thought she'd fit right in." Deborah flipped through the mail she had picked up at the diner. At least in these new circumstances, there was now much less junk mail.

"You know her from somewhere?"

"Why?" Deborah looked up.

"Seems to me that it would be a bit hard to tell all that from the condition that she's in now. You must have had a good interview to start with."

Sara meandered back out. "You do know she's an unwilling contract, don't you?" She frowned at Deborah, her blue eyes sharp with the question. Both Beth and Karen looked up in surprise and then turned to Deborah for confirmation.

"Yeah. She said she got shanghaied, filed a protest but got overruled." Sara shook her head in dismay. "She was in a bad spot," Deborah went on to explain. "It occurred to me she might be grateful enough to give us the benefit of a doubt."

Beth looked disturbed. "She put up a good fight when we were trying to put her to bed," she mused. "Not exactly like she was giving us a doubt then."

"Well, think about it," Deborah said reasonably in Joanna's defense. "She's sick, doesn't know where she is, strangers trying to undress her. Coming from where she had, what would you do?" Deborah sat back in her chair, as she took them all in with a steady gaze.

Karen laughed humorlessly. "Oh, I'd kick, slug, fight, scream." She looked pointedly at Deborah's black eye but didn't say anything.

Sara looked up from the contract. "I didn't hear any screaming."

"You know my sweetie, she tends to overdramatize things a bit," Beth responded with a fond glance at Karen and a ruffling of the blond hair from which Karen ducked.

"Okay." Deborah pulled them back to the issue at hand. "How bad off is she? How long is she going to be down?"

"Not real bad. Rest, some good food. Maybe a couple of days, a week at the most."

"Okay, we'll go with that. Put a rotation on the sick room so she's not alone. She doesn't know us, the house habits. Don't want her to get scared right off. Guess that's it for this morning."

Karen laughed as she got up. "No, we'll scare her later when we put her in the work rotation." She glanced out the windows as she stretched, her arm going around Beth as she got up. "It's melting fast out there. She should be available just in time for the mud details."

Beth hit Karen on the shoulder and Karen collapsed her arms. "Be easy on her. The idea is to get her good and healthy for the summer work, not put her back in the infirmary just when we need her the most." Deborah shook her head as they left. Glad she knew they were lovers, otherwise the good-natured bickering would get on her nerves.

Deborah had stacked the papers across the once highly-polished desk and pulled the rosters down from the bookcase behind her, when she heard a soft throat clearing. She turned to see Sara still leaning against the doorframe. Her pose was casual, but her look wasn't. "What's up?"

"My question exactly," Sara retorted. She tapped the folded contract into the palm of her hand. "A restrictive unwilling contract? She falls under a completely different set of rules. Supervision, restriction. Reports. The whole nine yards. Whatever were you thinking? If you slept with your people, I'd say that you were thinking with your libido." She paused, surprise and amusement in her voice. "Why Deborah, you're blushing."

"Yeah. My libido." She looked out the window to see the snow dripping off the roof as it melted. "I don't know if that part of me exists anymore." She could say that even as the memory of holding Joanna in her arms at Anoka rushed back at her. She shut it off and brought her attention back to Sara.

"You're right. I wasn't thinking but it didn't concern my libido." Deborah pointed to the chair in front of the desk and Sara obediently sat down. Sara was fairly new to the house and while Deborah found her to be naturally discreet, they were still developing a working relationship. "I'd rather this didn't get out. I don't discuss any of these folks' backgrounds." Sara nodded. "I won Joanna's contract in a poker game."

Sara sat upright in surprise. "Someone used her contract for poker stakes? What kind of person would do that?"

"The kind who would beat her and abuse her." *Never mind all the other things he did. If I never see him again, it will be too soon.*

Sara leaned back in the chair, thoughtful for a moment. "It's not going to be well received that she's an unwilling contract." She looked down at the contract again. "Or that she's registered with the state." She looked up. "They might understand better if they knew the circumstances."

Deborah shook her head. "No. She's had her privacy ripped away enough. Her self-esteem needs to heal just as much as her body does. Let that be her story to tell, whenever and how she wants to. I can weather anything they think of me."

"Then I guess we'll manage one way or the other." She got to her feet and then paused. "Tell me one thing so I'm prepared for it. Do you think she'll be grateful?"

Images of an angry Joanna caused Deborah to shake her head. "When pigs fly."

Deborah sat back in the chair after Sara left the office. Joanna grateful? Maybe she would be after she healed somewhat. In the in between time, Deborah would be relieved if she didn't tear the place apart with anger and dissension. Joanna always had the persuasive skill to draw people to her side, something Deborah lacked. She knew she was more cut-and-dried, "you do this, I do this," but persuade people to her viewpoint? No, Deborah lacked that. Well, she thought in dismissal, I'll deal with it.

For now, there was other business to attend to. She had managed to get the information Marv had wanted and pass it along to Todd. There was just the matter of how much he was willing to pay. She didn't agree with everything he and his militia unit were doing but she had to admit he was useful. Whoever would have believed that this high school juvenile delinquent who was thought most likely to land up in jail or dead would be the one so many would depend upon to guard them against the worst hooligans as well provide the pipeline for supplies from areas too dangerous for them to visit? Back then Deborah had envied his brash cockiness and in-your-face attitude, something she couldn't do. He had been impressed by her refusal to be intimidated and then by her acceptance. They had become the kind of friends that neighbors scratched their heads over but they never bothered explaining. When Deborah returned, they had picked up where they left off. They had started out with her supplying him with information, books and the Internet research, and him in return, supplying her with provisions she needed. Now, she was the middle person in a supply-demand chain handling increased needs and diminishing supplies. One more method of survival.

It was working out well enough that she'd like to expand her circle of contacts but that meant being gone from the house more frequently and for longer. When she acquired Sara's contract, she felt she had hit the jackpot. Good communication skills, tactful, discreet, peacemaker. About the only drawback was that Bobbi came along as part of the package.

Bobbi. Deborah threw down her pencil.

She had promised herself that once she got on her feet, if anyone wanted to join her, she would take them in. Bobbi had been a college fling, a mistake, a learning experience. She hadn't seen her in years although she knew Bobbi was somewhere in the area. She'd had no desire to keep up the contact. When she had run into them, Bobbi and Sara, at the commune of all places, Bobbi had latched on to her like a long-lost friend. Deborah had felt obligated in spite of her instinct telling her that this was a mistake. She should have listened.

However, Bobbi could work hard when she wanted to. And she could be charming, when she wanted, but she was the most egocentric, self-serving woman Deborah had ever met. Bobbi used to stir things up, cause trouble, just to get the attention. She hadn't here. Yet.

And now Joanna was in the mix. She opened Joanna's contract again. Maybe when Joanna settled in, she would open up because there was definitely something fishy going on. Right now, Joanna wasn't going to talk to her.

She pulled the ledger down that served as her roster. She was awfully close to the limit of contracts she could hold and not be classed as a contract business. Twelve was her mental limit because that had been the size of family the house had been built for. Purely coincidence the state had picked that number too.

She hadn't wanted to get into state-registered contracts either, she reminded herself. Once she was on the state's radar there could be all manner of problems. Even though she was isolated and pretty far out but all it would take would be one snoop. Or, she reconsidered, one malcontent contract.

She began to make a list. One extra person meant additional clothing, bedding, food. Spring wasn't here yet but the cellar wasn't empty, meat was still hanging in the smokehouse. Expansion of the enterprise was a possibility, an improvement on the mere survival of the past two winters.

Her mind wandered back to Joanna. Touching her, having her in her arms, pressing against her. The feeling had triggered other memories as well. She thought she was over the anger, the grief, the forgetting. The passion, the loving. She had been, right up until the moment Joanna was in her arms.

She hadn't intended to do that. It was only to get her warm, give her reassurance. She would have done that to anyone in the house, she told herself. Yet there was the nagging little question in the back of her mind. *Are you so sure of that? Would holding someone else have set your heart pounding so?*

She flung herself out of the chair so abruptly that Sara came out of her area to see what the problem might be. "I think we need to do an inventory," Deborah ordered. "See how prepared we are until the spring garden comes in, what we need to prepare for the summer. Can you get it organized?"

"Sure, but don't you think it's a little early?"

Deborah shook her head. "No. The house is almost full. Besides, things may be changing, and I want to be prepared." She stacked her papers and threw them in the drawer. "I'm going to do a walk around. Do you know where Linda's working this morning?"

* * *

"The house is almost full," she repeated when she found Linda. "You know what it's like when it's hot and everyone's tired and there's nowhere to get away."

Linda nodded. "Meaning you."

Deborah shook her head. Linda Conners was an old old, friend who knew Deborah and her family. "No, not just me, any of us. We need a spot to get away. What do you think of those old rooms in the stables?"

Linda grasped the idea immediately and was delighted. "We could do the repairs. It wouldn't take much, mostly cosmetic. There were living quarters for the staff, horse master or something, whatever they called them in those days." She went on, thinking aloud. "There's a bedroom, a small bath. It's not great, but it's adequate." She looked at Deborah with yet another idea. "You know, if we did have some horses, it would solve one of our transportation problems. I, for one, wouldn't mind living out here."

"You and your horses," Deborah scoffed good-humoredly. And a good idea. Horses had always been Linda's passion. It had broken her heart when she had to sell the last one, and she had been a constant lobbyist that horses would solve some of Deborah's problems.

"A team of draft horses could work the fields, drive to town. There's enough pasture here. We're already growing hay for the cows. They'd add to the fertilizer, and you know you've got someone who would take care of them."

"And who might that be?" Deborah asked with a laugh to be met with Linda's wide grin. She could just see this little Peter Pan person with huge draft horses.

The stable had large roomy box stalls to house a few horses. Deborah walked into the feed room, currently used for storage. She could remember it as a quiet getaway from the house and from her grandfather. She turned around and looked at Linda who followed her in and stood at the door.

"It's been a long time, hasn't it?"

Deborah glanced at the corner where as teenagers they had once stacked bales of hay and covered them with a blanket to make a bed. "Yeah."

Linda watched her knowingly and changed the subject. "How was everything in town?"

Deborah shrugged. She turned around slowly, looking over the entire room. "Depressed. Stores closed. More For Sale signs up. Folks are going through the motions but not much optimism. Heard about food riots up north a ways."

"You would think construction would be good."

"You would think." She shook her head again and turned back to Linda. "Never thought I'd be here again."

"Either did I." Linda had a fond smile. "But here we are."

"Yeah," Deborah repeated. She shook off the feeling. She was looking at the past too much. She needed to focus on today and tomorrow and the next day.

"Get with Karen and see what has to be done here to get it livable before the growing season. We'll be tripping over each other and that always makes for short tempers. We need some space to spread out when we get into each other's hair."

"You going to hide out here?" Linda needled.

Deborah laughed. "Maybe so." She gave the room another glance and moved out into the aisle. "On the other hand, it's too damned close to the house. If I'm going to run away, it'll be far, far away."

Linda caught her arm as she went by. "Don't say that, Deb. We need you here."

"No, I'm no one special. I was just in the right place at the right time. Anyone else could do it as well." She glanced at Linda's hand on her arm.

"I don't think so." Linda removed her hand. "You always managed to be at the right place at the right time." She walked out into the aisle along with Deborah. "You have an aura of luck around you. You had it in high school. You'd do something and everyone else would get into trouble and you just slipped through. Like if a brick wall collapsed, you'd be in the spot that was the doorway."

Deborah shook her head. Linda had always thought that she had something special. Sometimes Deborah believed it too, but most of the time she was able to laugh it off. "If I had some aura of luck taking care of me, I'd be somewhere different than here."

"Memphis?"

Memphis again. Deborah thought of her efforts to escape memories that took her to Memphis. "Maybe someplace else," she said quietly. She shook off the memory and looked around again. "Get with Karen as soon as you can. See how much you can get done before we have to start spring planting."

"Yes, ma'am," Linda replied with a mock salute.

"Cut it out," Deborah growled as she paused at the door. "I've got enough comments about being a control freak without you going around saluting me."

She completed her walk around noting that the weather had changed. There was a warming wind, and she expected that the snows would melt quickly. Flooding? Maybe but they were far enough away from the river that she didn't worry. She looked over the barns and stock. Two cows, a heifer that should freshen this spring, some hogs, chickens, rabbits. She had milk, eggs, meat. Gardens. She gazed over the snow-covered acres. The orchard, apples, peaches, cherries. Those trees had survived years of neglect. They were slowly coming back. She turned back to the house. Women were going in for lunch now.

* * *

Joanna woke slowly, moving through layers. There were comfortable noises in the house. Rain on the roof, soothing in its own way. In her half sleep, she thought she was in college, back in the dorm. There were others awake, but there was nothing to alert her. No panic, no discomfort, no one yelling. She was unable to move, just the stage of comfort where it's all lost if there's any movement, and no matter how the sleeper tries, that stage of comfort could not be recaptured. She didn't want to move and lose it. She sank back into deep sleep.

She woke later, restless, hurting again. She didn't recognize the room but that wasn't unusual. She tried to get up and immediately someone was there, leaning over her. "Want to get up, baby? Use the pot? Let me help you."

Someone kind enough to help her, the line from some stage play, "dependent on the kindness of strangers" ran through her head. When she tried to stand, she realized just how weak she was. Moving took concentrated effort and then she felt like she was walking through water. She tried to see where she was, who was helping her but it took all her concentration to focus on putting one foot in front of the other.

"How about some soup?" the kind voice asked as she was tucked back into bed. "Just a couple of spoonfuls?" The soup was passed under her nose and her mouth watered. "Thought you might want some."

She obediently opened her mouth and swallowed several spoonfuls before she wanted to go back to sleep.

When she woke up the next time, she just lay there unmoving. She felt clearer in mind, enough for her thoughts to focus. She carefully turned her head and found her nurse, bodyguard, whatever in the rocking chair, bent over something.

Deborah's infirmary. She was able to identify the location. Deborah's house. Deborah the contract holder. She carefully and dispassionately picked the idea apart. Deborah her ex-lover. Deborah who the one time they had met, cut her dead, denied even knowing her. Deborah, now running a farm, holding contracts. Holding *her* contract.

The woman was knitting. Joanna watched her idly. She didn't look abused. She was dressed in jeans and sweater, thin but not starved, light complexion. No bruises. There was a light knock on the door and Joanna closed her eyes. Someone came in, there was the squeak of the chair as her sitter got up and came over.

"Any change?"

"Still sleeping."

Someone leaned over her, a hand lightly on her forehead. She kept herself relaxed, breathing evenly.

"She do any more talking?"

"Not while I've been here. Has she been?"

"Restless like, muttering about having to go somewhere, had to make contact with someone."

There was a moment's silence. "Poor woman. Wonder if there's anyone out there looking for her."

"No idea. Deborah may know, but she's not saying much."

There was a soft chuckle. "Does she ever?" But the tone was still friendly, not hostile, Joanna realized. "That's some shiner she's got, did you notice?"

"How could anyone miss it? She's going to be sporting that for a while." They stepped away from the bed. "What do you think she's planning?" There was a pause and then the voice went on. "She's not saying anything."

"I don't know. You would think if she was going the state route…" She trailed off. "Well, I guess she'll tell us when she's ready."

"Guess so," came the returning comment. "And we'll just take it as it comes. Why don't you go, get out of here. I know you hate this part. I'll cover you."

"Thanks. I owe you one."

Joanna didn't move as she heard the steps across the wood floor, the door open and shut. When she dared to half open her eyes, the new person was sitting in the rocker, pulling yarn and knitting needles out of a bag.

Joanna cringed at the thought she might have been talking. Yes, she supposed there were people looking for her. Unfortunately not all of them were friendly. The difficulty lay in the ability to tell the difference. And how could she make contact now? She had no idea where she was, no sure idea about Deborah. So someone gave Deborah a shiner. Boy she would have liked to have seen that. The Deborah she remembered wasn't very physical. So much for one big happy family. She rubbed her face. That was the thing about holders, all the lies were difficult to maintain. Sooner or later, the truth came out. Unbidden thoughts of Gentry came up. She closed her eyes tightly and moaned softly. She had thought it had been rough before he had taken over her contract.

She flinched, cried out at the touch, jerking up to a sitting position and pulling away.

"It's all right, you're safe. No one's going to hurt you." The woman showed her outspread hands. "You were moaning. Are you hurting?"

Joanna looked at the hands and up at the woman. Had she moaned? She had thought… She didn't know what she had thought. She shook her head.

"We're not going to hurt you," the woman reassured her. "You've been asleep a lot. Are you ready to eat something?"

Eat? Yes, that sounded good. She was going to have to get back on her feet. Vulnerability meant that you could be exploited, robbed or even killed. "Yes." She found her voice was a croak.

"Some soup? It's probably chicken. That sound okay?"

Joanna nodded.

"Good. I'll get some."

Alone, Joanna thought. Although she wasn't sure what she would do alone. She watched the woman go over to the door, and she left it open, just stepped outside and called.

"Sue? Can you bring some soup up here? Our patient's awake."

"Right away."

The woman returned. "Sue will be so pleased you're awake. She's been in a state these past days, conferring with Beth, making sure that she always had hot soup for you when you were ready to eat."

Joanna made no comment but the woman went on to explain anyway.

"She's been working with Beth to make a healthier soup, but she hasn't had the chance to test it on anyone who's been sick." She moved around the room to bring forth a table and set it by the bed. "She said it'll be a chance to test it and fatten you up. She said that you were even thinner than she was."

"Short rations?" Joanna asked, remembering Deborah saying there was enough food. Maybe yet another lie.

"Not this year, we had good crops last year and got a lot put up. About time with the weather we've had." She pulled down a shawl from the shelf and threw it around Joanna's shoulders. "No sense you getting cold, don't want you back into the sick bed. No, Sue's just one of those people with a high metabolism. On the go constantly and never still."

True enough, Joanna decided when the skinny blonde came in with the tray. She set down soup, corn bread and tea in front of Joanna and then hovered, watching every bite Joanna took.

"Is it all right? Seasoned okay? I didn't want to make it too spicy since you haven't been eating much. Or too rich. It is all right, isn't it?"

"It's very good," Joanna assured her softly, reasoning the one person to avoid offending was the one handing out the food. Still, the woman was so full of nervous energy Joanna was exhausted being around her. And eating took a lot of energy.

Slowly Joanna regained her strength. Sue was in constant attendance, watching to make sure she ate.

As the days went by, she noticed she was left alone occasionally but she could hear people in the hallway. And then she was left alone at night. She began to relax a little. She had time to think about how she had gotten here and what she could do about it. She still didn't know how she felt about Deborah. So she looked up every time the door opened, both hopeful and afraid, and always disappointed because it was never Deborah.

* * *

"How's Joanna doing?" Deborah asked in the morning meeting.

Beth nodded. "Pretty good. I think she can leave the sick room." She glanced speculatively at Deborah. "It would have helped if you had dropped in to see her. She might be more reassured."

"About what?" Deborah looked up in true surprise. She had assumed that Joanna would be just as glad not to see her.

"She has no idea how she's going to fit in. And she keeps looking for you."

"She said that?" Deborah frowned. That did not sound like the Joanna she had interviewed at the diner.

Beth shook her head. "No, she actually hasn't said much, but she looks up at the door every time it opens. You're the only one she knows here so I guess she's looking for you."

"Well, I've been busy." She didn't miss Beth's raised eyebrows at her curt dismissal and did feel badly about it but she was unsettled. Joanna's resurfacing into her life had been totally unexpected. While she had had no hesitation on taking Joanna out of a bad situation and truly did not regret her actions, Joanna's presence still triggered memories of what had been, what had been lost. She had long forbidden talk in the house of what-if situations believing it was demoralizing if not depressing. She herself had steadfastly looked forward, at what had to be done to survive, what actions had to be taken, and no looking back.

But Joanna had made her look back. Holding Joanna in her arms at Anoka, then watching over her those nights in the sick room, not only reminded her of past feelings about Joanna, but how she had felt about herself, her life, a life far different than the present.

She forced her attention back to the meeting. "How's the inventory coming?"

"We've got stores left, we're not finishing out the winter down to beans."

"Thank God!" Karen breathed.

Deborah shook her head. They had had some lean years with beans as their main subsistence and Karen was a meat-and-potatoes woman. Karen swore she'd never eat beans again. "Enough to carry us until the gardens come in?" Sara nodded and Deborah checked the item off her list. "What else?"

"There's stuff to repair, tools and such," Karen reported. "We can get most of it done but there are some things beyond us. Know a blacksmith?"

"One over by Pipe Creek. What have we got?" Deborah pulled out her ever-present notebook as Karen handed over the list. "How's the stable coming?"

"So-so," Karen answered. "You have any immediate plans for it?" Deborah shook her head.

"Does it have a lock?" Sara asked suddenly. Karen, Beth and Deborah all turned to look at her.

"Like locking the barn door after the horse is stolen? No horses, Sara."

"No locks either," Karen added. Sara shrugged and went back to her notes. However she hung around after Karen and Beth left.

Deborah was already pulling out her house list for the day. "When we move Joanna into the house, do you know where you're putting her?"

Sara shook her head. "No, in fact, that was something I wanted to talk to you about. Did you read those regulations I left on your desk for you?"

Deborah found the pages under her scattered magazines and look sheepishly up at Sara. "No."

Sara shook her head and gave an exasperated sigh. "What good—oh, never mind. You knew that Joanna has run away before, didn't you? Tell me that you read that much of her contract."

"Yes, I knew that."

"She got turned into the state for that and the state has the option of locking her up," Sara went on. "Something about failure to support or something."

"Seems stupid to lock someone up and have to support them when all they are doing is failing to fulfill a private contract, but yes, I knew that."

"Well, you know the state. They're afraid that it'll be a drain on the community or they'll end up contracted to two different people at the same time and that would be fraudulent. Anyway, they pass that responsibility back to the contract holder. That's you."

"Why do I get the feeling that I'm not going to like this?" Deborah sat back and made a tent of her fingers. "Go on."

"Joanna has to be locked in at night."

"So. We lock the house up at night."

"No. That's not enough. She has to be locked in, like in a room, restricted." Deborah's eyes narrowed as she began to see where Sara was going with this but Sara didn't back down. "I researched her contract. She has to be locked in at night and supervised by a noncontracted person. If she runs away this time, it's the third time. Any damages or charges she would incur while she's gone would be charged back to you."

Deborah muttered a strong profanity.

Sara continued, squirming in the chair. Deborah didn't believe in shooting the messenger but she had been known to be pretty fiery when upset. "As you know, we don't have any locked bedrooms in this house—" She stopped.

"Except mine," Deborah filled in for her. Of course, she had the master bedroom, the one right over her office, her private retreat, about the only spot in the house she could really consider her personal area. Everything in the house was technically hers but with everyone having their own room or at least sharing a room, and then the common areas, there was less and less that was really hers. There was no other spot that she could go and shut the world away except her bedroom and the adjoining sitting room, nursery, dressing room, whatever it had been in the past.

She took a deep breath, reminding herself Sara was only delivering the information. She wanted her to wade through rules and regulations and manage the house and do all those things for her and she was doing it. "You're telling me that I have to give up my room so that Joanna can be locked in at night."

Sara actually winced. "Yes," she said with great reluctance. "Unless you want to share the room with her."

"Share the room!"

"There is that other room you've got filled with storage stuff," Sara continued doggedly. Deborah had wanted her to run the house and manage the paperwork, so this was what she was supposed to do. "I know you keep saying that you need to clean it out and make a sitting room. You could easily turn it into a second bedroom."

"There has got to be another way." *There is no way I can share a room with Joanna.*

"I don't know how. We lock the pantry, and there's the storage downstairs, but nothing else. There just isn't another room that we can lock up and still be considered close enough for you to supervise." She looked at Deborah strangely. "Is there a problem with her sharing your room? I know you've been avoiding her." She stopped at the jerk of Deborah's head.

Deborah looked away. Sometimes Sara was a bit too perceptive. It was quite one thing when she used her to read everyone else in the house, but quite another when Sara's gaze and astuteness fell on her. "Joanna's last holder used her sexually. I've assured her that that won't happen here. Having her in the bedroom with me at night seems to negate that."

"Is she family? Would that occur to her? I mean, no one here would think that you would." She broke off suddenly. "Deborah, are you sure there isn't something else going on?"

"Yes, she's family. And yes, that would occur to her. It already has." Deborah ignored the last question. "And I'm glad that it wouldn't occur to anyone else but Joanna's come from a vastly different experience. As far as she's concerned, the only good contract holder is a dead one."

"Good God, Deborah. Are you saying it would be dangerous for you to be locked in there with her?"

"No, I used the wrong comparison." Deborah shook her head. *At least, I hope it was the wrong one.* "Any other good news?" she asked glumly. Maybe if she thought about something else, another solution would come to her. She glanced up when Sara didn't answer right away and she didn't look happy. "Come on, out with it. How much worse can it get?"

"In light of what you've said, probably pretty bad." Sara leaned forward. "Because Joanna's run away and she's up for that third strike, her supervision needs to be almost constant. If we had any other kind of operation here, it wouldn't be so bad, but we're a farm. Lots of open areas, lots of independent work. I mean, it's nothing for one of us to be working fence—well not me. You don't send me out to do things like that, but for someone to be checking the fences and to be out alone for hours at a time."

"You're wandering, Sara. Must be pretty bad. Spill it."

"She needs direct supervision by a noncontracted person at all times."

"Shit. Damn. Fuck." Deborah closed her eyes. *The whole purpose of putting you in charge of the house was so I could get away more. Now you're telling me I'm more pinned down than ever!* She gave mental chuckle. *Like Todd says, no good deed unrewarded.*

She opened her eyes to see Sara braced and realized she couldn't take her frustration out on her. She took a deep breath. "I need to take a walk." *I need to think about this.*

"It's still raining."

"So?" Deborah got to her feet. "Actually, I may need to take a long walk. If I don't make it back for dinner, don't worry and just keep a plate warm. I'll be back."

"Where are you going?"

Deborah shook her head. "I don't know. Just walking." She recognized Sara's confusion and realized if she was learning how Sara worked, Sara needed to be aware how she worked. "I need to think, and this is what I do. If you say I took a walk, everyone will understand."

"All right," Sara said but she sounded dubious.

* * *

Deborah didn't return until after supper, almost true dark. She could hear everyone in the living room as she hung up her coat to dry. She needed to do this first, before she changed her mind, before some little corner of her mind insisted there had to be another way. If there was another *acceptable* way, she had not been able to come up with it.

"Listen up, ladies," Deborah announced as she walked into the living room. "Got some assignments for you." She gave Karen an apologetic look. This was horning in on her authority. "I do believe this rain will continue tomorrow so I've got a very delicate task for you." She tried to put a humorous spin on it but she didn't feel good about it. "I've decided my storage room needs to be cleaned out."

"Hot damn!" she heard and "About time." She narrowed her eyes, mostly in good humor but there was that little bit of resentment too.

"I know you all think I've used that space up there for my pack rat treasures which several of you have made less-than-gentle suggestions about what I might do with." There were more than a few chuckles since Deborah's standard response for something she didn't want to throw away but had no place to store it was the room off her bedroom. "I guess you folks win. I need that room cleaned out. Any volunteers?"

"Me!" Linda said immediately.

Deborah fastened a withering glare on Linda who only laughed along with everyone else. Linda was the direct opposite of Deborah. She threw away everything. Deborah looked around for allies. "Now I know a lot of you have thought I'm entirely too much of a hoarder but there are useful things in that room."

"That is true," Brea said in careful measured tones. "Maybe they haven't been available *when* we needed them because you couldn't find them, but, I for one will admit, that sooner or later, they do appear." She glanced around in case anyone missed her point. "Usually when we were looking for something else." There was general laugher then. "I'll volunteer," she said when the laughter settled down. "And I won't let Linda throw *everything* away. On one condition."

Deborah gave her a wary look. Brea's plain speaking could hit her in some tender spots. "And that might be?"

"You are not involved. You stay out of there. You stay clear. Otherwise, we won't be cleaning it out, we'll just be moving it to some other place, and for the life of me, I don't know where that might be!"

"You've got me over a barrel," Deborah admitted reluctantly. "I'll stay out of it." She made an ugly face. "But you know you're just throwing my life away."

"You've had a damn cluttered life," Brea retorted.

Oh, if you only knew everything I've lost. "Okay," Deborah agreed as she thought of her Memphis home buried in the earthquake. "I'll let you folks take care of it, but please, be generous."

"Great!" Karen sat up far too eagerly for Deborah's comfort. She rubbed her hands together and for the moment seemed ready to spring into action right then and there. "This is like those reality organization shows that used to be on television. Is there a television crew around somewhere to get this on film?"

"I'll even volunteer, Deborah," Peg said with some laughter. "That'll give you some protection."

Deborah sighed in resignation. As much as she hated turning the task over to others, she knew she could never do the job. That's why the room was stuffed to start with.

"Good." She drew a deep breath. "Then there's the next part. I know there's extra furniture around here somewhere, in the attic, or in one of the sheds. I need furniture moved in to make that room a bedroom."

The laughter faded. Curious glances were exchanged and then everyone looked to her. She definitely had everyone's attention.

"As you know, we've got a new member in the house. Beth tells me that she's ready to get out of the infirmary. Her name is Joanna Davis, by the way. Joanna's an unwilling contract, state-registered, in case you haven't heard. That's all I'm going to say except that I'm familiar with her story and have found nothing there that would put any of us in danger. Anything else is her story to tell, not mine. What I will say is that she falls under different rules and regulations. She needs to be under my supervision more closely than anyone else we've had in the house. She also needs to be locked in at night. Consequently, she and I are going to have a lot of togetherness down to and including sharing sleeping quarters."

She paused and while she could see the questions on their faces, no one said anything. "I want," she said carefully just to make it clear, "Joanna to be treated just like anyone else. She may be difficult, distrustful even, but I think when we show consideration, she'll heal and be a valuable member of the house."

There was an uneasy silence over the room for a moment. Not exactly welcoming, Deborah thought as she waited for someone to speak. She tried to read them but all she could see was discomfort and a deliberate blandness.

"Are we still going to have a party?" Sue said finally.

"Of course." Deborah was relieved at the question being about something so regular. "She'll be out tomorrow?" She looked to Beth who nodded. "So tomorrow night? Will that give you enough time to get everything done? The room? Food? Play time?" She watched everyone suddenly perk up. Any excuse for a party would do. Between that and the chance to tear her room apart might be enough distraction that Joanna sharing a room would be a minor detail. She hoped.

"Good. Now Sue, did you keep a plate for me? I'm famished."

"Yes, of course." Sue leaped to her feet. "It's in the warming oven. Just some stew." She rushed by Deborah already muttering. "I can put that ham in to soak tonight. And I think there's still some apples left. Sweet potatoes. I wonder if there's any maple syrup left or did I use the last of it."

Deborah breathed a sigh of relief.

* * *

Joanna was out of bed, wrapped in a robe and sitting in the rocker when Beth brought in her breakfast. "I think you're ready to free up the infirmary." Clothes hung over Beth's arm—jeans, sweater, shirt, underwear. "You feel okay?"

"I guess so." Joanna wondered how much choice she had. She got up and met Beth, taking the clothes as Beth took the tray to the small table. The jeans were not hers—these were heavier.

There was the silk undershirt, underwear, a T-shirt, the pullover sweater. She wasn't eager to leave the sickroom which had become a comfortable cocoon for her. "You're the doctor." She laid the clothes on the bed as Beth fussed over the place setting. "Where am I going? What will I be doing?"

"Not my bailiwick," Beth sidestepped. "I've simply said you were fit to be out of here. No heavy duty, still get plenty of rest. I'd rather not see you back in here any time soon."

"Fine by me."

Beth left a few minutes later, leaving Joanna alone. *Removing herself from interrogation,* Joanna surmised. She examined the clothes before she ate her eggs, oatmeal, stewed apples. Decent quality used clothing with still a lot of wear left. Different shoes, she noted. Well, those running shoes had run their last mile a long time ago. She dawdled over breakfast until it dawned on her it was probably going to be Deborah coming to collect her and assign her to whatever she might be doing. She shoved the tray back on the table and got to her feet. The last thing she wanted was for Deborah to catch her in the nightshirt and have to wait for her to dress or even worse, to catch her half dressed.

She was standing at the window looking over the muddy fields when there was a light rap at the door. There were still patches of dirty snow here and there, but the fields were mostly clear. She could finally realize what had bothered her all week. These were open fields. It looked like anyone working in them could just walk away.

"Snow's almost gone," Deborah commented, coming up behind her. She put her arm over Joanna's shoulder and leaned against the window frame. "Land goes over to that grove of trees, the boundary," she said, pointing.

Joanna resented Deborah's entry into her personal space, but what did she expect from a holder? She glanced over her shoulder and then did a double take at the cut over Deborah's eye and the faint bruise.

Deborah didn't seem to notice as she stepped back. "Beth tells me you're ready to get out of here. You feel up to it?"

"I guess so."

"Clothes fit okay?" Deborah looked her up and down.

"Pretty much," Joanna answered as she examined Deborah's worn jeans and sweatshirt in turn. Not exactly how she thought the holder would dress. Joanna hesitated. Some holders charged for every little thing and added it to the contract balance. "Is this something I'm going to have to pay for?"

Deborah raised a questioning eyebrow. "No, I provide work clothes. Now, if you want something else, extras or something fancy, you'll have to get it yourself."

And how would I pay for that? But Joanna kept the question to herself, not sure she would like Deborah's answer.

"So you ready to clear this place and see what the rest of the house is like?"

"My time is your time," Joanna returned dryly.

Deborah did give her a smile at that and with a wave of the arm, indicated the door. "Let's go downstairs then. Conversations like this do better in my office."

She pointed to the corkscrew stairs and followed Joanna down. "It's still early in the season. We're not geared up for heavy work yet, so you'll still have enough time to get in shape."

Wonder what the heavy stuff is like? Joanna waited for Deborah at the bottom of the stairs. She glanced around at the rough brick floor, the open doorway to the kitchen. There was someone working at a huge island bench that wouldn't have been part of the original house.

"This way," Deborah said as they went through. The woman in the kitchen looked up at her, glanced at Deborah and then went back to work but Joanna saw her look up again with a curious gaze as they left the room.

"The dining room and social area," Deborah said as they went through the sizeable adjoining room. Joanna took in the large oval table surrounded by chairs on the left, the mixed furniture consisting of a couple of couches, easy chairs and a coffee table, on the right. There was a fireplace on the far wall. The furniture was worn. There were holes in the plaster walls that needed painting. The floors were hardwood with scattered rugs. However it wasn't institutionalized and there was a comfortable homey feeling. It confused her because while it didn't look like anything she would associate with Deborah, it didn't look like any contract holder's house she had ever seen before either.

"Foyer," Deborah announced as they went into the front area, woven carpet, open to the second floor, the large double doors, the fancy curved stairs through the archway. A sharp burst of laughter came from upstairs and Deborah glanced upward with a resigned look. She shook her head but she continued on.

"My office." She opened the door and indicated Joanna to go in ahead.

Joanna walked into a formal office, heavy wooden, highly polished furnishings, carpeted floor. There were chairs in front of the desk, a credenza and bookshelves behind the desk. Blinds and curtains on the windows. It was old, definitely from a more formal time but now well worn in.

"Take a seat," Deborah invited as she shut the door behind them.

Uncertainly Joanna took a chair in front of the desk as Deborah searched for a file. This wasn't the type of interview she was expecting.

"Your file had a lot of transfers," Deborah commented as she took her place at her desk. She looked up when Joanna said nothing. "No comment?"

"No."

Deborah opened up the file and flipped through the pages. "I am going to assume that many of those transfers were part of his scams but some seem to predate his acquiring your contract." She looked up at Joanna. "I don't believe in such transactions. I like to think the agreement I make with someone is carried out, and I can't be sure of that if the contract is sold. Too many things can happen and then I have nothing to say about it."

Control freak.

"Consequently I don't sell contracts, I only buy them." She went back to flipping through the pages. "I see you've got about five years to go, not counting the damages that are tacked on. Is that your understanding?"

"That's what they're trying for but it'll be set aside."

"That is, of course, a possibility, but I wouldn't hold my breath." She sat back in the chair, crossed her legs, and looked at Joanna directly. "So until that happens, you're going to be here."

Or until I make it this time.

"We work on a rotation, everyone does a little bit of everything unless there are issues or pressing duties. I never thought it fair for someone to get stuck with all the nasty work or that just one person was the only one who knew how to do something. At the same time, everyone does have their specialties, some more useful than others."

She paused as if giving Joanna time to speak or maybe volunteer her specialty. *I don't think you'd like my specialty*, Joanna thought and said nothing.

"We'll be working you into the labor rotation, probably various jobs as we feel you out, find out what you can do and what you can't."

Shit work, Joanna interpreted. "I don't know anything about farming."

Deborah shrugged. "You're not the only one. It's a learning experience. What kind of work did you do after the Great Earthquake, before you got into trouble?"

Joanna shook her head—not an area she wanted to discuss. "Nothing that matters now."

Deborah didn't push it. So many jobs had disappeared. "You'll have to pull your own weight—slackers won't be tolerated. We don't have the time or energy for people who play games."

There was a loud crash from the room above them and both of the women flinched. Deborah looked at the ceiling and sighed before she turned her attention back to Joanna.

"It's not a bad life, Joanna. Better than some."

There were heavy footsteps above them and Deborah moved restlessly. "You'll be treated like everyone else as much as possible considering the restrictions of your contract. You know that there're restrictions, don't you?"

"Yes," Joanna said evenly. She was never quite sure what was really required by law and what had just been demanded of her.

"You know I have to lock you up at night."

Joanna nodded. Sometimes that was good, sometimes not. She wasn't sure how it would apply in this house. Admittedly she hadn't seen the sleeping quarters but it seemed unlikely that there would be anything which met the legal requirements. Most private housing didn't.

Deborah continued but Joanna recognized the tone. Deborah had rehearsed this part. "This house has three rooms with locks that are available for such conditions. The pantry, which is not appropriate. There's a storeroom in the cellar, affectionately called the dungeon which will not be used, and my bedroom."

Joanna stared at her with dawning comprehension, disbelief. *She can't mean what I think that means.* "I'm so sorry for the inconvenience of giving up your room, but I didn't make the law," she managed to say with a forced casualness.

Deborah chuckled as if she knew Joanna was bluffing. "Inconvenient, yes, but I'm not giving up my room. You're just going to be in there with me." She met Joanna's gaze almost as a challenge.

Oh my God, he didn't even keep me this close!

"There's a small room attached to mine, the master bedroom," Deborah continued. "I suppose it was originally a nursery or the lady's dressing room. I'm having it cleaned out. You'll sleep in there."

Joanna's mouth went dry. Her fledgling good thoughts about being there evaporated almost before they had materialized. She couldn't even protest. Unbidden, the memories of Deborah casually touching her at the diner, stripping her at the warehouse in spite of the cold, holding her in her arms flooded Joanna. After all Deborah's noble words, she was just like every other contract holder. Joanna would be *available.* She realized that Deborah was watching her as if she expected an outburst so she deliberately relaxed. She swallowed as she tried to stabilize her emotions. She had been prepared to be abused all those other times, but she had expected better from Deborah. "I see," was all she could come up with.

Deborah watched her for a moment and then continued. "Because it is the master bedroom, there's a lock on the door. I think it'll be enough to satisfy the legal requirements. Technically you will be locked in for the night."

"I thought you said…" Joanna broke off. Just what choice did she have? And Deborah already knew how she'd been used in the past. "You lied to me."

"No, I didn't." Deborah's eyes narrowed at Joanna's implication. "I promised you a bed by yourself. I'm not splitting hairs. I'm not Gentry. Sexual or any other personal services aren't required. We're simply sharing a room because you need to be supervised by a noncontracted person, I'm the only one here, and I have a room with a lock."

Joanna glared at Deborah in defiant disbelief. *Like you think anyone's actually going to believe that?* As angry as she was at the possibility, she remembered Deborah's hands on her, her touch, the gentleness she had displayed in the infirmary.

"I don't sleep with women I contract with," Deborah went on. "I find it blurs the lines. I don't beat anyone. I don't lock them in closets. I don't trade them out and I have never sold any contract I've acquired. You're with me for the duration."

Joanna heard the fine words, but she had heard them before. Oh, Deborah was being careful, but she was still a contract holder. She heard the power and the control. Soon that power would be exercised.

"Anything else?" Joanna said coldly when it was clear that Deborah was expecting some response from her. There were the sounds of many feet overhead.

Deborah stood up which also brought Joanna to her feet. "I think maybe this finishes this part of our conversation. How about we take a walk? It looks like the rain has let up. Give you a chance to see the grounds, get some fresh air. You up for it?"

"That would be fine," Joanna answered in a tight voice. This room was too small and it was closing in on her. All she could see and hear and feel was Deborah. God, would there be no escape from this woman? She took a deep breath, clamping down on her anger. Seeing what kind of setup this would be would be good, what would be expected of her. She had this vague memory of open fields but she had been too ill to remember much. And as long as Deborah was going through this fiction of being the concerned contract holder, then she could oblige with the narrative of the cooperative contractee.

Deborah looked her up and down, noting the shoes. "We'll pick up jackets and boots at the back porch."

They went through the house again, this time avoiding the now busy kitchen and out the side door. Deborah simply pulled two jackets off the nails on the side porch, tossed one to Joanna. "These," she said, pointing to a row of boots under the bench.

"It's turned muddy out there and housekeeping wouldn't like us tracking it in." She toed off her own shoes and pulled out what were clearly her calf-high leather boots. "Pick a pair that fits."

The farm wasn't huge by any means, too small to support a family in normal times but larger than a hobby farm. Seventy-five acres, Deborah had said. The buildings were old, weathered and a little run-down. Machinery was stored in the sheds, but not used since the fuel was prohibitively expensive. A small concrete block building was the milk house. The chicken houses were small sheds fenced off separately. A long low shed accommodated the hogs rooting in the mud. Workshop. Smokehouse. Laundry. Stables.

The walk cleared Joanna's brain and she gave only halfway attention to Deborah's farm tour. She was more interested in the road that came down the hill and continued on, and the neighbors' roofs she could see in the distance. There weren't many. The farm seemed rather isolated, which had its good points, and she guessed, its bad points. A body could just walk away without much trouble. She speculated on that as she looked off into the distance and then turned to find Deborah watching her.

"We're a little isolated," Deborah said, as if she had been reading Joanna's mind. "We sit in a pocket of some sort. Weather-wise, storms hit either north of us about thirty miles, south of us about twenty. And we're out of some wind pattern so we don't have an airborne problem. Don't get many drifters through here so we miss that issue. Hooligans may follow the train tracks but we're just far enough away that we haven't been bothered." She frowned as she scanned the horizon. "I don't complain about that."

This was another side of Deborah that Joanna had never seen before—where she came from. Deborah had simply said it was a small town, farming background. She had wanted more so she left. She had never suggested a visit or even talked about it much. Now she looked so at home as she walked through the mud, pointing out improvements she had made, even voicing plans she had for the future that Joanna couldn't imagine her ever having been in the city.

"You're proud of all this," Joanna ventured to comment as they went around the stable and walked back to the house through the orchard.

Deborah looked back across the outbuildings behind the large brick house. She paused when they reached the pillars that marked the sidewalk entrance to the front door. "Yeah," she said slowly. "I guess so. It's been in my family for generations. I can feel them surrounding me, protecting." She looked off at the road and across the fields. "For a long time, I thought I was just holding on to it because I was selfish, some family heritage I just wasn't ready to let go of. And now." She turned back to Joanna. "Now it holds others safe, a new kind of family. It's functional again." Her face turned steely as she gazed off into the distance. "And I intend to survive."

"Off the backs of contracts," Joanna couldn't resist throwing in.

Deborah turned back to her in some surprise, some amusement. "Is that how you see it?"

"Is there any other way?" Joanna asked unable to keep the bitterness from her voice.

"Yes," Deborah answered. She searched Joanna's face. "It might be my conceit, my ego, but I figure you increase your chances of survival when you become part of the House of Steele." Her face turned steely again. "I don't intend to lose anyone of you."

"Because of us or in spite of us?" Joanna muttered but Deborah had already turned away. She wasn't even sure if Deborah heard her.

She had. "Probably both," she said over her shoulder as she cut across the yard. "Let's go in, should be lunchtime."

There was a bit of a stir when Joanna and Deborah walked into the dining room. Deborah led the way to the buffet table set up against the wall. "Because of schedules at midday, lunch's always off the buffet. It's sometimes on the run. Dinner's at six usually and we're all at the table. Breakfast is at seven, also at the table. It all depends on the schedule. Like during the summer in the heavy season, we end up eating a little later." She picked up a plate and looked over the serving bowls. "I kept you out there too long. I'm afraid we're going to get the leftovers. It might not be as much as you got in the infirmary."

Joanna picked up a plate, glancing around at people watching her. "I can live with that. It's better than I've had in some time."

Deborah had already noted that those who had been ready to vacate were suddenly taking more food or just lingering. Their curiosity was understandable. Generally new women didn't collapse at the door and weren't so bruised.

"Regular meals might take some getting used to."

"How come?" Deborah asked without thinking, but when Joanna didn't answer, she paused to look at her.

"I wasn't exactly at the top of his priority list," Joanna said finally, minutely examining what she was putting on her plate. "And," she added, "a lot of the places we were traveling through didn't have much food." She indicated the buffet with a wave of a serving spoon. "All of this come from this farm?"

"Pretty much. Not totally. We're not self-sufficient yet but we've made a good start." She pointed to a small table in the corner of the dining room. "Over there." Even after they took their seats, Deborah continued the questions. "So where have you been traveling?" When there was no answer forthcoming, she looked up, her expression very open, as if there were no reason why Joanna might not want to tell.

"You just ask anything, don't you? And expect me to answer."

"Why not? Are you hiding something?"

"No." Joanna went back to eating but her entire manner changed again.

Time to change the subject, Deborah thought but she made a mental note to follow up on this later. "I don't think I mentioned it but there's a party tonight."

"A party?" Joanna looked up in surprise.

"We have an introduction party whenever we get a new member of the house. Gives you a chance to meet everyone on a more informal basis than at the dinner table or on a work detail." The dismay on Joanna's face was unmistakable. "It's not so bad." Everyone tells you a little bit about herself. There's cake, ice cream maybe, punch."

"Liquor?" Joanna asked facetiously.

"Probably. I'm not sure what's still in stock downstairs. It's too cold for sangria but I don't know, mulled cider." Joanna looked at her strangely. "It's up to the cooks." She paused. "It's been a long boring winter. We'll take any occasion for a party. New people mean new stories, and then you can listen to all those stories that everyone knows by heart. You'll be a new listener."

"Oh, great," Joanna muttered.

"I'm sure that everyone will be captivated by your charming personality and you'll have a good time."

"I feel like fresh meat thrown to the wolves."

Deborah chuckled. "Well, that too. I imagine that might be a little hampered by the fact that you're sleeping in the master bedroom."

"You just had to bring that up, didn't you?"

Deborah finished eating and deliberately set her silverware on her plate. "Joanna," she said very carefully, "I need to make something clear. I don't control that part of your life. If there's someone here who strikes your fancy and you want to either indulge your libido or have a relationship, I don't control that. I don't think it'll happen suddenly because usually anyone coming in takes some time to get their footing. On the opposite side of the coin, I don't have any predators here, anyone who's just dying for 'fresh meat' as you put it. But you are new and that's an attraction. You are physically attractive, in spite of the bruises and they will heal. You always had a certain open charm about you that drew people to you. I think that's a basic part of you and if it's been sublimated because of your surroundings, I suspect it will come back when you feel safe again. In short, I don't expect you'll be celibate."

"I thought you said that didn't happen with your contracts."

Deborah noticed how Joanna had referred to the people as contracts. Interesting. "No, what I said was that *I* don't sleep with the people I have contracts with. Who *they* sleep with is their business. The only other rule I have about it is no one gets coerced. Both my managers, who you'll meet later this afternoon, may have some authority but not over the individuals. Karen is the land manager—she does work rotation schedules but she's been in a relationship for years. I suspect if she stepped outside that relationship she'd welcome anything I might do as compared to what Beth might do."

"The doctor?"

"She's not a doctor, just a nurse practitioner but yes, that Beth. The house manager is Sara who is more inclined to do a perimeter walk rather than hurt your feelings."

Joanna looked away. "And you," she said as if it was being dragged from her. "Have you slept with any of them, maybe before you made up the contract?"

Deborah's tone was cold and final. "I don't see that it's any of your concern." She met Joanna's surprised gaze head on. "Now if you're done eating, let's go upstairs and inspect your new quarters."

* * *

Joanna stood off in a corner as several women cleared the room of boxes and miscellaneous furniture. When Deborah had said she had used it for storage, Joanna had visualized some dank and dark little room. Instead it was a decent size with a window on one side and a chimney on the other. The only drawback was that about half the wall between her and Deborah's area was an open archway. Still it was a lot better than what she had expected.

"Where to?" Karen, the dishwater blonde, asked as she paused with a stack of boxes. A large woman, she'd make a good guard, Joanna decided but Deborah had said she was the land manager.

Deborah gave the boxes a rueful look. "Move them down to the office," Deborah finally decided. "Did you find a bed in the attic?"

"There's a three-quarter size bed up there," Linda offered. She was the short strawberry blonde, and she gave Joanna a friendly smile when Deborah wasn't looking.

"That sound all right to you?"

"That'll be fine." Joanna still had no clue how to relate to this group. Every group had its hierarchy, some fluid, some rigid. Regardless, they all looked to Deborah for direction.

"Good." Deborah turned to Linda. "Set the bed up along this wall. It'll give maximum privacy and be warm enough in winter."

Joanna had offered to help but Karen shook her head. Joanna didn't know if she was still considered too sick to work or whether everyone else was a team and she wasn't on it. Once again, she was an outsider; and if she was tied to Deborah, she'd probably remain an outsider. Not exactly the way to fit in with the group. So she stood in the corner and watched as Karen, Linda, Sue and Brea brought down the bed, a small trunk and a chair and put them in the center of the room.

She looked up just in time to see Deborah turn away from looking at her. Everyone could feel the tension in the room. Joanna watched several of the women exchange looks. Deborah might say that she didn't sleep with women contracted with her, but Joanna wasn't so certain. And once the door was locked at night, who was going to know? And who would believe her?

Joanna turned away to look out the window. She didn't think she could have stood a room with no window. Thank God she had a view. She closed her eyes. She didn't have the strength now, but she had a view of the open fields. They gave her hope. She would survive.

"You okay, Joanna?" Deborah walked up to her, looking out the window as if to see what Joanna might see.

"I'm fine." She turned to meet Deborah's questioning gaze with as much defiance as she could muster. *Never let them see you scared.* She had learned that much. *Never show a weakness.*

"You need anything else here?"

A door, Joanna thought as she turned around through the archway into Deborah's area. She shook her head.

"Well, thank you, women. I'm sure that Joanna can rearrange things to her satisfaction now that you've delivered the goods."

Once they were all out and the door was closed, Deborah turned back to Joanna. "Is there anything you particularly need? Do you get cold at night?"

"I'm fine," Joanna replied. She glanced at the linens tossed on the bed. Another thing Joanna had learned, never ask for anything. Never trust a contract holder. She met Deborah's gaze. No, she would show her she could deal with anything Deborah would throw at her. But Deborah had this knowing gaze, part amusement, part acceptance of Joanna's challenge.

"Don't paint yourself into a corner, Joanna," Deborah said quietly. "Life is difficult enough." She turned away and went back to her area. "I'm going downstairs. My office is right below us. You can probably get settled better if I'm not breathing over your shoulder. If you need anything, let me know. We've got lots of stuff stored away."

"You trust me in your room alone?" Joanna went to the archway. Deborah picked up the key and dropped it in her breast pocket.

"Why not?" She turned around to look at Joanna. "It's not just my room anymore. It's our room." She glanced around and then came back to Joanna. "You might want to take a nap anyway. This is your first day out of the infirmary and with the party tonight, it might be late."

Joanna watched with disbelief as Deborah went out the door. Surely this was a test of some sort. Deborah wouldn't be so foolish just to trust her, just like that. She went to the door after she heard Deborah go down the steps. Cautiously she opened the door but the hall was empty. She closed it softly, uncertain.

She looked around Deborah's room. A high four-poster double bed covered with a quilt, an old-fashioned highboy dresser, a rocker in the corner, bedside tables with lamps. Just right there, handy. She shivered. In some ways, she suddenly longed for a locked closet. At least it had a door.

She made up her bed, feeling frozen. Deborah was isolated here, she had set up her own little fiefdom. No one to look in on her. No near neighbors to see what she was doing. A safe little pocket. Joanna made her bed, sheets soft from multiple washings. A straight-backed chair. A trunk to hold what? Her belongings? She didn't have any. She folded the quilt across the foot of the bed, her stomach tied up in knots.

She glanced out her window again. It looked like it might be easy to walk away but where was she going to walk to? There was the train but she didn't know where it went and besides, it didn't exactly make a stop. She closed her eyes. A party?

She lay down, trying to sleep at Deborah's reasonable suggestion, but sleep eluded her. She told herself she was nervous, anxious about the party, about meeting everyone but she knew her anxiety centered about what would happen after the party, after they came upstairs, after the door was closed.

CHAPTER SIX

"You ready?" Deborah stuck her head inside Joanna's room, glancing around to see what she had done with it. If she had done anything. Some didn't when they first moved in, as if afraid it would be taken from them. For some, it took time.

"I guess so." Joanna sat on the side of the bed, pulling her shoes on and tying them.

"Everyone enjoys a party," Deborah explained as they went down the curved stairs at the front of the house. "Any excuse will do, but it's special when we welcome new members to the house. Don't expect this every day."

The dining room was festive, the big table was already set with the better china, and a centerpiece. Amazing the length they would go to for a party, Deborah thought as she caught sight of the old WELCOME sign put up over the door. Must have been Sue's doing. Karen took her spot at the back door. Beth sat just inside the door, Linda over by the windows. Rae was tuning her guitar. There was an air of excitement, relaxation and fun. Deborah hated it. The only way she had been able to deal with these parties was to distance herself, see them as almost strangers, employees that she had to deal with rather than family members. That was how she could make her way to the front of the room, checking where everyone was. She pointed Joanna off to one side over by the window. She herself moved to the empty love seat that had been shoved between two foyer doors and sat on one arm. It didn't take long for everyone to find a seat and get settled.

"All right women," she announced. "Let's get started." She looked around at them as if she didn't see them every day, remembering when each one of them came in. Sue came running in from the kitchen and sat at the end of the bench. Deborah waited a moment, bracing herself.

"I know we've had a lot of surprises this past week. We were looking for spring and got a blizzard instead. Looked for some quiet downtime and instead, we got some excitement to take care of those winter doldrums." There were expressions of agreement around the room, which relieved her. The house was at capacity now. She just might need that room in the stable before this was over.

"I know I've been a bit distracted since I came back. The purpose of this tonight is to introduce our new resident but I thought I'd give you an update from town as long as we're all here and I have your attention." She glanced around the room, trying to think of things that they would want to hear. "The diner the Lincoln Land Co-op bought last fall, Natures' Bounty, it's still open. So they've pretty much survived the winter."

She saw the nods of relief. She and the Lincoln Land Co-op, LLC for short, were the only women-identified groups in this conservative patriarchal community. As long as the other group survived, they didn't feel so alone. In spite of some harsh disagreements in the past, they were both pragmatic enough to know they needed each other even if they didn't always like it.

"They're still talking about getting the rail service up and running all the way to Kokomo, still looking for the money for rail repairs. The bank's still open but they're talking about going to chits, local money, to hold on to real cash. The county's still solvent. Unemployment's still up. The school's supposed to open again. What else?"

"How's the state?"

"Insolvent." Deborah didn't have anything else she could say.

"And the Fed?"

"Well, hanging on, down to the basics. But can't look to them for any help for anything. Guess some people see that they're not a hindrance anymore but it leaves a lot of folks hanging." She paused, decided everything sounded pretty bleak. "Courts are still running—that's good. Military is still there."

"Power grid?" Karen asked.

"Spotty. Not real dependable. And it's diverted for essentials. Did hear the hospital reopened in Malone."

"Any clinics?" Beth asked.

"The one in Riverside is still open from what I heard." She pulled her thoughts together. "Okay, that's enough of the bad news."

"Any good news?" Brea asked caustically.

"Well." Deborah had to think. "We're one of the few counties who haven't been taken over." She gave a cynical smile. "No emergency managers. Guess there were advantages to being one of the state's poorest counties. We didn't have much to lose and what we had, we knew how to keep. We already knew how to tie a knot in the rope and hold on to get by. Guess you could say, we're holding our own."

"Whoopie," Bobbi said sarcastically.

Deborah shook her head. "Still got a roof over our heads and food on the table. Shelter from the storms and—" She paused, looked around the room at all the faces. "And someone to miss us if we disappear." She thought about but didn't report a couple of homeless folk who had frozen sometime during the winter and had just been discovered with spring thaw.

"So," she said abruptly, "that's done. Now to get to the purpose of our celebration tonight." She saw Bobbi grimace and turn away. She was never going to accept being on contract, would never see it as anything to celebrate.

"In case anyone's been stuck on the back forty and isn't aware, we have a new resident. Just so you know, Joanna and I ran into each other at the diner while Mother Nature did her best to let us know that winter was not finished. One thing led to another and in the end, Joanna will be with us for a while." She looked for Joanna, who looked terribly uncomfortable and it occurred to her that Joanna had probably been put on display more than once. She didn't have to draw this out and make her feel worse.

"Joanna, come on up here." She got to her feet and held her hand out. For a moment, she held her breath as everyone turned to Joanna, who hesitated. Then, as she had at the diner, Joanna got to her feet and walked up to Deborah, glaring at her. Evidently she remembered the moment also. Deborah took hold of Joanna's hand, lacing their fingers together in an effort to convince her it wasn't the same. She could feel her tension, feel the iciness that Joanna always had when she was nervous.

"This is Joanna Davis," Deborah went on smoothly as she viewed the curious faces. She needed to answer the unspoken questions before the rumors started. "Joanna's in a slightly different situation to all of you in that she didn't choose to come on contract. Sometimes events happen that we don't have any control over, we all know that. Sometimes it doesn't go the way we want and we have to fight for ourselves. Joanna's proven she's a fighter," Deborah said evenly as she held Joanna's hand firmly lest she pull away.

"That being said, Joanna falls under different rules and regulations, some of which I'm sure you've already noticed. But other than those requirements, which I cannot control, Joanna will be treated the same as you all. And I expect you to treat her that same way too. She has had some bad experiences so I trust that all of you will welcome her as each of you were welcomed and reassured." She pulled Joanna's hand to turn her to face her and much to Joanna's surprise, she pulled her into her arms for a welcoming hug. "Joanna Davis, welcome to the House of Steele."

Joanna resisted, looking shocked, putting her hands up on Deborah's shoulders in resistance. Deborah hoped no one noticed. Deborah released her, holding on long enough to steady her, meeting her startled gaze before she indicated the love seat and turned back to the group.

"Ladies, the floor is yours for introductions."

Joanna half turned in surprise as Deborah walked around the group and went into the kitchen.

This was always part of it also, Deborah wasn't even sure when it had started. In stages, mostly. At first the introductions had taken place at the dinner table but that seemed too confining. And dear old Hetty had said that it was cause for a celebration, hence the party feeling, the formal dinner, the cake, the punch. The welcoming hug had been Sue's doing. She had been so overjoyed at her acceptance, and Sue being Sue, had thrown herself in Deborah's arms. And when the presentation was over, it was time for Deborah to leave. Part of it had been her desire to escape and the other part was realizing that no one would be able to speak freely if she were in the room. Well, she thought they would but their words might be suspect to the new person because the contract holder was right there. So Deborah left. She would serve up the dinner. She sliced the ham, and pulled the parsnips, the potatoes, both sweet and white, from the warming oven. For being hard-pressed for time, Sue had done a good job. She even had a cake on the pedestal plate, having pulled everything out to welcome the newest. Deborah carried dishes to the table, catching part of the introductions, and hoping Joanna wouldn't expect meals like this every day. She ladled the mulled cider into the punch bowl to carry into the room as the introductions started.

* * *

Joanna sank into the love seat, shocked by Deborah's presentation, by her hug. Joanna had been labeled a troublemaker or worse so often, she wasn't sure how to react as being described as someone who was simply fighting for herself. Validation.

The now familiar tall, strong-looking woman who looked like she could pull guard duty stood up. Dressed in jeans, flannel shirt and boots, she looked even more rugged and intimidating. "Welcome, Joanna" she announced in a surprisingly friendly voice. "My name's Karen LaMont—the Mountain." She gave a self-conscious grin. "I'm the land manager," Karen went on, "and I get to assign work details so I guess we'll be dealing with each other. I had the privilege or misfortune—I've never decided which—of being the first to contract with Deborah." She met Joanna's gaze. "This wasn't something I wanted or aspired to, so I know how it feels. I don't pretend to think that it's a great situation but I do realize it could be a whole lot worse." She paused and looked around the room as if daring anyone to argue with her. "Now, I'm not going to tell you that Deborah is charming and easy to get along with. We all watch our step when she slams doors. We don't try to be logical when she's unreasonable. We even shut up when she rants and raves. On the other hand, we've got shelter. We've had food on the table, maybe not always what we like and maybe we're damn tired of beans, but there's been food. We've bitched about the hard work but she's been right there beside us. For the most part, she tells us where we're going and how we're going to get there. Sometimes there's kicking and fighting and screaming but so far, we are all here, *all* of us." She looked around the room again.

"What I'm saying is Deborah's always been straight with us, and we've appreciated it. We have faith in her. Whatever she's done, she had a good reason. That's all I'm gonna say." And she sat down abruptly.

Interesting endorsement, Joanna thought as she wondered if Deborah listened in. She probably liked the description. "Thank you, Karen," she said in a quiet voice. "I'll try to remember that."

The woman sitting beside Karen stood up, and Joanna recognized her. "Welcome, Joanna. I'm Beth Mitchell and you already know what I do."

"Yes," Joanna said with some of her old humor. "You tried to poison me."

Beth laughed and blushed as others in the group laughed. "Well, it does keep people out of the infirmary. I'm second on the seniority roster of Deborah's contracts. And she's not so bad in spite of what Karen says. I say that because I've seen Karen do some stomping and swearing and yelling too. She's really pretty open. I may be under contract to her but I'm free to practice healing on others in the area. It's not like I'm confined to the grounds. And I've even earned some money of my own. I'm not going to tell you I'm not looking forward to the end of our contract, but—" There she paused. "I've seen lots of sights around here in my travels. I know it could be worse." She gave Joanna a speculating look. "If you give her a chance, I don't think she'll fail you."

Remains to be seen, Joanna thought as she thanked Beth. "And thank you for the healing," she added as an afterthought. She hoped she wouldn't see the inside of the infirmary again but at least Beth did have the training.

The next one up was the mild-mannered rather bland-looking sandy-haired woman. They must be going down the seniority line, Joanna thought with some dismay as she realized she would be last. "Welcome, Joanna. I'm Peg—not Margaret—Rock, ex-military." She had a slight accent that said she wasn't local. Joanna couldn't quite place it. "I got stranded here, about as far out of my element as I can be. Stranger to the area, and you know how small towns take to strangers nowadays." Joanna nodded without saying anything and Peg went on. "So I appreciate meeting Deborah, her offering first a friendship and then offering me a hand when I needed one." Joanna nodded again. "Never been on a farm before, never wanted to be for that matter. But I'm here, I'm learning." She shook her head. "Can't complain. Welcome aboard."

Brief, Joanna thought. Didn't really tell much. "Thank you, Peg. I can't say I know much about farming either. When Deborah asked, I told her all I knew was growing plants in a pot on the patio."

Peg laughed. "Bet she told you about wearing coveralls and chewing straw."

"Yeah, she did," Joanna said. "I suppose I should have told her about those plants on the patio."

"Weren't anything illegal, were they?" someone called out.

"No," Joanna admitted. "Wouldn't have mattered anyway. They died."

"Make notes, Karen! Don't put her in the garden!"

Joanna began to relax as they went down the line. She still couldn't understand why anyone would voluntarily go on contract but they were putting on a good front. Others got to their feet, welcoming her, and she began to sort them out. There was Brea, a good Midwesterner who was a great baker, and a brewmaster when need be. She could be blunt as a hammer on her opinions. Rae, the potter who also played the guitar, could write some stinging satire. Linda, who was quiet, soft-spoken, and would rather spend time in the barn with her animals than in the house. Sue, a flaky little blonde who could take any raw produce and turn out a great meal. Kelly, dark-haired and looked sullen and brooding. Last, were Sara and Bobbi, the most recent additions. Sara introduced herself as House Manager, gracious, welcoming, inviting Joanna to ask for anything she needed. Bobbi was sullen, giving minimum information about herself and barely a welcome.

* * *

"Dinner's up," Deborah called, with no one realizing that Joanna hadn't introduced herself. Eager for dinner and eager to mix with the new woman the group gathered around Joanna to welcome her. Deborah watched. She was always amazed how they unfailingly managed to bring the newcomer into the fold.

Dinner was festive, but Deborah didn't eat much. The night was young, and she withdrew.

At some time or another during the eating, the drinking, the story telling, the singing, everyone touched the newcomer. Maybe it was a hug, at least a handshake, whatever, but they all touched Joanna. That seemed to be the bonding. It had been disconcerting for some of them. Brea had backpedaled so much she had spent most of that evening backed into a corner. Some of them had cried, as they had been searching for a place to belong for so long. She wondered how Joanna would handle it.

"I sense the real story lurking in the background," Linda commented as she came to help Deborah clear the table after dinner. "Anything you want to share?"

"Sure," Deborah drawled. "I found someone I couldn't resist." She turned to meet the gaze of her high school chum and shrugged with a smile.

Linda shook her head as she watched Joanna. "You sure you haven't bitten off more than you can chew?"

"Hope not." Deborah took plates to the kitchen.

Linda followed her with another stack as she gave Deborah a concerned look. "You got burnt once, Deb. Gluttony was never your style."

"Lightning doesn't strike the same place twice."

"The hell it doesn't." Linda set her stack down. "I need to check the barn, with luck we'll increase our stock tonight."

Deborah nodded and watched Linda pick up her jacket from the back porch. Gossip must be going well if Linda was coming back with something like this. Not that as close-mouthed as Linda was she would say anything. Nothing like a houseful of women for the gossip. She watched Sara disentangle herself from the group and work her way toward Deborah. "Having a good time?" she asked as Sara made it to the table.

Sara tilted her head. "It's been interesting, very interesting." She refilled her punch.

"How so?" Deborah turned back to the group, watching who spoke to whom, who was getting chummy, how Joanna was being received.

"Carolyn would be surprised."

Deborah gave Sara a look of sharp interest at the name of the commune leader. She had run into Sara and Bobbi at the commune just when their bid for membership had been turned down. Deborah could identify with the feeling of commune rejection, which might have contributed to her agreement to contract with them. "What makes you say that?"

"Consensus building takes time. She spends a lot of time persuading members. You make the decision and it's done. This house is much stronger, more stable than the commune. I think she'd be jealous of what you've achieved."

Deborah gave a small chuckle. If this had come from anyone else, she would think that her ego was being pandered to. "I think Carolyn might want a good many things that I have, but she would never be jealous. She's definitely a consensus person in a consensus group. My philosophy is sometimes you just don't have the time to persuade. Someone needs to make the decision so it gets done. So she thinks I run a dictatorship, have people to wait on me, provide my every comfort, so that I don't have to work."

"Obviously, Carolyn's never been here."

"No, she might get contaminated."

"Is that her statement or yours?"

"It's her attitude. In fact, it's the attitude of the commune."

Deborah's voice turned rueful. "I wasn't tactful. They threw me out when I told them they were going to talk themselves to death. So every success I have is just a slap in their collective faces." She sipped her punch. "My signing contracts just put me beyond the pale."

"Well," Sara said tactfully, aware that she had brought up a sore subject, "I suppose I should leave you alone." She turned away.

Deborah started at Joanna's voice behind her. "You might have warned me you were going to hug me."

"Didn't want to scare you. Thought it might freak you out. It's part of the 'welcome ceremony.'"

Joanna refilled her cup. "I must admit, you have done a marvelous job on them. They believe they are sitting on your coattail and will go down the drain if you do. Therefore, the group must survive." She sipped her drink. "Anyone ever oppose you?"

"Depends. Arguments sometimes. Shouting matches."

"But the bottom line is you get your way." She gazed innocently over the lip of her cup at Deborah.

"I'd be a fool if I didn't listen to their arguments," Deborah said evenly. "And I told you once, I'm not a fool."

"Humm," Joanna mused as she wandered away.

* * *

Joanna sidled out of the room, glancing around to see if anyone noticed her departure. Deborah had been right: she was the main attraction and everyone wanted to talk to her. She didn't know what they wanted from her. How could twelve people make a room so hot? She needed to find someplace cooler, catch her breath. She looked around to see where she was. The foyer. There was Deborah's office, the door closed. She turned to the other direction, the wide circular wooden stairs. And right in front of her: the double front doors.

She glanced over her shoulder. Everyone was chatting and milling around as if they hadn't just seen each other at supper. She walked to the front door. Deborah said they were locked up at night. Do you suppose? She reached out to take hold of the brass knob, the old-fashioned key lock, turn, open. She glanced over her shoulder again. The step was wet but the snow was mostly gone. Patches of it reflected enough light that she could see the path. She stepped along it, barely breathing. Alone. Outside. The night was still cold but not bitter. The only light fell through the open door. The sky was clear. She looked up, captivated by the sight of all the stars, picking out constellations.

"Beautiful, aren't they?"

She jerked, spilling her drink. She turned to see the doe-eyed tall woman leaning against the column. *Jeez, everyone's watching me, need to remember that.*

"Very," she answered, her heart dropping to her stomach. She was still trying to sort people out, and she needed to be more cautious. Even with a group this small, especially with a group this small, there were alliances. Anyone of them might bear tales to Deborah, and would Deborah think it likely that she had just stepped out for a breath of air?

"I'm Bobbi. You probably just remember me as a blur. I remember what it was like. But then I've only been here for about a month or so." She held out her hand and Joanna took it, not sure whether there would be a hug or not. "No hugs," Bobbi said with a grin. "I think that's a little forward but…" She shrugged.

"So you've been here for a month," Joanna said carefully, trying not to feel guilty. "How's it been?" She remembered that Bobbi hadn't said much about herself.

Bobbi took a breath as if to collect her thoughts. "Hard to say at this point. Everyone's been telling us that it's the slow period, not much to do. They keep telling us to enjoy it because once the work starts, it's nonstop." She didn't look convinced. "All I know is they've been keeping us pretty busy for it being a slack time."

Joanna returned her gaze, determined not to get rattled. She had done nothing wrong. Deborah hadn't confined her to the house. Worse than someone running to Deborah would be to be blackmailed, especially for something she hadn't done. "That's about what Deborah told me," she said, trying to keep a casual conversation going. "Karen assigns the labor?"

"Yes." Bobbi turned around to look into the house, to the tall woman in rapt discussion with Brea. "She's pretty fair, evenhanded. Doesn't play favorites. At least I haven't seen that. She can come on pretty strong, won't take excuses."

"She have the final say?"

"Haven't seen her overruled yet. Course I've heard that she and Deborah have had arguments in the past, but I haven't seen them." She examined her glass of punch.

"Oh, is it safe to argue with Deborah?" Joanna was curious.

"If you like arguing, shouting." Bobbi's tone grew chillier. "If you like being lambasted, raked over the coals. She likes to keep the upper hand." She finished her drink and moved toward the door. "I'm sure you'll find out. You ready to come in? Rae's getting ready to play. She has a good voice, writes some decent stuff." She paused as if giving Joanna the opportunity to refuse.

God, I've got to be careful, Joanna reminded herself. *Instead of one, I've got eleven.* "Yes," she replied. "It's getting chilly out here." But she knew that all her shaking was not from the cold. Together they wandered back inside to the fireplace where Rae was sitting. Joanna drew back as Bobbi took a seat by Sara.

"Here, Joanna," someone said and she turned to see Peg pat the bench beside her. "Come sit with me."

Joanna nodded as she took the seat.

"You okay?" Peg asked quietly as Rae tuned her guitar. If she noticed Joanna's shaking, she ignored it. "You feeling better?"

"Yes. At least physically."

"Good. Nothing like feeling like shit when there's so many new things to deal with."

That's for sure, Joanna thought, looking for something to say. She really hated parties like this.

"Can I give you a piece of advice?" Peg didn't look at her as she spoke.

"Sure, why not?" She wasn't about to turn down any information she could get.

"I've been dumped in strange places unexpectedly a lot in my lifetime," Peg spoke quietly, continuing to watch Rae get comfortable on the hearth. There was a calming quality to her voice, as if she knew how frightened, how nervous Joanna was. "Don't jump to conclusions about anything or anyone. Take your time to get your footing, the lay of the land so to speak." She looked around the room. "There's a lot of personalities here, and Deborah's a complex person. She has good intentions."

"Good intentions don't always work out."

"That's true. But sometimes they are better than nothing. Deborah's managed to keep things going." She paused. "She's a strong personality, but she's not the only one here. Sometimes that can get volatile."

"How does she deal with strong personalities?"

"She struggles. We all do. But it's Deborah who has the vision so sometimes she sees things that we don't see."

"Sounds like it could be difficult."

"Nothing's easy anymore." She glanced at Joanna. "At least Deborah's trying." She gave a soft laugh. "Sometimes very trying." She looked at Joanna, her glance resting on the cut that hadn't quite healed and then going to Joanna's shoulders as if she could see her bruises. Joanna stiffened. "You're not the first one to be ill-treated," she said in an even quieter tone. "It'll take a while to get over it, but it is behind you. Nothing like that will happen here."

"You speak from experience, I suppose," Joanna retorted in a flippant tone.

"Yes," Peg said so firmly that Joanna turned to look at her. "Firsthand experience." She nodded in confirmation as she got to her feet. "Deborah's a lot of things but she's not an abuser. I'm going after some punch. Do you want some?" Joanna shook her head.

She only half listened to Rae who did have a decent voice and played the guitar well. She turned as she saw Bobbi talking to Deborah. She looked away, her heart pounding. First day, barely introduced and she was in trouble already. She stared at the fireplace.

I didn't do anything. I wasn't even trying to escape. Why would I do that? I don't know where I'm at, where anything, anyplace is. Does she think I'm such a fool I would just walk away from the house in this weather with nothing?

She looked back to see Deborah coming across the room

toward her. She thought she was going to be sick.

"How are you doing?"

Joanna nodded, as any other answer was unthinkable. She scooted over on the bench for Deborah to sit down.

"You're looking a little worn. This is your first day up and about," Deborah said easily. "Don't exhaust yourself for appearance's sake. It's not like you're not going to see these folks again."

Joanna glanced at her, not sure what Deborah was trying to say. Maybe Bobbi didn't say anything? Was that a possibility?

"Whenever you're ready to retire, Joanna, just let me know, and we can go up together."

"Afraid to leave me alone?" she asked with what she hoped was a light tone.

"I'm not ready to leave you down here alone, and I'm afraid if I locked you in upstairs, you'd fret and worry about what was going to happen when I did come in. Seems to me that the best thing would be to retire together."

Joanna nodded. So Deborah wasn't going to let her out of her sight.

Deborah patted her on the knee. "You let me know whenever you've reached your saturation point." She got up and left.

Joanna closed her eyes. Oh, Deborah would just be on Joanna's ass all the time and then pounce at the first infraction. Joanna buried her face in her hands. She wanted to believe Peg's words that she might be safe here. And her action had been so innocent, just stepping outside. But she'd been caught. Deborah would now watch her until she did do something wrong. And even if Bobbi hadn't said anything, she now had the upper hand. Jeez! Not out of the infirmary twelve hours and she was trapped.

She looked up to find Bobbi watching her, her eyes bland, smiling enigmatically. When her gaze shifted, Joanna followed it to focus on Deborah. The cat with the canary had nothing on Bobbi at that point, and Joanna shivered.

She watched Deborah work the room, something Joanna did not recall her ever doing. Then Joanna realized the other difference in Deborah. She touched. She touched everyone.

Casual touches, not even invasive. Deborah put her arm around the waist of the little flirty blonde and she returned a spacey flirty look and leaned into her. The solid, no-nonsense woman got a hand on the arm, a finger in the shoulder during a discussion and got a hand waving in the face in return. Karen got an arm around the shoulder, Bobbi got a hair ruffling. That did not seem welcome although Bobbi did return a sickly grin. Peg—that was curious. Deborah touched her the least and yet it seemed the most intimate, a hand on her back as she passed Peg in the doorway. Joanna wondered how long they had known each other. Rae got a high five over something, one of her songs, Joanna thought, she hadn't really been listening. Beth got a hand resting on her arm during some conversation and Sara got a hand on her back, gently guiding out of the way. The Deborah Joanna remembered didn't like being touched. Yes, Deborah had changed.

* * *

Deborah stood by the foyer door. She was more than ready to retire but this was Joanna's night, and she needed to decide when to leave. There would be time enough in the future she would be at Deborah's beck and call. This was her opportunity to get her footing with these women, and it would not be easy. Because she was a different sort of contract, she wouldn't have the freedom to mix and to interact freely with them. One of the drawbacks of needing that constant supervision.

Deborah understood that everyone needed time away from her, time to blow off steam. She needed a break from them as well. But because of this damned contract restriction, she was going to be hampered on both sides. She watched with interest as Rae finished her song and Joanna got to her feet and made her way to the fireplace. She cleared her throat and everyone fell quiet.

"I want to thank all of you," Joanna said slowly, looking around the room. "I can't say that I'm happy to be here. Or even that I chose to be here. This is just where Fate has thrown me and I have to make whatever I can of it. All of you have made me feel welcome. Your understanding and acceptance has taken a good deal of the sting out of my circumstances." She gave a tentative smile and Deborah bit her lip. There was always something about Joanna that was open-hearted and honest and sincere. "I don't know what the future holds for me, but I wanted you all to know how much I have appreciated your kindness tonight." She glanced up and across the room at Deborah. She started to say something, then stopped and looked around the room. "Thank you," she said finally. "Thank you very much."

Then she sort of shrugged and moved off to one side amid appreciative comments and hands reaching out for her. She walked over to Deborah, stood before her.

"Are you ready to retire?"

"I think so."

Deborah spoke to the rest of the group. "I think you all know that Joanna's just out of the infirmary and we don't want her back in there. So we're retiring but that's no reason you have to. Just remember, we've still got a schedule and we've still got things to do."

"You mean you don't want to come down for breakfast and find us still here partying away?"

"Brea, if you can still do that, I'll know that Karen's been scheduling too lightly. Good night, ladies. We'll see you in the morning." She turned and followed Joanna up the stairs.

"How'd it go?" Deborah asked as she opened the bedroom door for Joanna.

"All right." Joanna walked into the darkness and stopped, unfamiliar in the dim light where the furniture was.

Deborah turned on the lamp on the dresser. Awkward there but at least at this location, the lamp cast some light into Joanna's area. She had forgotten about that. As a storage room, it had no light. She would have to do something about that eventually. She locked the door and tossed the key on the dresser. "You made a nice closing speech. I'm sure that won them over."

"I wasn't trying to win them over. I meant it." Joanna paused in front of the doorway to her sleeping area, expecting Deborah to make a move.

"I know." Deborah went around her bed, pulling down the

covers, pulling her nightshirt from beneath the pillow. "Your sincerity and openness always were your best traits." She shrugged. "Even when you were delivering bad news." She pulled off her shirt, looked up to see Joanna still there, obviously waiting. She had not anticipated Joanna standing there watching her undress. "Was there something else you wanted, Joanna?" she asked, deliberately stressing the "you." She stepped out of her short boots as she unfastened her pants and pushed them down. She looked up at Joanna questioningly.

Joanna drew back with a start, her face flushing. "No," she said sharply as she stepped back into her area.

"Then go to bed."

Joanna slowly undressed as she listened to Deborah's movements in the other room. She still didn't know if Bobbi had said anything to Deborah about her going out the front door. Deborah wouldn't be the first contractor to play a waiting game until Joanna's nerves were stretched taunt. She threw her clothes on the trunk that served as her dresser and pulled on the long nightshirt and knit shorts. She was still stiff and sore, as her back hadn't completely healed.

"Ready for the lights out?" Deborah called.

"Yes." Joanna crawled into bed and tried to find a comfortable position as the room went dark. She listened to Deborah's steps across the room, the squeak of the old-fashioned bedsprings. She listened to Deborah sigh as she settled and then there was silence. She could still hear the party downstairs.

She lay there, trying to put everything together—the women she had met tonight, whether Bobbi was going to say something. She supposed the best thing she could do would be to talk to Deborah about it, and then maybe she was making a mountain out of a molehill and she should say nothing. She closed her eyes.

"Joanna, come here."

She froze, caught between dismay and the relief in being right. Deborah was like every other holder. She squeezed her eyes shut, realizing she had believed Deborah, had wanted to believe. She lay very still, breathing even. Perhaps if she feigned sleep.

"Joanna, come here." The order was louder, harsher.

Cringing, but resigned, she got out of bed, shivering and not just from the icy floor. Deborah met her at the door. Deborah was dressed, dark clothing, dominant. She took Joanna's face in her hands, held her just so in spite of Joanna's hands covering hers, trying to pull her away.

"You promised," Joanna protested.

"You promised never to leave me," Deborah whispered harshly in reminder. She ran her tongue over Joanna's lips, tasting her.

"No, please, don't. Not this way." Joanna tried to pull back and Deborah held her.

"I let you go once. I'll not do it again. You can't run away from me."

"I wasn't running away."

"No?" Deborah stepped forward, boots loud against the wooden floor, forcing Joanna back into her room. "Then what were you doing outside? Why'd you go out the door?"

"I was hot, needed to cool off." Joanna stepped back but Deborah didn't let go of her, counterbalancing her, forcing her back, forcing her to grab hold of Deborah's wrists and hold on rather than fall. "I wasn't running away."

"Bobbi said you were." She pushed Joanna back. "Do you really think I'd let you go? After all this time, now that I have you again?"

"You promised," Joanna could only protest as the back of her legs hit the bed. She fell backward and Deborah moved over her. She could feel Deborah's knee between her legs. She pushed away. Not again, not this time. She let go of Deborah's wrists, pushed back with one hand, made a fist to swing, pulled back for some leverage and—

Deborah was gone. Joanna's swing was caught in the quilt and she rolled over, almost rolling off the bed in the tangle of covers. She cried out, and there was nothing. She struggled in the covers to get to a sitting position, looking around. Deborah couldn't have escaped so quickly.

Her heart was pounding. She could hear the blood rushing in her ears. As she calmed she could hear the party downstairs. She threw back the covers, determined that Deborah wasn't going to get away with this. She rushed into Deborah's room and stopped.

Deborah was stretched out on the bed, her back to Joanna's

area, half on her stomach, one leg drawn up, arm up under the pillow. Her breathing was even. She was sound asleep.

Joanna tiptoed around the bed. Deborah's clothes were thrown on the chair, her boots were under the chair also. Slippers were right there by the bed.

No, I know she was there. I felt her hands on me, her lips. She rubbed her mouth. Cautiously she reached out and lifted the covers. Deborah had always been a heavy sleeper. She was jolted, confused to see Deborah in her nightclothes.

"What the hell are you doing?" Deborah demanded with a swift movement that caught Joanna's wrist.

"I—I thought you came into my room." She didn't pull back from Deborah's grip.

"So what are you doing? Checking to see if I'm under the covers?" Deborah rose up on one elbow, still not getting up.

"I thought—I don't know." She stepped back. "Let me go." Deborah didn't let her go, but sat up. Had she been asleep? Had she fallen asleep without even realizing it and dreamed the whole thing? Oh, God…

"Thought what?"

"Let me go."

This time, Deborah did release her grip. "Are you all right?" she asked as she sat up. She rubbed her face, shook her head, old Deborah habits that at once seemed so familiar and yet so strange. "What happened?"

"Nothing."

"Nothing made you come in here and peek under my covers?"

Joanna flushed, this was going from bad to worse. "I thought you came into my room."

"And why would I do that?" Although from the look on Deborah's face, she knew exactly what Joanna thought.

Joanna shook her head, unwilling to accuse Deborah of something she now had doubts about.

"Well, I didn't."

"I must have been dreaming," Joanna said in a whisper.

Deborah gave her a long searching look. "Want to talk about it?"

"No," Joanna said shortly. "I'm sorry I woke you." She stepped back, not sure if she wanted Deborah to stop her or not. She could feel Deborah watching her as crawled back into bed. This was not a good start. She wrapped her arms around the pillow as if to ground herself. This was not a good start at all.

CHAPTER SEVEN

She was still trying to convince herself it was only a dream the next morning when Deborah called her. Even then, Deborah didn't come into her area, just stuck her head in. "Rise and shine."

Joanna leapt to her feet before she was even fully awake. The hardwood floor was freezing. It finished waking her up.

"Need to get you a throw rug by the bed," Deborah commented as she withdrew. "Remind me later." She returned to her area and Joanna reached for her clothing tossed over the trunk.

"Sleep all right?" Deborah called from the other room.

"Yes." Joanna wanted to forget her nightmare almost as much she wanted to forget the confrontation with Deborah. Both were unnerving.

"That's good." Deborah stuck her head back in the area. "Make your bed. You're not staying at a hotel now."

Joanna gritted her teeth. Did Deborah really think she was accustomed to being waited on? She hurriedly made up the bed, stuffed her nightshirt under the pillow. When she came out into

Deborah's area, Deborah was across the double bed, making up that side. Joanna immediately pulled up covers to help.

"You're not my servant, Joanna," Deborah said evenly. It sounded like a reproof.

"I just thought I'd help." They finished making the bed together.

"Thank you." Deborah acknowledged when Joanna stepped back.

A final look around the room and Deborah was ready to go out the door. She even jerked the door before she remembered that it was locked and had to retrieve the key from the dresser. She muttered darkly as she unlocked the door. Before she opened it though, she turned around to look at Joanna.

"Look at me," she ordered.

Joanna looked up at her, awaiting a scathing remark, something to put her in her place. Instead she found concern.

"You're not the first one who has come here and had bad dreams, Joanna. I just want you to know, if there's anything I can do to help, I will. I don't want you to think that you're the only one here who's suffered. I don't want you to feel alone."

Joanna clenched her jaw, unprepared for such sympathy. She couldn't say anything, could only meet Deborah's gaze with an iron will not to give way.

"Let's hit breakfast, get the day started."

"What will I be doing?" Joanna asked stiffly as she followed Deborah down the stairs.

"No idea. Karen assigns the work details after breakfast."

* * *

"Morning, ladies. I trust everyone got their beauty rest and didn't party hearty." She pointed Joanna to the empty chair in the middle of one side. "Looks like it's going to be a good day."

Joanna sat between Sara and Beth, nodding to those around the table as Deborah took her seat at the head. As soon as Deborah sat down, everyone started eating.

"Sleep good?" Beth asked as she passed the bowl along.

"Yeah, as much as you can in new surroundings."

"You'll get used to it, settle in. The infirmary is in a quieter spot. I was afraid we might have kept you awake since we were more at the front of the house."

"No. I could hear you but not enough to bother me. I fell asleep pretty quickly." *And dreamed.*

As they finished and everyone settled back, waiting, Karen pulled up her clipboard and went down the list. "I've put you in with housekeeping to start with, Joanna," Karen announced. "Beth has promised that she would kill me if I put you outside in the damp and you got sick again. You'll be working with Peg."

Joanna nodded and glanced at Peg smiling across the table from her.

"Deborah," Karen continued, "I assume that you're still going over plans so you'll be housebound?"

Deborah nodded without comment, and Karen continued passing out assignments.

The breakfast table broke up, everyone sliding their chairs back. Joanna glanced around, not certain if she was supposed to clear. "Those assigned to the kitchen take care of that," Sara said easily. "They clear the table, do the dishes. One of those jobs we all get to do in turns. Come on, I'll show you what you two will be doing today."

Sara led her to a small office off the kitchen. "We've got a book set up." She pulled the notebook out. "Not so much because it's complicated but everyone takes a turn at housekeeping. This makes sure that everything gets done. We've got a full house now so it would be easy to neglect something." She flipped through the pages. "It's not hard work, just lots of little bits. And unless Deborah gets a wild hair about something, it goes along smoothly."

"She get a wild hair often?"

"Mostly about supplies. Wants us to take food inventory, make sure there's enough and some to spare. Probably isn't a bad idea. We've had some pretty lean years."

Peg nodded in understanding, and Joanna followed suit. Deborah always had a flair for organizing.

"And we have a wish list, things we want or need. When she goes on her forages, she likes to have an idea of what's needed."

"She go on these often?" Perhaps there would be an opportunity yet.

"Depends on what's going on here. Slow time now, so she's free to get around, at least she was." Sara gave them both a stern look. "I 'spect that will be changing now."

"Since I'm along?" Joanna was quick to question.

Sara showed them the utility closet. "Yes, different rules. That might bring about some changes."

* * *

Changes. That was just what Deborah was thinking as she mapped out some of those changes. Having Joanna around was not going to be easy. It had been unsettling waking up with Joanna leaning over her. Sara's question about her safety in such close contact with one so adverse to contracts came floating back to her. *Was it going to be dangerous to be locked in with Joanna at night?* Joanna had been a pure pacifist. *Had been.* After everything she had gone through, was she still?

To keep her mind off Joanna, she pulled out her map of the property, rolled it out and moved the paperweights on the corners. She used it to plan the crop rotation for the year.

She heard Peg and Joanna on the stairs. It was a good pairing. Peg was nonthreatening and yet confident enough to take the lead. She'd done this sort of thing in the army, so she could handle Joanna. Keep Joanna inside a while, let her gain strength. She should be ready for outside work by planting time.

Corn, wheat, oats. Might be able to expand some this year. The gardens were going well. If the weather remained stable. Wished everyone could deal with eating rabbits. The first time they had rabbit stew, she thought there was going to be a revolt. "Floppy?" Sue had asked. Deborah hadn't realized the bunnies had been named. They still had rabbit occasionally but Deborah had noticed almost everyone suddenly turned into vegetarians. She traded the meat now. Still, they did breed well.

Her lists and her plans grew longer as the day went on. She still took her breaks, walked around the house to exercise, and to check on things, Joanna in particular. Peg was doing a good job keeping Joanna busy without exhausting her.

On one break Deborah watched Joanna clean the living room after the party last night. Poor planning, Deborah guessed. Guest of honor and the next day on the clean-up committee. She was still moving stiffly. Wonder if Peg would give her a rubdown. That woman could give wonderful massages.

Deborah had to admit, she missed those massages, like she missed a lot of other things she and Peg had had together. Who knew how long it might have continued on or even where it might have gone if Peg's situation hadn't changed when she lost her job at the hotel. A contract had seemed like the best solution. At least this way she still had benefits of Peg's experience and knowledge if nothing else. Peg had become a good part of the house but sometimes Deborah wondered what might have been.

Lunchtime and then Joanna was working upstairs, picking up the bed linens, laying out clean ones for everyone to make their own beds. Carrying laundry out to the washhouse, up and down stairs, a lot of walking. She was going to be tired. *Maybe too tired to dream*, Deborah hoped.

* * *

"I brought up a pot of tea," Deborah announced as she set up the teapot and cups on the table in front of the bedroom window, across from the foot of her bed. "I thought it might help you unwind."

She turned around to see Joanna leaning against the archway.

"I thought it might help you sleep."

Joanna took so long to think about it, Deborah thought she would refuse but she finally literally pushed herself from the wall. "All right."

"Here, sit in the rocker," Deborah offered as she poured the tea into mugs. The only chair, she made a mental note to bring in another. The only other seating option was her bed. It was entirely possible for Joanna to fall asleep where she sat and it would not be good if she fell asleep on Deborah's bed.

"You don't mind a herbal blend, something to relax you, help you sleep?"

"No." Joanna sat back in the rocker, watching Deborah fuss with the mugs. "Not that I think I'll need any help."

"Probably not," Deborah agreed, "but sometimes we can be too tired to sleep." She handed the mug to Joanna. "We used to do this to unwind at the end of the day. Remember? You want some honey in that?"

Joanna sipped the tea then held it in her lap as she rested her head against the back. "This is fine." She rocked the chair slightly. "I thought you were going to forget about everything we did."

Deborah took her mug and moved backward to sit on the foot of her bed. "All right then, I used to have a cup of tea with my lover before we went to bed. We had the opportunity to talk over the day and unwind. I think we slept better."

"And you think that will work now with me?"

"Can't hurt, can it?"

Joanna sipped the tea without speaking.

"How'd your day go?"

"All right." Joanna closed her eyes and rocked for a moment. "You've got quite a house. Come down through the family?"

Deborah toed off her shoes and drew up a leg as she leaned against the bedpost. "Yeah, they had them big in those days. Old Winslow had two wives, fifteen or sixteen kids. Don't grow them like that anymore."

"How do you decide who get the rooms with the double beds or the twins?"

"I let occupants hash it out. Sometimes they swap. Occasionally there's friction. There's less flexibility now that the house is full. There's no place to get away. It's better in the summer. Did you have any problems with Peg?"

Joanna shook her head. "Was I supposed to?"

"Army brat, daddy was a sergeant. Enlisted herself. Made sergeant. I don't think she ever really left."

"That why you can bounce a quarter off her bed?"

"Spit and polish. I hate drawing duty with her."

"You? Draw duty?"

"Hey, I'm just another pair of hands on labor rotation. I may have a reduced schedule but I'm still in there."

Joanna made no response but did drink her tea. Deborah could feel some of the tension leave the room. Maybe Joanna could sleep well and begin to relax. She watched as Joanna's eyes drooped, half closed.

Deborah finished her tea, got to her feet and put down her mug. Joanna sat still, waiting. Deborah came over to the rocking chair, took the mug out of Joanna's hand and put it on the table. Joanna took a deep breath, as if steeling herself. Deborah realized it was going to take forever to convince her she wasn't a predator. Deborah pulled Joanna to her feet and steered her to the archway and lightly shoved her into her area. "Go to bed," she ordered. "You're falling asleep."

Joanna stood there in confusion as Deborah went back, stacked the mugs on the tray to take down in the morning. Without looking back at Joanna, she went over to her bed and pulled down the covers. She undressed, ignoring Joanna still standing at the doorway. When she looked up, Joanna had retreated into her area. She shook her head as she pulled her nightshirt from under the pillow. This was going to be a long slow process. She turned off the light and slipped under the covers. She listened to Joanna's movements. Damn, she forgot the rug. She heard Joanna settle, and the house was quiet.

Both women slept.

* * *

Joanna was still on housekeeping with Peg the next day and the job of the day was pulling out all the canned goods and cleaning the storage cabinets. "Not entirely pleasant," Peg commented as she pulled out the back jars covered with dust and cobwebs, "but we get to see what's left to eat until the gardens come in."

"Quite a variety," Joanna commented as she looked over the jars.

"We insisted," Peg said. "Deborah is not the great meal planner. You put food down in front of her and she will eat it, almost all the time. Five minutes later you ask her what she ate and she has to think about it. She was doing the meal planning and frankly they were boring meals. She had a very limited repertoire. Something had to give."

"What gave?"

"First Hetty came in. Deborah stumbled across her on one of her trips to town. Hetty didn't have any family, nowhere to go. I think Deborah felt sorry for her. Brought her home. But when Hetty saw what the deal was, she insisted she could help. She organized the house, planned the meals, pretty much wrote the book. And she bullied Deborah something terrible."

Joanna couldn't quite imagine anyone bullying Deborah into anything. "How so?"

Peg pulled out more jars and wiped them down as Joanna scrubbed the cabinet. "Oh, Deborah wasn't always the way she is now."

No shit, Joanna thought. *You don't know how much of an understatement that is.* "How so?" she repeated.

"Oh, I'm not going to say that Deborah's such a great people person but she's a lot better than what she used to be. She could go for days without talking to anyone, off in her own little world, only coming out to give orders. It wasn't so bad when it was just Karen and Beth—they had each other. When I came, she was friendly for a while." Peg reorganized the jars, checking the year on the lids, and pulling the older ones to the front, the newer ones to the back. "But when others came, it got difficult. Everyone was sorta left to fend for themselves. Deborah was giving orders but there wasn't any structure. No one was really happy. And Deborah was an enigma."

"Hetty changed that?"

"Pretty much. Like meals, for example. Deborah wasn't eating with us, not because of any privilege thing," she added quickly. "She just wasn't sociable. She figured, I think, that we had each other at the table. She'd get a plate maybe later, at strange times. So meals were sorta—" She searched for the word. "Unstructured. Like a family with a busy schedule who never met for dinner, no cohesiveness. Hetty got her to the table. I mean, she went and got her, and said no one was eating until Deborah was at the table."

"I imagine that went over well," Joanna remembered Deborah never liked someone making her schedule. Actually, what she remembered was Deborah liked working alone best. She didn't do well in groups.

"Hmmmm, no. Imagine trying to have a decent meal with this impending explosion sitting at the head of the table. Not comfortable. And then Hetty insisted she have a conversation. But she kept at it and Deborah changed."

Irresistible force versus immoveable object. "So what happened to Hetty?"

"Pneumonia, last winter. Beth said there was something else wrong too, that the pneumonia was a kindness." She was silent a moment. "Don't get me wrong. Deborah was good one-on-one or she couldn't have persuaded anyone to sign a contract with her. She might be a little blunt but even that was good. You knew where you stood with her, even if you didn't like it. But you put her in a group and she's a completely different person. The first party that Hetty planned to welcome someone new, I think it might have been Brea, I thought Deborah was going to disappear on us." She shook her head. "I can't tell you how much she has changed."

"So why'd you sign a contract with her?"

Peg put in the last jars and opened up the next cabinet. "Didn't have anywhere else to go. Lost the little job I had. Stranger in town, you know what that's like."

"Yeah, I know." Joanna's stomach just cramped at the thought of the isolation from townspeople, the distance you couldn't cross, the barriers that were monumental.

"Deborah had talked to me about a contract once before, told her I couldn't stomach it. She said if I ever changed my mind, the door was open. So when it came down to whether I might survive the rest of the winter or not, I asked if the offer was still open."

"How bad was it?"

Peg shrugged. "Pretty bad. Bitter cold. No job. Didn't have a place to stay. Pretty damn bad."

"No, I mean, did Deborah change the offer? I mean, she held all the advantages if you were in a bad way."

Peg turned to look at Joanna. "Are you asking if she took advantage of the situation?"

"I guess so."

"No." Peg gave Joanna a questioning look. "No, she didn't. She made me the same offer she did when I had the advantage of walking away."

"Have you regretted it?"

"Regret? Well, if I had a wider choice, I would have passed. I didn't like contracts—just the concept of them gave me the willies. When I got out of the service, I said never again. In fact, part of Deborah's original argument was that she didn't think I'd be one to quibble so much. A contract wasn't so much different from an army enlistment except she wasn't asking me to lay down my life. She had a point but I still didn't buy it. But when it got down to the nitty-gritty, that seemed just like hair-splitting." She turned to look at Joanna. "How can I regret someone throwing me a lifeline when she could have just shrugged and walked away?"

She closed up that cabinet and then moved to yet another one. "If it had been a different season," she went on, "if I'd been in a different area, I like to think I'm pretty capable. But it wasn't, and I was here, and my options were limited. I wasn't quite ready to cash in my chips yet so no, I don't have any regrets."

If she noticed Joanna cringe at the poker reference, she didn't mention it.

Joanna mulled over Peg's story that afternoon while she pedaled on the exercise bike. She thought Peg had been kidding when she asked over lunch how she felt about riding a bike. Sue had come over and said they were running low of flour.

Peg nodded and turned to Joanna. "Can you ride a bike?"

Joanna made handlebar motions with her hands. "Voom-Voom?"

Peg laughed. "Not quite. No, more pedal until you're exhausted and have leg cramps and then do it some more."

"I suppose. Haven't done it for years. Are we going somewhere?" She immediately brightened at the thought of being able to get out and see the surroundings.

"Sorry, no such luck. All in one place."

The stationary bike was in one of the outbuildings. Stone floor, storage bins and the table with the mill fastened to it. A long belt went from the bike to the mill, run by pedal power.

"Deborah got a small one, she hadn't been planning on filling the house. At least it's not hand grinding anymore. She and Karen rigged up the bike so we can just sit there and pedal away. Grinds the flour. Wheat, oats, rye sometimes. Sometimes corn."

"Ahhh, I see."

By the time she finished, Joanna knew she would have leg cramps. She hadn't ridden since she was a kid, but it had been an automatic thing, leaving her time to think. Peg seemed comfortable being on contract and she didn't seem the type to be coerced into one. Maybe she didn't have much of a choice, but it wasn't Deborah who had controlled the conditions. Clearly, Peg believed that she wouldn't have survived otherwise. But couldn't Deborah have given her shelter out of charity, without a contract? Then again, Joanna wasn't sure. It was just an impression, but Joanna wasn't sure Peg would have taken charity. She would have felt she had to pay for what she got, one way or another. Which left the contract between them.

* * *

"I thought you looked tired *last* night." Deborah carried the tea tray as she followed Joanna up to the bedroom after dinner.

"Hmph." Joanna wasn't about to admit that her legs were aching as she went up the steps.

"Why didn't you and Peg take turns on the bike?" Deborah carried the tray over to the table.

"I told her I'd do it."

"You don't have to be a martyr, Joanna. There'll be time enough for that later in the growing season."

"You keep saying that. Are you trying to scare me?"

"Go change before you stiffen up."

Joanna wanted to protest and then decided it wasn't worth it. She heard Deborah pouring the tea.

"No, I'm not trying to scare you, just warn you. Farming is a lot of hard work. You probably could file a complaint with the labor board for cruel and inhuman punishment."

"Would they even bother with me?"

"Maybe—maybe not. Hard to say. Some boards are really good. Some, well, let's just say that they leave much to be desired." She turned when Joanna came out of her room. "I haven't had much to deal with them, but I don't think there've been many complaints."

"So no one here has complained?"

Deborah shook her head as she handed Joanna the mug.

"Do they know they can?"

"Full disclosure."

"You didn't tell me."

"I figured as much as you've been around, you knew."

"Not where the office is."

"Across from the courthouse on the town square."

"And everyone here is free to just go in and complain?"

Deborah held her hand, palm up. "Everyone knows where the tracks are, where the train goes. It's not like they're confined."

Joanna stood there, wondering just how much of what Deborah said was true. She absently sipped the tea and immediately choked, coughed and spat it out.

Deborah quickly set her mug down and reached for the towel to mop the floor. "Are you all right?"

"What is that?" Joanna held out her mug of tea in rejection. "Are you drugging me?"

"Ahh, well, yes, so to speak." Deborah stood up. "I thought you might be sore from all that exercise. I got some black haw from Beth. It's supposed to keep your muscles from going into spasms."

Joanna glared and Deborah looked amused. Joanna wasn't sure if it was because of the way she had reacted or for what she thought.

"I should have mentioned it," Deborah said blandly.

"That would have been nice," Joanna retorted. She set her mug on the table. "I suppose you have the same thing?"

"Didn't seem worth it to brew two different pots."

Joanna deliberately picked up Deborah's mug.

Deborah chuckled and shook her head as she took the mug she had given Joanna. "Have a seat. You know, Joanna," Deborah said slowly in a more serious tone, "it's in my best interest that even though you don't want to be here, you be as comfortable as you can be. I really don't expect you to like it. I understand your situation. But I'd rather you didn't fight it day in and day out."

Joanna could help but remember Peg's story just that morning about how Deborah resisted change. "Well, coming from you, that's pretty strange."

Deborah had the grace to look uncomfortable. "Probably so," she admitted. "I've never liked change and have had a hard time with it. But I've managed. So I know it can be done."

"What? The mighty Deborah has learned she might have been wrong?"

Deborah went back to looking amused. "Oh, I wouldn't go that far." She met Joanna's gaze directly. "But I have learned there's more than one right answer."

* * *

"How are you going to manage this?" Peg asked. "Seems to me you're going to have to curtail some of your activities."

Deborah stood on the side porch and watched Joanna beat the rug dragged across the clotheslines. A good way for her to get rid of her frustrations, Deborah considered.

Peg turned around slightly so she had her back to Joanna. "If she's attempted to escape, you can't just drag her around willy-nilly and show her all the layout. You'd be asking for trouble."

Her words finally sank in and Deborah slowly turned her gaze from Joanna to Peg. Had Joanna confided in Peg? She felt a jolt through her and with a small shock recognized it as jealousy.

"You know," Peg said casually, still in her soft voice, "the hotel was a regular hotbed of gossip. The staff learned a lot because we were treated like the furniture. Like when you're on contract, you don't get registered with the state for little things like insubordination. You've got to run away to get registered. So I guess that's what she did. And because she has to be under your supervision at all times, you're not going to be able to go anywhere without her." Her mild blue eyes seemed guileless as she looked up at Deborah. "And I would guess you aren't ready to let her know all the pies you have your fingers into."

Deborah said nothing as she examined Peg's bland face, wondering about Peg's motive and just what else she knew.

"Well Deborah, I never figured you came into town just to see me. And I told you at the first, everyone had you pegged being thick with Marv. Now they might have assumed it was romantic, or at least physical, but I knew that wasn't so."

"Being that I told you that right up front," Deborah said in as neutral a voice as she could manage. She deliberately turned her attention back to Joanna beating out the winter's dust from the rug, more than a little shocked at how much Peg had pieced together. She didn't know which shocked her more, Peg knowing or Peg never having said anything before this.

"That's true. But I didn't know you then. Took a while."

"And what did you find out?" *Yes, my dear, what have you found out?*

Peg looked at the ground for a moment, then back to Joanna. "You didn't treat me like a piece of furniture." She was quiet a moment as if deciding what to say. "Joanna seems to me to be real skittish about something."

Like our past relationship, Deborah thought. "She'll settle in once she realizes she's safe here. Keeping her busy will keep her from worrying about what's going to happen."

Peg turned back to face Deborah and she stepped closer. "Deborah, I don't know what you're doing with the militia," she said in a voice that didn't carry. "And I'm not sure that I want to, but I can see that it's working. You've built up a nice little pocket of peace and quiet here that's helping us survive. Whatever it is that you're doing, you need to keep doing it. If you can't drag Joanna around with you, then you need to find out what to do with her."

"That your pearls of wisdom of the day?" Deborah kept her voice even, not willing to give anything away.

Peg stepped back and relaxed a little. "That's it," she said back in her easygoing voice. "Come around tomorrow for the next installment."

"I'll do that." Deborah turned to go back inside. "Don't let her breathe in that dust too much. Don't need her down sick again."

Peg's comments disturbed her, made her wonder what else Peg had heard, what she had put together. She cut through the kitchen and grabbed a piece of nut bread, evading Sue slapping her hands. Once in her office she pulled down her calendar. She didn't think she'd been noticed. Peg sure blew that one away. She'd have to be more careful. And besides, Peg was right on target. With Joanna in tow, seeing people she needed to see would be difficult. For a couple of weeks, it wouldn't matter. That should give her time to see how Joanna was going to settle in. In the meantime, she might even be able to get Joanna to tell her what other areas of the state were like.

Now to get back to the planning. She pulled the account books down again, wishing not for the first time and probably not for the last time, that the computer accounting package had lasted longer. When the accounting package had crashed, she couldn't justify what it would have cost to replace it. She had gone back to keeping books by hand.

* * *

"Why are you doing this?" Joanna demanded that night when Deborah set the tea tray on the table. "Are you trying to soften me up?"

"In a way."

Joanna watched her as she poured the tea. "And what's the specialty tonight?"

"Oh, back to the regular stuff."

"Maybe I need to start preparing it."

"Fine with me." She turned and handed Joanna the mug. "How did the day go?"

"Am I going to get stuck with all the cleaning?"

"It's spring. Need to get a lot of the cleaning done before the ground dries so we can plant, get it out of the way." She didn't add Joanna was an extra hand and usually they didn't do the cleaning for another month.

"You didn't answer my question."

"I don't make the work assignments. You'll have to take that up with Karen." She watched Joanna's grimly set mouth. Evidently she wasn't ready to protest to Karen. A good sign, Deborah considered as she swirled the tea in her cup. "You've been working with Peg for a bit," she found herself asking. "How do you like working with her?"

Joanna sat down in the rocker and Deborah could see the routine developing. She felt a small measure of relief.

"Okay. She's direct, friendly. She has some quirks about neatness. I mean, you're not having a white glove inspection."

"That's the army in her." She paused again. "She easy to talk to?"

"Easy enough," Joanna said with annoying vagueness. She frowned as if trying to figure how to say something and Deborah waited with determined patience. "You do this with everyone, Deborah?"

"Do what?"

Joanna didn't look up. "Have nighttime talks like this with anyone else?"

"No," Deborah answered, a bit taken off guard. "But then I've never shared a room with anyone else before."

"You don't like it, do you?"

Deborah stopped to think before she answered. She hadn't expected this issue. "It's a solution."

"So, *are* you trying to soften me up?"

"For what?" When Joanna didn't answer, Deborah went on. "I don't recall you ever bending much once you made your mind up. I certainly don't think a few nights in a comfortable bed by yourself is going to do the trick. I'm just trying to make it tolerable. For both of us."

Joanna stood up and finished her tea and set the mug on the table. "I don't think that's all you're trying for, Deborah."

"I think you're reading too much into it."

Joanna shrugged. "Maybe so." She looked at Deborah directly, the challenge in her eyes. "I don't think so." She headed for her room. "The tea isn't going to work, Deborah. You might as well quit."

Deborah watched her go in some surprise. Here she had been expected her to say something about Peg. She was just being sensitive. Just because she had found Peg comfortable and easy to talk to didn't mean that everyone did. And instead, Joanna found the evening teatime suspicious. She smiled slowly. If it wasn't relaxing her, making her think of Deborah as something besides her contract holder, it wouldn't bother her. Quit indeed.

* * *

So Deborah didn't.

A week later, Joanna took stock. She had cleaned every room in the house, carried things downstairs to upstairs, carried things upstairs to downstairs. She even had been in the cellar and discovered the dungeon, its door complete with a little barred window. Just the sight of it made her shiver and wonder at its purpose.

She worked with some of the others—with Sue when she cleaned out the pots and pans cabinets and scrubbed the grills in the kitchen, with Bobbi in the laundry, where she learned how to use the manual washer in the hot and steamy washhouse. She had carried things up to the attic with Linda, finding furniture she could add to her room. She scrubbed the infirmary with Beth, an exacting taskmaster.

And every night when they went upstairs, Deborah invited Joanna to join her for tea. And every night Joanna declined and retreated to her room. She lay in bed, staring at the spiderweb of small cracks in the ceiling as she listened to Deborah in the rocker drinking her tea. Then Deborah would gather everything onto the tray, turn off the light and retire.

Joanna wasn't reassured. She was more convinced than ever she was going to be everyone's lackey and be forever at the bottom of the list. She was going to be stuck with the shit work. That had been her experience everywhere else and even though Deborah said all work was rotated here, she didn't see anyone doing the most menial of tasks. She was going to have to fight to gain any respect.

She glanced around the table. She was learning who had influence. Karen handed out the work details. Strong, but she didn't make a move without Deborah's permission. She'd heard they had arguments but she had yet to see anything even resembling a cross word. Sara, the house manager, was a Miss Goody Two-Shoes and knew on which side her bread was buttered. And Deborah? Joanna looked away. Deborah had said that she worked just like everyone else but she had yet to see her stir from the house to do anything.

"Weather should be good today, dryer at least. Fence line, Linda. Make sure that stretch didn't wash out. Check that back field and see how it's drying out." Linda nodded to Karen. Karen went down the line, more work outside but not for all.

"Joanna, putting you outside today. Chicken houses need to be cleaned. Sorry for the dirty work but…" She shrugged.

Just like I thought, shit work. "No."

"Excuse me?" Karen looked up in surprise. She sounded like no one had ever refused work before. The entire table fell silent and everyone looked at her.

"I said no," Joanna said more firmly.

Karen took a breath but before she could speak, Deborah spoke. "I'll take care of this, Karen," she said in a calm voice. "Just go on." She didn't even seem disturbed as she sat back to finish her morning drink. She didn't look at Joanna either which should have been reassuring but somehow it wasn't.

Karen eyed Joanna but she went on down the table in the midst of a heavy silence. When she was finished, no one moved, everyone looking toward Deborah. Except Joanna. Even if she wanted to see how angry Deborah was, she wouldn't let herself look.

"Sue, how's the inventory coming?"

Sue was still staring at Joanna and it took an elbow from Bobbi for her to jerk back to the table. "Inventory? Fine. I should finish it up today. We'll need more jars for this summer if we're to have a bigger garden. You might want to put that on your list when you do your wanderings."

Deborah nodded. "I'll see what I can do. Sara, have we finished with the winter reports?"

"Yes," Sara said with a puzzled glance. "I should have first quarter reports done today. They'll be ready in the morning."

"That's good. Thank you. Linda, what's the status of the stable?"

"Roof is patched. We haven't finished the plumbing yet. We should finish laying the line today or tomorrow. Ground's still soft without being muddy enough to fall in." She looked at Deborah curiously, glancing at Joanna.

"Stalls done?"

"Stallion stall is. Need some glass for that high window so it's a little chilly but it's useable."

Deborah nodded in satisfaction. "Okay, ladies. Looks like spring is coming. Let's get started." She stood up signaling everyone else to scatter. "Joanna, come with me."

Joanna was braced as she followed Deborah into her office.

"Have a seat."

Joanna sat in front of the desk prepared for the scolding, and even ready to take punishment. It didn't come. Deborah simply moved around the desk and began to riffle through papers. She only looked up when there was a soft knock at the door.

Deborah raised her eyebrows in surprise as Sara came in. She glanced at Joanna and then back to Sara. "I found that paper you asked about. You were right. I had it. I'm sorry. Was that all you needed?"

"Well, yes, but you've got that first deadline coming up."

Deborah nodded. "Just keep reminding me. I'd rather not go down to the wire but…" She stopped and didn't finish. Sara nodded as she took the paper from Deborah's hand and went into her office.

Deborah started stacking papers and putting them back in piles which made Joanna breathe easier. Deborah still didn't like confrontation. Joanna had seen nothing to indicate Deborah was into physical punishment. She sat back in the chair and watched Deborah clean off her desk.

"Okay," Deborah said finally after she put papers away. She got to her feet and looked over the desk. She nodded and then as an afterthought, pulled open the drawer to pull something out and stuff it in her pocket. "Ready?" she asked brightly as she looked at Joanna.

Joanna got to her feet. "I guess so."

"Good of you. I'm out of here, Sara. See you later."

"Have a good day."

Joanna followed Deborah through the house. She wanted to say something, to explain she wasn't going to start at the bottom and catch all the worst details, but Deborah was moving too fast. They paused in the kitchen. Bobbi had the dish detail this morning. Deborah checked the board for the lunch menu, stopped Sue and spoke to her while Joanna stood. Then Deborah said, "Come on," and they went out the back door.

"Better grab a jacket. You might need it later."

Obediently, and curious, Joanna grabbed one of the light jackets and hurried to catch up with Deborah. Deborah headed straight for the stable and Joanna guessed that she was going to inspect the Linda's work. She seemed satisfied as she walked around the building. Then she slid open the door for the stallion's stall.

"Why the stallion's stall?" Joanna felt confident enough to ask.

Deborah grabbed the bars that ran up from the partial wall to the ceiling. "Stallions can get a little overbearing, especially when one of the mares comes into season," she explained absently. "Family had some highly strung horses at one time. Needed to have a secure stall. Some of the stock had been excellent breeding, valuable bloodlines, at least in these parts. Like all valuable stock, had to be locked up." She pulled open the wide door and it slid down the rollers smoothly. "They did a good job." She turned around to Joanna. "What do you think?"

Joanna walked into the large roomy stall, the firm dirt floor, bare now but presumably usually covered with straw. The feed box, the high window out of a horse's reach could be opened for airing. "You've got some good workers."

"Yeah." Deborah slid the door shut. "Unfortunately it doesn't look like you're one of them." She shot the bolt home and pulled a lock from her pocket.

Joanna jerked around, only seeing the barrier. "You're not locking me in here!"

Deborah shook her head. "Either you are to be supervised closely or under lock and key. I've got work to do today and I don't have time to spend supervising you."

Joanna rushed forward to grab the bars but doors and bars built to hold in a stallion weren't going to bend to her. "Are you doing this just because I refused that shit work Karen assigned me?"

Deborah stepped away from the door. "What do you think?"

Joanna shook the bars for all the good it did her. "I'll work, but I'm not getting caught with all the shit work."

"Why not? You think you're better than anyone else?"

Joanna pushed away from the door. If that was the way that Deborah wanted to play it, that's the way she would do it.

"Have a good day," Deborah said on the way out.

The stall was fourteen steps by fourteen steps. The ground was hard but it was dry. The only saving grace was that there was a bale of straw that Joanna could sit on. She could stand this, she reasoned. He had locked her in a closet when they had been on the road and he wanted to go somewhere without her. This wasn't claustrophobic and dark, and it was warm enough. She could hear voices as the women worked around the grounds. It was sunny after days of rain so there was lots more work outside. This could be a lot worse. She could deal with it.

* * *

The next morning was the same. Karen assigned and Joanna refused. Deborah shrugged. Neither Deborah nor Joanna said anything as she was escorted to the stable and locked in.

"Sorry about this." Karen brought lunch to Deborah, who paused in her labors cleaning the brooder house. The effort of cleaning up wasn't worth the time to go inside for lunch so Deborah sat under the shade tree with her plate. Karen crouched down beside her. "I didn't think she'd refuse. No one else ever has."

"Everyone else has come in more or less willingly. They knew there was work involved and that was part of the deal. Joanna's an unwilling contract. She'll have to find a way to work it out in her mind."

"What are you going to do?"

Deborah watched the chickens scratch in the yard. "I imagine it gets pretty boring counting boards. She's not expending any energy so she gets short rations. She's isolated. Might take a while but she'll come around."

"Sooner or later?"

"Sooner or later."

Karen stared at the ground for a minute. "Did you know she used to be a TV reporter?"

Deborah turned to look at Karen, a bit surprised that it had come out so soon. "How'd you find that out?"

"Sara kept thinking she looked familiar—so did I. The bruises threw me off, her face was swollen. I used to be a news junkie once upon a time." She gazed off at the distance. "The hair, her haircut. She always had it short. It's longer now, really makes her look different." She shook her head. "Didn't think that was her name though. Wonder what happened."

Deborah dismissed the question. "Probably the same thing that happened to all of us."

"She did some real good stuff. Took a stance on major issues. I hated it when she got cut." She looked off into the distance. "Did you watch her?" Deborah shook her head but Karen wasn't watching. "Got mentioned as the best newcomer that first year, went from news to specialty stuff. Research was first-rate. If she said it, she had the stuff to back it up, very powerful. Her investigations caused some people a lot of damage."

Deborah sighed. She really wasn't in the mood to hear about any of Joanna's exploits. She handed the plate back to Karen. "How's the work schedule going?"

"Cold frames are doing good, got seedlings in. They'll be ready to plant. Think we'll have another cold snap?"

"Maybe. It's only late March." She looked at the sky, clouds being blown away quickly. "Think the snow is over though. Rain comes next."

"Remember the rain we had two years ago. I thought we'd have to build an ark."

Deborah got to her feet, stretching and flexing her back, turning her head one way then the other. "Check the roofs for leaks. Even if we can't get them repaired before the rains start, mark them with paint."

Karen stood up and took Deborah's plate. "What about Joanna?"

"What about her?"

"What do you want to do?"

"Ride it out," Deborah said. "Sooner or later, she'll get tired of it and get with the program." She picked up the pitchfork and glanced at Karen.

"Sooner or later." Karen took the plate, pursed her lips and turned away.

* * *

Joanna wrapped her arms around herself. She had forgotten her jacket this morning. The weather had been warmer and Deborah usually let her out in the late afternoon. They had ceased speaking or rather Deborah wasn't speaking. That particular mood of Deborah's hadn't changed.

Now it was almost totally dark and Joanna shivered. Was Deborah escalating the punishment and going to keep her here all night? Joanna paced the length of the stall. All Deborah had to do was to assign her something besides shit work. She wasn't stupid. All right, she didn't know farming but there were things that she could do.

She turned at a sound and saw a light, Deborah coming. Maybe she should apologize. Damn, wasn't there any middle ground? She moved to meet Deborah at the door as she unlocked and slid the door open.

"We're tired of you sandbagging," came this rough, muffled voice and Joanna realized with a shock that it wasn't Deborah. Joanna jerked around but she couldn't see whose hands grabbed her. There was more than one of them, two, no, three but they were just shadows.

"'Bout time you learn this is a one-for-all, all-for-one operation."

She lost her balance but she didn't hit the ground. She had participated in enough protests. She went limp.

"Oh, no you don't. None of that passive shit. We've been in protest actions too."

She was dragged to her feet, a hand under each armpit and carried along.

"Tired of working like dogs while you sitting here resting on your laurels."

"Deborah," she protested, vainly realizing that she was being dragged away from the house.

"Deborah's busy," one of them hissed. "Doing her work, your work. Who the hell do you think you are?"

She started to struggle then, not sure what they were going to do to her. She kicked out, hit something solid before her legs were knocked out from under her.

"Got energy enough, guess you've made a full recovery."

They threw her in the horse tank and she came up sputtering. The water wasn't ice cold, the days had been warm enough to warm it but being soaking wet in the evening chill wasn't good. When they pulled her out, she went into defense mode, striking out. She hit someone, soft tissue, and there was a satisfying "umph." She managed to get free but they surrounded her. She still couldn't see who they were, and she had some fleeting thought Deborah had sent them. She was tackled and went to her knees, winded, and as she curled protectively, she was picked up again.

"Let her catch her breath," someone said. They paused and she tried to get her bearings. They weren't releasing her but let her get to her feet as they shoved her along.

"No room for prima donnas here, babe," they said as they shoved her into the compost pile, newly turned over and enriched with leavings from the brooder house. "We all eat, so we all work, every last one of us."

She was sick at that, half crying too, partially from rage, partially from humiliation. She didn't struggle so much after they hauled her back up. They half dragged and shoved her around to the front of the house. Someone opened the door, another pushed her in where she stumbled and fell to the floor. The door behind her slammed loudly, alerting the others. Joanna was aware of everyone either at the doorway, or leaning over the upstairs banister looking down.

"What the fuck is going on!" an irritated Deborah exclaimed as she came out of her office, stopping short and then drawing back at the pungent odor. "What the hell happened to you?"

Without looking at anyone, Joanna got to her feet and moved toward the stairs. If only the floor would open up and she could disappear.

"Oh, hell no," Deborah exclaimed before Joanna could reach the stairs. "I've had to smell that shit all day long. You're not taking that smell into our bedroom."

Joanna stopped. She didn't make any protest, just stopped. Deborah's surprise, true surprise as Joanna knew because Deborah could never produce false emotion, convinced her Deborah hadn't ordered this.

Deborah stepped around Joanna to the foot of the stairs. "Hey! Someone up there?"

"I am." Sara came to the top of the steps.

"Toss me one of those big towels." She looked around at faces at the foyer door. "Go back to what you were doing." Then she waited until Sara tossed the big folded towel.

Joanna couldn't move. She thought she had been through everything but this was humiliating beyond anything that had ever happened to her. Her supposed peers had done this. Even though they hadn't spoken to her these past few days, she had thought they were afraid to give her any support because of Deborah. Now she saw their resentment and antagonism.

"Come on," Deborah ordered after shutting up her office. "You need to get cleaned up. God!" She opened the outside door and Joanna didn't protest. Joanna shivered as she followed Deborah around the house, not even asking where they were headed. "Are you hurt?"

"No." Joanna noticed Deborah didn't ask who had done this. They went to the washhouse where there was an outside shower. Deborah stopped. "They did laundry today. There should be enough hot water left but I wouldn't linger."

A shower. Outside. At night. Joanna didn't bother to protest. She wanted out of these clothes. She shed them not caring if Deborah was standing there, watching her. Deborah ducked into the building, returned with the crock of soft soap. Joanna took a big handful before she pulled the lever for the shower.

She hadn't expected retaliation from anyone but Deborah. That was a serious miscalculation on her part. Now she was really at the bottom of the pecking order and everyone knew it. It wasn't enough that there had been three of them, they had to make it public. She wasn't sure who it was but she would figure it out. But everyone had seen her. She wasn't even given the option of sneaking in, cleaning up in private. She had been publicly humiliated. By the time she finished lathering and washing off, the water was cold. The last flush of water to rinse her hair was like ice but she knew better than to complain. She took the towel from Deborah, drying off as much as she could and wrapping the damp towel around her.

"You ready?"

She nodded.

They went in the back door where the kitchen crew was getting ready for the next morning. She wouldn't look up but she could feel everyone's averted gaze. She saw Deborah pick something up off the counter and then continue.

Almost everyone else was in the sitting room, and Deborah led her through the house to go up the front stairs rather than the back ones. Joanna drew her silence around her. She wouldn't fall apart, wouldn't break, wouldn't buckle in front of them.

Once in the bedroom and the door closed she sagged a little. She just wanted to crawl into bed and make the world go away.

"Get into your nightclothes."

Joanna pulled on sweatpants and light shirt. She was numb as she crawled onto the bed and sat there cross-legged in the middle of the bed, trying to make sense of it all.

Deborah came in with a mug of hot liquid, tea with some of Beth's herbs. "Drink up. It'll help warm you."

Joanna took the mug but she didn't drink.

Deborah crouched down in front of her. "Who did this, Jo?"

Joanna looked up at her. Deborah looked concerned, intent. If Deborah really didn't know, and Joanna began to think for sure Deborah didn't, she wasn't going to compound her problems by saying who she thought it was. She shook her head.

"Jo, I can't allow things like this to happen. You could have been hurt."

"I'm not hurt," Joanna said tonelessly.

"Someone needs to be punished."

"I don't know who they were and if—"

"There was more than one?"

Joanna clamped her mouth shut.

Deborah examined Joanna's pale face. She wasn't sure how much she needed or wanted to get into this. She knew Joanna had to make her own way, and there were some things she could not help.

"All right," she said finally. "I won't ask who, but tell me what happened."

Joanna delayed so long that Deborah thought this would be a taboo subject too but finally Joanna spoke. "When they unlocked the door, I thought you had just been delayed. Usually you don't leave me out there so late."

True, Deborah thought, but tonight it seemed like there was just one damned thing after another. Sue had asked something about the food stores, Sara had wanted some information for the paperwork and it wouldn't wait until morning. Karen had a question about scheduling. It was like everyone had been in a conspiracy to keep her occupied. A conspiracy… Damn, they were all in on it.

"They grabbed me when I came out. Dumped me in the horse tank." She shrugged her shoulders, shivered. "Dragged me to the compost pile, threw me in, rolled me around." She closed her eyes. "Brought me to the front door, shoved me in. You know the rest."

Deborah nodded. A message. Not to her. Deborah thought that there might be some resentment because she was letting Joanna off the hook about refusing duty. Evidently there was, just not directed toward her. "Anyone say anything?"

"Called me a prima donna, said I must think that I was too good to work here."

Oh, that must have hurt, always proud of your work ethic, weren't you, Jo?

"Said I was sandbagging."

"You must have realized that there would be some resentment when you refused work."

"I'm not starting at the bottom," Joanna said in a low voice. "I'm a state-registered contract. I'm the last contract you'll take if you meant what you said about not falling into another classification. That means I'll always be at the bottom of the pecking order and I'm not going to do everyone's shit work."

"There is no pecking order, Jo. Work assignments aren't handed out by seniority."

"Yeah. Like I believe that. Who's above me in seniority?"

"Sara and Bobbi."

"So Sara's exempt because she's the house manager. Quite a plum, wouldn't you say? That leaves Bobbi. And tell me, was it Bobbi who got caught cleaning out the chicken houses when I refused to?"

"No, she was assigned elsewhere." Deborah could see Joanna's argument but she thought she'd let her get to the point her own way.

"And who got stuck with the chickens? Who's on your shit list now?"

"I've been doing it."

"You!" Joanna almost spilled her tea.

"Like I told you," Deborah said mildly, "either you're supervised outside or you're locked up, so we'll be assigned tasks together. It's taken longer to do with just one of us, but I should finish up tomorrow." She was almost amused at Joanna's slack jaw. *I wonder what she thought I'd be doing while she was cleaning after the chickens.* She saw the confusion, the puzzlement in Joanna's eyes.

"We're going to be together quite a bit, Jo. And I'm in the labor rotation just like you are. So yeah, there will be nasty work and good jobs as well. I don't like locking you up but I had to. That's a last resort as far as I'm concerned."

Joanna looked down at her tea.

"What are you going to do?"

"Nothing I can do." Joanna looked up at her. "You don't know who it was. It was clearly a message to you. I might ask what are you going to do."

"Do you have any idea who they were?"

Deborah shook her head. *But I think everyone knew and it was a united message.* This was something she needed to stay out of. It was between Joanna and the others. They had to settle it. She stood up. "You think about it," she suggested. "Drink up your tea, get warm. Get some sleep." She paused but Joanna made no protest, said nothing. "I've got to go downstairs and finish up some stuff. Are you going to be all right if I lock you in here?"

Without looking at her, Joanna nodded.

"Okay. I shouldn't be too long." She turned to go to her room but paused and looked back at Joanna. "Joanna, tomorrow's another day. Just don't paint yourself into a corner. You're too smart to do that, I know. Just don't be stubborn enough to do it to prove a point."

Joanna made no comment so Deborah went on. She didn't like leaving Joanna but she needed to maintain some distance. She had known that bringing Joanna into the house would stir things up but this was a surprising turn of events.

Breakfast should be interesting, she thought as she went downstairs.

* * *

The next morning, the interesting events started right away.

"Rise and shine," Deborah called when she heard no indication Joanna was up. She normally didn't go into Joanna's sleeping area but there was still no sound by the time she had finished dressing. She stepped in to find Joanna curled up on her side, the covers almost over her head. "Come on, Joanna. Time to get up."

Joanna shook her head. "I can't. I can't face them." Her voice was muffled under the covers.

Mornings were never Deborah's best time. She jerked the covers off Joanna. "Get up." Joanna didn't move. Deborah rolled her over on her back and took hold of Joanna's T-shirt. She unceremoniously pulled her up first to a sitting position and then jerked her to her feet. "You get your sorry ass out of bed and get dressed. You are not hiding in here and I'm not turning my bedroom into a jail cell."

Joanna half fell against Deborah. She turned her face away, her hands out to push away from Deborah. "I can't."

"Fuck that notion!" Deborah threw open Joanna's trunk so violently the lid crashed against the wall. She pulled clothes out right and left, tossing pants, shirt and underwear on the bed. "Get dressed." She turned on Joanna. "You've never been a coward before. I see no reason to start now."

"They think I'm shirking!"

"And hiding in here is going to change their mind?"

She stood over Joanna as she dressed, almost pushed her out the door. A quick task of morning ablutions and they were ready to go downstairs. Deborah never let Joanna out of reach, giving her no chance to hide. They hit the bottom of the stairs and Joanna paused.

"Stand up straight," Deborah hissed. "Hold your head up. Damn it, Joanna, where the hell's your spine? Gentry *raped* you and you didn't act this spineless!"

At that comparison, Joanna turned on her and Deborah glared. She was trembling with rage but standing straight as they walked into the dining room side by side.

"Good morning," Deborah greeted mildly with some tight effort as Joanna took her seat. "Everyone have a good night?" She glanced around the table everyone watching. *Sometimes*, she thought, *there is a pack mentality. I just didn't expect to see it at my table.*

No one was fooled by her calm tone. Joanna wouldn't look at anyone, a mistake, Deborah thought. She had some idea who had instigated it all. Perhaps it had been necessary. It was the first thing they had done as an independent group. That said something, she supposed. Maybe Joanna was a catalyst.

Sara stepped in and said something to start morning conversation. Deborah watched Joanna keep her eyes on her plate. This was not a good start. If she was going to be a victim, she had made a very bad miscalculation. On the other hand, maybe she did think she was going to be at the bottom of the pecking order. Maybe she had been on the bottom too long.

The conversation resumed, although it was strained. There were always those who were wide awake at breakfast and those who just didn't talk much until lunch. Joanna's silence wasn't that unusual but there was an air of expectation, slight tension around the table. Karen eventually pulled up her clipboard.

"Ahh, yes." Karen ruffled through the pages, glancing at Deborah. If she was looking for guidance, Deborah gave her none. She had supported Karen making assignments all this time. Now was the time to see if Karen could deal with resistance. "Linda, how's that pipe line?"

"We need some fittings. It's down until we get some."

"Okay. Can you help Peg finish out those cold frames?"

"Sure."

"Sue, how're the seeds coming?"

"It would help if we had some more cold frames with glass."

"Okay, I'll see what we can do. Deborah, how's the chickens?"

"Should be done today. I think we need new nesting boxes when the cold frames get done."

"Okay. Joanna, are you working with the chickens today?"

There was a long pause and Deborah just held her breath. She felt like the table held a collective breath.

"Yes," Joanna answered in a small, clipped, hard voice.

If Deborah wasn't mistaken, a soft collective sigh of relief went around the table.

The crisis was past. Deborah watched, looking for any signs of triumph but while there was relief in everyone, no glances were exchanged. And everyone scattered quickly as soon as assignments were given out.

Bobbi was already pulling her plate away and stacking it by the time Joanna stood. Karen and Beth had their heads together, and Sara was conferring with Peg.

"Let's get started," Deborah ordered. She guessed everyone was avoiding her just as much as the uncomfortable space. Nothing like this had ever happened and they would be questioning how she was going to address it.

Once they were outside, she led Joanna to the work shed where she had left boots and coveralls. She merely pointed to the second set of coveralls, but Joanna wasn't ready for that. She was right in Deborah's face when Deborah turned.

"Don't you ever talk to me that way again, Deborah. I don't care if you are my contract holder. I'm not one of your spineless people here who you can just walk all over."

"I don't have spineless people here," Deborah spat back. "I would have thought you would have figured that out after last night. And any time you act like an ass, I'll call you on it. I told you from the beginning you'll pull your weight. No one here gets a free ride. Now let's get to work. I'm damned tired of this chicken shit."

Joanna glared at her, and Deborah glared back. *No babe, you're not running this show. And if you haven't figured that out yet, you need to learn it quick because I really don't want to get ugly with you.*

The moment stretched and Joanna finally turned and picked up the coveralls. Deborah finished dressing and picked up the pitchfork and shovel. "Bring that wheelbarrow." They finished shortly after lunch, again which Deborah worked through. Joanna didn't ask for any quarter although this was clearly a task she hated.

Deborah had another issue on her mind. For the first time, she felt out of the loop, and she didn't like it. She had been able to predict how the others would react, but now? Was she so distracted by Joanna that she had missed something? Was Joanna the problem or was it there were so many in the house that she was losing that personal interaction? She wanted to protect Joanna but she knew she couldn't. What she didn't know was if or when she needed to step in.

They finished in silence, and then cleaned up, still in silence. Deborah was still mulling everything over as they went to lunch. Almost everyone else had eaten and had gone, an inadvertent blessing. She did her best thinking in silence and isolation.

Joanna went over to the small table by the window. As long as she was in sight, Deborah was comfortable. Joanna was unlikely to bolt out the door. Something was nagging Deborah. When Peg stuck her head in the dining room, it crystallized. Glancing around to see that Joanna was still eating, Deborah casually stepped around the tables and caught Peg alone in the kitchen, carrying pans from the stove to the sink.

"You wouldn't know anything about Joanna stumbling into the horse tank and then the compost pile, would you, Peg?"

Peg cocked an eyebrow at her. "Me? Whatever would give you that idea?"

"Just seemed to have a military flavor to it, you know, have the awkward one in the unit brought into line so the unit functioned."

"I've heard tell of things like that happening," Peg said blandly.

"And the likelihood of this happening again?"

"Most smart awkward ones learn quickly."

"I hope so," Deborah commented, giving her the eye. "There could be repercussions."

"There usually are." Peg stepped around Deborah and moved back toward the sink. She didn't look back.

CHAPTER EIGHT

"You need to make a trip into town," Sara reminded Deborah after lunch three days later.

Deborah was finishing up her paperwork. Her figures indicated that she might have broken even this past year. "Why?" She only lent half an ear to Sara.

"Since Joanna's state-registered, the state needs to know where she is. There should be an office at the courthouse."

"Yeah…" Deborah continued with her figures.

"Deborah." This time Sara waited until Deborah looked up. "It's coming down to the wire. You need to go."

"Go where?" Deborah shook her head a little, wondering what Sara was talking about.

Sara gave an exasperated sigh. "To town. To register Joanna. So the state doesn't put her on the AWOL list."

That. Deborah went back to her list. "All right. I'll go in the next day or so. Shouldn't take long, can catch the early run and be back in the afternoon." She could maybe sneak in a little side trip, take care of some outstanding matters. And, besides, a break from everyone would be a good time to clear her head about how to manage Joanna's supervision. She had managed to get by one crisis, but she didn't think it would be the only one. And there was still the matter of her side business in town with Marvin. Peg's words nagged at her.

"Deborah!" Sara positioned her backside on the corner of the desk, deliberately sitting on Deborah's lists. "Will you listen to me?"

Deborah threw down the pencil and leaned back in the chair. "You're just not going to let me finish this, are you?"

"I let you finish this and then you'll run out to check on something and I won't see you until dinner time like you have for the past several days. This needs to get on your schedule."

"I said I'd go in the next day or two."

"Joanna needs to go with you."

"No."

"No? What do you mean no?"

"Just what I said. Joanna isn't coming along. I can catch the early train and be back right after lunch. Joanna can spend the day in the stable or in her room."

Sara looked at her incredulously. "You're not serious."

"Yes, I am."

"Deborah, you can't do that."

"And why not?"

"You've told her she'd be treated like everyone else. When you locked her up last week, it was because she refused an assignment. You can't lock her up when she hasn't done anything wrong. You'll lose all credibility. Not just with her but with everyone else."

"I don't see it would be a problem. She has to be supervised or locked up. I'm not here, so she would be locked up. What's the problem?"

"And what happens if you get delayed?"

"It's a quick trip. Nothing's going to happen."

"You were delayed the last time. I know, it was a snowstorm and we're past that."

"Hope so."

"But anything could happen and then she'd be locked in and no supervisor on the grounds." She shook her head. "I don't think it's a good idea, Deborah."

"Nothing's going to happen," Deborah said as she pulled the papers out from under Sara. "Don't worry about it."

Sara got up and took a deep breath. "I don't think you have choice." Deborah looked up at her in sharp warning and while Sara stepped back, she went on. "The regulations say she has to be supervised by a noncontracted person. You're the only one on the place. Do you really want to take that chance of something happening when you're not even on the grounds? You've got a lot at risk now, and you're risking us."

Deborah pushed back from the desk. "Are you telling me I have to take her with me?"

"I'm telling you the penalties are there if you leave her unsupervised and something happens. I'm not willing to run the risk, and I'll bet no one else in the house would be either if they knew." She stared down Deborah's glare. "Deborah, you don't have that choice anymore."

"And you think you can tell me what to do?" Deborah bristled.

"You put me in this position to dot your i's and cross your t's. I'd be remiss if I didn't bring this to your attention. And no, it's not me telling you to do this. I'm just the messenger."

Deborah hadn't realized just how much she wanted to get away from Joanna until Sara said she couldn't. As much as she wanted to berate Sara, she knew that wouldn't be fair. "You're just not going to let me have any time alone, are you?" *Or any time away from her.*

"Wasn't me who took her on. I asked if you knew what you were getting into. Even by then, it was a little late in the game."

Deborah's eyes narrowed. All her ideas, fantasies of getting away, taking care of other issues vaporized. She was trapped. "If I say that we'll go in tomorrow, will you leave me alone so I can these charts done?" she said icily.

"If you say that you *and Joanna* are going in tomorrow," Sara replied firmly, "I'll be glad to put it on your schedule and leave you alone."

"Joanna and I will be going into Richmond tomorrow to make sure she is registered at the courthouse," Deborah said in cold, measured tones. "Now why don't you go away so I can get this done."

"Yes, ma'am," Sara agreed and she left.

Deborah threw down the pencil, all her concentration broken. These damn rules and regulations were going to kill her, she muttered to herself. Joanna had been sullen and abrasive since everyone had ganged up on her. She had done what she was told but she was barely civil and prickly besides. Deborah had considered some isolation might improve her mood. Certainly she herself was looking forward to having some time alone. She got up and stalked out of the office and through the house.

"There you are," she said when she finally found Joanna in the potting shed with Linda. Joanna jerked around at her tone, spilling a can of seeds across the table.

"Sorry about that," Deborah had the grace to apologize at Linda's dirty look. Seeds were precious and spilling them was careless. She shifted her attention back to Joanna. "When you get a break there, I need you to find Rae and both of you come see me. Need to make you a go-to-town outfit."

"Yes ma'am."

"Is this going against my contract?" Joanna asked when she and Rae learned what Deborah had wanted. The two outfits lay across Deborah's bed, similar in quality and style to that which she had worn at the diner.

"No," Deborah said irritably. "Try that one on," she said, pointing to the green one. "You should know better by now."

Joanna changed as Rae picked up the pieces, examined the seams, the stitching. "I just ask because this isn't basic clothing, and special clothes were always charged against my contract."

"That's because Gentry was a cheap SOB," Deborah growled, "and I'm getting tired of being compared to him." She picked up the jacket, checked the zipper, the pockets. "I don't want you going into town looking like I dress you in rags."

* * *

"Ladies, women," Deborah addressed them after dinner that night. "A little business meeting." She waited until she had their attention. "I can't seem to get all my ducks in a row. I seem to be picking up contracts on my way *back* from town rather than going *into* town, so now I need to make another trip. If anyone needs anything, better let me know. For those of you sticking here with nothing to do, here's something to chew on.

"The farm has hit the break-even point, by which I mean to say that we've managed to support ourselves. We have put food up and for the first time, we're not coming into the growing season living on beans."

"Thank God!" someone said.

"We've got growing stock, we've managed to stay healthy, thanks to some of Beth's god-awful concoctions. We've made it through another winter. I think this year we need to expand a bit, see if we can turn a profit. There are several ways we can do this, but I'd like to hear your ideas."

Brea leaned forward. "You said profit."

"Thought it was a nice goal."

"Where does that profit go? Your pocket?"

"Part of it would, yes. I've laid out a lot for the past two years, some of that needs to be replaced for hard times. And there's the general good, I'm sure there's any number of things you'd like to see here that would help all of us."

"For instance?" Brea questioned.

"I wouldn't mind a more dependable hot water system for hot showers," Deborah offered.

"All right!" Karen concurred and there were other murmurs of agreement.

"I'm sure there would be a list of things if you set your mind to it. I'm open to suggestions. But there has to be a way to make that profit before we spend it." She looked around the room as Brea sat down. "So, ladies, that gives you something to think about while I'm gone. We'll meet and talk about it when I get back."

* * *

The courthouse clock was striking two when Deborah and Joanna walked into the Columbia Hotel. From the outside it was deceiving, a single door through a narrow hallway leading to an open room with marble floors and the huge old-fashioned wooden registration desk. Pictures of days gone by hung on the walls, and one could easily believe they had stepped back in time.

Joanna could feel the walls closing in on her as she followed Deborah. The trip in had been bad enough. Deborah's mood had not improved. As eager as she was to leave the farm, Joanna was not overjoyed to return to Richmond. She'd had a very different role to play the last time she was here with Gentry and his scams, and she wasn't sure she wanted to face anyone, never mind see how Deborah might deal with them. Her heart sank when Deborah headed for the hotel across from the courthouse where Gentry had made his headquarters for the few days they had stayed.

As she strode to the registration desk Deborah slipped off her knapsack and set it down on the marble floor. "Afternoon, James. Need a room for two."

"Good afternoon, Ms. Steele." The clerk turned the registration book around for Deborah to sign. "Didn't expect to see you back so soon."

She signed both her and Joanna's names and turned the book back. "Corner front room available?"

"I do believe so." James glanced at the registration and paused in his reaching for the key. He cleared his throat uncomfortably. "Ahhh, I'm sorry, this person is not welcome on these premises."

"How so?" Deborah said distractedly, already reaching for her knapsack.

"She's not allowed to stay here."

Deborah looked up to see the clerk sweating profusely. Joanna stared straight ahead and wouldn't meet her eye. "Are you telling me that I cannot bring a member of my household with me and stay here?" She didn't raise her voice but the challenge was clear.

"No, no, ma'am," the clerk stammered, recognizing an unhappy significant client. "J-just that one."

"Is there a problem?" asked the manager coming out of his inner office.

Deborah drummed her fingers on the desk as the clerk stammered out the situation. The manager, looked at his regular well-paying guest, glanced disdainfully at Joanna and then back to Deborah. "Won't you step into my office so we can discuss this?" he invited.

"No," Deborah said flatly, "I will not."

Joanna recognized the tone. Deborah was way past annoyance. She was not going to be conciliatory or amenable.

"Perhaps we can step to one side? There seems to have been a bit of a disturbance the last time this person stayed here."

Disturbance! I could have been killed and you wouldn't lift a hand.

"What kind of disturbance?" Deborah demanded. She didn't raise her voice but her annoyance was clear to the manager.

"Ahhhh, I'd really rather not say."

I bet you wouldn't, ruin the reputation of your nice little hotel. But you and I both know better so don't give me that shit. "I think you had better," Deborah's voice was as demanding as Joanna had ever heard.

"Ahhhh." The manager shot Joanna a look that said this was all her fault. Joanna said nothing and remained motionless. She had learned the hard way that she could not influence such matters. "Shall we say a struggle over the person's attention?"

"You mean she was being fought over?"

"Well, yes. We do have our reputation to consider, Ms. Steele. In this day and age, we can't be too careful."

Deborah didn't even hesitate. "And then I take it Mr. Gentry is on the list of undesirables."

The manager drew back. "I really couldn't say," he replied in his most tactful manner. "We do try to protect our clients."

"You already did say," Deborah snapped. She reached behind her for Joanna's wristbands, holding her hands up. "You see these bands?" The manager glanced at them and then back to Deborah, nodding hesitantly. "Do you know how much free will these leave her? And you're going to tell me *she's* not welcome on these premises when her contract holder who was responsible for her then, *is* a welcome guest? Mr. Mathews, if you're worried about your hotel being turned into a brothel, you're looking at the wrong end of the stick. And you're right: you do have your reputation on the line. Because if I have to find another place to stay whenever I come to town, no matter what member of my household I bring with me, I will be glad to make it clear exactly as to the reasons why."

Joanna clenched her jaw as she tried to keep an emotional distance. She should be used to people talking about her when she stood right there. At least this time, someone was sticking up for her but, she wondered if Deborah was sticking up *for* her or merely because she was part of the Steele household.

"Oh," Mr. Mathews grasped the only straw he could find. "I'm so sorry, I didn't realize Ms. Davis is now a *member* of your household. Of course, you and your entire household are welcome at any time, Ms. Steele. I'm sorry Jim didn't understand that when you signed in." Joanna watched and listened as Mr. Mathews backpedaled as smoothly as he could. When he handed Deborah the key, she turned away, picking up her knapsack. "Let's go," she said to Joanna.

Deborah unlocked the door and stood aside for Joanna to go in first. Joanna stopped in the center of the room. Deborah followed her in and tossed her bag on the bed before she turned to Joanna, taking her bag from her hand and throwing it also on the bed.

"What happened?" she demanded harshly as she turned around.

Joanna faced her defiantly but remained silent.

Deborah made a sound of exasperation. "Well, something did," she snapped. "Now am I going to run into this attitude all over town? Because if so, I want to know about it and not get blind-sided."

"You deal with it?" Joanna burst out. "Like this is a reflection on you?"

"In a manner of speaking, yes, since you're part of my house. And yes, it's a reflection on you, just not one you can control."

Joanna glared at her. Just one more humiliation after another.

"Like I told you at the diner, Joanna—you're a woman on contract. You're vulnerable. You're under my roof now and you have my protection. I won't have any of my people treated badly, and I won't have them talked about."

"As if you can stop gossip!"

"Oh, there will always be gossip but I'll be damned if it'll be thrown in my face, or in your face. I don't have any control about what happened before. I'm damned sorry, but that is done, finished! No one in my house will be treated with anything but respect."

"And that's just going to happen because you demand it?"

Deborah took a breath. "It will to begin with," she said evenly. "Because that is what I demand. The rest is what you earn. So what are you going to do?"

Joanna caught her breath. This was the second time Deborah had caught her off guard, asking for, no, demanding cooperation.

"Joanna, I can demand respect from everyone for everyone in my house. You're the only one who can command respect for yourself. Now I don't know what you're going to do. I can't *make* you do anything in this regard. You've been treated badly but now you've got the opportunity to have some control over how you're treated."

Joanna didn't know what to say.

They faced each other in silence. Then Deborah reached out and took hold of Joanna's hand. "Tell me what really happened, Joanna," she said in a quieter sympathetic tone. "Tell me."

Joanna pulled her hands away and Deborah let her go. Joanna walked over to the window and looked down at the street. "I told him when he brought me back that I wasn't going to do it anymore." An act of defiance. Maybe she had hoped that he would turn her in. Prison had to be better than what she was enduring with him.

"That couldn't have gone over well."

"He said I'd do it or face the consequences."

"And you actually thought he'd stop?" Deborah's incredulity was apparent.

"No." Joanna looked down in resignation. "I didn't. I just knew I couldn't deal with it anymore. The last poker winner…" She trailed off. "He took me back, demanded his money back. They got into a big argument." She stopped.

"And then you got a beating for not cooperating," Deborah supplied what the likely outcome was.

"The management finally intervened because of the noise."

"Son of a bitch," Deborah said quietly.

"I think he would have killed me if management hadn't stepped in."

"So when he tossed your contract in the pot at the diner you went along with it."

"I didn't know it was you, but yes. I decided I really wasn't ready to die."

Deborah shook her head. "Well," she said after a moment. "I'm glad you're still alive. And now, you don't have to make choices like that anymore."

"Don't I?" Joanna turned around and her gaze slid past Deborah to the bed behind her.

Deborah frowned and turned around to see what Joanna was looking at. The beautifully-covered queen bed seemed to take up so much of the room. And it was the only bed in the room. The significance of it suddenly dawned on Deborah and she turned back to Joanna who had that knowing look about her.

"You don't think," she started but one look at Joanna's knowing gaze and she knew what Joanna thought. "I always take this room because it overlooks the street," she protested.

"You don't have to explain." Joanna turned away but Deborah caught her arm. Joanna turned back. "You're the holder. Whatever you want. Who am I to protest?"

"I told you I don't do such things," Deborah said in a tight voice.

Joanna gave her a weary look and seemed to sag. "No, Deborah, you probably don't. If I've seen anything in the past few weeks, I've seen how much and how little you've changed. When you set out to do something, and come hell or high water, you do it. That's the same. You may have changed how you get there—try to persuade instead of order, get people on your side, but you're still determined to get your own way." She paused and looked Deborah up and down.

"Some people think that's a virtue." She sounded a little defensive.

"And what about you?" Joanna said quietly. "Do you ever regret anything?"

"The past can't be changed. There's no sense torturing yourself over decisions made," Deborah said firmly without emotion.

"No," Joanna agreed. "The past can't be changed. But it can be learned from."

"Really?" Deborah retorted. "I guess we've learned different lessons then."

"And what did you learn?"

"That when two people don't want the same thing, the relationship isn't going to work. When they have different values, they aren't even speaking the same language."

Somehow, Joanna realized, the discussion had changed from contracts in general to the personal.

"I promised you a bed by yourself," Deborah said abruptly. "I'll tell them we need another room, one with two beds."

Joanna sighed in resignation. "I know you're not going to do anything, Deborah. That's over and done with. And you never were one to take advantage. Unless you don't trust yourself, just stay here. If you change the room, it's only going to make it an issue, and I'm already an issue. Don't make it worse."

Deborah looked at her as if trying to find some hidden meaning. "Fine," she agreed. "We'll stay here. Make a pit stop if you must. We need to hit the courthouse before they close. I'm sure it's not going to be a quick duck in and duck out. Nothing else has been that easy in dealing with you. I don't expect this will be any different."

If she saw Joanna flinch she didn't seem to care.

* * *

The streets were in early dusk by the time they returned to the hotel and the nighttime chill was settling in. Joanna was drained. Deborah could understand why. Joanna had always been able to draw people to her, to command their attention. Now to be sidelined, to be talked about, around and over as if she didn't exist had to be galling. That she was able to tolerate it told Deborah more than anything what she had gone through.

Deborah herself was in a pretty mellow mood. All the irritation about the trip and Joanna coming along had been dissipated in dealing with first the hotel manager and then with the contract registration office. She shook her head. She had never thought Judy was particularly tactful—she had gone to school with her—and she was the same heavyset, shortsighted, not too bright personality now that she was then. Only now she had a little authority in a plain county office with white walls, broken computers and cracked linoleum. She had discussed Joanna as if that person wasn't standing right there. She complained about information which Joanna could have supplied—if she had been asked—but evidently signing a contract meant a person gave up their humanity.

Finally Deborah had politely asked to see the supervisor, who wasn't available even though Deborah could see her sitting in her office. When Deborah stood, she was sure Judy thought the interview was over. But when Deborah leaned over the desk, her hands flat on Judy's papers, Judy pushed her chair back.

"Judy, either you go get the supervisor or I'm going to walk over you to her office, and I'll be glad to share with her how helpful you have been. I do not intend to put up with your bullshit any longer."

"You can't do that!"

"Have you ever known me to make an idle threat?"

Judy rose, backing away into the supervisor's office.

"You always treat county employees like that?" Joanna asked in a low voice.

"Judy and I have issues," Deborah said, not taking her eyes away from Judy. She sat back down when the supervisor came out the door. "Old issues."

Frances was one of those ageless women who looked like they had been around forever, and usually had, knew the system inside out and were as efficient as a computer, sometimes even more. She was helpful as long as you didn't ask her to bend the rules or God forbid, break them. She dressed primly, her gray-streaked dark hair pulled back severely, and pursed her lips when challenged. She also had the personality of a statue. Other than that, she and Deborah got along like cats given catnip.

Unfortunately Frances wasn't much more help than Judy, although at least Deborah knew it wasn't a personal issue. She had finally thrown in the towel.

"I'll have my lawyer take care of this," Deborah said as she got up. "If you can't get your act together for me, then we'll see what you can do for him." She gave Frances a withering look. "I understand this might be a new situation for you, but you should be able to handle it. So don't give me this crap that the procedures aren't set up." She might have been more conciliatory if she hadn't been pissed to start with. She felt justified being irritated, and being able to turn the entire matter over to someone else was a relief. Maybe he could get further than she could.

"Any preferences for dinner?" she asked Joanna as they crossed the street.

"Don't care," Joanna said wearily. "As long as I don't have to clean it, dress it, chop it, cook it or clean up afterward."

"I think we can avoid that," Deborah answered with a chuckle and a mental note to move Joanna out of the kitchen for a while. "You look tired. Ready for an early night?"

"With the chickens," Joanna responded and then she grimaced.

This time Deborah did laugh.

They hit the dining room relatively late, so it was mostly empty, and Deborah made a point of getting a more private table. Any diners out this late would be looking for more than a late dinner and she didn't want to invite any trolling. She noticed a few glances Joanna's way but they moved along when she fastened her gaze on them. Joanna seemed oblivious and Deborah did nothing to bring it to her attention.

"Are we going to have much to do tomorrow?"

"Probably." Deborah toyed with her food. "See the lawyer, and I want to check a few folks out. And I'll introduce you around town so people know who you are, that you're part of Steele House."

Joanna didn't look overjoyed at that prospect. "You could go without me," she said in a low voice. "It wouldn't be the first time I was locked in at the hotel."

"I won't do that," Deborah said, wondering how often she would have to repeat that line and blithely ignoring the fact she had intended to do exactly that at home. *That was different*, she told herself when she remembered. *That was on home grounds, not in public.* "I'm not going to hide you away."

"Are you sure that's a good idea? Might reflect badly on you. People get the wrong idea."

Deborah gave a cynical laugh. "Joanna, if I were worried about what people thought, I wouldn't have contracts to start with." She sobered and looked at her sympathetically. "I know it's going to be hard on you. I wish it could be easier. You're not the person Gentry tried to make you out to be. I want people here to see who you really are."

"It might be nice if you asked me what I wanted," Joanna muttered low enough that she could be ignored.

"All right," Deborah acknowledged. "What *do* you want—besides not being on contract?"

"Maybe I just want to survive."

"I think that's what we all want," Deborah said seriously. *But it sounds, my dear, like you've had a taste of just how hard surviving might be.* "The question is how? By hiding? By carving out our own space? By lying low? By running away? Or by fighting back?" She paused and Joanna said nothing. "I don't know any safe spots to hide. I'm not prone to running away, and besides I wouldn't know where to run. This is my home. I'm perfectly willing to carve out space for those who want to join me and survive. And I'll fight to hold this space. I might even die doing so."

Joanna looked up at her in surprise.

"Oh, yes, I've had threats. We're not living in the same world anymore, and I know there are people who would kill for what I've got. They're too lazy and stupid to figure out how to get the things they need to survive except by stealing or killing." She shook her head. "This is a time of survival of the fittest, but I just hope that as a society, we don't lose our humanity."

"You think having contracts is an example of humanity?" Joanna asked quietly, cautiously.

"As long as they are agreed to on both sides. It's just a measure of commitment." She gave Joanna a curious glance at this turn of conversation. "I couldn't deal with contracts that were forced, whether for debt or anything else. I know contracts are abused. I can't see anything that justifies that."

"But you're part of that system."

"Yes." She paused. She really didn't talk about contracts much with anyone, at least not the philosophy of them. "I think," she said slowly, "it's a means of survival. I hope when times are better, contracts will just disappear. I'm glad there are people who oppose them—we always need checks and balances. That doesn't mean I'm not doing what I think is best for me."

"Foot in both camps, Deborah?"

Deborah shook her head. "No. I just don't think things are so black and white anymore. Lots of gray areas." She glanced at Joanna's plate of meat loaf, potatoes, beans, a standard Midwestern meal. "You done?"

They left the table, paid the bill. Joanna wasn't saying much.

"Could you survive without contracts?" Joanna asked as they went through the lobby and up the stairs.

"Maybe," Deborah admitted. "I had the house. I had started the gardens before anyone came. Had a couple of break-ins that rattled me. That was one of the things that made me consider the commune. That didn't work. So I had to find something that did. Considered having someone else there instead of being a lone woman in this big house might be safer."

"Wasn't there another way to do that?"

"Tried a couple of things. Contracts worked the best." Deborah locked the door behind them. "I really didn't wake up one morning and say Aha! Contracts are the answer. That first one kept me awake nights before I did it."

"They didn't after that?"

Deborah shrugged her shoulders. "Not so much."

"So what was the difference? I mean, one contract, two contracts, a dozen, two dozen. What's the difference?"

"I don't know. I think everyone's different. I figured out what I could deal with, drew my lines."

"And what are they?" Joanna demanded. Deborah turned at her tone.

"You think I don't have any, Joanna?"

"I don't know. Do you?"

"I just said I did." She didn't know how to answer, didn't know if Joanna was trying to be belligerent or just curious or if she really was just trying to understand. "Like I said, it was just a commitment. But once you do something often enough, it takes on a life of its own, so I had to figure out a limit. The law says twelve is the number where it ceases to be a family operation so to speak. But for me, it's my dining room table."

"Your table?"

"Seats twelve. So twelve was family. As long as I could seat everyone around the table, they were family. Anything more was something else. And I didn't want to go there."

"That's—that's an arbitrary number. That's about as ridiculous as anything I've ever heard."

Deborah shrugged her shoulders. "Table seats twelve, house sleeps twelve. My family limit. Works for me. That's all I'm concerned about."

Joanna's jaw dropped. "You mean," she calculated quickly, "if you'd had twelve in the house, you wouldn't have taken my contract? Or—or if you had a smaller house?"

Deborah frowned. She had thought of those circumstances. "Wouldn't have covered the bet," she said reluctantly.

"Even though…" Joanna trailed off.

Deborah met her gaze. "Gotta be a boundary somewhere," Deborah said lightly. "Hard choices sometimes. Nothing's easy anymore."

She turned around and picked up her knapsack. "You want to use the bathroom first? Get to soak in a hot tub as long as you want. No one pounding on the door to get in." She pulled out her nightclothes.

"Luxury," Joanna answered tonelessly.

"Take advantage when you can." She sat on the bed and pulled off her boots, then moved to the chair and pulled her journal from the knapsack. She looked up at Joanna who still stood in the middle of the room.

"Jo. Don't worry about things that didn't happen. I did get your contract."

Joanna gave a start and then looked at Deborah.

"Go get that bath," Deborah said as she stretched out her legs. "The future's worrying enough. Don't look back. It's scary or at least demoralizing." She opened her journal and flipped through to an empty page. When she looked up, Joanna was closing the door to the bathroom.

She tilted her head back and examined the ceiling. She could give advice so easily about what to do. How many times had she lain awake, wondering if she had made the right choice? She might as well have flipped a coin. Which she had on occasion. Saved her a headache. She closed her eyes. Sometimes she was so tired.

* * *

Why had she thought this would be easy? Being around Joanna twenty-four hours a day, seeing her hurting, listening to her cry at night, remembering how it used to be. She had always thought she was stronger than Joanna, wanted to protect her. And now.

She curled up, feeling Joanna against her back. Things hadn't changed, she still got cold at night and wanted to cuddle, just like she used to. Deborah felt Joanna's arm wrap around her and she leaned back.

"You okay?" she asked quietly. She felt Joanna nod and she rolled over, facing her. Tentatively she reached up to brush Joanna's hair back, watching Joanna watch her. She still looked so vulnerable, defenseless.

"I'm so sorry you've been hurt," Deborah whispered. She stroked Joanna's face, running her fingers over the healed bruises, over her eyebrows, cupping her cheek. "I would have done anything in the world to keep you safe."

"I know," Joanna answered in a whisper as she drew Deborah's hand down, kissed the palm. "But you're here now." She moved closer, watching Deborah with trusting eyes. Deborah brought Joanna's hand to her lips, kissed her knuckles. She couldn't even say who made the first move, only conscious of their lips meeting, arms wrapped around each other.

"I missed you so much," Deborah confessed. "Everyone I ever loved since has been measured against you."

Joanna made no return confession but Deborah didn't care. She had always known she was only part of Joanna's life while Joanna was her life.

"Please," Joanna whispered. "I want to feel safe again." She wound her arms around Deborah's neck, pulled her closer.

"As safe as I can keep you," Deborah promised as she kissed Joanna's neck. Joanna was warm from her bath, the bubble bath she used. She filled Deborah's senses as clothing disappeared, as she felt Joanna yield to her. Nothing had changed, everything was as she remembered, the mole Joanna had on her shoulder, the way her breast filled Deborah's hand, the way she arched her back to press against Deborah.

They still fit together, even Joanna's hands on Deborah's shoulders, pushing her downward and Deborah's teasing resistance. She tongue teased Joanna's nipple, first right then left as Joanna moved against her, opening her legs, wanting. She kissed down Joanna's rib cage, across her belly, hip to hip.

"Please," Joanna whimpered, "don't torment me."

And Deborah couldn't refuse her, not when she had waited so long herself. Everything was too fragile, too unreal. She didn't know how this was happening but she wouldn't question. She only knew she had the woman she loved again and that was all that mattered.

She settled between Joanna's legs, could smell her, taste her. Joanna raised her hips, offering and Deborah kissed the inside of her legs, tasting the moisture, her heart pounding, feeling Joanna's hand on the back of her head, wanting her.

Pop!

* * *

Joanna closed the bathroom door and filled the tub. Privacy. It was one thing for Deborah to tell her not to think about what might have happened. Easy for her. She hadn't suffered like she had. Joanna closed her eyes even as she realized the paradox. She hated being on contract but it could be worse. And for Deborah to say so casually she would have passed on acquiring her contract. When she knew Joanna. When she could see how Joanna had been treated. When she even agreed that Joanna shouldn't be on contract.

Joanna stripped. Her wounds had healed, she was regaining her strength as well as her weight. She held out her hand. Her nerves were better. She didn't feel like crying as much. She slept through the night with no nightmares. She was beginning to think beyond the next day. She stepped into the tub, sinking into the hot water, her head laid back against the rim. Luxury. The only thing missing was the bath oil. She closed her eyes. Once upon a time… But she had learned not to do that. Torture.

What was she going to do now? Joanna had to cooperate and work. She sank beneath the water. She had misjudged everyone. She had thought they worked because Deborah made them. No, they worked collaboratively. Why? Because their work fed them. They might be eating at Deborah's table but it was *their* work. Was it really possible contracts could be cooperative?

She sat up suddenly, splashing water out on the floor. No. She refused to think that. Contracts were benefiting the holder. Now she had the facts, the *knowledge*, the experience of just what contracts meant, she could do so much more. If she could get back. But Deborah was a formidable barrier.

When she stepped back into the bedroom dressed in her sweats, warm and tingly from the hot bath, her skin puckered from the long soak, she walked over to stand before Deborah. She didn't look so formidable now, her legs stretched out, her head resting against the back of the chair, eyes closed in sleep. The journal had fallen to one side, the pen cap on the floor. Deborah looked tired and vulnerable.

Joanna bent down and picked up the pen cap from where it rolled almost under the bed, gently pulled the journal free from Deborah's limp hand and the pen from her fingers. She moved back to lay the journal on the low dresser and in doing so, saw the room key. She caught her breath, quickly looking over her shoulder to check if Deborah was truly asleep.

Her knapsack was waiting there, packed for a two-day trip, as was Deborah's. Joanna knew there was cash in the side pocket. Her mouth went dry at the possibility. Never had there been such a good opportunity. She looked back again. Possibly a setup? Would Deborah do that? Did she have the nerve?

Deborah stirred and Joanna froze. She looked over her shoulder again but Deborah only turned slightly, then her breathing evened out. Joanna thought surely her heart pounding was loud enough to wake the dead. She bit her lip, hating the temptation before her. Choices. Every other time she had the opportunity with just seconds to decide. Now, she had time to consider. Choices have consequences. She could hear Deborah's words warning her.

No, she decided. She wasn't ready. She didn't know the geography yet. Didn't have a plan. If, she gazed longingly at the key, she passed this time, Deborah might trust her, or at least begin to. And there would be other opportunities, better opportunities, if she were trusted. She backed away from the dresser, moved around the bed and pulled down the covers, sitting on the side of the bed. She was shaking, already second-guessing herself.

"Enjoy your bath?"

Joanna started. Deborah's eyes were half closed and she hadn't moved. Joanna had no idea if she had just woken or if she had been awake and watching.

"Yes," she answered breathlessly.

Deborah got to her feet, and stood there a moment, like she didn't know where she was at. She looked at the chair, the bed, Joanna, then looked around the room and then back at Joanna.

"Your journal?" Joanna assumed she was looking for it. "I put it on the dresser." Joanna indicated the location with a wave of her hand.

Deborah looked at the chair, the floor, Joanna, then the dresser. Curiously she turned back to Joanna. "I didn't even feel you take it," she said simply, giving Joanna no indication how long she had been awake. "I just put my head back a moment, to think."

"I filled the tub for you," Joanna said slowly. Deborah was so uncertain about something, making Joanna wonder if she had been watching her. "It should still be hot enough. A nice long soak will probably help you too."

"I must have dreamed," Deborah muttered. She rubbed her face, ran her hands through her hair. "A hot bath will probably put me to sleep," she said as she stretched, deliberately. "If I'm not out in twenty minutes, you'd better check on me."

Joanna nodded as she eyed the journal tend the key on the dresser. She was almost relieved when Deborah picked up the key when she went by and stuffed it into her pocket. Joanna lay back on the bed and stared at the ceiling, relieved at not having to make the decision.

* * *

Deborah sat in the tub until she was thoroughly chilled. She could still feel Joanna's touch although she knew it wasn't real. It was only her own longing, her own dreams. She had established her own rules of conduct regarding contracts from the beginning, before there was any temptation. And now when there was so much she wanted right there before her, beside her, she knew she couldn't yield. She could give Joanna safety but that was all she could give her and still be true to herself. And if Joanna hated her for holding her contract, she'd hate her more for abusing it.

She was cold when she crawled into bed and it had nothing to do with the room temperature. She had been relieved when she came out and found Joanna asleep already. This might be the hardest thing she had even done, this putting Joanna back in the box and locking it tight.

CHAPTER NINE

"Good God, Deborah, it's bad enough that you're into contracts, now you've got to get a state contract," was her lawyer's reaction. His broad square face was flushed as he watched Deborah pace in front of his desk. It wasn't his day in court so he was dressed more casually in a plaid sports shirt and khaki pants, with a leather jacket hanging on the coat-tree in the corner.

"Roger, I'm not into contracts—I'm into farming. I happen to contract for labor, the same as sports teams did way back when, the way anyone did for a short-term project with independent contractors."

"But they are totally under your control!"

"What else do I have to pay them but room and board in this cash-poor economy?" Deborah reported testily. He ought to know that. His nice dream of that law degree supporting the family farm hadn't worked out. Now he was living on the farm and practicing law on the side. Such were the dreams of her generation.

"You're simply asking for trouble."

"And I'm paying you to keep me out of it."

He pulled the papers across the desk to examine them again. "Tell me, is this a one-shot deal or is it just the forerunner?"

"Forerunner of what?" She stopped in front of his desk to look at him.

"Getting into state contracts?"

"Why would anyone bother?" Deborah snapped as she pulled one of the chairs around and threw herself into it. From this angle, she could still see Joanna in the outer room. "This one was a one-deal time and while I'm not ready to give her up, why anyone would buy into that system is beyond me. The red tape is a nightmare."

"Then you haven't heard the rumors. There's a lot of talk going around that Consolidated is trying to move into the area."

"Private prisons…" Deborah mused. She looked back across the desk as he continued grimly.

"Yep. They are also getting into the contract process centers. They look for poor rural counties who need the cash influx. Brings jobs, lots of business."

"Dirty business you mean. Consolidated's been big on talk but not so much on delivery. Just transfers big city problems out to the country and then when they go flat, the county is left with the problems."

"The money they're dangling looks awfully good."

"Who's dangling?"

"Fellow by the name of Gentry."

Deborah sat bolt upright. "Son of a bitch!"

"You know him?"

"We've had dealings."

"I don't know where else he's been but he's talking good for here."

"I don't know either, but I can find out." She got up and went to the door to the outer room. Joanna sat there reading some old magazines. "Joanna, could you step in here, please." Deborah tried to keep the angry edge out of her voice but Joanna gave her a startled look and immediately moved.

"Roger, I'd like you to meet the newest member of my household, Joanna Davis. Joanna, this is Roger Henderson. Besides my lawyer, he's my cousin's husband."

Roger got to his feet. "Good to meet you, Ms. Davis." He frowned slightly. "Joanna Davis?" he repeated. He gave Joanna a sharp look in puzzlement. "You look familiar." He ignored Joanna's outstretched hand as he turned to Deborah.

"What?" Deborah said sharply as she watched Joanna drop her hand. She had never known Roger to snub someone. If news had already traveled from the hotel, if Roger was taking offense at the gossip, she would have her work really cut out for her.

"Have we met before, Ms. Davis?" Roger said slowly as he turned back to Joanna. He was still giving Joanna a quizzical look.

"No, I don't think so," Joanna said cautiously.

Roger belatedly waved both women to take a seat. "Joanna Davis," he repeated, digesting the information. "Well." He shook his head, still puzzled. "I'm sorry, forgive my manners." He held out his hand and Joanna shook it warily.

Roger scratched his chin. He shook his head, his gaze going from one woman to the other.

"Gentry was Joanna's previous contract holder. He used her contract in a poker game."

"And you won," Roger replied. "As usual."

"Ms. Davis," Roger addressed Joanna directly. "A word of warning," he said seriously. "Never play poker with this woman. And if perhaps you do get suckered in to doing so, never bet more than you are prepared to lose. She has phenomenal luck. And she can bluff."

"Joanna," Deborah moved in to change the subject, "we were wondering if you might share some information with us."

"If I can," Joanna said carefully, looking from one to the other.

"You said that Gentry kept you on the road a lot. Can you tell us where you've been?"

Joanna looked relieved and shook her head. "I really don't know. There were a lot of little towns, rural areas. Some of them I'd never heard of before." She looked from Deborah to Roger.

"Any name at all?" Roger asked.

"Vernon." Roger scribbled it down. "Rock Creek, Run, something like that. Burlington. All of them were on rail spurs, most of them out in the middle of nowhere."

Roger and Deborah looked at each other. "We may have some problems," Roger said slowly.

"What was he doing?" Deborah asked, directing her question to Joanna.

"Scouting for some investment company. They're moving away from St. Louis, to safer ground. Brings them back this way, at least that was what I gathered. He didn't talk business around me."

"No, I guess he wouldn't," Deborah said shortly.

"Is that bad news?" Joanna finally ventured.

Deborah gave a big sigh. "Employment, money brought in, that could be good, but yeah, I think it's bad news." She turned to Roger. "What's your view?"

"I don't like it." He shook his head. "It's one thing for something like this," and he flipped through Joanna's papers, "another on that scale."

"In for a penny, in for a pound," Deborah said bitterly, blew out a long breath and shook her head. "Well, that's something to think about, Roger." She stood up, which immediately brought the other two to their feet. "I need that contract straightened out, nailed firm, buttoned down, i's dotted and t's crossed. I don't want any problem with it. Now or in the future."

"We'll get it done."

"I don't want to spend a lot of time in town. There's too much going on at home. Town is a waste of time."

"You know," Roger said slowly, "you might want to keep in closer contact, Deborah. Things may be getting interesting." He absently tapped the paper on the desk.

"Damn. I live out there to stay out of things like this. You know that."

"I think you might want to be in this loop." Deborah gave him a dirty look but she didn't argue. He turned his attention to Joanna. "It was good meeting you, Ms. Davis, and thank you for the information. I hope," he paused, glancing at Deborah. "I hope your stay with us goes quickly."

"What was that all about?" Joanna asked as they walked back downtown.

"Gentry's scouting for a location for Consolidated to open a contract processing center." Joanna stopped dead in her tracks. "You didn't know, did you? No, I didn't think so. Come on, let's go eat lunch. There's a few other places that we have to go see but I think first we need to talk."

"I don't have any appetite."

"Then eat to live."

Joanna was still silent when they stopped at the small side-street diner with the name of Nature's Bounty painted on the glass. Deborah guided her to one of the booths in the back away from the windows. Deborah put in an order for both of them.

"You're familiar with Consolidated," Deborah said when the waitress had delivered their meals.

"Yes." Her answer was clipped and short.

Deborah picked up the leaflet left on all the tables. "I hear they're pretty bad."

"You could say that." Joanna's words were noncommittal but her tone wasn't.

Something else to pick your brains about, Deborah considered. *Sure wish you'd open up.* "Seems like you really got around," she commented, but Joanna only avoided eye contact and looked away. Shit. Deborah read the leaflet and slid it over to Joanna. "They're organizing already," she commented. "Must sound a bit more promising on coming here than Roger thought."

Joanna read the leaflet announcing a public meeting to fight against the location of a contract processing center the following night at the United Church. There would be speakers outlining what a processing center did—signing up people to go on contract as well as handling the sale of those contracts to buyers. "Are you going?" Joanna asked as she pushed the leaflet back to Deborah.

"She's not welcome," came a husky voice from the aisle and the tall redhead slid into the booth, crowding Joanna over to the wall. She hardly gave Joanna a second glance as she grabbed the leaflet from under Deborah's hand.

"Well, hello, Carolyn." Deborah gave the woman, denim-clad, in both jeans and oversize shirt with rolled-up sleeves, a friendly if guarded greeting. She hadn't expected a warm open-armed welcome from her and she wasn't disappointed.

"Don't even bother trying to go, Deborah. I'll be the first one to throw you out."

And I'll just bet you could do it, Deborah thought as she looked over the thin woman. Her thinness was deceptive. But it wasn't Deborah's intention to have a confrontation, so she kept her tone mild. "It says it's an open meeting. Everyone who has an interest."

"In opposing Consolidated." Carolyn said in a grating voice. "We don't need any contract holders there to report on us."

"It wouldn't hurt your argument to have a contract holder be opposed to Consolidated. Makes it look like you're opposing the company and not the practice. Would give you a stronger argument."

Carolyn wasn't mollified. "Judy said you registered a state contract." Deborah gave a noncommittal shrug. The speed of gossip in this town was phenomenal. "Is this the contract Luella said you won in a poker game over at her place?"

Deborah just glanced up at her without answering. Joanna focused all her attention on the table in front of her and wrapped her hands around the glass of water.

Carolyn shook her head. "You just get in deeper and deeper, don't you Deborah? I would think that you'd be in hog heaven with a processing center right here in your backyard."

"Just because I have contracts doesn't mean that I approve of how Consolidated handles them. And Consolidated's not the type of company I want for a neighbor."

Carolyn tried to stare Deborah down but she wasn't budging. "You know, Deborah," Carolyn said finally, "sooner or later you're going to get your head out of the sand."

"I don't think my head's in the sand. You just haven't shown me anything better. Contracts right now are a means of survival for a lot of people. Consolidated's something else. Now if you want to keep them out, you're going to have to get their history. They've got a bad record of doing snow jobs, big promises and bad delivery. They're going to need the railroad for the supply line to a big city. I guess that's why our line is getting fixed. Find out what their failure rate is. They have the habit of coming in, getting lots of government money to build things and then pull out, leaving the county holding the bag without completing anything. And find out who's investing." She pulled the leaflet out of Carolyn's hands to look at it again.

"I don't need you to tell me how to organize a protest."

"Maybe not, but you need to tailor it to this area. Philosophical and moral arguments aren't going to cut it. You need to argue money and employment and survival."

Carolyn drummed her fingers on the table as she stared at Deborah while the waitress served their lunch. Carolyn left with the waitress, taking the flyer. "Okay, if you show up, I won't have you thrown out. Better to watch you anyway."

"I'm not the one you need to watch," Deborah retorted. "The ones you need to watch, you won't even see." Carolyn grunted and walked away.

"Who was that?" Joanna asked.

"Carolyn Miller. She runs the commune some miles from here. This diner is their business, such as it is."

"That the commune that you keep clashing with?"

"Yeah."

"You still get attracted to women holding the opposing viewpoints, don't you?"

"What can I say? I like to argue."

Joanna ate a little more. "I apologize, Deborah. I thought you were stuck out here in the boonies and didn't know anything that was going on. You seem quite in touch."

"Not enough, it seems." She pulled the flyer back to her, frowned at it.

"What are you going to do?"

"I don't know. I'll have to think about it." She went back to eating. "I think we'll spend some more time in town."

The rest of the afternoon was spent visiting everyone in town with whom Deborah had an account, and in this cash-poor economy, there was a lot of bartering. Most of it, Joanna learned to her discomfort was sitting around and shooting the breeze with people she didn't know, talking about things she knew nothing. She felt like a five-year-old tagging along in Daddy's footsteps. She didn't like it. "God, how many people do you know in this town?" she muttered to Deborah as they were leaving the hardware store. "And how many of them are related to you?"

"Not enough and about half." Deborah paused as she opened the door for the woman coming in. They made the rounds of other stores, Deborah just dropping in to chat a bit, introduce Joanna as part of her household. Joanna noticed that several of the men gave her the once-over but they always turned most respectful when Deborah eyed them. She was relieved when they finally made it back to the hotel.

"God, I haven't talked to so many people in years." Deborah kicked off her boots and threw herself onto the bed. Joanna turned around in surprise. "My granddad used to do it. Every Saturday he'd come to town and spend the day, talking, visiting. I'd tag along, bored as hell but," she chuckled at the memory, "the old men would think I was cute, give me a nickel and I'd go buy me some candy. Now I know they were getting rid of me to talk about things that weren't suitable for little girl ears. And now I know how he managed to stay one step ahead of the game and know so much."

"So what did you learn?"

"Carolyn's going to have her hands full. There're men drooling over the opportunity for work, having a bit of security. They're not going to like her for delivering bad news or for killing an opportunity. It might get ugly before it's finished."

"And how do you stand?"

"Good question. I don't know. I don't like Consolidated's record. I certainly don't like Gentry. I don't like the idea of them being in my backyard."

"But they're all right in someone else's?"

Deborah shook her head. "No, I don't have that philosophy either. I just don't see things in black and white, there's a lot of gray."

"Still sitting on that fence, aren't you, Deborah."

"Yeah, for right now, I guess." She turned to look at Joanna. She patted the bed beside her. "Lie down for a while." Joanna slipped off her shoes and obediently lay down. "I'm sorry, I'm sure I totally bored you today and exhausted you besides. But on the other hand, now enough people know that you belong to the House of Steele, so they'll think less of anything else they hear."

"And it won't reflect badly on you." Deborah shrugged. "I don't understand you," Joanna continued slowly. "On one hand you don't care what people think or at least you say you don't, and on the other hand, we go all over town to make sure that you get your side of the story out first."

"A paradox, isn't it?"

"Yeah. Makes it very hard for people to know what side you're on."

"Well, I hope people like Gentry see me the same way you do then."

"And who knows where you really stand?"

"No one."

* * *

"Here's your paperwork, all buttoned down and nicely tied," Roger said the next afternoon. "I'll have the will updated, you can sign it the next time you come in to town. You will be in town more frequently, won't you?"

"Probably," Deborah said absently. She frowned, looking back at Joanna sitting outside. "Tell me, what's the deal about someone getting shanghaied onto a contract?"

Roger sat back in the chair, seemingly surprised at the change of subject. "Happens. Some localities are getting their name for it." He followed Deborah's gaze toward Joanna and then back. "So far they've been held up in court."

"What do you think about them?"

"Dirty trick. Get an unwilling contract. Makes a bad reputation for the area."

"Anyone doing anything about it?"

Roger made a tent of his fingers, looked at Deborah speculatively before he spoke. "I've heard tell of a class action but I haven't seen anything. Takes someone to get the ball rolling or be a test case."

Deborah slowly nodded. "Let me know if that ball gets rolling."

"Is that her claim? Not that I can see her walking willingly into a contract but you never can tell. Stranger things have happened."

"True enough." Deborah turned to go. "Just keep me posted on that. And yes, if there's a class action, make sure she's included."

"Trying to get rid of her already?"

"No. I just don't think it's fair. It's hard enough when you agree to a contract, even harder when you don't see any other way. I can't imagine what it's like to be forced into one."

"All right." He walked Deborah to the door. "I'll let you know if I hear anything." He nodded to Joanna. "Good meeting you, Ms. Davis. Sorry it couldn't be under different circumstances."

Joanna got to her feet, nodded at him as Deborah headed for the outer door.

"Are we going to the meeting tonight?" Joanna asked as they walked back downtown.

"No, I think it's too soon. I'd be surprised if anything gets done tonight other than just the organization letting off steam, airing what everyone knows or what they think they know. I've said my piece to Carolyn and she'll use it for what it's worth."

"That was the purpose of lunch yesterday?"

"Yeah. I figured Carolyn would be hanging around. The commune owns the diner." She stepped around a puddle. "Carolyn and I disagree on contracts, but I don't think she believes I would abuse anyone. That's a whole different ball game. And if she heard anything to the contrary, I think that she'd defend you, if not me."

"You have a clear picture of how to use people, don't you, Deborah?"

"No, not clear at all. I figure it's just part of a network, maybe not of friends but women who want to stay alive. Carolyn and I don't see eye to eye about a lot of things, but she knew I was right even as they voted me out of the commune. She covered me for quite a few months. For the past couple of years, I've supplied them with produce that they otherwise would not have had access to. She's a good strong woman."

"You hit on her?"

Deborah laughed. "No, she made it clear that she wasn't interested, more's the pity. But I wouldn't deny that woman enriched my fantasy life for quite a few months." She glanced at Joanna, amused and encouraged. As much as she had dreaded this trip with Joanna, and as badly as it had started, something was different. She took it as an encouraging sign Joanna's acceptance of being on contract with her.

"Now, one more thing before we leave." She wondered if Joanna would really believe what she was about to say. "Anyone you want to contact?"

Joanna stopped dead, staring incredulously at Deborah. "What—what do you mean?"

Deborah cocked an eyebrow. Joanna might not believe her but it still seemed like the considerate thing to do. "You must have someone somewhere who's worried about you. A lover, friends at least. Family. Communication isn't one hundred percent dependable but it's pretty good. You can send a message letting them know that you're safe."

"Safe? What? That I got shanghaied and now I'm working as a contract laborer on some two-bit farm for God knows how long?"

Deborah's eyes narrowed at Joanna's description and she bit back the first words she wanted to spit out. "If someone I loved was missing," she said instead, "I'd be overjoyed just to learn they were alive." She paused. "But the choice is yours. You know your situation best." When Joanna glared at her without responding, she turned back downtown.

"Let's see if we can catch the early train. I think I've had about all the bad news that I can stand on one trip. You have any objections?"

"My time is your time," Joanna replied through gritted teeth.

Deborah took Joanna's response as a no regarding communication and gave it a mental shrug. Another note to make in the Joanna file and puzzle about later.

* * *

They did catch the early train and it did stop at the Lincoln Diner, an arrangement that Luella had nurtured through the years of serving good food to the railroad crews. They got the first choice of everything and first-class service. Still, Deborah was a little surprised when the first three things that she and Joanna ordered were already gone. When the order finally settled, Deborah requested a word with Luella.

"What's up?" the older heavyset woman greeted her as she slid into the booth after bringing their plates over.

"How's your food supply chain holding out?" Deborah was right to the point with one eye on Joanna's eating and the other eye on the train crew finishing up their meal.

Luella shook her head. "Harder and harder."

"I'm expanding," Deborah said flatly. "I think we can grow more of the garden items and have enough to sell. Would you be interested? No supplier to go through."

"Truck farming," Luella confirmed. She looked away but Deborah knew that meant she was considering it. "Depends. Which vegetables? I don't need no fancy stuff, just plain regular."

"Now's the time to speak up," Deborah said. "We're in the planning stages. You can be in on this." She watched the first of the train crew push back their plates. Luella saw it too and was already getting up.

"You come back next couple of days," she said as she left the table. "We'll talk about this more."

Deborah nodded, turning to Joanna. "Chow down, we've got about three more minutes."

* * *

"Well, ladies," Deborah was saying in greeting as Joanna sat down at the dinner table. "I see you survived nicely without us. I trust it was an uneventful time."

"How are things in town?" Linda asked before anyone could answer.

"About the same," Deborah replied as they began to pass the dishes. Joanna wondered just what Deborah would report. "Business opportunities might be coming, got the population stirred up a bit but it's only a possibility."

"How possible?" Brea asked.

Deborah shook her head. "Hard to tell at this point. You know how rumors go." She sounded very noncommittal. "Remains to be seen."

"Chance to do any selling?" Brea asked.

Deborah wagged her head. "Maybe, maybe not. Did talk to Luella about the possibility of supplying the diner. She was running out of food, and indicated an interest."

"She solvent?" Linda asked. "I know she's a good cook and the train's running more regular."

"From everything I've seen and heard," Deborah replied. "Might be a good way to start our selling. You gals come up with any ideas?"

"How do you feel about goats?"

Deborah looked up at Linda in surprise and turned up her nose. "I'm more of a beef person."

"Goats don't take the resources cattle do, they can survive on less. They produce milk."

Deborah rolled her eyes around as she did when she was thinking. Joanna watched to see just how flexible Deborah might be with this. "Think there might be enough of a market? This is the middle of beef and pork country."

"It's possible—meat's meat. If it can be had, might be better than possum or coon."

"True enough," Deborah replied with a grimace. She glanced around the table. "We put goat on the table, you all gonna turn into vegetarians like you did with the bunnies?"

"That's not fair," Sue spoke up. "Those bunnies were cute."

"Nothing's that cute when you're hungry," Deborah observed. "Anything else?"

Karen hunched forward. "We think we can expand the gardens if you think you can sell the produce. If the trains are running more, then we can pack it into town. But there's no sense doing all that work if the market isn't there."

"Oh, the market's there. People always have to eat. Whether the money's there is another story."

"Barter?" Sara interjected.

"For?" Deborah came back with. "No sense taking stuff we can't use. What do we need?" No one answered.

"Got to be something. Even if it's only work as a trade-off. We've had good luck with the gardens," Brea pointed out.

"The orchard looks good," Linda chimed in. "We had good crops last fall, peaches, apples. I found an old cider press in the shed. If we made cider, it'll be a way to take care of our surplus."

Ideas circled the table and Joanna listened without contributing. Everyone else except Bobbi, who sat back saying little, had a suggestion. She was city-bred, a bureaucrat, and this was probably as much out of her league as it was out of Joanna's.

"What do you think, Joanna?"

Joanna came back with a start, as she hadn't been paying attention. "What?"

"You've been around the state more. What's the food situation?"

Joanna was loath to volunteer anything. "There were food riots down in the southern part of the state, a lot of hungry people. With the transportation infrastructure broken, can't always get food in. With the population centers in the east and then all the misplaced folks, demand exceeds the supply."

"So transportation's the problem," Rae pointed out.

"And if people don't have the money, how are they going to pay?" Deborah asked.

"It isn't always the money," Joanna said sharply, forgetting herself. She swallowed when everyone turned to look at her. "People are starving in other parts of the country," she protested at the various expressions. "You people here have more food on the table now than some areas have seen in days." She watched the guilty expressions avoid her. She looked at Deborah who met her gaze with acknowledgment.

"Yes," Deborah said quietly. "I've heard that it's still bad in other areas, very bad. And you're right, it's not always the money. But there has to be give and take, sometimes it's about pride, and for some people, pride is all they've got."

Joanna clamped her mouth shut.

"And we can't feel guilty because we have something which others don't," Deborah went on casually. "This is what we've worked for. This is rebuilding and if we can share it, that's great. Our doing without won't help anyone." There was silence around the table. "Isn't that our point?" Deborah went on. "To survive, and to help others survive. Our economy, our government in lots of ways, has tanked. But it can be rebuilt."

"What," Joanna spat out. She hadn't realized how guilty she felt for being comfortable. "So the rich can get richer, and the poor, poorer?"

Deborah didn't seem perturbed. "Hungry is hungry and I've never seen anyone get much sustenance from cold hard cash. You can't eat cash. Maybe this time, if we as a society rebuild carefully, we won't make a god of the almighty dollar. And maybe we won't be so greedy. Maybe God or the powers that be were sending us a message with all these disasters. I don't know. I'm not sure anyone does." She looked around the table. "I'm not into charity. Like I said, I think everyone has pride so they have to feel like they're paying something. But I'm not necessarily after the cash either. There's a middle ground."

"Where?" Peg asked reasonably.

"Wherever we find it." Deborah looked around the table. "Now did you come up with anything else?"

Joanna barely listened to the ideas that were floated around the table. She had seen too many homeless, too many go hungry, too many food lines, people ripe for the pickings by others who had resources to exploit them. She had seen people die and no one do anything. Now it just seemed like these women were taking advantage of people in desperate need. She hated being part of it. When she had finished eating, she abruptly got up and stormed away.

She went out the back door to attend to the chickens, her responsibility now. She had no idea whether it had been Karen's or Deborah's quirky sense of humor or just plain retaliation. Someone else would have taken care of them in her absence but she still went to check on them. As soon as she appeared, they all came running toward her. She leaned on the fence, where Peg found her.

"You okay?"

"I guess so." Joanna looked across the field, a peaceful—looking view that contrasted with her turmoil. "You just don't know."

"Joanna, we all came from hard times, some harder than others. So, are we supposed to feel guilty when we're eating because someone somewhere is hungry? Do you suppose someone felt guilty when we only had beans to eat or had coon on the table?"

"Coon?" Joanna jerked around but from the look on Peg's face, she wasn't kidding.

"Karen's a big meat-and-potatoes person. Beans don't do much for her and those first years, we ate a lot of beans. Deborah's hoarding the chickens, for the eggs, and coaxing the setting hen so we can have more little chicks. Karen's counting eggs and trying to figure out which hen isn't laying so she can stew her. She was ready to kill a chicken if they didn't get some meat. About then, eggs went missing. Deborah thought it might be Karen." Peg smiled as she told the story but there was a grimness behind the smile. "Deborah took to guarding the chickens, discovered it was a coon, so she killed it and decided to serve it up."

"Coon? Rodent, masked face?"

Peg nodded.

"How it was?" Joanna asked cautiously. She wasn't sure she wanted to know and then she suddenly appreciated the advantage of working in the kitchen. At least then it wouldn't be mystery meat.

Peg gazed across the chicken yard. "Tough, she didn't cook it long enough. Next one was better. She stewed it." She shrugged her shoulders. "Hard times. We were pretty lean for a while." She fell silent.

Joanna tried to imagine it. Yes, she had been hungry but coon? "Did you eat it?" she asked suddenly.

Peg gave a mirthless laugh, pushed away from the fence and clapped Joanna on the shoulder. "Ahh, honey, I was in the army. If it didn't move, I ate it and didn't ask questions." She didn't take her hand from Joanna's shoulder.

"So I shouldn't feel guilty for eating regularly?" She glanced at Peg.

"We won't save anyone by starving ourselves, and if we can spread it around, well, we might help others survive."

"It's not fair."

"No." And Peg didn't elaborate.

They stood in silence for a few more minutes then Peg casually said, "Everyone's out in the shed, having a little meeting while Deborah's in her office. They'd like us to join them."

Joanna turned her head to see Peg in the dusk. "What kind of meeting?"

Peg gave a shrug. "Just a meeting. We do that occasionally when Deborah's occupied."

About Deborah? Away from Deborah? Joanna was surprised. "Why didn't you just have it while we were gone?"

"'Cause you couldn't be there. Didn't want to exclude you." Peg's voice was casual but Joanna could hear a certain tension. "I suspect it also had a lot to do with the fact you're the one who went to town with her."

Joanna's mouth went dry. "Does she know about these meetings?"

Peg raised an eyebrow but she didn't answer directly. "What do you think?" She turned and looked toward the house. "I suspect she does." She turned to go. "Do you want to go? I figured it'd be just what you've been looking for."

"Are you going?"

"Wouldn't miss it for the world."

Joanna went with Peg to the far stable, tucked to one side so voices wouldn't carry. No one was talking much as they came in and Brea slipped outside as soon as Peg and Joanna took a seat.

Joanna saw impassive faces examining her. She had the belated thought that if they doubted what Deborah had told them, they now had her to verify it. Deborah would know that. A tightrope stretched over an unknown abyss.

"Joanna," Sara began in her quiet soothing voice. "We know that Deborah was in a pissy mood when she left but came back in a fairly good mood. She didn't say much about her trip to town this time. We were just wondering if anything happened."

Joanna shrugged noncommittally. "I'm not sure if I'm the one to ask." Several quickly spoke in protest and Joanna held up her hand. "Yeah, I was there, but I don't know the town. I'm not sure I would have recognized anything significant." She looked around the circle. "We went to the hotel." She wasn't sure she wanted to mention that fiasco. "They weren't particularly happy to see me, so Deborah got to be irritable with them." Chuckles went around the circle because they all knew what it was like to irritate Deborah when she was in a bad frame of mind. "We went to the courthouse where it wasn't much better. They didn't know what was going on and Deborah was caustic with them."

"Judy still working there?" Linda asked.

"Yeah. She was the one. I thought Deborah was going to crawl over the desk. I take it there's some issues between them."

Linda nodded and Peg spoke up beside her. "Old issues."

"Deborah talked to Judy's supervisor, said her lawyer would take care of it. I guess he did. We didn't have to go back." She continued with an abbreviated recap. Eyebrows rose when she said they ate at Nature's Bounty and Carolyn stopped by.

"So you met Carolyn?" Bobbi asked.

"Well, I wouldn't say we've met. She was going right for Deborah, something about an anticontract meeting and that she was threatening to toss Deborah out if she showed up." She realized that Deborah had omitted any discussion of a contract processing facility coming in and decided it might be better if she didn't mention it, at least for now. "I don't think she gave me more than a casual glance."

"Oh, some meeting happening. About time," Bobbi commented. "What was Deborah's response?"

"Not against it," Joanna could say truthfully. "She just didn't think Carolyn was going to get very far. She still maintains contracts are a matter of survival."

That went down with varying degrees of acceptance.

"Did you see anyone else?" Linda asked slowly.

"Everyone," Joanna said flatly. "Deborah talked to more people than I can remember, and talked, flirted, argued with anyone and everyone. Don't ask if I can remember anyone because after the first three places, it was a blur."

Glances were exchanged but she had no idea why, and she had the uneasy feeling she was being interrogated. She wasn't sure she liked it.

"Anyone else?"

"No one special, except the lawyer."

"How was everything at the Bounty?" Peg asked thoughtfully. "Service okay? Enough food? Look like they were doing good business?"

"Service was okay, I guess. Not up to the same level as Luella's. Even that's having problems. First couple of things we ordered, she didn't have. That's why she was so interested when Deborah said she was expanding."

"Carolyn's place, the Bounty," Sue commented. "How'd it look? I mean, was it clean, bright? Look like they had business going?"

Joanna shook her head. "Looked poor, like they were struggling. Wasn't anyone else in there while we were there." She saw the glances exchanged. "Why?"

"It'll be bad if the diner goes under," Peg said slowly.

"Why? I thought it was run by the commune and Deborah didn't like the commune."

Peg straightened up. "She doesn't, but they're a buffer. They're on the fringes ideology-wise, draw a lot of attention. As long as folks are looking at them, they're not looking at Deborah."

And Deborah doesn't want to be watched, never did. "Hmmmm," was all Joanna could comment.

"Go anywhere else?" Karen said, seeming to Joanna to feign disinterest. Joanna was beginning to feel annoyed.

"Diner, town—hotel, courthouse, lawyer, all over. Back to the diner, home." She looked around, trying to read them, trying to understand what they weren't saying.

"See a tall dark-haired, good-looking guy, lanky, laid-back?"

Joanna turned to Peg. "Todd Lancaster? A friend of Deborah's?" Peg looked askance, and there was guarded interest as well as surprise. "I met him at the diner when Deborah won my contract originally. No, I didn't see him this trip. Should I have?"

Peg shrugged and frowned. "Just wondering."

"Look," Joanna said suddenly, "I get the feeling you're all fishing, and I'm the lake. I don't know what you're looking for, but—" she shook her head as she looked around at them, "I don't know there's anything more I can tell you."

Sara leaned forward. "It's not that we doubt what Deborah tells us, but we think she leaves things out." She looked at Joanna knowingly. "That's the part we want to know, what she leaves out."

"So go along with her next time," Joanna said sharply. "Deborah tells me that you're not confined here. Or was she lying to me?" She faced them defiantly.

"No, she wasn't lying," Linda said slowly. "But we never know when we go along, how tailored it is for us. And while Beth does go out, she goes wherever she's needed to do doctoring. Her trips give us some information but not necessarily what Deborah does.

You're going to be going with her all the time, and she can't tailor all of it."

"Can't you go out by yourselves?"

"Sure," Karen said, "but where are we going to go? We don't have a lot of cash in our pockets. We're still outsiders in the area, most of us. We don't have Deborah's network."

"Whose fault is that?"

"No one's," Linda answered. "She just has the in because she was raised here and gets out a lot."

Joanna looked around the circle, fixed her gaze on Linda. "But you're local, you know people. You must have friends around here."

Linda did not move from leaning against the wall, her hands clasped across her stomach. "Deborah and I never looked at things quite the same way. We're tight with each other but we never had the same circle of friends. And we still don't."

"So she doesn't confide in you?"

Linda gave a slow smile. "Deborah doesn't confide in anybody."

"We'd like to know what she's planning," Karen cut in.

"And you think she's going to tell me?" Joanna asked in disbelief.

"No, but we see you as an intelligent woman who can certainly draw conclusions from where Deborah goes and who she sees," Sara said slowly.

"Are you asking me to spy on her?"

"No…" Sara said in a drawn out way. "We'd like some hint about what she's not saying."

"Why?" Joanna's tone was sharp. This was a completely different side of the group than she'd seen before.

"We're all gambling on Deborah's success. Our survival depends on it. If we don't know what she's up to, we're acting blindly. I don't know about the others, I'm not fond of acting blindly. And while Deborah's pulled us through so far, maybe we want a little more assurance that it will continue."

"Then why don't you ask her?" Joanna retorted.

"We don't think she'll tell us and we need to know more," Beth said. "We're hoping you can tell us the things that we're missing."

Joanna stood up abruptly. This was too much on top of the trip with Deborah. "I don't know what I can tell you. Like I said, I don't know the area. And I don't know the people. Deborah leads me around like a puppy on a leash."

"But you'll learn, won't you?" Bobbi said in a tone that seemed half-warning, half-threatening.

"I don't know if I can tell you anything," Joanna said flatly. "And as far as I can see, if you trust Deborah so much, then you can ask her."

Bobbi gave a low mocking laugh. "Deborah's not going to tell us anything. I've never seen a more close-mouthed individual."

"It's probably part of her survival mechanism," Joanna countered tartly. She looked around the room, seeing everyone in a new light. "I can't tell you anything." *And I'm not sure I would if I could.*

"I'm leaving. I don't want to deal with this tonight. I've told you what kind of trip I had. You can take the information any way you want." She started toward the door.

"Joanna, don't say anything to Deborah about this."

Joanna turned around to look back at them. "I might be real new here, and don't know everything that goes on but do you really think all of you disappear at the same time and Deborah doesn't notice? Get real. If you've been meeting clandestinely, it's because she lets you." *Or doesn't think you can do anything to damage her.* "I'm going to bed. And no, I'm not saying anything."

She walked across the yard, unsure how she felt about all of this. Relieved, she decided. They were still thinking for themselves and not just indiscriminately trusting Deborah make the decisions for them. It made her uneasy but she couldn't quite decide why. Walking into the kitchen, she almost ran into Deborah, standing over the kettle. She stopped short.

Deborah looked up. "Isn't it the truth a watched pot never boils?" She gave Joanna a questioning look. "You okay?"

Joanna nodded uncertainly.

"I'm always out of sorts when I get back home, shifting gears I guess. Probably call it a night early. You okay with that?"

"I think so. I'm tired too." She nodded at the kettle. "I'll take care of that. You done in the office?"

Deborah yawned. "Going over expansion plans, wondering what would sell best. But I'm not making sense even to me. You bring that upstairs?"

"Yeah." She paused. "Mind if I join you with a cup tonight?"

"That would be nice."

CHAPTER TEN

Deborah was slicing potatoes into hot grease in the cast-iron skillet as she watched the ham on the griddle across the back of the stove. She was beginning to enjoy breakfast duty. The house was quiet. Those assigned to taking care of the stock were already out. She had left Joanna sleeping, safely locked in. Getting up before everyone else was the closest she could come to truly being alone now, and she relished the luxury. A small price to pay for less sleep.

Ham, eggs, potatoes, corncakes, coffee cake in the oven—the aromas would wake people up soon and the stove had chased off the morning chill. She glanced at the clock when she heard someone on the stairs. She heard the front door open, wondering who else would be up this early and going out the front door. She heard it shut and someone coming through the dining room.

"Deborah?" Sara came into the kitchen, already dressed and ready for the day. "Someone's out front to see you."

"What are you doing up so early?" Sara was one of the house night owls and was rarely awake at this hour.

"Couldn't sleep. I heard someone knocking at the front door when I came down the stairs. It's Carolyn." Deborah's eyebrows went up in surprise. "I've put her in your office," Sara went on. "I'll bring in some coffee in a few minutes." She was already getting down the coffee cups and a tray from the cabinet. "Is the coffee cake about done?"

"Just about, I slid it in right before I put the potatoes on."

Curious, she thought as she headed for her office. This was a first. Something had to be really important to bring Carolyn visiting. Short of the commune burning down, she couldn't think of a thing. She paused at the door, listening to the house, before going in.

"Well, will wonders never cease!" Deborah greeted her visitor in a hearty tone. "And what brings you to greet the wolf in her den at such an early hour?" Carolyn jerked around from examining the bookcase, looking startled. Deborah wasn't sure whether to be amused or insulted. She was curious. Deborah closed the door firmly.

"Go ahead and gloat, Deborah," Carolyn said immediately. "Get it out of your system. You can add to it that the board would probably kill me if they knew I had come out here anyway, just on principle."

Curiouser and curiouser. Carolyn look uncomfortable. "Well, then, if it makes the board uneasy, by all means, have a seat. Just what brings you out here and so early besides?"

Deborah indicated the chair in front of the desk where Carolyn's jacket was already thrown.

"Just like you: right to the point. No friendly niceties. Still blunt to the point of rudeness."

"It would never occur to me that you might walk all the way out here just for a social chit-chat, Carolyn." She turned the other chair around so she wouldn't be sitting behind the desk. The thought did occur to her that she was being a far from gracious hostess. For whatever reason Carolyn had for coming here, there was no sense rubbing her nose in it. At least not until she knew what the reason might be. She was saved from making more blunt comments by a soft rap at the door.

Sara stood there with a tray containing a carafe of coffee, another of hot water, with the little cluster of tea bags, two cups, coffee cake on a cake plate and two plates, forks. Deborah glared at her but let her come in and place the tray on the desk. How was she going to convince Carolyn she wasn't waited on hand and foot by her people when Sara did things like this?

Be nice, Sara mouthed as she faced Deborah, her back to Carolyn for that instance. *Be polite. Don't be caustic.*

"Thank you, Sara." Deborah continued to glower, saw Sara out and took a deep breath. Sara's advice was good. Carolyn wouldn't have come without knowing it would be difficult. They had been at each other for too many years.

Deborah turned back to see Carolyn still standing at the chair, uncertain now. Sara was right—there was no reason to be antagonistic. "Have a seat, Carolyn," she said more warmly. "You're right. I am blunt but I don't mean to be rude. Would you like some coffee? Tea? You look like you've been up most of the night."

"Tea, if you have it," said Carolyn as she sat down. "I took advantage of the moonlight, walked over. Be nice to catch the train back. And I've got to get back before I'm missed." She took the tea from Deborah, cautiously sipped, then blew before she sipped again. She closed her eyes for a moment, as if to gather courage or her thoughts.

Deborah sliced the still-warm coffee cake and put a piece on the plate. There had been a time when she and Carolyn had gotten along. They didn't always agree but were able to agree to disagree. Then Deborah had started signing contracts, which was totally unacceptable to Carolyn.

"I have a favor to ask," Carolyn said finally without looking at Deborah. "A personal one," she added.

Deborah set the coffee cake down on the desk in amazement.

"I don't know if it is something you would want to do," Carolyn continued. "But I thought you might be willing." She stopped again.

Such hesitancy was unlike Carolyn. Deborah recognized Carolyn's discomfort, also unusual. "I guess, Carolyn," she said slowly, doing her best to be receptive, knowing instinctively that Carolyn could easily change her mind about this and say nothing more, "the only way you'll find out is to ask."

Carolyn took the plate of coffee cake, toyed with it but didn't taste it. "You're familiar with ACTS, aren't you?" she said finally.

ACTS again, Deborah thought. Against Contracted Temporary Services. Joanna had asked if she had heard of ACTS. "Most contract holders have," she said dryly. ACTS was irritating initially, as they presented a good argument. However their extreme views now had become downright aggravating. Her contact with them had been limited and she didn't know much about them.

"Yes, I thought you might have. There were some ACTS people at the organizational meeting the other night."

Deborah nodded. ACTS members attending hadn't occurred to her, but Consolidated planning a processing center would certainly have drawn their attention. And, Deborah considered with some annoyance, it probably meant that she might now be a target for ACTS activities as well. That was another mark to hold against Gentry. "Have a decent turnout?" she managed to ask offhandedly.

Carolyn nodded, a little more confidently. "Fair enough, but this is another issue. It has nothing to do with our organizing against Consolidated. I'm only asking you because you have access to sources that we can't get to."

Deborah sat back, saying nothing. She noted the we pronoun, but it was no surprise that Carolyn was a member of ACTS, if in fact that's what the "we" referred to. Whatever the issue, she was going to have to let Carolyn get to it in her own way. She leaned on her chair arms, held her coffee cup and told herself to be patient. "Go on."

"You've made your stand on contracts," Carolyn stumbled on. "I don't want to go into that again. We're not going to change each other's minds." She leaned forward to set her tea on the desk. "But at the same time, you've been outspoken against abuse to the contracts. I thought—because of that, you might…" She stopped.

"What do you want, Carolyn? Just spit it out and stop beating around the bush."

"I don't know how familiar you are with any of the ACTS leaders."

"I have tried to avoid that."

Carolyn nodded. "Okay, I can see why you would." She tried again. "A while back, one of the leaders, a woman, which is why I think you might help us, started getting threats." Carolyn stopped again.

"That wouldn't be unexpected," Deborah said. Carolyn straightened up, bristling. Deborah held her hand up to forestall anything Carolyn might say. "Not acceptable, but yes, I can imagine some people would be pretty upset."

Mollified, Carolyn settled back into the chair. "Upset," she repeated. "Yes, that's a good word." She took a calming breath. "It got pretty bad, evidently there were a couple of really nasty confrontations."

I can imagine, Deborah thought, even as she realized Carolyn was trying to elicit her sympathy, a difficult task considering the subject. Carolyn knew that a woman being threatened would pull Deborah's cooperation, regardless of her feelings about ACTS.

"The decision was finally made that maybe she needed to drop out of sight—for a while at least. She was a bit too recognizable—she used to have national exposure. She was going to head up to Canada for a while."

"That sounds reasonable," Deborah said noncommittally.

"She didn't make it."

The plot thickens. Deborah shifted in her chair. "She get killed?" Deborah really didn't think so. That would have been newsworthy and she did not remember hearing such.

Carolyn gave her a dirty look. "Back to being blunt, aren't you?" She shook her head. "No, not that we know of. She just disappeared. There were several checkpoints she was to stop at, sort of like the Underground Railroad."

"Like those that runaway contracts use," Deborah suggested evenly. She saw no sense in hiding what she knew. Some contract holders actively pursued broken contracts. She never saw sense in it herself. She included a termination clause in her contracts, an easy out for either side rather than having to deal with runaways. She had heard runaways headed for Canada. It sounded perfectly reasonable to her so she assumed there was a method.

Carolyn ignored Deborah's suggestion, neither confirming nor denying. She stopped speaking again.

Deborah didn't see they were getting any closer to the favor and Carolyn was obviously rethinking the issue. Maybe bluntness did work better, at least between her and Carolyn. "So you have a national figure using an underground railroad to go to Canada," she summarized. "And she disappears. Where did she start out from?"

"St. Louis, heading up through Wisconsin."

Deborah considered the geography. What had once been a couple of hours away was now much further, but none of these places were in her backyard. "So what makes you think she ended up here in Indiana? And if she's not here, what do you want me to do? I think it would be a stretch to think that I'd have any knowledge."

"You must have contacts. Contract holders talk to each other. If she did go on contract for whatever reason, she would be hidden and never surface." She hadn't discounted the idea that the woman could have been killed and Deborah could read that valid fear easily enough. "There would be no way that we could locate her, especially if the contract holder knew who she was and wanted to either eliminate her or hide her."

"And you think I could search among the contract holders?"

"Well, yes."

Deborah set her cup on the desk. "And what do you think I can do? Go around asking if anyone has settled old scores with one of the ACTS activists? If they might be sheltering her for some reason? As if they would tell me. Good God, Carolyn. You think that we've got some sort of contract database?"

Carolyn wouldn't look at Deborah. "I know you deal with a different bunch of people and sometimes they like to brag. I thought you might have heard something." Deborah stared at Carolyn uncertain whether to be angry or to laugh at her.

"I thought," Carolyn went on, "you've always advocated for women, even when they're on contract. I thought you might be sympathetic. And there was the fact that this woman is openly gay. She was getting some really ugly hate mail, from a whole gauntlet of people, not just contract holders, but a lot of the militia, as well as the fundamentalists who weren't exactly members of her fan club."

"Anyone else want to do her in?" Deborah asked sarcastically. Carolyn said nothing. Deborah shook her head. It wasn't exactly something she would care to step into. She stretched out her legs and stared at her boots. On the other hand, Carolyn had said that this was a personal favor. Finding someone in this situation would be a challenge, and she might get some mileage out of it. Having Carolyn owe her wouldn't hurt, and ACTS? "They know who I am?"

"I gave your name to the executive board." She paused. "One of them spoke up, said your name was familiar. She couldn't remember how or why."

Interesting. She'd have to think about that later. Right now, if she did take this on, where would she start? "And pray tell, when did all this happen?"

"She missed her Thanksgiving checkpoint."

"Thanksgiving!" Deborah exploded. "My God, woman, that was over six months ago. She could be decomposing in a grave by now." Carolyn winced terribly and Deborah had the fleeting thought she might have gone too far.

"Last year," Carolyn amended.

"Last year? Like eighteen months ago?"

Carolyn nodded, not looking at Deborah.

"Good God!" Deborah looked at Carolyn in disbelief. "What kind of organization…" She trailed off, shaking her head. "For someone so important, you sure as hell lost track of her fast enough. Remind me to never look to you for safe conduct." She watched Carolyn in silence for several minutes. She couldn't believe that any organization wanting to get one of their leaders to safety in Canada would let them drop out of sight this long before they started a search.

"You think," she said finally, "she is on contract somewhere. And that's why you can't check, because you need a contract holder to do the nosing around but not anyone who might be remotely related to ACTS."

Deborah watched Carolyn reach for the tea, nibble at the cake. There was something else there that Carolyn didn't want to talk about. Deborah sat back in the chair. "Carolyn," she said finally, "even if there was some central place where I could check, do you really think that kind of information is going to be out in the open?"

"No," Carolyn said slowly. Clearly she was having an internal debate about how much to tell Deborah. "We know she was caught by the early winter last year and just settled in to wait it out. By spring she had disappeared. So something happened over the winter."

"That's still a year," Deborah said.

"There was some evidence that she got on contract but she had necessarily assumed another identity."

What vulnerability, Deborah thought. "What else can you tell me?" she asked with a resigned sigh. To her surprise, Carolyn shook her head. "What? Not even a name?"

"I don't know what name she was traveling under. And I won't tell you her name. No one wants to advertise she's missing. In case she's at risk, her identity needs to remain hidden."

"Carolyn, be reasonable. You can't have me be on the lookout for an unknown woman with no name who may or may not be on contract." Carolyn shook her head. "So I've just got to be on the lookout for someone boasting about having an erstwhile celebrity as a contract?" Carolyn nodded. "Fuck! Talk about a needle in a haystack." Deborah got up and walked around her desk. "I hope to hell that ACTS is better organized than it seems, Carolyn." She sat down behind the desk and thought about it. "The threats," she said finally. "Anyone go back and check them out?"

Carolyn straightened up. "They were checked out. Most of them were just noise. Some were quasi-serious but they checked out." She took another breath. "We know there weren't any accidents, no Jane Does just waiting to be claimed."

Wonder if Joanna would know anything? Deborah drummed her fingers on the desk. "Anything else?"

"There's militia units all through there. I don't know if you have any contacts. Ours around here seem pretty small time."

Deborah said nothing. Militia units were a closed group about as much as the contract holders were, but they exchanged information. Good. If Carolyn didn't realize how linked they were, Deborah wasn't going to enlighten her.

"Anyway, I thought it was a possibility. I thought you might, seeing that it was a woman, that maybe…"

"I need something more, Carolyn," Deborah said evenly. "You can't have me on the lookout for some woman who may or may not be under contract, who may or may not be abused, who may or may not be against contracts. Shit, you could pull out half the women in this house and they would fit." *Maybe even all of them.*

Carolyn looked unhappy. "I don't know more. As I said, they don't want to advertise she's missing. They certainly don't want the wrong people to find her."

"No, I guess that could be very bad." Deborah frowned. She supposed she could do some nosing around. Some yahoo would be sure to brag if he had someone like that in his hands. "How'd my name come up?"

Carolyn twisted in her seat. "I said I knew someone who might check for us, someone definitely not an ACTS member, who had contacts. I said I thought you could be trusted."

Carolyn vouched for me, well, that's something. "If you're going to trust me to look for someone, you're going to have to trust me with more information than what you've provided," Deborah pointed out. "Something. A name, any name, an area."

Carolyn looked away. "I don't know." The clock struck the hour and she jumped to her feet. "I've got to get back, catch that train. If I miss it, I'll be walking back. Right now no one knows where I'm at." She pulled her coat back on, and glancing at Deborah, said, "I'll see what I can funnel to you, but if you ever let on that it came from me…"

"Yeah, I know. There'll be hell to pay." Deborah stood up and came around the desk. "Can't tell you how many conversations I've had that end like this."

She stood on the porch watching Carolyn walk up the road while she heard everyone gather at the breakfast table. Deborah shook her head. She closed the door and went up the stairs. Time to unlock Joanna and get the day started.

* * *

Joanna sat back on her haunches and wiped the sweat off her face. Midmorning and it was already hot. She couldn't imagine how miserable she would have been if she'd worn the long-sleeved shirt and long pants Beth had recommended instead of the shorts and tank top. She looked up and down the thick rows of strawberry plants to see how far she still had to go as she set the woven boxes into the center of the path for pick up later. She paused to get a breath, picking a berry from one of the boxes, absently hulling it with a thumbnail and popping it in her mouth. Sweet, juicy, warm. A treat from the garden. They grew so well and with little input. Deborah had said they had always been there.

"You doing okay?"

Joanna grimaced. From anyone else, she would have taken it as a rebuke that she was shirking but not from Peg. Peg always sounded like she was truly concerned about Joanna's well-being. "Sore knees, aching back, sunburned neck. About normal I'd say."

Peg laughed. "Yeah, it's not exactly a day at the spa." She wiped her face with her handkerchief. "But at least it seems more rewarding than a lot of other jobs."

"There is that," Joanna agreed. "And I must admit, I've looked at our food in a different light." Joanna got up stiffly and walked to the end of the row to get water from the cooler. She took a few sips, and poured the rest over her handkerchief and tied it around her neck. The cool water trickled down her back and down between her breasts.

She looked at a lot of things in a different light, gazing across to see Deborah also working her way down the row. She had never seen a contract holder work as hard as the contracts, and she did have to give Deborah credit. Deborah was right out there doing everything, which meant, more often than not, Joanna was also there doing everything alongside her. It was hard to complain about shit jobs when she looked beside her to see Deborah doing the same work. True, there were times when she had the easier house tasks when Deborah had office work, but lately that sort of work was getting more difficult. There was canning coming in and working over a hot stove wasn't any better than working in the field. There were days when she thought she would melt and the dog days of summer weren't even close. Two, almost three months here, and she was beginning to appreciate a different point of view. Of farming, of Deborah, of contracts.

"Joanna!" She turned to look at Peg. "When you come back this way, bring some more baskets, will you, please?"

Joanna nodded. Peg could fill up the baskets faster than either she or Deborah could, but at least she was safe in the strawberry patch. Red strawberries were easy to recognize but she had trouble with other plants. She still was of the mind that a green plant was a green plant, and had a hard time telling which was to be pampered and which needed to be weeded out. She dropped the cup back into the water cooler and picked up the stack of pint baskets.

There were parts of the gardens she was not allowed into, a distinction she shared only with Bobbi. Bobbi had even been tossed out of the strawberry patch when someone caught her pulling the runners off the new strawberry plants. "How was I supposed to know?" she had whined. "No one ever told me." Joanna hadn't made that mistake, at least she hadn't before someone had discovered what Bobbi was doing. So Joanna did get snagged for picking the bright red berries and she was relieved she could do something. She still wasn't fond of farming but with limitations, she was willing to do the work. She did like eating. And she understood the connection. Even now as she carried baskets down to Peg, stepping carefully between the plants, she could imagine strawberry shortcake, strawberry jam, strawberry cake, and someone had even mentioned strawberry ice cream.

Now she could understand the work cooperation between Deborah and these women. When they sat down at the dinner table, they knew Deborah wasn't providing them with the food set before them. They were feeding themselves. They had done the hard work. The harvesting and the canning. They had fed the chickens, slopped the hogs, done the labor. Deborah might have provided the land, the means, certainly the planning and sometimes the skill but she hadn't done it alone. And they were quick to point out when someone wasn't pulling their weight. That was the part Joanna had missed with the fiasco of her refusing to work. She still cringed at the memory.

She heard the digs at Bobbi who hated farming with a passion and didn't let a day go by without some comment that this was really beneath her. Her displeasure was largely ignored now, but Joanna realized she did not want to be seen like that. True, there was a lot she didn't know but she made it a point not to complain about any job she was given and at least give it a good try.

She took care of the chickens, feeding twice a day, letting them out in the morning, shutting them up at night, gathering eggs. She couldn't say she was fond of them, especially one old hen who seemed to have it in for her, but she gritted her teeth and did it. Then she was peculiarly pleased when Deborah complimented her, said that Karen had reported egg production up, less strife among the chickens who were strangely sensitive to loud noises and angry ravings. She wasn't sure how she felt about it when the chickens all came running at her when she went out with the basket of cracked corn. Bobbi had asked how she could stand it. She had always been afraid they were going to start pecking on her feet and she had gone around stamping her feet all the time to keep them away. Joanna had shrugged. At least she could do *something* Bobbi couldn't and now had some standing in the group.

"Watch it!" Peg warned suddenly. "Snake."

Joanna froze and watched the black snake slither under the short stems and make his getaway from them. Snakes didn't bother her much, not like Rae who had screamed running down the row upsetting baskets of berries in an effort to get away from the snake who was surely slithering as quickly as possible from the loud noise. Rae didn't come back to the berry patch often anymore either.

Now Joanna glanced up at Peg, still picking but keeping one eye on the lookout. She liked working with Peg. The woman had a very calming presence and didn't say much, but there was an air of competence and assurance about her. Joanna had been surprised to find out she hadn't been raised on a farm. She talked about several places she had lived but that was just incidentally. In fact, she didn't have much to say about her past.

Joanna set her full basket of berries out of the row to be picked up later. She had to admit it was nice being part of the group. With *him*, she had been isolated, moving around too much, no friends, no support. And before, well, there were meetings and gatherings, and yes, there were friends, but not like this. There was a togetherness, a family feeling in this group.

She had worked with almost everyone by now and she still wasn't sure who her attackers had been. It had bothered her at first but it lessened as time went on. After the attack, after she had finished cleaning the chicken house out, everyone had started talking to her again. There had even been some pointed teasing about chickens when she was assigned them, even about her "vacation," her confinement in the stable, and it took a few days before it sank in to Joanna that they weren't being unkind. This had happened, this was the reaction. It was all out in the open and now she was back in the fold. Now she was part of the group.

The only thing that bothered her slightly were her debriefings, which she had taken to calling the group's interrogation after a trip away with Deborah. How could she explain that Deborah just seemed to be neighborly, stopping in to see families, see how they were doing, exchanging gossip? They went to Richmond about every two weeks, and made weekly trips to Luella's. Sometimes, to Joanna's frustration, Deborah just went up to the diner for a cup of coffee. The goal seemed to be to sell produce but Joanna suspected there was something else going on.

She had thought, began to hope maybe, they might stop at the commune, the Lincoln Land Co-op, she had learned was its formal name. She was beginning to hear more about it, both from the members of the household and outsiders, rarely from Deborah. Joanna began to think the commune, and more specifically Carolyn, might be able to help her, if she could ever talk to her, make contact with her. She was anticontract, that was for certain, but whether she would be able to actually help, Joanna had no idea.

Joanna hadn't given up the idea of escape but it was harder to hold on to. Deborah had been right: the work was hard, exhaustingly so. Maybe she didn't have the energy to think of how to get away. Maybe she didn't feel so abused when she looked around and saw that everyone was working just as hard as she was, if not harder. It was simple—if they worked hard, there was food on the table. They had good times, someone was always telling a story and they were all from different walks so stories were interesting. Good-natured discussions with different points of view. They had impromptu parties. They played. If she could ignore the contracts, she could almost...

"Joanna."

She looked up into the sunlight to see Deborah standing over her, ominous and menacing. She blinked, sunspots in front of her eyes. It was just Deborah blocking the sun, not menacing at all.

"You need to go inside, you're all red, sunburnt."

"I'm all right."

"No," Deborah said shortly. "There's no need for you to get heat stroke. Go see Beth. Now."

Joanna looked from Deborah to Peg and back. She didn't want to be thought a shirker.

"I'll finish the row," Peg said easily. "Just about done anyhow. This is about where I started yesterday."

"Vinegar water," Beth said when she saw the sunburn. "I told you to cover up more, wear something heavier. You're too fair to be outside that much so soon. I'll have Karen put you on housekeeping for a day or two."

"God, no, don't, please. I hate housekeeping."

"You need to be out of the sun for a bit, let that tan. Cooking detail?"

"Not after I burned the beans. The only thing Sue lets me do in the kitchen is dishes."

Beth leaned over to ask in a low voice. "Tell me: did Karen bribe you?"

Joanna frowned and then remembered Karen's aversion to beans. She laughed. "No. Just my mind wandering."

Beth straightened up. "Wouldn't have been surprised. How about laundry duty then?"

Joanna shrugged her shoulders. "I guess if those are my choices."

* * *

Joanna showed up at the washhouse the next morning after breakfast. She hadn't been exactly overjoyed to discover she was working with Bobbi. She never felt completely comfortable with the woman since that first night at the introduction party when she walked out the front door and Bobbi had followed her. She still wasn't sure whether Bobbi had told Deborah, although Deborah had never mentioned it.

"Morning," she greeted Bobbi as she was pulling the tubs down.

Bobbi looked over her shoulder, first at Joanna and then behind her. "Morning," she greeted as she set up the tubs. "You lose your keeper today or she just let you off the leash?"

Joanna shook her head. The way Bobbi always brought up Deborah's supervision grated. No one else mentioned it but Bobbi never failed to. "I suppose she's around," she commented as she started to work. She pulled forth the James washer from the corner and thought how nice it would be if the hot water supply could be expanded the way Deborah had hinted at. She started filling the tubs to soak the dirtiest clothes.

Bobbi seemed to have taken upon herself the responsibility of watching her if Deborah weren't in sight. Joanna acknowledged Deborah might well have instructed someone to do so but she didn't think Bobbi would be Deborah's choice, and she thought she would have told her about it. Aside from that, Bobbi never had a good word to say about Deborah. Not that Joanna was a member of Deborah's fan club but she was beginning to see Deborah in her own light, and not as a contract holder.

"I have to give you credit," Bobbi said smoothly as she agitated the clothes. "You've settled in real well." She paused a moment as if making sure she had Joanna's attention. "I mean you're joined to Deborah at the hip for the most part, and it can't be easy."

Joanna went on working. Easy wasn't how she would have described it but at the same time, she knew how bad being a contract could be. Deborah had promised to treat Joanna as well as anyone else in the house, and she had kept her word. And she managed her legal obligations without being heavy-handed about it.

"I mean, it wouldn't be easy under most circumstances, even if you were only just opposed to contracts on principle. But from your position and everything you've done to actively campaign against contracts, well, it's got to be galling."

Joanna froze. Of all the places she had expected this to seep out, it wasn't from here. She held her breath and Bobbi went on.

"So I can see that you would want to keep a low profile. Deborah's not exactly known for being easy on those who challenge her."

"Oh?" Joanna said in what she hoped was a neutral tone without turning around.

"You know," Bobbi continued in that sly insinuating voice, "I've been helping Karen make the deliveries to the diner."

Only because she can keep an eye on you and you can't screw it up.

"I've had a chance to talk to some of the regulars there."

"I'm surprised you'd talk to anyone so far beneath you."

"Yeah, well, sometimes you get good information that way." Bobbi seemed to ignore or be oblivious to Joanna's meaning. "Did you know that Deborah killed someone?"

Joanna paused and then she remembered Hetty and the impression Deborah had left at the diner. "Rumors. Innuendo. I heard that one about Hetty and I know that's not true."

"No." Bobbi stopped agitating the washer in her excitement about the story. "It was some guy, not long after she came back. Well, maybe not right after but pretty early. She was living alone then, and he'd been doing some work for her. He'd been bragging to his buddies that he'd show that dyke what a man could do."

Just the tone chilled Joanna.

"He was a real asshole, you know, the kind who says all a dyke needs is a good fuck."

"I'm familiar with that," Joanna said icily. She paused, listening intently.

"Then he disappeared. Just gone. They did an investigation 'cause he worked for Deborah last and she was the last one to see him. She said he got ugly and she fired him. He left, and she hadn't seen him since. But, get this, one of his jobs was to pour some cement, a foundation for one of the buildings. Just fresh laid." Bobbi got into her story eagerly.

Joanna's heart raced. She had just about convinced herself that Deborah couldn't be violent. "So," she said evenly. "Did they dig up the foundation?"

"At first she wouldn't let them, said she'd just laid that cement and she wasn't going to have it torn up. Sheriff went and got a court order. She was real pissed about that." Bobbi sounded so smug.

"And what'd they find?"

"Nothing. She made them cart all that cement to a ditch she was filling in and pour the foundation again. She got real ugly about it before her lawyer settled her down."

"So did they ever find him?"

"Nope, never did. And the whole county thinks Deborah killed him. They might be saying that he deserved it, and that she was probably justified, but just the same, she killed him."

Joanna went back to washing. "Sounds like a story you tell kids to make them behave."

"Yeah, maybe so. But there's always that question now, isn't there? And let me tell you, from the things I've heard, no one really wants to cross her."

"Pshaw! You listen to too much gossip, Bobbi. And you're too quick to believe the bad things about her."

"I just know that she couldn't own something like this and be left alone if there wasn't some heavy protection around. And I don't think she's one likely to say 'oh pretty please, leave me and my girls alone.'"

Yes, Bobbi had a point with that, Joanna considered. No one bothered their crops or stock in spite of their isolation. And just the image of Deborah saying "pretty please" for anything to anyone was enough to make Joanna laugh. She turned on Bobbi with some contempt. "Something I don't understand, Bobbi. Why are you so eager to tear Deborah down? Especially when you're hiding behind her—" She stopped, almost said skirts, "shirttails. You really want to see her fail? And if she does, what the hell are you going to do?"

"Well, I—I just get tired of her being so high and mighty."

"What's wrong, Bobbi?" Joanna came back with. "I think you're jealous."

"What's there to be jealous of?" Bobbi demanded.

"Because Deborah managed to hold on and not lose everything," Joanna said flatly. "I may not like how she's done it, and there may have been other ways or even better ways, but she hasn't just dried up and disappeared. She's done what she said she would do. And like you said, she's not one to be crossed. So if I were you, I'd stop snapping at her heels. Sooner or later, she's going to get tired of it and deal with it."

"And what about you?" Bobbi sneered. "What'll you do when she finds out about you?"

"Well, I guess we'll just wait and see, won't we? Unless you're going to go running to her and tell. You seem like that kind of talebearer. But I tell you, I'd rather deal with Deborah face to face rather than some little sneak who's constantly at my back."

Karen stuck her head in the door just then. "Are we having problems?"

"No," Bobbi said quickly.

"Yes," Joanna said firmly. She stepped away from the washer. "Assign me somewhere else today—I don't care where or what. Just not with her."

* * *

Deborah was in her office after dinner. Joanna, she knew, was on kitchen duty, so she was secure. She frowned at the list of names on her list, all the contract holders she knew of in the county. She had been approached last year about joining an organization of contract holders, but had told them she wasn't interested. Now she regretted her point-blank refusal. The mystery woman wasn't in the region, not that she expected her to be if she'd been traveling in Illinois. If so, no one was bragging, and she hadn't heard of anyone new. But in the surrounding counties there were larger communities, more industry. More troubles. She could go there, but she didn't relish the idea. Traveling was troublesome, although trains were beginning to run more. And she didn't like drawing attention to herself or her holdings.

She looked up at the soft knock on her door. "Karen, what's up?"

"Can we talk?"

"Sure." She closed the folder and sat back, surprised when Karen closed the door. "Something wrong?"

"Got a problem." Karen pulled the straight chair forward and turned it around to sit on it backward, her folded arms across the back. "Joanna asked to be reassigned today."

Deborah raised her eyebrows but said nothing.

"She was working with Bobbi in the laundry."

Bobbi again. Deborah didn't say anything but she mentally kicked herself for ever acquiring Bobbi on contract. Karen squirmed, clearly uncomfortable. "What happened?"

"I don't know. Joanna didn't say. When I walked by, I heard Joanna saying something about a confrontation but not enough to know anything. When I stuck my head in, Bobbi said there wasn't a problem but Joanna requested to do something else, anything else."

"So she wasn't refusing to work?"

"No. In fact, I put her in the hog lot and you know that's crappy work. She never said anything, just went to work."

"Any idea what it was about?" Karen shook her head. "So how's she doing otherwise?"

"Great. She's a willing worker now, never complains. She gets along with everyone. Now she's got the score, she fits right in. Except with Bobbi."

"Well, she's hardly exceptional there."

"No," Karen agreed. "That's for sure. Wish Bobbi would get the score. She's about as useful as tits on a boar hog." She shook her head and rested her chin on her folded arms.

"Sounds like you handled it all right if that's what you're asking. If you're asking for another solution, I don't have one. You've done a good job planning the work force."

"Sure it wouldn't help if you had a talk with Bobbi?"

"Most definitely not," Deborah replied. "I'm sure that would make it worse. And in case the thought even crosses your mind, a little unit discipline like what happened to Joanna had better not happen." Karen gave her a questioning glance. Deborah went on. "Bobbi's just the type to go running to the labor board. They'll just open a can of worms that I don't want to deal with."

Karen frowned. "I suppose you're right. And yes, she'd squeal like a stuck pig. But she's a troublemaker. Most of us have figured that out but I'm not sure about Joanna. She's settled down quite a bit but there's still something there spooking her. I don't know what buttons Bobbi pushes but I'd bet my bottom dollar—if I had one—that if anyone could find Joanna's buttons, Bobbi can. She is one conniving bitch."

"Okay. I'll see if I can say something to Joanna tonight, find out something. But don't hold your breath. She's not likely to turn anyone in, even someone like Bobbi."

"More's the pity."

When Karen left, Deborah mused. Joanna and Bobbi. What to do?

* * *

"How was your day?" Deborah asked as she and Joanna went up the front stairs that night.

"So-so. Back feels better, skin's tight. Peg said I looked like a lobster, broiled. She gave me a rubdown."

"Yes," Deborah said absently. "She gives good rubdowns."

Joanna turned. "How do you know?"

Ooops, Deborah thought. "She's given me a few," she said casually as they went into the bedroom and Deborah locked the door. She ignored Joanna's puzzled look as she tried to remember if Peg had ever given anyone at the house a back rub. She couldn't remember, and the longer she thought about it, the more certain she was that Peg hadn't. And vaguely she remembered Peg saying how intimate she considered back rubs. So she had given Joanna a back rub. Now that was interesting…

CHAPTER ELEVEN

After the dishes were done Deborah stepped out on the side porch and stretched. The cool breeze after a hot day was a welcome respite from the gardening. The additional crops were coming in and she was gratified as she glanced over the stack of boxes and baskets in the corner ready for the next morning's picking. Luella was taking everything for the diner that they could grow and Sue was organizing the canning for their own supplies. Karen wondered if they needed another root cellar but Deborah didn't think so. At least not this year.

Then again, extra stores for the winter might not be bad, be able to sell some. From what she had seen as she wandered around the countryside, not everyone had such a good cropping. The idea was just beginning to go around the county that she might set the standard for some time to come.

She leaned against the column and gazed off into the distance. A lot of folks had thought they would coast through a short bad time. Deborah had never thought that. She had thought that recovery after the Great Earthquake and the resulting collapse would take a long time and had made plans accordingly. If she was wrong, so much the better, but so far she hadn't been.

More and more of her neighbors were agreeing with her, to her surprise. They were slowly changing their expectations and even more surprising to her, they were changing their opinions about contracts. She provided the example that owning a contract was not necessarily an evil thing. Acquiring Joanna's contract at the diner had been seen as a kindly rescue by several folk. Gentry had left a bad taste in their mouths.

She wished Joanna could see it as a rescue, although she had been better, more settled, more secure the past couple of weeks. She didn't act as if Deborah was going to jump her bones at the first opportunity. She was turning into a steady worker. She didn't complain. She was responsible. Deborah was cautiously letting down her guard around her.

Then there was this other thing, Carolyn's missing woman. Besides the advantages of doing a favor for Carolyn, this search was forcing her to reach out and make contact with other contract holders. Most of them were small holders, like herself. They were just trying to help people survive. This outreach bit was not something she would have done under normal circumstances, she smiled ruefully, but she had to admit that she took some enjoyment from it.

Now maybe it was time to go a little further afield in her search but she didn't know what to do with Joanna. As Sara had so tactfully pointed out, she couldn't just lock her up and leave her, and she wasn't sure Joanna would be welcomed in some of the places she thought about going, nor whether Joanna would be comfortable with it.

"A penny for your thoughts?"

She turned around to see Linda. "Hey. What's up?"

Linda glanced around to check that they were quite alone. She pulled an envelope from her hip pocket. "Found this on the back gate when I went after that blamed goat you brought back. That stupid creature I swear to God can climb a fence."

"Can't be too stupid then." Deborah examined both sides of the envelope. The paper was dry and brittle as if it had been dampened by the morning dew and then baked dry. "He must know what we've got planned for him and wants to make his getaway while he has the chance."

"Well, he's one creature I won't mind having on the dinner table."

Deborah slit the envelope and pulled out the folded paper. After she read it, she folded it back and tucked it into her pocket.

"Good news? Bad news?"

"Yeah, a bit of both." Deborah frowned. "Marv's on his way back through." She frowned as she considered. "Wants to meet, probably needs something else. I need to see him, but I'd like to do so alone. I'll need to sort out Joanna's supervision." Deborah looked back at the sky. "Think we'll get any rain soon?"

"Don't think so. Wish we would. It'd be easier than watering the gardens."

"Think Crockett'll be cutting hay?"

Linda pursed her lips. "A bit early but maybe. It was wet enough earlier for good growing and now it's dry. Might be cutting before the rains come again. Why?"

"He's got all those sons, only one daughter. Wonder if he'd like some kitchen help for a couple of days during the haying?"

Linda nodded. "Could be but I wouldn't send Joanna alone. I don't think either side would be comfortable. Maybe Peg?"

"Think she could bridge the gap?"

"I think Joanna's comfortable enough with her. And face it, stepping into the Mennonite society might be pretty strange for her. She doesn't strike me as adaptable. But Peg is."

"Actually, I think she'd do pretty good at Crockett's, a damn sight better than with Marv." She opened the door to the house. "That might be the best solution all around. Why don't you wander over there and feel him out, see if he'd be comfortable. If I went over and asked, he'd think that I think his womenfolk can't manage. If you hint as to the mutual benefit, then he might agree."

"What about locking her up?"

"He's out in the middle of nowhere. You know as soon as it gets dark, they lock everything up as tight as a drum just on general principle."

"Okay, I'll go over in the morning. He had a lead about some stock anyway. Wouldn't seem strange me just dropping in."

The next morning while Deborah was on the breakfast detail, she caught Peg to one side. "Got a project for you," she said casually. "If you're willing to do it."

"What's that?"

"I need to make a side trip." No need to explain to Peg what any of her side trips were. "And I can't take Joanna with me on this one." Peg nodded in understanding. "I'm loaning her over to Hiram Crockett. He's doing some haying, could use the kitchen help. I'm afraid it might freak her out if she goes by herself, but she'll be reassured if you go along. I know you don't usually do kitchen work but I thought you might."

Was that a leap of eagerness in her face? Deborah wondered but the expression was so fleeting, she wasn't sure.

"I think I might be able to handle that," Peg said in her same casual easy tones. "That going to meet the conditions?"

"She'll be working with the family so she'll be supervised. Come dark, they lock everything up, they're so afraid of someone stealing something. That'll meet the guidelines. I shouldn't take long, two days, maybe three at the most."

Peg nodded, thoughtfully. "You think she'll be comfortable with that?"

"Oh," Deborah couldn't resist jabbing, "I imagine you'll do your best to make her comfortable."

Peg's eyes widened in surprise, and something like an understanding passed between them. "I wouldn't want to step on anyone's toes," she said obliquely.

"Oh, you'll know about it if you do." Deborah turned back to the oven to pull out the coffee cake. "I'll let you know when you're going."

* * *

Five days later Peg and Joanna were dropping backpacks on the twin beds in the small plain room at the Crockett residence. "Deborah do things like this often?" Joanna asked. She hadn't wanted to question Deborah.

"Occasionally," Peg answered without being specific. "Part of being a good neighbor. You know, do favors when there's a need." She looked around, taking in the small table, the dry sink with the double bowl and double pitcher. Probably a room converted for their use. That was all right, their stay was temporary.

Yes, but who is doing whom the favor? Joanna wondered as she slipped out of her shoes. "It would have been nice if she had asked instead of just assuming we would be fine doing it."

Peg shrugged. "Probably had a lot to do with who was available."

"Or," Joanna said in bitter tones, "who might fill all the requirements of the law so she could go off somewhere else without me."

Peg turned and gave Joanna a questioning look. "There is also that possibility."

"So how did you get stuck with me? Did she just order or did you volunteer?"

"Well, I wouldn't have said she laid out an order and she certainly didn't ask for volunteers, but I would have volunteered."

"You what? You would have?" Joanna turned around to face the woman.

"You're pretty nice to work with," Peg went on. "Have some conversation skills, aren't afraid to hold your own position. Have a sense of humor." She smiled. "Seems to me I could do a whole lot worse."

Joanna gave her a quick look, surprised, and then went back to the unpacking. "Thanks," she said ruefully. "That makes me feel halfway human. I know I haven't always been good to work with."

"Told you that first night: take your time, feel your way. You've done pretty good. From what I've gathered, where you came from didn't exactly encourage a cooperative frame of mind."

"Not hardly." Joanna washed her hands and face at the bowl. She looked into the mirror. So much had changed since then.

"So you've had the time to figure things out. And adjust. You're settling in nicely from what I can see."

"That's what Bobbi said."

Peg's head came up sharply. "Bobbi said what?"

"That I was settling in nicely."

"Well, you have, but I'm surprised Bobbi would be aware of such things."

"Bobbi seems to be aware of a lot of things," Joanna muttered half under her breath.

"Bobbi been giving you any trouble?"

Joanna shrugged.

"I know sometimes she can be really irritating. She's just one of those people who lost so much and hasn't been able to find a place for herself."

"She's not the only one who has lost everything," Joanna said tartly. "But she's the only one who goes around stirring up trouble."

Peg pursed her lips. "She does do that." She hesitated. "But you didn't answer my question. Has she been giving you any trouble?"

Joanna shook her head, unready to confide in anyone, even Peg. "She just rubs me the wrong way, like she wants to be one up. What do you think of her?"

Peg closed her bag. "I think she's a troublemaker. But she's here so I deal with her."

Quite a statement for someone who works hard to treat everyone alike, Joanna thought.

Peg brushed back her hair and looked around the room. "Don't let her needle you too badly. Deborah seems to have her mark even if she keeps her around. Now, I guess we'd better go meet our supervisors and see what we can do to help them through their haymaking."

* * *

Joanna lay on her back and stared at the ceiling of the converted milk house. She wasn't fond of being locked in but she took solace in the fact that the house as well as some of the outer buildings were also locked up tight each night. She considered that it might be more difficult for Peg who wasn't accustomed to being so restricted.

"You still awake?" came Peg's voice out of the darkness.

"Yeah." She didn't even turn toward Peg, lying along the right angle wall to her. A cement block table stood in the corner and both single beds came off the sides. "What's wrong? Can't sleep?"

"Not used to going to bed this early. Deborah has a lights out but doesn't mean we can't be up." She heard Peg move around in the bed.

"They do things differently here."

"Probably because they were never set up for electricity to start with. Like all of us, Deborah had all the conveniences and had to adjust to being without."

Because she couldn't see Peg in the darkness, Joanna felt able to ask casually, "Do you know where Deborah went that she didn't want to take me?"

Peg's answer was a split second too long in coming. "No." But then she continued. "That is not exactly right. She goes a couple of places where she doesn't take anyone."

"How come?"

Peg gave a deprecating chuckle. "Well, I 'spect because she doesn't want us to know about them."

"I just wondered," Joanna said slowly, imagining contract houses, finding information on ACTS. Just the thought unsettled her.

"There was talk," Peg said casually, "that she had a girlfriend stashed away somewhere."

"A girlfriend!" Joanna half sat up.

Peg laughed. "Well, it is possible, Joanna. I mean, Deborah's not celibate. Maybe long dry spells, but she's not dead."

Joanna clamped down on the jolt of feeling that raced through her. Was that jealousy? "I thought…I mean."

"That because she said she wasn't sleeping with anyone contracted with her, she wasn't sleeping with *anyone*?" Peg's voice changed direction and Joanna could imagine her rolling over on her side. "Deborah doesn't strike me as the type to kiss and tell."

Joanna didn't know what to say.

"But all of us can have lovers. Why should she deprive herself?"

"I don't know," Joanna stumbled. "I guess I just never thought about it."

"Like imagining your parents having sex?" Peg teased.

"Not exactly," Joanna said as she thought about Deborah being with someone. Actually, she could imagine all too well Deborah being with someone. She just wasn't sure how she felt about it. And that surprised her.

"I mean, haven't you thought about being with someone?"

She'd been dealing with too much for that feeling to come back, although, she admitted, thoughts were beginning to flit through her mind upon occasion. "Who would want me?" she said with some bitterness. Her recent experiences had changed her, and she wasn't sure how she would feel or react if someone did touch her.

"Probably any number of women," Peg responded. Her voice sounded closer.

Joanna shook her head. "No." She closed her eyes, even though she knew Peg couldn't see her. "Not if they knew." She stopped, her mouth dry.

"Knew what?"

Maybe it was because it was dark. Maybe it was because she spent so much time with Peg and she was so nonjudgmental. Maybe it was just because it was time to talk and they were away from the house. "The places I've been, the things I've done." Joanna turned away from Peg as memories flooded her. "No one would want that."

"Well I can't judge what I don't know," Peg said easily, "but I can't imagine you doing anything terrible."

Joanna could just picture the sandy-haired woman, lying on her side, her head propped up on her folded arm. Peg was so wholesome looking, like nothing bad had ever touched her, everyone's pal and never upset. She was competent, easygoing, and now as Joanna thought about it, easy on the eyes. She had this lightly tanned skin that never seemed to darken, light golden honey. Joanna shook her head. She didn't need to go down that path.

"And as for the things that might have been done *to* you," Peg went on, "well, you're hardly responsible for that." Peg's voice was very relaxed, very casual, very supportive. "And if you want to talk about it, I'm willing to listen, but that isn't going to change my feeling about you."

"And what feeling is that?" Joanna asked faintly.

"That you're a survivor, a strong woman who has been wounded and is healing."

Joanna made a choked sound. A strong woman? "No." She swallowed. "Not strong."

"You've survived," Peg pointed out. "Some don't. Actually a lot don't."

"Survived?" Joanna spat out. "And you know how I survived? By being in a lot of beds. With a lot of people." There was a long silence and Joanna closed her eyes. She knew her history would stop any discussion.

Then Peg spoke quietly in the darkness. "Before I came here, before I contracted with Deborah, I was in a pretty bad way. No job, no family. I didn't know anyone here. This was as far as a bus ticket brought me. Before they stopped running." She spoke quietly as if she didn't want to startle Joanna. "I told you that before."

"Yes."

"I got a job at the hotel. Chambermaid. But it wasn't enough to put a roof over my head. Just enough for food. So I was homeless. And I did okay, as long as the weather was good. Got to shower at the hotel, wash clothes. Occasionally I even got an empty bed. But not always." She took a deep breath and Joanna could hear the tension. "We had a real bad winter a couple of years ago."

"I remember," Joanna said softly.

Peg took another deep breath. "I ended up sleeping with a lot of people just to have shelter for the night. I don't think I sold myself cheap. My only other choice was freezing to death and I wasn't ready to die."

"Ahh." Joanna made a sigh, her head lowered. "You do understand."

"I'm not proud of what I did, Joanna." She paused for a moment and then went on. "To steal Deborah's favorite line, we do a lot of things we never thought we'd ever do just in order to survive."

"I'm sorry."

"Don't be sorry for me," Peg responded quickly in defense.

"No." Joanna rolled over, looking toward Peg's voice. "That's not what I meant. I'm just sorry that you had to go through that. That's all." She reached out her hand. "I understand. And I think

you probably do understand what happened to me. But I still—"
She stopped. She was surprised to feel tears, and she couldn't
speak.

"What?" Peg asked, and she was closer.

Joanna shook her head, still unable to get the words out.

"What Joanna?" and Peg was right there, her hand reaching,
brushing back Joanna's hair. Joanna reached up and Peg caught
her hand. "Tell me. It's all right, we're alone here. I know, there
are no secrets at the house but we're not there. Tell me."

Joanna shook her head, and began to cry. To her shock, Peg
slipped in beside her and took her into her arms.

"It's all right," Peg assured her. "Go ahead, cry." She held her,
stroked her hair. The tears were like a dam bursting and Peg just
held her, letting her cry.

"I don't know why this is hitting me now," she sobbed.

"Because you're ready for it," Peg soothed. "And you feel safe."
She wrapped her arms about Joanna and held her. "You've had the
time to decompress some."

"This is foolish," Joanna still sobbed.

"No, this is natural. Because you've been hurt and you haven't
had time to deal with it. Now you have."

Joanna cried until finally she couldn't cry anymore. But she
couldn't talk either, and Peg just held her, made quiet soothing
sounds until finally Joanna fell asleep.

When she woke the next morning, she was still enclosed in
Peg's arms, their legs entangled. Peg was asleep and Joanna didn't
dare move, afraid to wake her. She couldn't get out. The bed was
wider than a single but not much more. She could feel the wall
at her back. She examined the easy-sleeping Peg. Joanna envied
her—she always seemed so calm and yet in control. Nothing
seemed to bother her. She moved slightly and Peg stirred. Joanna
knew they would have to get up soon, but she wanted to watch
Peg as long as she could.

She reached up to brush Peg's lips lightly and Peg moved,
quickly catching her wrists. Joanna froze, sure she had made a
mistake but Peg brought Joanna's hand to her lips, kissed her
knuckles. She didn't open her eyes.

"We need—" She was interrupted by the knock at the door.

"Good morning," the Crockett girl called as she unlocked the door.

Joanna froze, waiting for the door to open but Peg didn't move.

"Are you awake?"

"We're awake," Peg called. "We'll be there shortly, Gretchen." She didn't stop watching Joanna as they heard Gretchen retreat. "I guess we need to get up."

"I guess so," Joanna replied but she didn't withdraw her hand.

Peg kissed her hand again, then let go. "Gonna be a busy day," she said quietly as she caressed Joanna's cheek. She bent forward so their foreheads touched. "You ready for it?"

Joanna nodded, still not wanting to speak, not wanting to break the comfortable feeling between them. Then Peg was out of bed, on her feet and gathering her clothes. "Rise and shine, darlin'," she said briskly. "Another day, another dollar." She grinned.

* * *

That night Joanna wasn't even sure the previous night had happened. Peg was just as considerate yet impersonal as ever. Joanna wasn't sure what she expected—some glance, some indication that something had occurred between them. Maybe Peg was merely being kind. Maybe that was just the way Peg was.

The day was long, hot and busy. By the time they got through dinner, dishes washed and put away, it was time to start supper. There wasn't a restful moment the whole day and by the time they walked to their room, Joanna was exhausted.

"How many more days of this?" she asked.

"I don't know," Peg answered. "Gretchen, do you think they'll be finished tomorrow?"

"I think so." She opened the door. "I'm sorry about having to lock you in."

"Don't worry about it," Peg said easily. "We have a houseful at home. This is the most private, quiet time we've had in months."

Gretchen gave a small laugh uncertain how to take that comment but she closed the door behind them and locked it.

"You do that so easily," Joanna commented.

"Do what?"

"Make people comfortable."

"Well, there's no sense making her feel bad about something she has no control over." She pulled off her shirt to wipe her face, her arms, her shoulders. "And you know our house is never this quiet—well maybe at two in the morning, but I don't want to stay up that late for a quiet time." She used the washcloth at the basin to wipe herself down again.

"True enough." Joanna rubbed her face. Her shoulders ached from carrying heavy platters and bowls to the table from the kitchen. Those men could eat. She would love to have a full bath she considered as she waited for Peg to finish.

"Are you feeling better than you did last night?" Peg dried herself and moved out of the way for Joanna.

"More or less." Joanna quickly washed off at the basin. "Certainly tired."

"Probably just as much from crying as the work today." Peg turned her back to strip off her sports bra, to slip into her oversized T-shirt she used as a nightshirt.

"Well, yeah," Joanna said uneasily.

"Are you feeling bad because you cried in front of me?"

"Well, maybe," Joanna admitted. "I mean, yes, I've cried in front of people before, but no one ever held me while I cried. Not for a long time."

"I didn't want you to feel alone or on display." Peg was sitting on one leg on the bed when Joanna turned back.

How was it, Joanna wondered, that some women, meaning Peg, could work out in the field, work in the kitchen, whatever, do a quick sponge bath and look like they had stepped out of a leisurely bath, both refreshed and refreshing? She looked so demure and modest in the faint lantern light while Joanna felt grungy and fragmented and haphazard.

Joanna gave a wan smile. "You succeeded. You're very soothing. I appreciate your concern." There, she could put it off, just treat it like Peg was being supportive of anyone else in the house. She pulled the tank top from her pack, much too immodest to wear here during the day but she needed the coolness at night. She was still self-conscious about her bruises, her wounds, even though they were healed so she turned her back to pull off her shirt and slip into the tank top.

Peg gave a low laugh of reassurance. "Please, Joanna, don't think it was all one-sided. I am sorry you were upset. I can understand and empathize with how you felt, but at the same time, it was a pleasure to hold you." There was a warmth in her voice that made Joanna catch her breath.

Joanna turned back in surprise, Peg's meaning unmistakable. "I—I don't know what to say."

"Well, at least you didn't get indignant and rush out of the room."

"A little difficult when the door is locked," Joanna found the wit to say.

"Okay, indignant," Peg corrected herself. She got up and came over to stand before Joanna. She took hold of her hands. "I've been thinking all day it might be pleasant to do it again." She brought Joanna's hand to her lips, kissed the back of her hand.

Could have fooled me. "With or without tears?" Joanna managed to get out.

"Without would be nice, but with is okay. If you want to or need to, just as long as I'm not the one making you cry unhappy tears."

Joanna stood still, not sure what she wanted, but when Peg drew her close, she made no protest at either the arm around her or Peg's lips meeting hers. Then she suddenly put her hand up on Peg's shoulder, pushing her gently away. "Peg."

Peg stepped back immediately but she didn't let go. She had a questioning look.

"I'm not—" Joanna started. "I'm not protesting," she went on quickly. She didn't want Peg to get the wrong idea. "I just—"

"Just?" She pulled Joanna to her. They stood in the middle of the room, looking at each other. "You can say no if you want to," Peg said quietly.

Joanna swallowed. "I don't think I want to." She wasn't sure, part of her was afraid and another part of her knew there was nothing to fear with Peg. "I don't know how I'll react," she whispered.

"That's okay," Peg whispered. "Just don't be anxious, and I'll stop whenever you want."

Her lips were soft and warm, her hands gentle as she ran her fingers through Joanna's hair. Joanna didn't know what to do with her hands, didn't know what to feel as Peg's hands roamed, caressing lightly. She turned her face away and Peg's kisses trailed along her jawline and down her neck. She moaned, moving into Peg's arms, as she felt Peg's hand on her breast. She let Peg lead her to the bed, and said nothing until Peg reached for the light. "No, please. Leave it on. I want to see you."

"Okay." She stood beside the bed, pulled off her nightshirt and stood there, letting Joanna see her. Joanna shivered, then quickly sat up and took off her tank top, her panties too. Peg stretched out beside her, one arm around her, sliding one leg between Joanna's. "You can touch," she said lightly. She bent down to kiss Joanna lightly. "Everything okay?"

Joanna nodded, shivering slightly, moving under Peg. She closed her eyes, feeling Peg along the length of her.

"You're beautiful," Peg whispered in her ear. "You have beautiful eyes. I love watching you." She stroked Joanna's face, coaxing, reassuring.

They lay together, whispering, kissing, touching, and slowly Joanna relaxed, felt more at ease. "Did you plan this?"

Peg buried her face against Joanna's neck. "No, but I take advantage of opportunities. Which is not to say I haven't been wondering how I could get you alone."

"Hmmmm." Joanna slowly ran her hands over Peg's smooth flesh. She closed her eyes, blocking out memories, trying to stay in the present. "I didn't think anyone would be interested in me."

"Difficult. You were a bit prickly to start with." She moved down to Joanna's breast. Joanna arched her back, pushing up. "That seems to be gone now."

"No, I don't feel prickly at all." She took a deep breath. "Can I—can I touch you?"

"My pleasure."

Joanna turned Peg over on her back and then caught her as they almost rolled off the bed. Peg grabbed her and they were in a tangle of arms and grips that seemed to break the ice.

Peg moved more to the center of the bed, and Joanna knelt beside her, leaning over her, her hair brushing over Peg's breasts. Peg was patient, letting Joanna set the pace, explore her, take her time. Only when Joanna's hand was buried in her, when her face was buried against Peg's neck, when she said breathlessly "Touch me," did Peg slowly touch her, stroke her.

"Oh, God," Joanna breathed as she opened up, her fears dissipating as her desire grew.

"You all right?" Peg checked.

"Yes. No."

Peg hesitated. "No?"

"Oh, God! Don't stop!" Joanna gasped and moved against her. "Yes, I'm all right, oh, God, this is more than all right."

Hours later they lay entwined in each other's arms. "We need to get some sleep," Joanna said sleepily.

"Probably so," Peg answered as she ran her hand down Joanna's back.

"I mean it," Joanna said, grabbing her hand and pulling it around to rest between her breasts. "We've still got tomorrow to get through."

"And then we go home," Peg pointed out.

"And this will be over."

"There are ways," Peg whispered. "Trust me, there are ways." But Joanna was already asleep.

CHAPTER TWELVE

"Guess we're going home today, not tomorrow," Peg commented as they stepped out of the hot kitchen the next morning. Joanna looked at her quizzically and followed her gaze as she nodded toward Deborah standing at the barn talking to Crockett. Joanna looked back at Peg quickly, searching for any disappointment or dismay in the calm face. She was not at all eager to return. The work detail had reaped unexpected benefits besides just getting away from Deborah.

"What?" Peg gave a sly grin. "You not ready to go home?"

"The privacy has had its advantages." She was actually able to give Peg a self-conscious grin.

Peg gave a low pleased laugh as Deborah approached.

"Ready?" Deborah said in greeting. Wherever she had been, whatever she had done, she did not look well-rested.

"I guess so." Both women picked up their knapsacks.

"Good, I'm ready to get home and get a decent night's sleep in my own bed." She started off immediately and both women fell in behind her. "Oh, before I forget it." Deborah turned around to face them, walking backward. She pulled coins out of her pocket. "Here." She split the coins and handed them to both Peg and Joanna.

Peg nodded her thanks and stuffed the coins in her pocket but Joanna looked at them in amazement. She hadn't seen cash for a while. That had been part of her problem. She hadn't had any money, any actual cold hard cash, in over a year. "What's this?"

"Crockett didn't want to claim it as a favor. I think he was afraid I might call it in sometime and he wouldn't be able to refuse. So he paid me for your labor. Wasn't my labor. Figured it was yours so you deserve the cash."

"You're paying us?"

"Yes." As if she knew what Joanna was getting ready to say, she went on in short order. "You complaining?"

"No! No, not at all." Joanna stuffed the coins into her pocket. "Just—just surprised."

Deborah shook her head and turned around. "Let's get home. I haven't had a decent night's sleep since we left."

Joanna watched her. No sleep? Well, if she had seen a girlfriend as Peg suggested, the visit clearly had not gone well. No, Joanna suspected something else. And just the thought of what it might be made her uneasy.

She watched Deborah set off at a pace that reinforced her desire to be home. She didn't feel Peg fall into step beside her until Peg's hand slipped into hers.

"Surprised?"

She turned to see Peg's pleased face. She nodded. "Did you know?"

"I knew there was a chance. Deborah's passed along the money other times. Sometimes I think she feels bad that she doesn't have enough cash to pay us anything."

"Nothing? Nothing at all?" Joanna hadn't known that. Her contract certainly wasn't for labor. She looked at Deborah again.

"Nada. But she was clear from the beginning. She was laying out cash for our support, for the farm, without knowing what might come up. That's why everyone was so surprised when she said she thought we'd make a profit. She's been taking the financial risk, we've been taking the Deborah risk."

"The Deborah risk," Joanna repeated. "Where's she get her cash?"

Peg shook her head. "She's never explained. I know it hasn't been from the farm because we've barely been making it."

"She acts like we're all dirt poor."

"We are, land poor, at least," Peg pointed out. "Even if we've been living on a cashless basis, there's still things like taxes, and things we can't grow or barter for. She's been able to get what we absolutely needed but it's been tight."

"She hoarding it away somewhere?"

"Now does she look like she's been living it up somewhere?" Peg asked loudly enough for Deborah to look back over her shoulder. Peg dropped her voice. "You've been out and about with her. She spending wildly?"

"Hardly," Joanna admitted. "Takes care of the basics. That's it."

"She's got a trade line somewhere. She comes back with the strangest things. Those solar panels, Karen said they came in piecemeal. She's always said she'll get more, but they're not from around here. Without them, we wouldn't have any power in the house."

"I thought all that came from Before."

Peg shook her head. "When I came, the house had power. She was working fast to get it off the grid. Sure enough, that bad winter I told you about?" Joanna nodded. "It took the lines down. She was at the end of the line. They wanted to bill her to put them back way out here. She told them to forget it. She and Karen put up the panels that summer." Peg shook her head. "Bad summer. Karen doesn't like to talk about it. I thought they'd kill each other. Frustration and so much to do. Deborah really has a terrible temper. Just keeps it under control most of the time."

"I know," Joanna said without thinking. As soon as she said it, she regretted it. She glanced at Peg to see if she had caught it but Peg was looking ahead.

"Then that was the year of the beans." Peg shook her head. "We all laugh at Karen, the way she turns green at beans, but damn, it was bad."

"I'm surprised she stayed."

Peg shrugged. "She said she didn't have anywhere to go. And by the time she got done, she figured after all the effort, she might as well stick around and get some of the benefits."

"Will you two step it up?" Deborah called over her shoulder. "At this rate, it's going to be midnight before we get home."

They were welcomed home with open arms and Joanna was relieved to see Peg peppered with as many questions as she was. She managed to have the briefest moment alone with her as everyone was coming in for dinner.

"You're not going to say anything, are you?" She didn't know if she could deal with the teasing, the knowing glances, what Deborah might say.

"Trust me," Peg whispered. "I'm the soul of discretion."

They took their seats across from each other at the dinner table and Joanna settled in. For the first time, she felt comfortable, like she had come home. She caught herself at the thought. Was she really beginning to think of this as home?

* * *

She gave that question serious consideration in the days that followed and she felt split in two. There was the Joanna who did her tasks, who ended up working with Peg a lot more, and because Deborah seemed distracted and even perhaps more trusting, stole some private time with Peg. And there was the other Joanna, who counted her little pile of coins each night, a reminder of her determination to leave.

Clothes were one problem. She would need her bracelets to be covered. No one noticed them anymore because she was part of the House of Steele and everyone in the area knew that. Deborah had made sure of that. She might be able to slide through the local area although they would expect Deborah to be around. However, once she got out beyond that, her bracelets would mark her as a state contract. She needed long sleeves, ridiculous in this heat. Or she could try to remove them.

"Can I get rid of these?" she asked Deborah one night over their evening tea.

Deborah gave her a long contemplative look. "I'm afraid not," she said finally. "That's not my choice, by the way. Why?"

"They're in the way. Dirt gets under them, water. Irritates the skin. An annoyance."

"I think that might have been the point," Deborah said dryly. She put her feet up on the footstool, pleased that another chair to her liking had been found in one of the storage rooms. "I'll see what I can do."

Deborah, she admitted, was as accommodating as she could be, considering the circumstances. There was even a part of Joanna who felt she might be betraying Deborah if she escaped, but she dismissed the feeling. Deborah was a contract holder. And Joanna didn't want to be on contract. She had been surprised and relieved that Deborah was as lenient and trusting as she was. More and more, she was able to do work out of Deborah's sight. She had noted that to Peg one morning in the haymow as Deborah worked outside.

"I told you," Peg said quietly from where they were lounging in the hayloft. They took their private moments when and where they could, and the haymow was a spot where they could lay in each other's arms. "Deborah's not a jailer. She'd be a lot more accommodating if you'd just tell her."

"No!" Joanna sat up. "God, can't I have something that's private! She's there all the time, everywhere! I'd just like to have something apart."

"You've never lived in a group setting before, have you?" Peg lay back and pulled Joanna down.

"No." Joanna settled back into Peg's arms, her head on Peg's shoulder. "Oh, I camped with a group on vacations. This all-the-time deal isn't my cup of tea."

Peg ran her fingers through Joanna's short locks. "I'm glad you finally let Linda cut your hair. Frames your face better, looks nicer."

More recognizable, Joanna thought with dismay. "Cooler," she said simply. *Besides, if I leave, my description will be with long hair. I'll just have to take the risk of someone recognizing me from before.* She tightened her arms around Peg. *Who am I kidding? I'm a forgotten person. No one's looking for me. Who's going to recognize me after all this time?*

She buried her face in Peg's shoulder, then abruptly rose up over her to look down into her face. Peg's hazel eyes were calm, accepting.

"Do you know what a touchstone you have become for me?"

"Everyone needs someone at their back."

Joanna bent down. Peg's kisses were always so welcoming, so warm. Her hands sliding up under her shirt were so firm, so exciting. They made her forget so much, gave her a feeling things were normal. They broke apart at the sound of someone coming in down below. Joanna pulled back but Peg just held her.

"What's up?" they heard Deborah say.

"Need some straw for the plant bedding. Those berries'll get sunburnt." It sounded like Linda.

"Why don't you do it later?"

"Because I want to do it before the afternoon heat." The voice was coming at the foot of the ladder.

"There's a bale at the stable." Deborah was also at the foot of the ladder. A long silence followed and then Linda spoke.

"Okay, but I'll probably need more." Her voice retreated.

Deborah waited several minutes. "Peg. Joanna."

"Yes, ma'am," Peg answered without moving.

"Fork down some more straw when you get done up there."

"Will do."

They listened to her retreat, a door close.

"She knows." Joanna turned back to Peg with the sudden realization.

Peg smiled and brushed back Joanna's hair. "Don't worry about it. We're up here moving hay. Just what she told us to do." She pulled Joanna back. "Now where were we?"

* * *

Joanna found work details around the house and grounds useful now. When she stashed things away, somewhere along the line, she was alone long enough to retrieve them and pack them away. It took time, and she counseled herself to be patient. Slowly her treasures grew.

An aluminum water bottle with a tight lid. The season had been hot enough they were all carrying water bottles as they worked. They worked through the heat of the day which seemed hotter and dryer than any of them remembered. Hats for the shade, often dunked into water for cooling. If a water bottle didn't make it back to the kitchen, well, they were always stumbling over one someone had dropped in the garden or in the field. It would show up. An extra set of clothes—pants, a long-sleeved shirt, long enough to cover those bracelets. A short-sleeved shirt for other times. Or to wear in layers. Socks, underwear, shoes. Now that was the hard part. Extra shoes were hard to come by, and she decided she'd simply have to pick a day when she wore her strongest shoes. Food, at least enough for a few days, was the easiest. They had been making fruit leathers. Sue was experimenting with dried meats and her samples were all over the place, with invitations for them to try and critique. She'd never miss a few of them.

And unaware, Sue aided her. She had also been making granola and energy bars. She had argued it was a convenient and nutritious way to preserve food. *Very helpful,* Joanna thought as she sampled freely and stored most of them.

A knapsack. It wasn't in the best shape so when she said she needed it for chicken feed, Karen let her have it. While it was definitely beat-up, torn and ragged, Joanna knew it wouldn't attract attention as much as anything valuable.

Her largest problem, she realized as she sat cross-legged on her bed early in the morning while Deborah was downstairs preparing breakfast, was that she wasn't certain in which direction to go. Should she go south and try to meet up with ACTS people? Or continue north and cross the border. South would take her into areas she had seen while traveling with Deborah but it would increase her chances of discovery. North, while it was unknown, she wouldn't be less likely to be recognized.

Originally the plan had been to go to Wisconsin but, she reasoned that was too far especially without a map. If she could get up to Michigan, Port Huron would be the closest route, but she'd have to go around Detroit. Would it be safer to go all the way up state and clear into Ontario at Sault St. Marie? Or would it be better to through Ohio, perhaps? No. Michigan. She could follow the Eel River up to Fort Wayne. If she couldn't make contact there, then the St. Joe would take her up further. And she knew, in a vague sort of way, the direction of the river. She hadn't been that way before, but on the other hand, no one would look for her in that direction. No one would think she would be heading up for Canada. A map, what she wouldn't give for a map.

She was browsing in the bookcase in the living room one evening, restless, wanting to get moving. The old books held little interest for her. "What're these?" she asked absently.

Linda looked over her shoulder. "Deborah's genealogy. Her grandmother was real big on it. Most old people are."

Joanna was surprised and she admitted in some small corner of her mind, jealous that Linda knew so much about Deborah. "I'm surprised they're not packed away for safekeeping."

Linda shook her head. "She was afraid they'd get weather-damaged if they were in the attic. She had some packed away there and when the roof leaked, well, she lost a bunch. Gotta remember, once upon a time, she was a librarian. Books were her life. Family books, well, she takes good care of them."

Joanna pulled an oversized book out, a reprint from something back in the 1880s. Her heart almost stopped when she flipped it open. There was a county map, the rivers, the roads. She looked up quickly to see if anyone noticed but the day had been long and tiring. Everyone was relaxing a bit before bed. There was a line drawing, a sketch really, of this place. The buildings weren't all there but then this was over a hundred years ago. Deborah had said it was old but still she was surprised. The house, the barn, other buildings that were now gone or replaced.

Even more important were the property lines at the back of the place. She saw that the roads were pretty much the same also. New interstate went through there but still. Cross it and then there was the river. She swallowed, fearful that everyone in the room could feel her excitement. She carefully folded the corner of the page down and put the book back on the shelf. She was going to need to look at it again but she had to settle it in her mind.

Absently she walked to the office. "I'm really tired," she told Deborah. "Do you mind if I just go on to bed?"

Deborah looked up briefly but she shook her head. "I'll be up in a bit. It's been a long day, hasn't it?"

Joanna nodded, trying hard to remain casual. She needed to use the time alone to pull out the paper and pencil she had hidden and make notes while she still had it firmly in mind. This was the last piece. Now all she needed was the time.

* * *

"You'll never get away with it."

Joanna jerked around from the cellar door but it was only Bobbi. "What's it to you?"

"Deborah will blow a gasket." She leaned against the door and folded her arms as Joanna continued to stuff food into her backpack.

"So run away and tell her," Joanna shot back. "You're such a tattletale, I thought that'd be the first thing you would do. It's not like Deborah ever shoots the messenger."

"No," Bobbi mocked. "I think I'll just sit back and watch the fun."

Joanna sandwiched in the last of the food and pulled the cover over it. She bounced it a couple of times to settle before she buckled the straps. "You do that, Bobbi."

"How long do you think you'll manage?" Bobbi's words were a taunt.

"You know what will really be fun?" She walked right up to Bobbi but Bobbi didn't move. "Thinking of the hot seat you've put yourself into because right now you have so few choices. You can run like hell for Deborah to try to stop me. You can wait until I'm gone and tell her that you knew about it. I imagine that will go over big. Or you can wait and see if she brings me back. I can't wait to tell her not only that you knew about me and what I was planning, but that you snooped around and kept me apprised of her search."

"She wouldn't believe you." Bobbi straightened up.

"What? With all the crap you've been putting out, you think Deborah would believe you over me? Now get out of my way."

She pushed by Bobbi and headed for the stairs. There was silence behind her and then she heard Bobbi's quick steps.

"You can't," she said in a rush. "You'll never get away with it. Deborah will never let you go." She grabbed Joanna's arm.

Joanna turned on her and pushed her away. When Bobbi fell backward, Joanna followed her. "This isn't up to Deborah Steele! She holds my contract but Deborah Steele is not my master! Or my mistress! She does not own me and I don't owe her a damned thing."

Even as she said that, she could hear Peg quietly pointing out *She got you out of a bad situation.*

Joanna went up the cellar steps, pausing as she lifted the door to look around and see who might be in the vicinity. She could make an excuse for being in the cellar but it would be so much easier if she didn't have to. Now if she could just get off the grounds before Bobbi alerted anyone. She turned her head to hear that Bobbi's steps were going the other direction, toward the stairs inside the house. She should have time.

She made her way through the orchard, over the stone wall. She heard Karen coming so she crouched down. It certainly wouldn't occur to anyone she might take off. They were all quite content to remain as Deborah's serfs.

Bobbi was right about one thing—Deborah wouldn't let her go. She might not be able to sleep with her, but she did have possession of her. Such sweet revenge for Joanna leaving her all those years ago. And she might have managed to convince everyone else that she had their safety and well-being in mind but she didn't convince Joanna. No, Deborah had set up her own little kingdom, and everyone was at her beck and call. Bobbi's comments that Deborah was visiting all the contract holders sealed it for her.

As she crossed over the last fence, she saw a figure coming after her. It had to be Bobbi, as the woman had such an awkward run. She hurried through the fence and started down the gully.

"Joanna! Joanna! Wait up! Wait for me!"

Not bloody likely, Joanna thought as she threw herself headlong down the steep slope. That had to be the bridge where she and Peg had sat and talked for so long. Which meant the river.

She was halfway up the far side of the gully when Bobbi came into view on the opposite bank.

Joanna glanced over her shoulder without responding, thinking, "but you haven't caught me." She kept working up the steep slope even as she heard Bobbi crash down. If there was anyone following her, they could certainly track her by the noise alone.

She was almost to top when Bobbi scrambled up close enough to grab her foot. "Joanna, wait up?"

"What the hell for?" Joanna kicked Bobbi's hand off. "For the rest of your goon squad to catch up?"

Bobbi slid down a few feet but she came right back up. "There isn't anyone else coming."

"Why not?" Joanna reached for the sapling and managed to pull herself up. "You going to take credit all by your lonesome, think that will redeem yourself in Deborah's eyes."

"I couldn't find Deborah. She's holed up in her office," Bobbi confessed. "If you'll just come back now, you can get back before she even knows you're gone."

"I'm not going back. So you can just go on back and tell her all you want."

Bobbi shook her head as she came up over the edge and pulled herself up. "No, no. If you're not going back, I'm not going either. I'm not going to face her."

Joanna looked at Bobbi with new contempt. "You really are scared of her, aren't you?" she sneered.

Bobbi looked away.

"And what did she ever do to you to make you so scared?" Even at that point, as much as she wanted to hear anything bad about Deborah, she couldn't believe she had hurt anyone. "Well?" she demanded harshly.

"She yelled at me."

"Yelled at you!" Memories of being beaten made Joanna almost choke. "You're scared of her because she yelled at you?"

"There's stories around that she killed some guy," Bobbi muttered. "And I've seen her mad, not that yelling bit she does, but that cold, dark anger. I've heard her say what she would do to anyone who tried to take this place away from her. I've seen her with that look that she could kill someone. She's looked at me that way."

Joanna laughed. She couldn't help herself. Good God! All the same, she had seen Deborah enraged, but that was when they were younger. And she could imagine that if pushed, Deborah was well capable of all Bobbi said. But to think that she might be enraged at this mealy mousey thing was, was, well, she would have thought it just a waste of energy.

"I thought you two were lovers at one time," Joanna taunted. Although she knew they had been. Many years ago, Deborah had told her about a Bobbi when she was at college.

"That was a long time ago." Bobbi got to her feet. "She was real different then."

Well, Joanna had to agree with that. She wondered what Deborah had ever seen in her. "Yeah," she agreed instead, "a lot of things have changed since then." She pulled her notes from her pocket and checked her sketch, looked up to see where the sun was. She would have loved a compass. With luck on her side, she may not be missed until lunchtime. With bad luck, well, she needed to put some distance between her and the house. She started off again, having caught her breath.

"Wait!"

Joanna didn't pause. "I don't care what you do, Bobbi. You're not stopping me." She needed to cross that next field to hit the remnant of the interstate and follow it to the river.

When she reached the neighbor's field, Bobbi was right there. "I'm going with you."

"Whatever. Just don't expect me to take care of you."

* * *

Deborah sat on the back step, away from the group canning in the kitchen. These days, she took every opportunity she could to be alone, now a relative term. She was shelling peas, automatically splitting the pods, raking her thumb down to empty the peas into the pan and tossing the pods into the bushel basket to go to compost. She could hear the conversation in the kitchen behind her, and she could overlook the grounds, so she knew where everyone was.

"Hey!"

She looked up to see Karen crossing the yard. She had taken the early morning run of vegetables to the diner. This thing with Luella was working out quite well. "Hey, yourself. How's Luella this morning?"

"Good. Likes our stuff. She's wanting more. Need to talk to you about some expanding. And what are we going to do in cold weather? She was asking about that this morning—so she's already thinking about this as a year-round deal." She came up, dropped the backpack and stretched. "Oh, there was a package there for you that someone dropped off. And I picked up the mail too."

Deborah wiped her hands on her pants before she took the envelope. There was no return address but she recognized Carolyn's writing. She flipped through the other mail noticing something from the lawyer and then turned her attention to the envelope from Carolyn. She slit the opening.

"What's that?"

Deborah shook her head—it had been a coon's age since she had seen one of these. "A CD," Deborah said absently as she pulled up the envelope flap.

"*Sorry,*" she read, "*this was the best I could do.*"

"What good's that to you? You got anything left that can read it?"

Deborah put aside the peas and got to her feet. "I need to see this." She picked up the mail and the pan of peas and went into the house. She dropped the peas off in the kitchen and went on to her office.

"Sara," she called as she hit the door. Sara was immediately there. "Where's my laptop?"

"Your laptop?"

"Yes," Deborah said impatiently. She knew it was old and beaten up but in its day it had been the top of the line. And she had babied it, coaxed it, as one of the last remnants of her previous life. One of the first things she had bought when she was stranded here was a solar pack to charge her cell phone and her computer. The cell phone had died. She hadn't been able to adapt the solar panel to anything besides the computer and more important issues had taken her attention. Nevertheless, she occasionally pulled out the laptop, kept it charged, and nursed it along. There wasn't a lot she could do with it nowadays. She had reluctantly gone back to pen and paper, but maybe she could read this disc. After banging around the office, she found the laptop in a safe place in the back of the credenza.

"When was the last time you used this?"

"Oh, God, I can't remember. I spent many a winter night that first winter playing games." She pulled out the solar pack. "Once upon a time, I thought I couldn't live without it. I was so dependent on it."

"Yeah, well, weren't we all?"

Deborah hooked it up, fumbling with the cables that she once would have been able to sort out in her sleep. The battery needed to be charged. She crawled back down under the credenza to find the solar pack. When she got back up, Sara was at the desk, holding the disc.

"Just what's so important that you've got to dig out the laptop?"

"No idea, but I figured if someone sent me this, I need to look at it." She hooked up the solar pack to the laptop and went out to the sunny front porch. A few hours in the sunlight should solve that problem. When she came back in, Sara handed her a notice.

"You need to read this."

Deborah read the letter from Henderson. "Damn, somebody finally did it," she muttered as she read of the class action for setting aside forced contracts. "Great." She looked up the see Sara's questioning gaze. "Joanna might have her problems solved," she said, folding up the notice again.

"That'll be good," Sara agreed and then she looked again at Deborah. "Won't it?"

Deborah nodded but considered the repercussions. *And I'll lose her again.* "Yeah," she said with resignation. "Can't imagine what it's like to be locked into something you abhor." Something suddenly registered and she quickly unfolded the notice again. "Tomorrow's the deadline? Shit, that doesn't give us much time." She looked up at Sara. "Could you go find Joanna and ask her to come here? We need to discuss this, probably go into town. But don't tell her what it is." She gave a small mental shrug. At least she would be able to be the one to give her the good news. She started fetching the papers the lawyer would need.

The sound of someone running through the house alerted her even before Sara threw open the door. Sara didn't run—it wasn't in her nature. Deborah met her at the door. "What's wrong?"

"I can't find Joanna."

"Can't find?" Deborah went cold. She knew immediately that Joanna was gone and she cursed herself for being lulled into the belief that Joanna wouldn't do this to her.

"I looked everywhere. She's supposed to be on laundry. She might have—"

"Call everyone in," Deborah ordered sharply. "Use the dinner bell. And where's Peg?"

Sara looked flustered as she shook her head. "She's—she's on—on moving the cows to the other pasture."

"I want her. Have everyone gather in the dining room, see if anyone else is missing. I need to see Linda right away. Have Karen on standby." She went up the stairs two at a time. If Joanna had hightailed it, she wouldn't leave with nothing. As angry as she was, she hesitated at the archway into Joanna's area. She might keep Joanna under lock and key because that was the law but she believed everyone needed private space. She had never stepped into Joanna's area without cause and never when Joanna wasn't there.

Well, this is cause, she told herself as she entered the plainly-furnished sleeping area. She went through Joanna's things. The longer she searched the angrier she got and she might have started tearing things up in fury had Linda not knocked on the door.

"What's up? Sara sounded a little—what's wrong, Deborah?"

"Joanna's flown the coop," Deborah said tersely as she brushed by Linda in the doorway. "And we'll have to find her before someone else does or there will be hell to pay." She went down the stairs with Linda following. "I need you to do something for me, and I can't send anyone else."

"What? Where?"

As they crossed the foyer to Deborah's office, they could hear the excited conversations at the end of the house. Right now, Deborah had to get Linda on task. She moved behind her desk and pulled out stationery.

"I need you to catch the train into town." She glanced at the clock. "I think you can just catch the midday. You know Roger Henderson? He's got his office on High Water Street." She looked up and Linda nodded. "Good." She stopped talking and wrote in bold strokes.

"Roger—get Joanna Davis included on the class action. Just to be on the safe side, also file to include Joanna Braaford—double AA—be sure to get the spelling right. This should give you the authority. If you need anything else, let me know ASAP and I'll get any information to you." She signed it with a bold flourish and blew on the ink to dry it.

"I need to have this in his hands today. Tell him to use the wire, whatever he needs to get this filed—I'll stand the cost but try not to cut off my leg." She folded the note, stuffed it in an envelope and handed it over. She looked up. "He knows you, knows you're a county resident, that you're not likely to be a runaway. He won't question you delivering this but under no circumstances say anything about Joanna taking off. Not to anyone. Tell him I couldn't possibly leave." She stopped, trying to think of some excuse for her not to be taking this to the lawyer. She couldn't think of any. "Tell him—I don't know what—just whatever you come up with, be sure to tell me."

Linda nodded unhesitatingly, but looked troubled. "Where would she go?"

"I don't have the foggiest idea. I was working out back so she didn't go by me. And Karen was at the diner this morning and didn't see anything of her in that direction."

"The river?"

"She's never been that way." Deborah was already closing up her desk and heading for the door. "I'm doing a head count, so come along but I want you out of here and on your way ASAP. And don't bother talking to anyone about this, in or out of the house."

"Of course not," Linda said quickly. "You know I wouldn't."

Deborah stopped and looked at her. Linda was an old, old friend and once she wouldn't have given it a second thought, but now, Joanna had created an air of mistrust. Deborah was a contract holder and Linda was on contract. She saw the hurt on

Linda's face and she wondered which of them had changed. "I know, Linda. I'm just really pissed. And upset." She glanced at the envelope. "If I didn't trust you, I wouldn't be sending you on this task." She was already turning to the dining room. "Let's go see who's missing."

"Head count!" she called in a loud voice as she entered the dining room. It was enough to silence everyone and they all turned toward her. The last time she'd called a head count, they had been out in the wood lot and a sudden snowstorm had blown up. By the time they had made it to the house, it was a white-out and Linda had staggered in just as they were going back out in search.

She looked around the table quickly—three missing. Joanna, Bobbi who under other circumstances would have had Deborah dancing in glee, and then there was Peg. Peg's absence was almost a second punch.

"All right," she demanded. "Who saw who last? When and where?"

Karen led off. "Assigned Joanna and Bobbi to laundry. Joanna finished the chickens. Did she bring the eggs in?" She turned to Rae.

She questioned them all, where they had been working, what they had seen. Since they were all in different parts of the farm, she had hoped someone had seen something. They traced Joanna to the washroom and then someone recalled seeing Joanna and Bobbi heading for the barn. Said something about needing more rope for the clothesline.

"And Peg?" Deborah demanded in a cold voice.

"I'm right here." Peg came in the door, slapping her gloves together. She stopped when she saw everyone gathered around the table. "What's going on? I heard the dinner bell—thought it was early for lunch."

"Joanna's missing," Deborah said tersely, still not sure that Peg knew nothing about this. "And so is Bobbi. Have you seen them this morning?"

Peg's jaw dropped a little, the surprise and shock on her face quickly covered up. She didn't know, Deborah decided. "Not since breakfast. I thought—I mean, Joanna was on laundry."

"Yeah, well, I guess we'll have dirty clothes for a bit longer." Deborah unrolled a plat map onto the table. Peg knew the area. "Peg," she said and her voice was sharp and cold. "You've been taking Joanna all over the place. Did you take her to the river?"

"No!" Peg sounded appropriately horrified. She shook her head when Deborah looked up at her. She stuffed her gloves in her hip pocket and came over to look at Deborah's plat map. "The closest we got was the back bridge." She pointed to the spot on the map. "She asked what was over there by the trees and I said the river, but that was just in passing, I don't think…" She trailed off, her mouth set in a grim line.

Deborah glanced at Linda. "You need to go." Linda nodded without comment and picked up a Windbreaker as she went out the door. The women around the table glanced at each other but no one spoke.

"All right, who was on kitchen duty? Did either of them come in to get anything?" continued Deborah.

"I was," Sue answered quickly. "And no, I didn't seem them this morning, but there were some things missing out of the pantry." Deborah looked up at her and she went on quickly. "Just little things, some apples, hard-boiled eggs, ham. I thought someone was out in the field today and just took a lunch. It didn't occur to me."

"No, of course not." Deborah went back to the map. "They probably wouldn't go through Anoka since Karen was coming in that way. Do either of them know anything about what lies to the east?"

"Bobbi and I came in that way," Sara volunteered. "She knows the commune is in that direction. I don't think she'd go there."

When everyone hashed out what they knew, the consensus on where the women were headed was the river.

"Todd was right," Deborah muttered to herself as she organized the group. "No good deed goes unpunished. Beth, Sara, you stay here. If they come back, keep them here." She glanced around at the group, her eyes resting on Peg.

"I'll stay here if you want," Peg said evenly.

Deborah shook her head. If they did run into trouble Peg's army experience would be helpful. Of all of them, she had the best training. "If they do go to the river, there's a bigger chance they may run into hooligans. Brea, you're coming. Rae, I want you to secure the house just in case we're followed back by unwelcome visitors. Sue, you keep the home fires burning." She looked around the table, head counting. "The rest of you, stay here."

She went to the foyer, running down a mental list of everything that could possibly happen. Marv had said town gangs were branching out, looking for food and whatever else they lacked, and the railroads and the rivers were good highways for them. She tripped the lock to the hidden panel by the front doors. Grandfather Winslow was a suspicious old coot, and there were hidden panels throughout the house, handy places to hide all sorts of things.

She pulled out two revolvers, one gun belt, one shoulder holster, ammunition. She'd never had to use them before. She saw the shocked looks when she carried them back into the dining room.

"Is that necessary?" Sara burst out.

"Probably not." She held them both out for Peg to choose one. "But rather than be unprepared, I'm taking them." She saw Karen step back, she really hated using the guns although she would use the sawed-off shotgun if necessary.

Peg took the shoulder holster and slipped it on so casually it got everyone's attention. In stark contrast, Deborah handled the gun belt awkwardly. Peg checked both the revolvers and handed one back to Deborah, shaking her head in some dismay.

"Karen, you and Peg go over to the bridge via the road, and continue down river. Brea and I'll do a straight shot across the fields. We should both end up about the same place on the river. I'm guessing, Logan's Landing. What do you think?"

"Probably so," Karen answered. "Straight line. And it's fordable there."

"Let's go."

"Clarification." Peg didn't move as Deborah started for the door. "This is just for our own protection, right?"

"Of course." Deborah looked at her and then around at the group. "I'm pissed," she said, "really, royally pissed. That doesn't mean I'm planning on shooting anyone. It means that I've heard that more people are coming in to the area and not all of them are friendly. The river's a highway now, and I don't intend to lead anyone undesirable back home. Now does that rest your minds? Now, let's go," she said in a tight voice. She would deal with all those other feelings later. Right now, the objective was to catch Joanna before she got away.

* * *

They were found at the river, arguing under the chestnut tree, out in the open, where anyone could see them. Deborah scanned up and down the river, but she saw no boat traffic. Marv said he used watercraft a lot, and that his boys accessed the river across her land. Logan's Landing had once been much bigger than just the small boat launch it was now. Once upon a time, there was goods shipping here, and a community store.

She wasn't so worried about the local militia stumbling across Joanna. Marv, the leader, wouldn't hurt her, just hold her for Deborah, but he'd sure extract payment for the favor. That wouldn't be good, but she could deal with him. But some of his boys though, that could be unpleasant.

Joanna saw them first and, without hesitation, took off running upstream. Bobbi didn't see them until she turned to see what caused Joanna's flight. She started running in the opposite direction, perhaps reasoning that everyone would chase Joanna. Deborah motioned Karen and Peg after her, while she and Brea chased after Joanna. Deborah tackled her. Joanna hit the ground, rolled over onto her back and kicked out. Deborah caught that one on the shoulder but by then her adrenaline had kicked in. She grabbed Joanna's leg, twisted and dragged her toward her.

"God damn it, Jo. Give it up!"

"You're not taking me back!" She kicked again and Deborah had to let her go.

Joanna sprang to her feet with Deborah scrambling after her, catching her by the ankle and pulling her foot out from under her. Any thought of capturing Joanna without hurting her was fading fast as she slammed her into the ground and then landed on her before she could roll over.

"Damn it, Jo. I'm not letting you get away. Now if you want this real ugly, I'll hog tie you and we'll carry you back. Is that what you want?"

CHAPTER THIRTEEN

"She's all right," Beth reported when she came in from the stable. "She'll be a little sore, she got jerked around some but nothing worse." She looked at Deborah uneasily.

"Thank you, Beth," Deborah said simply. She had withdrawn to her office, letting the rest of the house deal with their issues. She was still coldly furious and a little heartsick. The house had never been so cut along contract holder and contracted worker lines. She saw these people as family and the contract was just a formality, hoping that because each of them had made the decision to join her, they felt likewise. She acknowledged that families sometimes fight, sometimes don't get along, sometimes don't speak to each other. Sometimes members even run away. But they don't struggle the way Joanna did. They don't fight like they had to escape. And Deborah had never had to lay hands on anyone in the house before this.

"Are you all right?" Beth asked.

"I'm fine," Deborah answered automatically. "Go ahead and check everyone else over. I'm sure everyone's upset. Just generally make yourself available. Thanks Beth."

Beth withdrew, shutting the door firmly behind her.

Deborah sat there. She hadn't expected Joanna to be so, so volatile. Her fault. She had been lulled into the idea that since she had known Joanna previously, and rescued her, she would be grateful. Her mistake. Joanna was a state contract. She had run away time and time again. She didn't want to be on contract, for which Deborah couldn't blame her. But none of it was Deborah's doing. What was she supposed to do? Leave Joanna in that situation? Just walk away and ignore her, knowing that she was being abused? It had been a no-win situation. Had it been anyone else, anyone but Joanna, she could have walked away, could treat her as a troublesome contract.

There was a light rap on the door. "Come in," Deborah said with a sigh.

"I brought in your laptop," Sara said with the computer in hand. "The battery's charged. I didn't know if you still wanted to bother with it now, but regardless, it shouldn't be outside."

Deborah got up from her desk. "Yeah, maybe that will give me something else to think about." She glanced at Sara, knowing the others confided in her. But being everyone's confidant didn't leave anyone for Sara to turn to. "Are you all right?"

"Well, I'm upset, I think everyone is." She sat down, sitting on the edge of the seat. She hesitated before she asked. "What are you going to do?"

"Damned if I know." Deborah set up the computer on the desk. "I'll have to think about it."

"Can I give you some advice?"

"Sure." Deborah turned the computer on, closed her eyes and held her breath. To her relief, the clicks and whirls indicated that the computer was still alive and well. She breathed a sigh and opened her eyes to see Sara watching her. "Go ahead. I'm all ears for anything and everything."

"Don't wait too long. Don't put this off. Everyone's waiting to see what you're going to do."

"Well, I don't know what I'm going to do," Deborah said simply. She sat back and stared at the screen. "I never thought that this would happen."

"And I know you feel worse because you thought that Joanna would be appreciative."

Deborah didn't move as she looked at Sara. "Yes," she admitted cautiously.

"You were the one who told me at the very beginning that you didn't think she would be—when pigs fly, I do believe you said."

Deborah went back to the screen. "Yes, I did say that. I would have been better off if I had remembered it." She had become complacent. Or avoiding it, she wasn't sure which. Either way, it had blown up in her face.

"Joanna's been healing over these past months," Sara temporized. "I think that maybe now she's getting back to her real personality. She strikes me as a very strong person. Only a strong person could have survived what she has without being broken. And such a person wouldn't like being on contract."

"I didn't put her on contract," Deborah said through gritted teeth.

"But you are her contract holder. You're the person she has to deal with. Even if you're not the cause, you are the one she has to look at every day and be reminded. It's unreasonable to think that she wouldn't feel ill toward you. Even if there were reasons not to blame you." Deborah looked up at Sara quickly. Her words implied there was another hidden meaning.

"You knew Joanna before, didn't you?" Sara asked carefully. Deborah didn't deny it but she didn't admit it either. "Both of you seem to know things about each other, things that just haven't come up since she's been here. Sometimes it's just little things I don't think either one of you realize." Sara gave Deborah a sympathetic look. "I imagine that makes it harder."

Deborah took a deep breath. She needed to cut this conversation off now, quickly before Sara probed too deeply. "Well, yes, it does," she said briskly. "But that's neither here nor there. She still has to be dealt with. And maybe I did think that she would be grateful. My mistake." Sara started to say something more and Deborah cut her off. "Leave it, Sara. I hadn't seen Joanna in years." *So many years.* "People change. Obviously I assumed too much. And now I have to correct that mistake. Before it gets worse."

She started searching across her desk, blinded for a moment by the memories of Joanna. She couldn't find the damned disc from Carolyn. She looked up and Sara handed it to her.

"Everyone's upset," Sara repeated. "But it's mainly because of Joanna. I think a lot of us were able to forget that we were on a contract. We just happened to all land here in an effort to survive. But Joanna made us look at it for what it was. It happened when she first came in and she wasn't happy about it, but then it all eased off. Now it's back in full force. You're going to need to do something, Deborah. You've been hiding from it too. I think that now you're going to have to bring the issue of us all being on a contract, out into the open. We're not really family."

"Okay." She loaded the disc and frowned at the screen as it loaded. The title appeared, *ACTS founders speak out!* There were five of them onstage. It had to be one of the early organizing rallies. She studied the three women, two men, dismissing the men. They looked as expected—young, idealistic, energized. There was panning of the crowd, a good turnout, maybe a couple of hundred. She leaned forward to turn up the sound just as the lead person came to the podium.

Deborah's mouth went dry as the camera came in for a close-up. The speaker was intense, impassioned, articulate, everything that made her the focus of the crowd. She had the honest, open look that made you believe her cause was just. Deborah stared at the screen, unable to do more than just swallow as she listened to contract holders being called to task.

"That sounds like Joanna." Sara got to her feet and came around the desk to stand by Deborah as she watched. "What is this?"

"It's an ACTS rally," Deborah said without emotion. She continued to watch, hypnotized, numb with shock. *Oh, God, Joanna's the one Carolyn's looking for. Joanna's the one who was heading for Canada because of death threats.* "These are the founders," she added. *God, why didn't I ask Joanna what she had been doing?*

"Oh my God, Joanna's one of the founders of ACTS? And she's here on contract?" Sara put her hand on Deborah's shoulder to steady herself, and then looked at Deborah. "Did you know?"

Deborah shook her head. "No, but I'm not surprised," she said in a hollow voice. "Joanna always did have charisma. You've seen that here. Sharp as a tack. Maybe not notice what she was wearing but logistically, she could pull something like this together without breaking a sweat." She paused. "She'd be wound up so tight she'd be bouncing off the walls but no one ever saw that, just that cool exterior. Nothing fazed her at that point, someone just had to pull her back before she burnt herself out."

As long as she talked, she didn't have to listen. She didn't have to hear how opposed Joanna was to her, how criminal she was, how she was power hungry, how she was taking advantage of people's misfortunes, how controlling she was. She finally leaned forward and muted the speakers but she couldn't bring herself to turn off the video, to see Joanna pace across the stage, impassioned, to see her fix her gaze on someone in the audience as if they were the only one in the world. Someone must have picked her wardrobe, as Joanna never would have chosen the tailored slacks, the white shell, the small earrings that cupped her ears, the matching necklace that hung just between the curve of her breasts. She watched as Joanna finished her speech and was hugged by her companions. She ducked her head as she raised her hand in acknowledgment of the applause. The video went black abruptly.

"Did you know this?" Sara demanded as Deborah leaned forward to pop the disc.

"No." Deborah stopped, holding it in her hand.

"My God," Sara repeated. "I remembered her on television as a reporter. I knew that she became an activist but I lost track. And frankly, the issue of contracts wasn't on my radar."

"Not on mine either. At the time."

"Deborah, are you all right?"

Deborah shook her head. "I need to think."

"What are you going to do?"

Deborah shook her head again. "I don't know," she said faintly. She sat back down, bowed her head in an effort to organize her thoughts but they kept going in a circle. She'd been attacked before because she had contracts. She had managed, at least locally, to speak of her contracts like family, which seemed to make it more acceptable. All the old families had had hired hands or live-in help that had been regarded as family, so a piece of paper was easy to gloss over. Outside of the area, well, Deborah didn't go there much. But all this coming from Joanna? That was an unexpected blow.

She got to her feet. "I need to take a walk."

"Deborah, it's getting late."

Deborah shook her head. "Everything's settled here for the time being. Joanna's locked up. Bobbi certainly won't want to run into me. The rest of the house needs to settle how they feel without staring me in the face." She powered down the laptop and closed it and then put it in the bottom desk drawer. "Don't say anything about this. To anyone. I'm relying on you. I need to…" She stopped. What did she need to do? To think about this.

"You take Joanna her meals out in the stable. I don't want anyone else having any contact with her, and certainly not a repeat of what happened the last time." She pulled open the desk drawer. "Here's the key if something happens, the barn catches fire or something. Otherwise, she stays there."

Deborah started up the stairs and halfway up, she stalled, realizing she couldn't go into the room she shared with Joanna. She had lain in bed and listened to Joanna toss and turn, moan in her sleep, and steeled herself against going in to comfort her. The night they had spent at the hotel had been heaven and hell, certainly hell enough for her to realize that she probably shouldn't repeat it. And she had foolishly thought the feeling of her blood pounding when they were at the warehouse on that first day had been just because she hadn't seen Joanna in such a long time and was appalled at her mistreatment.

"Deborah?"

Deborah turned to see Karen standing at the foot of the stairs, eyeing her in an uncertain perplexed way.

"Are you all right?"

Deborah pulled herself together. She needed to get out of here for a bit, get away. She couldn't think with everyone around and worse, couldn't act like everything was all right when she actually felt that the earth had just shifted beneath her feet. She turned around and went back down the stairs. "Yes. How about you? You were in the thick of things. Are you all right?"

"Just bruises. Joanna's got quite a kick."

"Probably played soccer." Deborah vaguely remembered a trophy. "What's up?"

"We've lost an afternoon's work, and now Linda's gone."

"She'll be back. What was on the schedule?"

Karen shook her head. "Not much."

Deborah examined Karen with new eyes. Karen was inexperienced in supervision. She had never had a managerial role before and only had this one because she had been there from the beginning. Everyone was probably coming to Karen as the work manager for some reassurance, but who did Karen have to go to besides Deborah?

"Just rework the schedules for a couple of days, Karen. Linda should be back tomorrow so she's no problem. Do without Joanna and Bobbi until I decide what to do with them. Keep everyone busy, that shouldn't be difficult should it?"

"Not hardly." Karen stuffed her hands in her hip pockets and stared at the ground.

Deborah picked up the jacket from the front coat hook. "I'm going out for a while."

"Taking a walk around, to think," Karen supplied as she came to the door.

Deborah gave a rueful laugh. "I'm getting too predictable," she said with a faint smile. "Yes, to think. I'll be back later. Hold the fort down while I'm gone."

"Be careful," Karen said at the door as Deborah left.

Deborah slung the jacket over her shoulder and started walking, out through the orchard, over the stile, past the buildings. When the sun went down and it got cooler, she put the jacket on. She shoved her hands in the pockets and kept walking, simply putting one foot in front of the other, not caring where. Only when she realized it was almost completely dark, did she look up to see where she might be.

She had been walking for over two hours, a walk so automatic, that she had taken so often, she hadn't needed to pay attention. Now she needed to focus and reach a safe place. By the time she reached the buildings, it was true dark and if they hadn't been painted white, she might not have been able to find them. She opened the side door to the garage and felt over the top of the doorframe, hoping that Linda hadn't gotten smart and moved the key. Then she felt her way over to the house, around the house to the back door and into the back porch.

No lights, but there were still candles in the drawer. The pantry was empty to avoid attracting rodents. The water pump on the back porch still worked though. She remembered how many hot summers she had walked over here and tasted the cool fresh spring water. She drank from habit and hung the tin cup back on the nail over the sink.

She was still numb but not as blank. She had been able to process during this walk, really not so far as the crow flies, just miles and miles on the roads. How many times had she and Linda met in the fields, halfway between the houses? How many times had she walked over here or met Linda halfway? That must have been why her feet came here automatically. She hadn't consciously planned to come this way.

She made her way to the living room, dripped some wax on the end table and anchored the candle. She took the seat in the recliner by the door and pushed herself back. The house was silent. She stared into the darkness almost dozing off. She sat up abruptly and blew out the candle. Linda wouldn't appreciate it if she burned the house down. She pushed herself back and closed her eyes. She was so tired, all she wanted to do was to go to sleep and maybe this whole thing would be a bad dream.

She awoke abruptly at some sound, not remembering where she was, when it was. The room was bright with blinding sunlight, and she turned at the pounding at the door before she recognized her surroundings. Then all the events of the past day came flooding back. Linda's house, she had walked over last night. She got out of the recliner, moving stiffly and unlocked the front door.

"Good morning," Linda greeted her in a cheery voice. "Or should I say afternoon?" She pulled out her pocket watch. "Yep, afternoon."

"Ohhh," Deborah moaned. She turned away. "It can't be that late. I never sleep like that anymore."

"Did it this time, girlfriend." Linda came in and took off the bag she had slung over her shoulder. "Brought you some food, didn't think that you'd find much over here. I cleaned out everything when I closed up the house." She handed the bag over to Deborah.

Deborah walked through to the kitchen, set the bag on the table and opened the knapsack. "Hot damn," she said, pulling out the thermos. "Better be tea. Need something besides plain water."

Linda moved around the kitchen pulling out a mug, a plate. "Thought you might need something. You took off yesterday without taking anything. By dark Karen was almost frantic. Sara and I had to sit on her to keep her from going out searching." She handed over the mug as Deborah opened and inhaled the contents of the thermos.

"But you knew where I went." She poured the liquid and drank. It was just the right temperature.

"Had a good idea." She leaned against the kitchen counter and folded her arms across her chest. She said nothing as Deborah unwrapped the ham and cheese biscuits. She waited until Deborah had eaten one of them before she spoke again. "Get everything figured out?"

Deborah shrugged. She still didn't know what she was going to do but she didn't feel so numb anymore. So Joanna had become an activist. She had always wanted to improve the world and thought she could make a contribution. Contracts were the issue. And God knows, certainly Deborah did, that contracts could be abused.

"You know," Linda cut into her thoughts, "gotta tell you. If ever Sara set her mind to it, she could be one hell of a poker player."

Deborah turned back to Linda. "How so?"

"She nabbed me before I even made it into the house from having been in town, wanted to know if I had seen you."

"So?"

"Then she announced at the supper table that you had run into me and told me that you'd be gone overnight and not to let anyone worry. You'd be back tomorrow, that is today. She announced that and didn't bat an eye. I figured anyone who could tell a bald-faced lie like that could certainly run a good bluff at poker."

"Sara doesn't gamble."

"Mighty good thing or you might lose your standing as a good bluffer."

Deborah gave a weak laugh, trying to picture Sara playing cards. The image just wouldn't fit. "Maybe I need to stay away a bit longer and see what else she can come up with."

Linda pointed a finger at her. "You do that, and I'm with you because I'm not going back there and telling her you're not coming."

"You could tell her you couldn't find me."

"She'd call me a liar, and I don't appreciate that. I'll do lots of things for you, but lying to Sara isn't one of them."

Deborah shook her head. Sara could be surprising. She could just see Sara telling everyone such a story, calming everyone, proceeding like everything was normal. "I don't think you'll have to do that." She slowly unwrapped another biscuit. "I need to go back there and settle things." She ate absently. "Did you get that authority to Henderson? Any problems?"

"Yes, I did, and no problems. And he got it filed just like you wanted. You file it for two people?" Deborah absently nodded. "Well, he thought it was strange but he went and did it. Said he'd have the information for you when you got to town."

"What'd you tell him as to why I wasn't there?"

"Said you were sick something awful, everyone was worried about you." She paused. "Wasn't so much of a lie. Everyone was real upset last night that you were gone."

Deborah looked at her in surprise. "Why?" She expected people to miss her but worry about her? No, she didn't expect anyone ever to worry about her.

"You don't just take off and disappear like that. Yeah, a walk around, everyone knows you do that in order to think. But you're always back by dark and you've never been gone this long. Upsets them. Makes them pissed off at Joanna and Bobbi."

"Oh, really?" The thought had never occurred to her anyone would be mad at Joanna and Bobbi.

"Well, why not? Even though Joanna made it clear from the first night she wasn't happy to be on contract, you're not the one who put her there. And from the looks of her when she came in, she hadn't been on any picnic. So why isn't she grateful instead of being a troublemaker? You've been more than fair with her. Some people just don't know when they're well off."

Deborah eyed Linda's indignation and smiled. "You say that because you know that you can walk away anytime." She looked around the room, the ceiling. "Roof over your head, place to sleep, work to do. It's easy to say be pissed at Joanna when you've got all those choices. You might feel differently if you didn't have any choice."

"You're right. I do. But there are others in your house who don't have anywhere else to go, and would have a hard time managing without you. They know better than to bite the hand that feeds them."

"They still made the choice. All right, maybe it wasn't much of a choice but they made it. No one forced them to sign on the dotted line. Joanna didn't even have that."

Linda fell silent, a faint look of disgust on her face. "You're still defending her, making excuses for her."

Deborah opened her mouth to speak and then closed it. Linda was only saying what Deborah had been feeling all through the previous night. "I suppose so. But I guess if I couldn't see her side of the deal, I'd be the kind of contract holder I don't want to be." She began to repack the knapsack. "Why did you sign a contract with me, Linda?" When Linda didn't answer right away, she turned around.

Linda had a look of disbelief. "Oh," she said finally. "Lots of reasons. Got tired of living alone. You came back like you'd forgotten how to live on a farm and I wanted to help. I was over at your place a lot anyway. You had some good ideas on wanting to help people." She gave a rueful deprecating chuckle. "Had to stick by so I could be there if you ran into trouble, so I could bail you out."

Deborah did manage to smile. "You could do all that without a contract."

"Couldn't live there. Everyone got upset, thought I was freeloading."

"Too independent for that. You gave up a lot of that independence when you signed that contract."

"I trusted you." The silence in the room hung heavy between them. Linda abruptly moved from the counter. "I trusted you then, and I trust you now. But you're going to have to come up with something about Joanna. And quickly. And besides Joanna, you've got one hell of a problem with Bobbi. That woman is about as useful on a farm as, as I don't know what. To give Joanna her due, she's a good worker and doesn't think labor's beneath her, once she figured out she wasn't being treated unfairly. She just doesn't want to be there." She moved around the house, locking the back door and going to the living room to pick up the candle and clean off the table. "Where's your jacket?" She came back to the kitchen and picked up the knapsack. "So what *are* you going to do about them?"

"I guess it will come to me when it comes," she answered as she stepped off the porch for the walk home together.

CHAPTER FOURTEEN

When there was a knock on the office door later that day, Deborah still didn't know what she was going to do. "Come in." She watched the stocky brunette enter, and not for the first time, she wondered what she had seen in her.

"You wanted to see me."

"Yes." Deborah made no move to come from behind her desk. This was one time she wanted the distance and the authority. Bobbi came in and closed the door quietly behind her. "Have a seat."

Bobbi still looked ravaged from the day before and seemed poised to flee at any sudden move Deborah might make. She didn't return Deborah's angry gaze.

"You really don't like it here, do you, Bobbi?" Deborah started out, stating the obvious.

"It wasn't what I went to college for," she replied quietly.

"Well, it wasn't what I majored in either." Deborah sat back in her chair. "Like any of us, you're a little out of your area of expertise. Like Sara, what was she, a French teacher?" Bobbi nodded. "Now she's a housekeeper. And Karen, engineering I think. And Brea, financial management. And Rae, real estate. Gee, I bet they all wanted to give it up and plant veggies for a living, muck out stalls. I'm sure it was on their ten-year life plan. Don't you?" Bobbi made no response and the silence lengthened. "When I ask a question, I really expect an answer, Bobbi. Do you think that this was in any of their life plans?"

"No."

Deborah nodded, acknowledging Bobbi's response. "But you, you *really* don't like it, do you? Or is it just me that you don't like?" She waited, and she waited.

"Maybe a bit of both," Bobbi said cautiously.

"Maybe so," Deborah agreed. "You know," she said as she picked up the letter opener and began to play with it. "I was really lucky. If I hadn't needed to be back here for family business, I would have been sitting in my favorite spot, in my office in the library, overlooking the pond, placing new orders and planning the spring book fair. My office was buried under tons of books and steel and cement. I doubt that I would have made it out alive but I would have been in a place that I loved. Where were you when the earthquake struck?"

"I wasn't in the earthquake zone," Bobbi said. "I was in a job interview. My company had eliminated my department. I had gone to Columbus for a promising interview, it was the second one."

"Did it come through?"

Bobbi shook her head. "No. I think there were over a hundred applicants for that one position."

"Hum, a shame," Deborah admitted. "Times are hard." She let it rest for a minute. "Like I said, I was lucky I was here. Out of the earthquake zone, had a few rattles but nothing like home. I lost my house, my job, lots of people I knew didn't make it. But I had to look at what I had. I had a farm, an opportunity to survive, might not be easy, but at least I had a place to lay my head and a way to put food on the table. All in all, I thought I was damn lucky. It was more than a lot of people had."

"Yes," Bobbi agreed slowly. "It was."

"And I thought that since I was so lucky it was miserly not to share it. I had more than enough so I decided in those first few days when all that terrible news was coming out of Memphis, I thought I could share it all. Well, that didn't turn out the way I thought it would, but I did promise myself one thing. I needed to help anyone I ever had ties with, especially family. That was part of being in a supporting network. Not that I was tripping over family up here, gay family that is. Blood family, I had more than enough of, but I thought the gay family, the lesbian family needed to be supported. Some of our networks weren't strong and a lot of us didn't have supportive families." She watched Bobbi squirm. She knew Bobbi's family was not supportive, something Bobbi had always bemoaned.

"So when you and Sara came along, I felt obligated. Not that you had done so much for me. At college, you thought you were going to teach me the ways of the world and when I rejected them, well I was ungrateful and a county hick, not worthy of your attention. You really were a manipulative bitch, convincing all your friends that I was an ignorant little bumpkin. And for some reason, God help me, I don't have the faintest idea why now, I thought you were pretty neat. You had traveled, you were smart and you were cute. And you did teach me some new things in bed. But you weren't the first one there." She chuckled at Bobbi's startled look.

"Whatever there was," she went on as she put the letter opener back in the pencil holder, "I felt like I had the obligation. Even when you bitched and moaned and were just in general a pain in the ass. I knew you embroidered stories, you always did like to inflate yourself. I just don't feel so inclined to give you the benefit of a doubt anymore." She watched Bobbi squirm. "But, I am inclined to do something else, something I've never done before."

"You can't sell my contract!" Bobbi said quickly. "Part of your reputation is that you buy contracts, you don't sell them."

"That's true. You've done your homework." God, she wanted to wipe that smug look off Bobbi's face. "But there is a termination clause in the contract. I can cut you loose."

"Cut me loose?" Bobbi leaped to her feet. "You can't do that."

Deborah sat back, satisfied that she had Bobbi's full attention. "I most certainly can. It's in the contract that either party can terminate it. Not state contracts, but the civil ones that most of you have here. I didn't satisfy a debt for you that you're working off. I'm not taking over a government responsibility for you. I haven't taken over a loan for you. It's simply a civil contract offering room and board for your unskilled labor, and an as yet undefined share of any profits. You don't like the work—you said it over and over again. You have proven yourself to be a troublemaker of the first magnitude. You don't have a skilled trade that I need. I don't need you."

"But where will I go? What will I do?"

"I don't care."

"Deborah, you can't do this to me. You contracted with Sara and me together. Are you cutting her loose too?"

"No, I contracted you both at the same time, but not together. You were not partners with her. You have separate contracts."

"Deborah, you can't do this to me," Bobbi entreated, her eyes filling with tears.

"Why not? Give me one good reason." Deborah even laughed, an ugly laugh. "Hell, I'll be generous, magnanimous even: give me one *bad* reason and I'll reconsider it."

Bobbi began to cry. "Please, Deborah, you know I'm perfectly useless out there now."

"Yeah, I know it. I don't think you know it."

"Please, Deborah. I'll do anything, anything at all. I'll shut my mouth. I'll never complain about one damn thing again. I'll do any task you set me to. I'll take on every shit task—" She stopped there for an instant and sobbed. On a farm, there was lots of shit work. "Please don't let me go. I'm so sorry. I really didn't mean to egg Joanna on. I was just talking through my hat. I just wanted—"

"Wanted what?" Deborah said in a tired voice.

"I just wanted to be somebody besides the fuck-up." She cried. "You don't know what it's like to know you screw up everything, even the shit work. How in the hell can someone screw up mucking up cow shit?" And she cried.

Deborah watched her and didn't feel the faintest bit of sympathy, which only told her that it had been a big mistake to take Bobbi on to start with. "All right, stop crying," she said finally. Bobbi slowly got control of herself. "And after that little crying jag, am I supposed to have pity on you?"

"Yes."

"Why?"

"Because you loved me once."

"Please, don't remind me. I'm beginning to think I've had the shittiest judgment in women and should have joined a nunnery." *But then I found Joanna.*

"Because you may need me."

Deborah stared at the ceiling. Was there no limit to Bobbi's conceit? "And how, pray tell, might I need you?"

"Because I worked in psych in police departments and whether you like it or not, you're going to have to deal with all sorts of people."

"First I've heard of it, Bobbi, and from what I've seen of you, you must have been fired for incompetence then, because you are the most manipulating, conniving woman I've ever seen."

Bobbi swallowed. "Which makes me an asset if I'm working for you, doesn't it?" Deborah said nothing. "You said to give you a reason, even a bad one. Will you reconsider expelling me?" Bobbi waited. "Please, Deborah. I'll make amends. I've been an ass, I'll agree. Please, give me another chance."

Deborah tapped her finger on the chair arm. She shook her head, examining those hazel eyes.

"Please." Bobbi barely kept from crying again.

"I'll reconsider," she said finally.

"Oh, God, thank you. You won't regret this, really, Deborah, really, you won't."

"I said I'd reconsider, Bobbi. I didn't say I have changed my mind. Now get out of here before I do." Bobbi bolted for the door. "And Bobbi, you're on *really* thin ice. No stories, no exaggerations, no undermining morale, no whining. I don't want to be around you when you're not working. And don't talk to me."

Bobbi nodded so energetically that all Deborah could think of was those little bobbing head figurines.

"Out," she ordered and Bobbi was gone. *One down, one to go.*

* * *

Deborah walked around a bit, not sure at all what she had to say to Joanna. She had started for the stable but then she veered off and walked around to the barn. She saw everyone working. Some nodded and she absently nodded back, but no one spoke to her. Everything had changed in ways she never would have imagined. She had been furious when they had found Joanna and Bobbi—furious and relieved and frightened. For the first time she understood parents who snatched their children from danger and then threatened to kill them for scaring them so.

Some part of her had been smug that they hadn't gone very far, but another part of her was appalled that they were so close to disappearing completely. She had been speechless in her fury, not daring to even vent how angry she was, and that, she gathered slowly, was what had everyone on edge. It was quite one thing for her to send Bobbi to her room. The sniveling little bitch was too scared to stick her head outside the door. It was quite another for her to manhandle Joanna back to the house and then to lock her in the stable. She had never before done anything like this to anyone contracted to her. She didn't know what she would have done if Joanna had struggled more.

Yes, she did. She would have taken her down, tied and gagged her if necessary, praying all the while that none of the locals saw Joanna and Bobbi clearly fleeing.

She had walked around the barn and the sheds, circled all the outbuildings until she came to the stone wall. She stood there a moment in contemplation. She turned and looked over the buildings, the gardens where everyone was working, where she should be working. She wanted to walk away, that feeling again, but now there was nowhere to walk to. She shook off uneasiness and started for the stable.

Just like the time Joanna had revolted over the chickens, Joanna again sat on a bale of hay in the stallion's stall, with its bars above the chest high wall reaching to the ceiling. It was airy, light and not as isolated as the sleeping quarters in the corner. The sliding door had a locked deadbolt so it served the purpose. Not the purpose of a get-away space that Deborah had proposed or that Linda and Karen had refurbished the building for, but like everything else on the farm, it was adaptable.

Deborah stood at the door for a moment. Joanna glanced at her and then looked away. She looked comfortable enough on the hay bale, leaning against the wall, casually chewing on a piece of grass. But Deborah could see her tension, the apprehension. "You open for company?" Deborah greeted.

Joanna shrugged without looking at Deborah. "My time is your time."

Deborah slid the door closed behind her. She still wasn't sure what she was going to say, so her first words surprised her. "Why, Jo? Why'd you run away?"

Joanna gave her a quick surprised look and then quickly looked away. She frowned but she made no answer.

"Why?" Deborah repeated as she advanced to the middle of the stall.

"I told you," Joanna finally said stolidly, without looking at her. "I don't want to be on contract."

As if I can control that! "Did I treat you badly? Were you ill-used? Tell me, Joanna, what did I do wrong?" Joanna said nothing, and Deborah shook her head. "I win you in a poker game, like some prized chit. I take you away from abuse and mistreatment. I bring you into my house, shelter you, feed you, clothe you. You're not abused. You're not beaten. You're not raped." She paused, trying to stay philosophical and not be angry or wounded. "I give you much more freedom than the law allows. You make friends, you take a lover." Joanna jerked around at that, surprise all over her face. Deborah met Joanna's wide eyes. *Didn't you think I knew?* "So tell me, why did you run?"

Surprise settled into stubbornness as Joanna repeated in the most reasonable voice, "I told you in the beginning, I don't want to be on contract."

Deborah looked down at the straw-covered floor a moment, exhaled. "And sitting in a jail cell for the next five years would be better than here with me?" She looked around, saw the other bale by the door, and sat down. She needed to put aside her personal feelings. No matter how she felt, what Joanna did affected them all and there were others that Deborah had to consider here.

"Did you really think that you could make it to Canada?" Joanna's head came up. "The underground has been watched, not so much for you specifically. After all, when you started out, you weren't on contract. Were the threats so horrific, Joanna?"

"What do you know about them?" Joanna demanded as she sat up.

Deborah sat back, stretched out her legs, crossed her ankles. This could be a long conversation. "Enough to know that you thought Canadian weather might be better for your health." She remembered the initial shock at Carolyn's CD and then the realization that she had been so stupid, so blind as to not wonder what Joanna had been doing these past years. "Why didn't you tell me about ACTS?"

Joanna made no reply.

Deborah examined the toes of her boots. "My mistake was taking you at face value. I thought if you had a safe place, you'd consider it a sanctuary. I'm not foolish enough to think that it's a piece of cake here. There's a lot of hard work. We're isolated. There's a lot of things we do without. But, so far, we've managed to stay out of the limelight and be relatively safe and secure."

"Because you deal with the militia so you're not bothered," Joanna retorted.

Deborah shrugged. She knew Joanna was guessing but she saw no reason for denying it, or confirming it. "Militia, military, someone always wants the upper hand. Take your pick. If you want to survive, you do what's necessary. I told you, I intend to survive."

"That's not the way it's supposed to be!"

Deborah looked up with the anger she reserved for those people who don't deal with reality. "That's the way it *is*, Joanna. And you might want to change it—hell, you might even be able to, but right now, right here, that's the way it is."

Joanna glared back and Deborah finally shook her head. This was an area they were always going to disagree on. She sat up, leaned forward, her elbows on her knees. There was no sense going over and over this again. She even thought that, given time, Joanna's arguments would win. Just not right now. "You have piss-poor timing besides," she commented.

"How's that?"

"I discovered you missing because I got a notice in about your contract. There's been a class action filed to set aside all shanghaied contracts." *That got her interest* she thought as Joanna sat up. And because she was still annoyed, Deborah added, "Mail being what it is and the fact that I'm not known for having forced contracts, I didn't get the notice until very late. Deadline was yesterday."

Joanna froze, her hopes dashed. "You, you deliberately kept me out of it!" Her fists clenched and Deborah felt vaguely satisfied.

"I wasn't the one who wasn't available," she said mildly. "And then, when I went to find you, I had more pressing matters on my plate, like tracking down two runaways before someone else caught them and caused a whole lot of problems." She watched Joanna's face grow even paler and she had the idle thought that Joanna's dark eyes against her white face gave her a tousled moppet look. Charming, endearing, infuriating.

"No, Joanna," she said resignedly as she tossed down pieces of the hay she had been pulling from the bale. "I sent Linda in to Richmond to see Henderson and get you included in the filing while I went in search for you. Having your contract declared null and void wouldn't do you much good if you were sitting in jail for failing to honor it and being charged with the damages."

"They would have set that aside."

"In a pig's eye, they would. They'd have dragged it all out until your time served was over and then apologized and said all sorts of flowery things, but the fact would be that you'd been in jail for five years." She looked up at Joanna in faint disgust. "You still don't get it do you, Jo? You can complain about the system and you can even move it—I'll give you credit, you'll probably get it changed, but in this case, here and now, contracts are going to exist because they are a means of survival. And until survival is easier, then this is what's going to happen. Trying to circumvent the system or break it isn't going to work."

"Keeps you sitting in a pretty spot!"

Is that what you call it? "And you." Joanna bristled and took a deep breath but Deborah cut her off. She didn't have time for another debate. "Look, we could debate this question forever and neither one of us is going to say anything new. This is where we're at, and this is what we have to deal with."

Joanna shut her mouth, a good sign, Deborah decided. At least she hadn't stopping thinking rationally. "Are you going to turn me in?" Joanna asked finally.

"Hell, no. I've seen those jails. If you saw them you'd think this," and she glanced around the straw-filled stall, "was a pleasure palace. They're dirty, under staffed, poorly maintained. Even if you were lucky enough to get to the prison farm, you'd still be at risk of rape and everything else that goes on there."

"Are you trying to scare me?"

"No." Deborah shook her head. "I'm willing to offer you a deal."

"Deal? What kind of deal?"

Deborah looked around, unable to look at Joanna. She hated to doubt her but she really wondered if she could trust her. "We need every pair of hands here for the growing season to make our commitments. This class action thing, it's not going to be settled quickly. If it's done by fall, I'll be surprised. But then again, someone's lit a fire so it may happen. Never can tell. You stay here, give me no problems, no headaches, wait until that gets decided. It gets set aside, I'll swallow any damages they put on and you'll be free to go, a free woman, wherever you want."

"And if it's not set aside?"

"I'll take you to Canada myself."

"What?" Joanna came to her feet.

"You heard me. There wouldn't be any problem traveling with someone who holds your contract. Once we cross over the border." She shrugged. "I put a bond on you. I'm not liable for any so-called damages you might do in Canada. We're free and clear. I come home."

"And what happens when I come back to the States?"

Deborah shook her head. "I have no idea. So many things could happen that I wouldn't even want to guess that far. Forecasting next year's weather would be easier." She examined her boots. "I wouldn't advise coming back for some time though. Could get real sticky." *Sticky, boy is that an understatement.* She fell silent, thinking of all the terrible possibilities. She finally looked up to see Joanna kneeling in the straw in front of her.

"Why, Deb, why are you offering me this?"

Don't touch, please don't touch. Deborah examined the face that she had fantasized about, dreamed about for years and then had closed the door on. She didn't dare move. "Do you think this has been easy on me? To see you at my table, in my house, in my bedroom? To know that what I see as a sanctuary for you, you see as a humiliation? To see that you have been hurt and could be hurt again? To feel you look at me and see me as representing something you despise? To want to do something for you and have to balance it against every other woman here, to catch myself and ask if I would do it for any of them? It would be so much easier if I simply knew that you were away, far, far away, but safe and secure."

"I didn't think it bothered you," Joanna said slowly. "I thought when you shut doors, they stayed shut."

"Might have been if I hadn't turned on the television every night and seen you." She looked away. "It was a great thing for you. You were right, it was the opportunity of a lifetime, a stepping stone that wouldn't come by again. It gave you everything you wanted."

Joanna bowed her head, not looking at Deborah.

"You did well, Joanna," Deborah said slowly. "I never begrudged your success. You took the opportunity and ran with it and didn't let it go to your head. You gained respect and position and influence without running over people or cutting people down. It was the right choice for you."

"And what about you?" Joanna looked up. "Was it the right choice for you?"

"I made my choices, and they were the right choices for me." She looked at Joanna sadly. "There were just never the right choices for us."

Joanna sat back on her heels, her hands on her thighs as Deborah moved back a bit, away from her. "So what now?"

"That depends on whether you take my offer or not."

"And if I don't?"

Deborah leaned forward. "Do you realize," she said intensely, "what could happen?"

Joanna drew back from her. "I run away, either I get there or I get caught, whatever."

"Whatever is right!" Deborah heatedly. "This would be your third time, so jail. I've already told you what the jails are like. If you get tossed in there by *anyone*, I get charged. This is a poor economy. *I* have to finance your support, for your board, as horrible as it might be. You think I'm well-off, but it's not in terms of cash or anything that can be liquidated. I've got land and I've got buildings, those are my assets. My only other assets that can be liquidated are contracts." She pointed off to the house. "Every one of those women has a contract with me and every one of those contracts could be sold to whoever has the cash to buy them. And there's a hell of a lot more contract holders like Gentry than there are like me. That's how your room and board for five years would need to be paid."

She got up from her seat, moving around Joanna now with no difficulty. "Damn it, Jo. In that respect, you haven't changed a bit. Show you the overall picture and you can put your finger on the problem. See the changes coming and see where they might lead us, good or bad. But I still had to stop you on the way out the door in the morning and make sure that you had money in your pocket for lunch, and make sure there were groceries in the cabinets. You just don't get the small picture, the consequences of *your* actions."

She paced around the stall, too angry now to speak. Joanna in turn, looked down to her lap, and said softly, "I didn't know. I didn't realize."

"Of course not," Deborah snapped and then took a deep breath. She really didn't think that Joanna was selfish or self-centered. She probably *didn't* know. And Deborah wouldn't have thought about it except for Sara pointing it out buried in the fine print. She came back over and crouched down in front of Joanna.

"Look, Jo. If it were up to me..." She reached out and raised Joanna's face to hers. "If it were just me, I'd pack your bags and give you an escort, but it's not just me. Every contract I've made has been with the understanding that we need each other. I have the local standing, the land, just not the labor. They provide that and in return have some sense of security. I can't put that at risk for all those women."

Joanna looked away. "And I remember you as being someone who didn't want to have anything she couldn't just walk away from, to be invisible, no responsibilities."

"Yeah. I remember her too, I just don't know where the hell she went." Deborah withdrew from Joanna and got to her feet. She paced up and down the length of the stall, occasionally eyeing Joanna, who hadn't moved. She wanted to give her time to consider, but the longer Joanna remained silent, the less optimistic she was. Finally she stopped behind her. "If you're going to take off, Joanna, tell me now. Give me time to get everything arranged."

"Arranged?" Joanna was on her feet, grabbing Deborah's arm. "What are you talking about?"

"Every contract I have has a thirty-day termination notice for either party. I can start canceling the contracts, turn everyone loose."

"But where would they go? What would they do?"

Deborah shook her head. "I don't know. One or two might have resources locally but then—" She shook her head again and stared at the ground. "The contracts we have would have to be ended. Luella's contract for us supplying her with food would default." She grew cold at the thought of all she was dismantling, everything she had spent the last years building up, everything they had worked for.

"But—but there's no place for those women to go. The diner, Luella's dependent on us. There would be a ripple effect, even the commune would be affected."

"Yes, I know."

"No, you can't make me responsible for that!"

"But you *are*." Deborah threw off Joanna's hand. "I won't have them sold when I promised they would be safe. And I'd much rather they at least have the freedom to make those choices instead of just be taken." She started thinking aloud. "Thirty days, give them notice tomorrow, we'd get some of the crops in. Send the notice to Carolyn. She might be able to set something up. Even without a contract, I think I could hire her in return for a share of the crops that would be harvested after thirty days." She started pacing, stepping around Joanna. "Linda's okay. Beth would have the clinic. If I gave her a severance, she might have enough to get her started, and then maybe she could do it. Sara. Sara? Henderson said he could use someone, not much, but better than nothing. Karen has Beth. Peg? Rae? Brea? I don't know."

"Stop it!" Joanna flung herself in front of Deborah. "You can't do this to me!"

"I'm not doing this to you, Joanna. This is what happens. These are the choices I have, and this is the choice that I would make. You give me your word and I go with it. You don't, and I make arrangements with the least collateral damage."

"You'd break your contract with them?" Joanna's voice rose.

"I'd break those contracts rather than see them sold! I promised them safety and security to the best of my ability. If I can't give them that, then the contract is broken. My cutting them loose is just a formality."

"You can't do that! You'd lose all your credibility!"

Deborah gave a mirthless laugh. "Hell, I'd be lucky if that was all I lost." She knew in the worst-case scenario, she could end up on contract to pay the debt.

It took a few moments for her meaning to sink in. "No, I won't have it!"

"What's wrong, Joanna? You left me with about this much the last time, just more invisible. What difference does it make?"

It ended with them facing each other, Joanna even more white-faced and Deborah feeling cold and grim and hard. "This is what being a contract holder means," Joanna said sneeringly. "Deciding about people's lives."

"No," Deborah came back immediately. "This is being responsible, keeping my word. I'm not a god. I can't control events. We hammered out an agreement and now I can't keep my part of it."

"You could lock me up."

"I could. But I won't. No one deserves that. And I'm no one's jailer."

Joanna closed her eyes. "What do you want me to do, Deborah?"

"I want you to decide," Deborah spat back in deliberate tones.

Joanna shook her head. "I can't consent to this."

Deborah's shoulders sagged. "Then that's what we'll do." She took a step toward the door.

"No!"

Deborah turned. "No? You mean you'll run immediately? You'd make me keep you under lock and key until—"

"No." Joanna hung her head in resignation. "No. I'll stay. I'll give you no problems. Then when the suit is decided, we'll see what happens."

"Look at me," Deborah ordered. "Tell me that."

Joanna looked up at her and Deborah could see the grief and the pain. She set her jaw, determined not to bend on this. There was too much risk for too many people.

"I give you my word, Deborah Steele," Joanna said clearly. "I won't run. I won't give you any problems. Until the suit is finalized, I'll be a willing contract to you."

Deborah let out a breath she didn't know she was holding. "Thank you, Joanna."

* * *

That evening around the dinner table was awkward. It was the first meal they were all together since the incident, well, all but Joanna who remained in isolation in her room. Her punishment aside, she was still a little too shaky to face everyone. As it was, conversation was forced and Bobbi was as awkward as ever, dropping silverware, knocking over her glass. She escaped at the first opportunity, muttering that she had to do something somewhere. Deborah really didn't care but when everyone else started to get up, she did speak.

"Can we talk for a moment?" Everyone settled back into their chairs. Deborah took a deep breath, not wanting to do this at all. A meeting would be easier but meetings were for the entire house. "I think this would be a good opportunity since neither Joanna nor Bobbi are here. I have an issue with you." She took a long deliberate look all around the table and found few to meet her gaze. "All of you. There is no way that Bobbi and Joanna could have planned taking off with none of you knowing anything about it. And now we have to deal with the effect it has on all of us. So I have to admit, I'm a little pissed with all of you."

"With us?" Karen burst out. "What did we do?"

"It's more what you didn't do," Deborah said slowly. "I know I've ignored Bobbi. We had a stormy ending to an unhealthy relationship. Still it was enough of a relationship that I felt the obligation to bring her into the house, but that didn't mean I liked her. I didn't expect she would do something like this—my fault. If she wanted to get out, I didn't think she'd go this far. Some of you had to know what they were planning or how she was bullying Joanna. So you share the responsibility for what happened. And it needn't have happened at all if someone had said something."

No one said anything for a few minutes. "Anyone need to say anything?" Deborah asked.

"We didn't feel like it was something we wanted to deal with. It didn't affect our relationship with you," Beth said.

"It didn't? It affected the house. It set off a nasty chain of events."

"It seemed like a personal issue between you and Bobbi, and Joanna, not a house issue," Linda said.

"And none of our personal issues affect how we interact with each other in the house?"

"Maybe it was just that we didn't want to interfere in someone else's contract," Sara said slowly, playing mediator. "We each know what we've negotiated with you but not what anyone else has. It's been a privacy issue when we all have given up a lot of our own."

"So you thought it was none of your business?" Deborah asked.

"Ahhh," Peg started out. She didn't look up at Deborah, didn't look at anyone as a matter of fact.

"All right," Karen said suddenly, leaning forward. "You're right. It would have been good for one of us to say something. Like Sara said, every one of us hammered out a contract with you, not the house. We're just a group of women who all have contracts with you. Now you've brought Joanna into the house. It was clear you were going in a different direction. I mean, if you're going to start taking on state contracts, that puts a different wash on it."

"I won Joanna's contract in a poker game." A ripple of surprise went around the table. "She was part of a scam run by a guy called Gentry." Deborah explained it all to the women. There was silence around the table as everyone took in this new information.

Deborah didn't say anything, idly tracing the weave in the embroidered cloth with her finger as she looked around at them.

"Uh-hum," Karen said as she finally had the explanation.

"I bet he didn't like that," Sue stated the obvious.

"No, I don't think he did. And unfortunately, he wasn't just passing through. He's made a big pitch for a contract processing center to be located here. That's what's producing all the railroad construction, and in turn, creating our market for the extra food."

"You mean, we're supporting a contract processing center?" Rae jumped to her feet, shoving back her chair.

"No, we're not," Deborah responded firmly. She didn't need a revolt on her hands on top of everything else. "For the record, I am not in favor of it. But if the railroads are repaired, it opens markets. If the markets are opened, there is an opportunity for this county, which is primarily farming. It always has been. No matter how bad the economy is, people have to eat. We've been hampered badly because the road system, the trucking system has been broken. If farming is viable again, people can eat, people can survive, and a contract processing center won't be so financially attractive. But we need the railroads."

"And if the processing center comes here?"

Deborah sighed. There was always that possibility, as much as she did not like it. "There will be employment, economic opportunities, a better life for a bunch of people," she said slowly, ticking off points. "There will be bad elements, lots of problems coming to the area. Taking advantage of people's bad luck. More crime."

"Anyway," she went on, "as you might guess, Carolyn has organized a group opposed to their location here. I think she may have a big battle."

"Are you going to help her?" Sara asked. The table suddenly grew quiet.

"There are..." Deborah stopped, not sure what word to describe her position. "Complications."

"Because you hold contracts," someone supplied.

"Well, that doesn't exactly give me a free ticket in. In fact, Carolyn's initial greeting was that she would throw me out. No, there are a lot of other factors involved." She paused. She didn't want to appear indecisive but right now she was. "I'm still mulling it over—"

"What's the indecision?" Rae exclaimed. "Processing centers are brutal!"

Deborah slowly nodded. "Yes," she agreed slowly. "So are lots of other things."

"You don't want to be a target," Beth said slowly as if coming to sudden clarity. She made it sound like cowardice.

"It would put the house in danger," Brea announced in quiet observation.

"Yeah, there's that," Deborah agreed.

"What kind of danger?" Karen asked.

Deborah took a deep breath and sat up. She might as well lay it on the line. "If there are any damages laid against me for anything, I don't have the cash. If I can't pay these damages, the government, such as it is, will seize my assets. I have land, buildings." She looked around the table. "And contracts." Everyone sat up. "Contracts are the most liquid."

There was silence after that as everyone considered the ramifications.

"You mean," Sue said, "that our contracts could be sold?"

Deborah nodded. "If Joanna had gone to jail, I would have been held responsible because of lax security. The law states I would have been responsible for paying the county or the state for Joanna's support for the term of the contract, which she would be serving in jail."

"Shit," someone muttered.

"Did Joanna know this?" Sara demanded. "Did she deliberately put us at risk?"

"She says she wasn't aware of it, and she probably wasn't. I wasn't aware of it either."

"And now?"

"Joanna's given me her word she will cooperate."

"Do you believe her?" Brea demanded.

Deborah nodded in spite of her misgivings. "Yes."

"What about Bobbi?" Peg asked slowly.

"Oh, Bobbi's a completely different story. I have no idea why she ran except she's a coward. She could give me thirty days' notice at any time and just go. But..." Deborah shrugged. "I have no idea how she reasoned it out. Except for needing all hands available, I wouldn't miss her." She glanced around the table. "As it is, she's begged for another chance. We're coming into the busy season. I, frankly, am inclined to give it to her but she's on my shit list for some time. I don't know if she'll cut it. She's never liked being here, thinks it's a real comedown."

"Well, if she'd just accept that her world has changed and get on with it, she and we'd be a lot better off!"

"Brea," Deborah said with a short laugh at the woman's bluntness. "Not everyone could do that. Bobbi's the only one here who can't accept where she's at."

"Well, if you want my opinion, maybe you should have thought twice about taking her on."

"Maybe so," Deborah conceded. She was relieved on two points. Everything was out in the open, well, not everything, but enough. Secondly, the table full of women seemed to be beginning to consider it their house as well as Deborah's. That would be a relief. "But I didn't and she's here." She paused, but no one spoke. Evidently she had given them enough to think about.

"Well, ladies, I've had my say. Anyone else have anything to add to it?" There was shaking of heads around the table. "Then I guess we need to get back to schedule."

Everyone pushed back their chairs, more subdued than before. *That'll give them something to think about tonight. Now one more issue.* "Peg, a word with you, please."

Peg gave her a short nod and came around the table.

"Let's walk," Deborah said as she pushed her chair under the table. She really didn't want this talk, and after watching Peg's face during this discussion, she wanted it even less. "The orchard?" Peg nodded and they went out the front door.

Did you know? Deborah wanted to ask. She wanted to ask it so badly that she clamped her jaws shut lest the question come blurting out like her initial question to Joanna. "This is awkward," she said finally. "I'm not sure what you know about Joanna's past."

"I know you were lovers," Peg said slowly as she paced beside Deborah.

"Yes, I thought you would put that together." She stopped at the length of the orchard. She turned to Peg but she couldn't see her clearly in the gathering dusk. That was probably just as well.

Do you love her? she wanted to ask. *Really love her? Does she love you? Are you good for each other? Do I even want to know?*

"I imagine you and Joanna now have some issues to discuss," Deborah said instead. "There may be things you don't know."

Peg took a breath but didn't say anything. She didn't look away from Deborah though. "Do I have your permission to speak freely, Deborah?"

Deborah compressed her lips rather than smile. Leave it to the army brat to fall back on the military formality. "No," she said with a sudden decision to stay out of this part of their lives. "I need you to do something for me," she said instead in an even voice. She fished into her breast pocket for the key to her room. "Like I said at the table, there're things I need to think about. I'm going to be ensconced in my office, probably for the night." She handed the key over to Peg who took it with a strange expression. "I want you to go tell Joanna that I won't be in tonight, I'll be downstairs. Bring me back the key whenever you're finished."

Peg opened her mouth and then closed it. "Do you expect me back right away?" she said carefully.

"I don't expect you back until morning."

"Is that an order?"

"No." Deborah drew the word out. "It's an opportunity. What you do with it is your choice."

"Deborah," Peg started.

"Don't." Deborah cut her off. She turned back to the house. "Joanna forgets to eat when she's wrestling with a problem. You might want to take something light with you to eat." She paused again. "And she can work herself into a state if she thinks she's in a safe spot. I don't know if you've seen her like that, but she can be pretty impressive."

"Deborah," Peg tried again.

"I think you need to go before she gets to the depressed state. Sometimes you have to use force to pull her out of it, and you never were good at that." Peg just continued to stand there and look at her. "Go, Peg. Now."

Abruptly Peg turned and left.

CHAPTER FIFTEEN

Joanna stood at the window of her bedroom, arms folded, watching the setting sun. All sorts of weird scenarios were going through her head. She could open the window, drop down to the ground. It was what, only a twenty-foot drop? Take off across the field. But she had given her word not to escape.

Maybe she'd break a leg when she dropped, an arm, her back. Then Deborah would be obligated to care for her without any profit in the deal. Just a passing thought. She wasn't into self-harming.

She leaned her forehead against the window, feeling the heat in the glass. She had come close, and might have made it if there had been just a little more time. Ironic that news of an opportunity for freedom had thwarted a real bid for it.

And now Deborah knew who she was, her connection with ACTS. Maybe Deborah was in with the group of contract holders who had threatened her way back then. Her accusing Deborah of being in cooperation with the militia hadn't brought forth any denial either.

Deborah had simply asked "Why?"

Joanna turned away from the window, barely glancing at the dinner plate Deborah had brought up. She was probably the topic at the dinner table tonight, Deborah outlining new policy and procedures, explaining how Joanna had put them all in danger. Now they would be watching her, all having a vested interest in her not escaping. But she had given her word.

She didn't understand the consequences of her escaping, and she wasn't sure that would have stopped her if she had known. She couldn't bear being trapped like this. She rubbed her face, wondering how she could endure the next months. She stood in the middle of the room, unable to think, unable to decide anything, unable to move. That's where she was when she heard the sound of the key in the door. She didn't care and didn't respond.

"Joanna? Are you all right?"

She looked up in true surprise as Peg took hold of her by the arms and turned her around.

"Joanna?"

"What are you doing here?"

"Deborah sent me up." Peg's face was full of concern, and for the first time her calmness and serenity seemed to be broken. "She said to tell you she was working things out, would be in her office probably most of the night."

Working things out, Joanna thought. It's already begun.

"She said she thought we might have things to discuss."

Joanna still looked at her blankly. "What things?"

"Have you eaten?" Peg asked instead of answering. She looked around the room, saw the meal on the table. "No, you haven't. No wonder. Deborah said you didn't eat when you were upset."

"Not hungry."

"Well, hungry or not, you're going to eat." Sliding her arm around Joanna she drew her over to the table.

"She's going to lock me up," Joanna said as she sat down.

"No, she's not. No more than what she already has."

"She's going to change that stall around and use that for a jail cell."

"I don't think so." Peg pulled the cover off the plate. "Come on, you need to eat. You can tell me what she said to you out there."

Joanna just sat there.

"She didn't hit you, did she?"

"No."

"Did she yell at you?"

Joanna shook her head. "No." And then she laughed slightly. "You know what's funny?"

"What?"

"I could have dealt with the yelling. I even thought she might beat me. And all I could think of was Bobbi saying she was scared of Deborah because Deborah had yelled at her once. Yelled at her." She laughed slightly, and then the laughter turned into a sob. "Oh, Peg, what am I going to do?"

Peg put her arms around Joanna's shoulders and held her. She brushed back Joanna's dark hair, laid her cheek against Joanna's head.

"I didn't mean to put anyone in any danger. Really I didn't."

"I know that," Peg said quietly. "And Deborah knows that too." She held Joanna a bit before she asked. "What did she say to you?"

Joanna was silent, trying to encapsulate the conversation, all the emotions. "She asked why."

"Why?" Peg repeated. "And you told her?"

"I didn't want to be on contract. Like I've been saying all along." Joanna pushed herself free and Peg let her go. "Why is that so hard for everyone to understand?"

"I think everyone understands it, Jo—"

"Don't call me Jo," Joanna burst out angrily. *That's what she calls me, no one else can.*

"All right," Peg went on smoothly. "What no one can understand is why you're blaming Deborah. She didn't put you on contract. She can't release you."

Joanna calmed herself, some of her fog lifting. "She says she will."

"She what?" Peg stepped back to look at Joanna's face. "Release you?"

Joanna rubbed her face, not even fully aware of what she was saying. Peg was so easy to talk to. Joanna relayed the pact that she and Deborah had made.

Peg said nothing and Joanna didn't look up to see her surprise. Finally, Peg spoke. "So you promised."

Joanna nodded.

Peg took a seat across the table from Joanna, a little breathless by this revelation. "So what's your problem? It seems like you'll have what you want, to be off the contract? Without being in any danger."

Joanna picked up her fork and sat there looking at her food without eating. "No true timeline, the court case could drag on and on. She knows that. But then, who knows, it could be settled quickly." She looked up at Peg with all seriousness. "You don't think she'll kill me in the meantime, do you?"

Peg gasped. "Kill you? Whatever are you talking about?"

"I've had death threats. They've been traced back to contract holders, militia units. Deborah's in with both of them."

"Death threats? Why in God's name would they want to kill you?"

Joanna blinked, realizing just what she was saying, recognized Peg's bewilderment. "Deborah didn't tell you?"

"Tell me what? She said she didn't know if you had told me anything about your past, said there might be some things I didn't know."

"That's all?"

Peg nodded. "So why the death threats? And why do you think Deborah's a danger to you?"

Joanna searched Peg's face, suddenly realizing what she had said. She debated and then shook it off. If she was in danger, there was nothing she could do about it here and now. "Joanna Davis isn't my real name. It's Braaford. I used to be a reporter."

Peg frowned as if trying to place her.

"After I was a reporter, I was an activist. I was, am one of ACTS founders." She held her breath.

Peg continued to frown and then as what Joanna said fell into place, she let out a long sigh of understanding. "And Deborah knew this?"

"Well, she knew who I was. We," she hesitated, "knew each other," she finished lamely, not ready to confess more than that. "She didn't know about ACTS, we had lost contact by then."

"Ah-ha."

"I don't know how she found out about my involvement with ACTS but, yeah, she knows." She began to eat then, as if just telling someone was a relief.

Peg sagged back in her chair. "How'd you get on contract then? If you don't mind my asking."

"I got stranded on my way to Canada, long story, and then I got shanghaied."

"So you're not doing this undercover then?"

"Good God no!" Joanna burst out with the most energy she had since Deborah brought her back to the house. "I've been beaten, raped, prostituted. I was passionate about my job but that was going a bit too far."

She looked up from her plate to see Peg's shock and she realized how she must have sounded. "I'm sorry. I know this sounds farfetched, and it's a lot I've held back from you. I'm sorry. I didn't know who I could trust."

"No," Peg said slowly, "I knew you were hiding something. I didn't imagine anything like this." She met Joanna's gaze and if she was disappointed, she hid it.

"I wanted to tell you. So many times, I wanted to confide in you. I was just too afraid. I saw too many others sell out."

Peg nodded silently.

"Then when I saw you at the landing, and you were carrying a gun, I thought you had chosen sides and I was glad I hadn't told you."

"And now?"

Joanna shrugged. "I don't know." She looked away. "Deborah knows. She's going to do whatever she's going to do and I can't stop her. There's nothing left of me that's worth selling." Peg groaned and Joanna looked back. "Not that I think you would have sold me out anyway. I just didn't trust anyone."

"Deborah's not going to kill you." Peg's voice was quiet reassurance.

Joanna gave a deprecating laugh. "Probably not. Just think of the propaganda she'd lose. I'm effectively neutralized. The most anticontract symbol in the country on contract." She frowned. "I just didn't want to die anonymously and no one ever know what happened to me."

"Rather be a dead martyr?"

Joanna looked up at her. "Well, yes. At least then I wouldn't have wasted my life." She caught herself. "Better that than being just a piece of paper with a body attached to it."

"You really think Deborah looks at you like that?"

Joanna drew a breath to answer and then stopped. "No," she said reluctantly. "Deborah still sees us as individuals. And she tries her best to treat us as such." She shifted in the chair. "But the long and the short of it is that it doesn't matter how Deborah sees us. She herself says the contracts—you, me, all of us—are assets." She shook her head in dismay. "What have we come to? Corporations are treated as people, and people are treated as assets." She was silent a moment, reflecting on Deborah's words. Abruptly she looked up. "So she knows about us."

Peg nodded. "Yes. I tried to tell you. There were just too many times we were able to get together. There had to be some arranging in the background." She cocked her head in that thoughtful way she had. She sat further back in the chair as if putting distance between them. "I have to ask this, Joanna, not because I really want to know the answer."

Joanna looked up at her expectantly.

"Was everything with me just a cover? Just a way you could be out of her reach so you could make your plans?"

"No!" Joanna leaned toward her. "Please don't think that. I would never treat you so offhandedly."

"But you took care that I didn't know your plans," Peg pointed out.

"I didn't want to put you in any danger," Joanna protested. "I didn't know how Deborah would react. If she was going to explode, I didn't want you in the line of fire."

"Deborah wouldn't do that to me," Peg said with certainty. "Because I wouldn't get in the line of fire." She looked around the room as it darkened. She turned on the lamp by the window. "She trusts me. And she trusted you."

"Trust? Are you so sure it was trust? Or that she didn't think we would dare do anything? Just one great big happy grateful family?"

Peg turned back to look at Joanna in some consternation. "Some of us feel exactly that. I told you what I came from. There are others here who had nothing and nowhere to go when Deborah took them in."

"At what price! Don't any of you think Deborah gets a whole lot of benefit from this? She might see us as people but do you really think she's doing this out of the goodness of her heart and generosity of her soul?"

"I don't think Deborah thinks in those terms, but you should know, shouldn't you?"

"What do you mean?" Joanna asked quickly.

Peg shrugged. "I don't think she took your contract because it was going to be an easy task. So what other reason did she have except she didn't like the treatment you were getting?"

Joanna's head went up. "I don't know what her motivations were."

"Would you rather she had left you there?" Joanna bit her lip, not ready to admit Deborah had done her a good turn but unable to deny it. "You know, Joanna," Peg said in a quiet reasonable voice, "you're going to have to come to terms with the fact that not all contracts are bad, that not all holders are cruel and self-serving and that Deborah did you a good turn in acquiring your contract."

"That good turn wouldn't have been necessary if contracts didn't exist to start with."

"Jesus Christ, Joanna, give the woman a break!" Peg exploded. Joanna drew back in surprise. "Contracts exist. You're pissed at Deborah because she holds your contract even though she didn't put you on it. You'd be pissed at her if she did terminate the contract because she can't do anything about anyone else's. And you'd really be pissed at her if she had just left you with that bastard. That's her three choices. Just what in the hell do you want her to do?"

Peg stood there watching Joanna before she spoke again. "Besides, you're not pissed at Deborah just because she holds contracts." Joanna turned around to look at her. "You're mad at her because you're in love with her."

Joanna gasped and an angry flush heated her. "In love with Deborah! Don't be ridiculous! Don't be insulting. You go too far, Peg." Peg said nothing, just watched her with her direct gaze. "What?" Joanna continued her protest. "I'm supposed to fall in love with Deborah because she 'rescued' me? I wouldn't have had to be rescued if contracts didn't exist. Or maybe because she took care of me when I was sick, or because she feeds me and puts a roof over my head. All the requirements of a good contract holder. No, I'm not in love with her."

Peg looked down at her hands and then back up at Joanna with pained eyes. "She wasn't always your contract holder, Joanna," she said quietly.

"What! What do you mean? I said we knew each other. I didn't say anything about being lovers!"

"You didn't have to. I could see it. It might have been a long time ago, and I don't know what happened, but I think you still love her."

Joanna's jaw dropped and she felt the ground move beneath her. "I don't know what you're talking about! But it's idiotic, Peg. There's nothing between Deborah and me, except this damn contract."

Peg looked at her in disbelief. Joanna's stare dared her to say more. Peg finally dropped her gaze and turned away, adjusting the lamp. "So," she said without turning back. "You gave your word that you would cooperate. Was that out of the goodness of your heart?"

"No," Joanna rasped back.

"Should she believe you?" Peg moved toward the center of the room, toward the door.

Joanna followed her. "And what do you mean by that?"

"You managed to keep your plans a secret once, thereby deceiving us all. What's to stop you from doing it again?"

Joanna took angry steps toward Peg. "You doubt my word? I thought you knew me well enough."

"I thought I did too but that was before all this happened. Now you're telling me you're really someone else, that you've got this whole past that you've never mentioned. While I can understand why you were hiding your identity, there was a lot of other stuff you were hiding as well." She shook her head. "Suddenly I don't know you at all." There was silence between them and then Peg went on. "Were you worried I might try to stop you if I knew?"

Joanna drew back to look at Peg. The two women stared at each other and Peg finally dropped her gaze. "I guess I need to go," she said quietly.

"Peg." Joanna took a step forward and Peg looked up quickly in anticipation. "You believe me, don't you?"

Peg took so long to answer that Joanna grew frightened. Peg had supported her in so many ways in the last months, she didn't know how she could go on if she lost her. "I don't know," Peg said finally. "I knew you were afraid, and I knew you were hiding something. But I thought you were beginning to trust me." She lifted her hand to prevent Joanna from saying anything. "Now I don't know."

Joanna swallowed, realizing she had half expected Deborah not to believe her but it never occurred to her that Peg might not. She had expected distrust from her contract holder, but not from her lover. "I wanted to, really I did. I've just had everything jerked out from under me so many times." She took a deep breath. "You have no idea what seeing Deborah again did to me. Here I am on contract, terrified most of the time. Then to see Deborah, someone I thought I knew once, respected, valued, and she's calmly betting the pot to be able own me. That she was part of that group of people who wanted me dead." She closed her eyes. "She represented everything I believed was bad and suddenly I'm supposed to trust her?" She wiped away tears. "Whatever was between Deborah and me was over a long time ago. We had different values then and we certainly have different values now. Yes, I deceived you, and her and everyone in the house, but I was petrified. I've been alone for a long time and could trust no one.

"But I trusted you, as much as I was capable of trusting. I told you honestly as much as I dared. Yes, I was beginning to trust you and maybe if I hadn't had Bobbi ragging me on some search Deborah was doing, I might have been able to confide in you more. All I could see was everything I feared closing in on me. Now everything's out in the open and I have nothing left to hide."

She looked at Peg, feeling like she had her heart in her hands. "Please believe me."

The minute dragged on into an eternity before Peg answered. "I don't know, Joanna. Everything's changed. I want to, but…"

"I know everyone's going to view me with suspicion. I know it's going to be hard, but please, give me the chance." She didn't want to cry now. "Peg, I've been so afraid." Right now she wanted Peg's arms around her. "I'm so sorry. I never wanted to deceive anyone I cared about. I always valued honesty."

Peg sighed, looked around the room everywhere except at Joanna. "Deborah keeps saying we do lots of things now we never thought we'd do." She went over and sat on the side of the bed. "I thought you had come to terms with being on contract, understood there were some circumstances…" She trailed off.

"I just saw so many terrible things," Joanna almost whispered.

"And you could say that you knew Deborah at one time, yet you still thought she would be abusive and controlling."

"People change. Deborah is so different from the woman I remember. She would have curled up and died rather than do what Deborah's doing now."

Peg made a derisive sound. "You badly underestimate Deborah's will to get through this."

Joanna shook her head. "No, that's the only thing I didn't underestimate. Her will to have her own way is the one thing that hasn't changed. I just never expected her to be concerned about anyone else's survival."

Peg seemed to consider that. "Even yours?" she asked finally.

Joanna held back her feeling of helplessness. "Maybe especially mine. Deborah's not a forgiving soul, and I walked out on her." She watched Peg's face for a glimmer of understanding. Or recognition that she knew what had happened all those years ago.

Peg sat back on the bed. "So you walked out on her once and now you've run away from her again. And she still takes your word that you'll stay and behave until the court case is decided." She shook her head. "Joanna, you have a shitty way of dealing with the women who love you."

"Yes, I guess I do."

"Why?"

Joanna shook her head. "I don't know."

"Do you expect me to believe you?"

"No, not really. But I'm hoping you'll give me a chance." She twisted her hands. "I don't know what Deborah's really going to do with me. I don't know how the others will look at me. But I'd really like the opportunity to make it up to you. Can you forgive me? Can we try again?"

Peg just looked away. "I don't know what you've got, Joanna, what it is in your makeup. Deborah's the most unforgiving soul I've ever met. There's people in this town she won't deal with because of something that happened years ago. But she takes your contract on. And now she takes your word you won't cause any problem." She looked back at Joanna, half-exasperated, half-angry. "I always said that if someone betrayed me, I wouldn't have anything to do with them ever again. But there's some part of me that keeps making excuses for you. I don't want you out of my life but I'm not sure I trust you in it either."

Joanna's heart skipped a beat, not sure what Peg was meaning.

Peg stood in front of Joanna. "I'm an idiot," she said in deprecation. "Or I'm in love." She took hold of Joanna's hands. "Maybe both, and I have no idea which is worse."

"I'll make it up to you," Joanna promised.

"Don't make promises you can't keep," Peg said seriously.

"I don't want to lose you."

"There are worse things," Peg pointed out. She brought Joanna's hands to her lips. "But we can try."

Joanna nodded, and they wrapped their arms around each other, standing in the center of Deborah's bedroom, wondering what their future would hold.

Bella Books, Inc.

Women. Books. Even Better Together.

P.O. Box 10543
Tallahassee, FL 32302

Phone: 800-729-4992
www.bellabooks.com